G. R. HALLIDAY

G. R. Halliday was born in Edinburgh and grew up near Stirling in Scotland. He spent his childhood obsessing over the unexplained mysteries his father investigated, which has proved excellent inspiration for *From the Shadows*. The book was shortlisted for the McIlvanney Debut Prize 2019. G. R. Halliday now lives in the rural Highlands outside of Inverness, where he is able to pursue his favourite pastimes of mountain climbing and swimming in the sea, before returning home to his band of semi-feral cats.

G. R. HALLIDAY

From the Shadows

VINTAGE

3 5 7 9 10 8 6 4 2

Vintage
20 Vauxhall Bridge Road,
London SW1V 2SA

Vintage is part of the Penguin Random House group of companies
whose addresses can be found at global.penguinrandomhouse.com.

Penguin
Random House
UK

Copyright © Highland Noir Ltd 2019

G. R. Halliday has asserted his right to be identified as the author of this
Work in accordance with the Copyright, Designs and Patents Act 1988

First published in the UK by Harvill Secker in 2019
First published by Vintage in 2020

penguin.co.uk/vintage

A CIP catalogue record for this book is available from the British Library

ISBN 9781529110791

Printed and bound in Great Britain by Clays Ltd, Elcograf S.p.A.

Penguin Random House is committed to a sustainable future for
our business, our readers and our planet. This book is made
from Forest Stewardship Council® certified paper.

MIX
Paper from
responsible sources
FSC® C018179

For Sarah

Friday

Chapter 1

The first autumn stars had appeared in the black sky above the Wester Ross mountains, but Robert didn't notice them. He didn't look up once as he wheeled his bike into the dark garage, swung the door closed and ran shivering towards the light at the front of the house. But the other person, the one who was watching from the shadows among the trees, did notice those stars. And knew immediately that they were a sign.

Robert hesitated on the doorstep then reached to his pocket for the mobile phone again. He knew he should wait, but the need to read back over the messages was desperate.

Were the messages really from his mum? It didn't make sense. And the phone. Taped to the handlebars of his mountain bike that morning when he'd left for school. That didn't make sense either. But then nothing seemed to make sense since she'd gone. It was like everything had tilted off by a degree. Robert touched the dark denim material of his pocket. Compulsively checking that the phone was still safe. He pulled his hand away, resisting the urge to read the messages again. He knew his dad would be listening out and he'd only try to interfere. Besides, it was Dad's fault she'd left anyway, wasn't it? He must have upset her somehow. He must have done something bad to make her leave.

Robert pushed at the front door. Unlocked, as it had been for weeks. Dad was still hoping she'd come back. *He still thinks she might want him.* There was a sound from inside, a soft shift of body against old sofa. He could picture his father craning his neck, hoping.

'It's me,' Robert shouted, one hand on the bannister.

'I thought you were coming straight home from school?' Even Dad's voice sounded weak now. Weak and pathetic. 'You're only sixteen. I told you to call so I know you're safe.'

'Yeah, well I didn't. Get over it.' *Of course he's weak. Why else would Mum have left if he wasn't?* Even as Robert thought this, he was swallowed up by horror as the alternative explanation came swimming up from his stomach: *She left because of you. No.*

He squeezed the phone in his pocket. This was proof. She had asked to meet him. Why would she do that if she'd left because of him? But his mother never called him Robert. Always Robbie, or Rob. So why would she change that now? He ran a hand over his short dark hair. He should speak to his dad, let him read what she had sent. *Maybe she's had ...* Robert searched around for the right words. A breakdown, depression.

He seized on the idea, a trace of light in the dark. That would explain it all. Why she left, the strange messages. She was probably ashamed, worried what they would think of her. Robert pictured himself gently putting his hand on her face. *It's OK, Mum, we're here for you.* He turned towards the living room, then stopped as he caught the stifled sound coming from the room. A strange new fear joined the constant ache in his stomach as he realised it was the sound of his father crying. He turned back and went quietly up the stairs.

Robert opened the door to his bedroom at the top of the stairs. A confusion of feelings churned in his stomach. Like he was old and worn down, young and powerless, all at the same time.

As he stepped into the room he caught the faint edge of a smell. Was it a perfume? From his mum? Robert shook his head at the idea – that was called wishful thinking. He turned as their dog came padding along the corridor. Ellie was an ageing Scottish deerhound with shaggy grey hair that hung down over her eyes. She nuzzled at Robert's leg then pushed past into the room. He ran a hand through her soft fur and watched as she lunged awkwardly onto his bed. Slowly rotating her long spiny body in a circle before collapsing on the bedspread.

Robert nudged the door until it caught on the carpet, then dropped his bag on the floor. There was homework to do. Exam preparation. He looked at the neglected study timetable pinned on the wall at the far end of the room. Before she'd gone he'd craved knowledge. He'd soaked up all the information he could use to get the hell out of Wester Ross. Tourists came to the north-west Highlands of Scotland and especially this area to go walking in the mountains. To visit the beaches. Robert had even heard of people coming to watch the stars and planets in the dark skies, far from any street lights. But just try living in a lonely glen in the middle of nowhere. He shook his head again, still looking at the study timetable. Now his mind was so filled with his mum there wasn't any room left to care for much else.

At his desk, his fingers moved to his pocket again. He stopped when he noticed a mug sitting by his darkened lamp. It was Dad's favourite mug, the white one with an old DIG FOR PLENTY logo on it.

He leaned over and clicked on the lamp, the phone momentarily forgotten. The mug was still warm. Hot chocolate. His favourite. Guilt bubbled in his stomach. This was Dad's way of showing that he understood, that he felt the same way. Robert took a mouthful of the thick, sweet liquid. And another. It hugged all his senses as he curled up on the bed beside Ellie. Her fur was calming against the bare flesh of his arm. He heard the low sound of the television from downstairs. It was comforting somehow, despite everything.

Ellie whined and tilted her head. Robert followed the dog's gaze towards the shadows at the end of the room, the window. The darkness almost seemed to stare back at him. He shivered at the idea and pulled the strange phone out from his pocket. He hesitated, then started typing before he could stop himself: 'I'd like to see you. When can we meet?' Send.

He dropped the phone onto the bed and ran his hand over Ellie's head. Over the fine fluff on her ears. He took in that distinctive smell she had, like warmth and security distilled. He stared at the fur above her eyes, blinked. Each strand of fur seemed to stand out, bright. He blinked for a second time. This time the dog almost seemed to blur in front of him.

She whined again. Suddenly she uncurled her body, jumped off the bed and moved stiffly to the window. She turned and caught his gaze, the whites of her eyes bigger than usual. She started to paw at the pile of his washing heaped beneath the windowsill.

'What is it, Ellie?'

Robert heard the slur in his own voice, felt saliva run down his chin. He reached a hand up to wipe his mouth, but his arm wouldn't respond. A tide of panic washed over him. He tried to sit up on the bed, but he couldn't move.

He screamed.

But the sound that came from his mouth was a whisper. He tried to stand up again. He experienced a moment of pure horror when he found that he couldn't even turn his neck or raise a finger.

'Dad. Please, help me,' he tried to shout. But the words lay dead in his throat.

Dad. Please.

All the hurtful things he'd said to his father.

The noise from the television died. Robert heard a click. His father was switching off the lights in the living room, in the downstairs hall.

Ellie barked. The lips around her yellowing canine teeth were trembling. Robert caught the faint edge of that smell again. He tried to swallow and felt the saliva run down his throat. A thick sweet taste, but with something else underneath it. A hint of bitterness. He tried to swallow again. Nothing. Could he breathe? His lungs felt tight, and panic set in.

Dad. Please! Help me.

Then there was the sound of his father's footsteps on the stairs. The familiar creak from the floorboard as he paused at the top, just outside Robert's bedroom. The door opened.

Daddy.

That old comfort against all the fears. The dark, the monsters.

'Rob.' It was his dad's voice coming from the doorway. 'I'm sorry – about everything, with Mum. You know you can speak to me ...'

Please help me, Dad. But the words were locked in Robert's throat and his back was facing the door so his father couldn't see his face.

'We can speak tomorrow.' His father sounded too broken and sad to seek a response from his son. 'Come, Ellie, down to bed.'

The dog whined, barked again. She wouldn't move.

Look at me, Dad. Please, look at me!

Robert heard his father take a step closer. 'Ellie. Come on.' His voice was louder, commanding. Reluctantly the dog turned from the window, obedient to her master. She paused at the foot of Robert's bed, whining, then passed from his sight.

Robert screamed and screamed.

But the noises never made it out of his mouth. He heard the door click shut, his father's footsteps fading down the corridor.

He stared into the dark at the end of the room. The taste of bitter hot chocolate burning in the saliva pooling around his tongue. That faint smell of perfume, lingering. He stared, unable to move as his eyes slowly adjusted to the low light.

There was a long moment of silence in the house. Then suddenly the phone buzzed on the bed beside him. But Robert couldn't move to read it. With his head locked into place, he forced his eyes as far left as they would go and saw one word appear on the screen: 'Now.'

The message was followed by a sound from the corner of the room by the window, where the curtain hung down to the floor. It was the sound of someone breathing heavily – sucking in deep lungfuls of air.

Then the soft shift of fabric sliding across carpet as the curtain began to move.

Robert stared into the dark. And a pale white face smiled back at him.

Saturday

Chapter 2

The naked body was placed in a particular position, its torso folded forward so the face was pressed into the boggy ground. Detective Inspector Monica Kennedy looked at the back of its head. Short dark hair; lower down on the back there were deep red cuts on skin that was horribly white and vulnerable. The smell of rotting meat. The smell her first boss, down in Glasgow, had said you never forget. How right he was.

She glanced around the rough croft land. It was close to the Minch, the sea that separates the west coast of the Scottish Highlands from the Outer Hebrides. Far across the water through the afternoon haze Monica could just see the sharp Cuillin mountains on Skye. Like a monster curled on the horizon.

The closest house was a quarter of a mile away. Far enough for someone to dump the body without being seen. They could come at night. Take their time. It's what she'd do. After eighteen years working serious crimes she knew she could get away with murder. It wasn't a fact she'd necessarily share with others – a topic of conversation over a pint of stout – but it was a comforting thought, really, when her job after all was to catch whoever had left the victim in this beautiful wilderness.

Monica looked down at the body again. Cuts, bruises and blood, but no obvious cause of death. A big part of her wanted to reach down, the motherly part of her needing to try to comfort – as if you can comfort the dead. She should know better. Instead she crouched down, the forensics suit stretched and then rustling as she leaned carefully in and smoothed away the strands of grass close to the victim's legs. The skin was bruised purple by the gathered blood. It meant the body had been placed here before the blood settled, or placed in this particular position at least.

Monica's eyes ran down the white of its back. It was a boy's back, she was certain, but she wouldn't voice this until they had confirmation. You could never say what you thought without upsetting someone or other. Not until about eight people had discussed and confirmed it. She shifted onto her knees, feeling the cold damp ground through the plasticky Tyvek suit. Then her eyes landed on something and the breath caught in her throat. She leaned in closer.

'For Christ's sake,' she muttered.

She stood up then. Stared down at the body for a second longer before walking towards the crowd of rubberneckers who had gathered by the road for this unexpected Saturday afternoon entertainment. An unfamiliar police officer turned towards her. He must be new, Monica thought. She'd been working back in the Highlands for over four years and made a point of trying to remember the uniformed officers' names and faces. She often failed, but the intention was well meant.

He did that familiar double take when he realised how tall she was. An unwelcome reminder that in the white suit she probably looked like some weird Halloween scarecrow set up in the field to frighten children, with her pale skin and her long arms and legs sticking out of the sleeves of the suit, which was really a size too small for her. Large felt bad enough. But shifting up to XL or 2XL …

Jesus. Monica shook her head and forced that sense of embarrassment at her size back under its rock where it belonged. This was a crime scene, probably a murder investigation, she was responsible for. And who didn't look terrible in one of those hideous suits anyway?

She took a deep breath and squirmed out of the thing like a snake shedding its skin. She folded it up, then dropped the bootees into the paper sack beside it ready for the forensics team to check. She thought of the microscopic fibres of evidence that she might have picked up from beside the body. Little particles of death desperately clinging to her forensic second skin.

The officer kept staring, his mouth open like maybe her strangeness was connected to the dead thing folded up over there. As if he'd slipped into a new, terrifying world.

'What is it?' she said, staring back hard at him with her brow folded. Part of her almost wanted him to make some comment about how stupid she looked.

He shook his head, eyes wide, face pale. He tried to say something but the words weren't coming out. She realised that maybe it was the first body he'd seen. Maybe he was in shock, and she felt half a moment of guilt. Well, he was lucky it was her and not her new colleague he was speaking to. Lucky that DC Crawford hadn't arrived from whatever it was he did at the weekend. From whoever's bed he'd found himself in. They were yet to even work on a case together since his promotion to the Major Investigation Team, but from the meetings they'd attended she'd seen how he went after weakness. Like he saw any hint of uncertainty in others as an opportunity to prove himself as a detective.

The officer tried to speak again but the words still wouldn't come. This time Monica took the weight off for him.

'Who found the body?'

'I was the first officer at the scene ... responding to an emergency call. They were out walking.' He motioned to a man and woman standing beside the flashing lights of a police car. The blue in the growing dark of the autumn afternoon was cold on their faces, making the day colder still.

Monica took the young couple in. Matching orange Gore-Tex jackets that would have cost three hundred pounds each, built for mountains they'd never visit. The dog at their feet was a black spaniel, sitting quietly, well trained. Shock was written clear across their faces. They were young professionals probably, doctors or lawyers. Monica dismissed them as suspects, another thought she'd have to keep to herself for now.

'Their dog, it came over and ... They saw the body.' The officer's shaking hand went to his forehead. 'I removed the suspects—' He took a breath, tried again. 'I removed the witnesses from the scene and detained them for questioning, then I cordoned off the area until ...'

Monica nodded. She should say something to reassure him, since he was obviously anxious he'd messed up somehow. But she decided not to. Maybe he had messed up and it would come out later.

She turned at the sound of a car pulling up at the edge of the field near the crowd. A silver Audi. Monica watched as Detective Constable Connor Crawford climbed out of the vehicle. He was a small and wiry man with dark red hair combed up into a thick quiff. There were female whispers in the office about him being 'fit' or 'hot'. But to Monica he looked preened, pampered even. Somehow like a strutting fox, appealing but not someone you should trust. He looked around, taking everything in as if he were sniffing for trouble.

Monica noticed that he was wearing the same brown suit as when he had left the office the previous afternoon. Except now it was crumpled from the pubs, nightclubs or whatever it was he got up to after work. Monica felt something like professional satisfaction that her profile of him seemed to be correct. *Well, you don't have to look for trouble, Crawford,* she thought. *It's found you, and it's lying right over there waiting.*

She turned away, let him come to her and watched as the forensics team worked to set their tent up. Watched as the white nylon snaked and rippled in the wind, almost alive against the darkening sky.

'We need to put out an alert for all young missing persons. Do you know of anyone who's gone missing locally?' Monica said to the young officer, who was still standing beside her.

He shook his head, eyes dancing up, back over Monica's shoulder towards the body. 'Who, who would do that?'

She sighed. Who indeed? And that voice at the back of her head piped up, *Who wouldn't? This whole world has gone to hell.*

Chapter 3

The rain hammered the roof of the Land Rover. Water leaked round the door edges and trickled into the vehicle. Michael Bach took a draw from his cigarette and flicked it out of the gap in the window. The smoke stuck to the damp interior, mixing with the heat of the engine.

His watch said it was 3 p.m., but the wide sky over the west coast of the Scottish Highlands said it was later, a lot later. The dark storm clouds covered the sun. Beinn Dearg, the mountain at the head of Loch Broom, was fading to purple, grey and black.

Time to go home. Instead, he lit another cigarette and once again went over the short phone conversation from the week before.

Can you meet me this morning?

We've got an appointment next week.

Please, it's really important.

Nichol Morgan was seventeen. The kid had his problems, no doubt about that, but he was one of the good ones. One of the ones Michael thought he had a better relationship with, as good as it can be when you're someone's social worker.

OK, Michael had replied eventually. *I'll meet you in an hour.*

Except he didn't. And now seven days had passed.

Sitting by the black sea loch, below the mountains, Michael watched the clouds breaking over the town of Ullapool. It was remote – a place for fishermen, hillwalkers, drinkers and misfits. But never for the faint-hearted. He thought of Nichol again and felt that pressure growing in his stomach. Shame. He remembered turning up outside Inverness train station two hours late, looking around for the kid. Calling his phone, texting him, waiting for the reply that never came.

He took another deep draw from the cigarette, the smoke burning his lungs.

The reply that didn't come until the next morning. He opened his phone and read the strange message again: 'The future is in the stars.'

A line from a book Nichol had been studying at school? Something from a sci-fi comic? Michael had texted back: 'Where are you? Is everything OK? Sorry I missed you yesterday.'

But there was nothing after that. No reply. No answer to any of the calls or the messages Michael had left.

Sometimes clients went missing. It was a fact of the job. Those were the ones who wanted out, who headed for Glasgow or London. Nichol was different though. Or seemed different anyway. But he went too – *or someone took him.*

Michael forced a laugh, to make the thought seem ridiculous. Who would have taken him?

'He's probably fine.' The words sounded dull and unconvincing in the empty vehicle, with the smoke sticking to the condensation on the glass, and the rain hitting the roof.

He made to start his engine as a red Volkswagen entered the car park. The glow of its body was eerie against the mist. Slowly the car pulled in front of Michael's space, blocking him in. Its lights like eyes in the gloom until they flashed, once, twice.

Michael zipped his jacket closed – his dad's jacket, he reminded himself – a Mountain Equipment down jacket from the 1970s. Faded red and blue, slightly too tight for his wide shoulders. He climbed out of his Land Rover and jogged towards the car, the rain pummelling at his hair and skin. As he drew closer he realised he knew the driver.

The man's name was Ben Fisher, DC Ben Fisher, a police detective. Youngest brother of one of Michael's old classmates. The last he had heard, his ex-classmate was working over in America. Strange how two people who'd grown up together could be experiencing such different lives at the same time.

DC Fisher wound his window down. His black hair neatly groomed in a side parting, even as his face scrunched behind his glasses against the rain. He was wearing a suit jacket – city clothes – betraying his unfamiliarity with the brutal west coast weather.

'Mr Bach?' Fisher said, not recognising Michael or resorting to proper procedure.

'That's right.' Michael held up a hand to shield his face from the rain.

'You filed a missing persons report on a young man named Nichol Morgan?'

Chapter 4

Michael followed the signs that led to the morgue. It was hidden away at the back of the building at the end of a maze of corridors and handleless doors – Raigmore Hospital's little secret: a murdered boy and God knew what else. He tried to ignore the thought and went to push the final doors open but then hesitated. Through the glass panel Michael could see the flight of stairs that led down to the morgue, down into the underworld.

A layer of sweat hugged his back – his thick jacket was too warm for indoors; the smell of floor cleaner, the smell of the hospital cutting through. Some memory trying to surface in his mind.

Michael shifted as a noise echoed down the corridor behind him. Footsteps squeaking off the linoleum floor. He realised that his hand was shaking, and a sudden childish impulse took hold: an urge to drop his head and run away. Instead he pushed his hand into his pocket and turned.

Michael was a large man, used to staring down at people, but the woman walking towards him had dark unblinking eyes that sat level with his own. *She must be six foot two*, he thought, and for a moment he forgot why he was standing outside the doors to a morgue. She walked with slightly stooped broad shoulders and wore a dark wool coat that fell to just above her knees. It flared out behind her as she moved, giving the strange sense that she was floating.

He blinked, looked again. She was around forty with black shoulder-length hair, a round face and pale skin. Very much at home here, close to the dead. He cleared his throat, forced a smile to cover up his discomfort.

'Michael Bach?' she said it like *back*, with a hint of an Inverness accent. She must have seen something on his face because she tilted her head as if he had sparked her interest. 'Thanks for coming, it's not ... an easy thing to do.' She let the words hang. 'It was a traumatic death. He's been outside overnight.' She paused again. Studied him, his response.

'You mean he's not going to look the way he did?' Michael said, wiping a hand across his face as the horror of what he'd just asked sank in.

She gave an almost imperceptible nod and waited as if to see whether he had anything else to say. When he didn't she leaned awkwardly past him, pushed the door open and led him down the stairs.

The body was lying on a metal table, covered by a sheet. A man dressed in surgical scrubs was standing behind it. Michael found himself staring down at the anonymous shape. There was a thing under there, an object that was once a boy. He gripped the lighter in his pocket tighter. No one spoke and after a few seconds the man folded the sheet back.

It wasn't Nichol.

Michael knew instantly because of the shape of the face. It was older and there was a little stubble. Nichol was still baby-skinned. This boy's face was swollen, strange, his soul replaced with something, with nothing: the worst-kept secret, the worst-kept surprise.

'It's not him.'

'You're certain?'

Michael looked again. He saw the marks of violence this time. What looked like a love bite on the boy's neck, burst blood vessels in his right eye. Someone did that to him, hurt him, chose to take his life away. For the first time Michael caught the smell of death and decay. His hand went to his mouth as he gagged, and he knew for certain then that the boy would be following him in the darkest corridors of his dreams. Back up those stairs and into the real world.

Outside the hospital a curious mist had now replaced the rain. It sat heavy, suffocating the car park. Michael went to light a cigarette and noticed his hand was still shaking.

'What happened to him?' Michael said. 'That wasn't ...'
Wasn't what?

'We're still in the early stages of the investigation. Thanks again for coming in,' the detective said, turning away from him.

'What happens now with Nichol?'

She stopped, looked back over her shoulder, silhouetted against the bright white entrance to the hospital. 'I'll get someone to give you a call.'

'I don't think he would just go off like this.'

She turned back to face him. 'I'm not being funny, but we hear that a lot when people go missing. It's difficult when someone's over the age of sixteen. Technically they're an adult.'

'There must be something you can do. I mean he could be in danger – you saw what happened to that boy in there.' Michael tried to keep the rising anger out of his voice.

'I've read the report on Nichol, Mr Bach. He was seen boarding a train. Unless I'm missing something, there's no suggestion of a crime having been committed.'

'He's only seventeen.'

Her hand went to her forehead, something behind her eyes, thoughts buzzing. Michael realised that she was weighing him up, judging him. 'Was there anything unusual with him? Before he disappeared?'

Michael stared at her. Those dark eyes, tiny laughter lines visible in the light from above the hospital door. Although it was hard to picture her laughing. He squeezed his brain, needing a reply, because this was exactly the type of question to shut an inquiry down. The inevitable response: *Nothing I can think of.*

'There was something.' He shuffled his memories of Nichol.

The detective tilted her head, both hands on her hips, her dark coat spread wide.

'A month – a few months ago – Nichol started carrying something around with him.' Michael felt the cigarette lighter in his pocket, gripped it in his fist.

'What was he carrying?'

'It was a rock. A black piece of rock.' Michael swallowed, knew that what he was saying sounded insignificant. He expected the detective to see straight through his stalling.

'Why was it strange?'

'I don't know.' He paused, suddenly embarrassed by what he was going to say. 'He used to rub it on his lips, almost kiss it.'

The detective watched him. Maybe she was about to say something, but then the door behind was pulled open again. A small, thin man emerged. He must have been in his late twenties or early thirties, although the wear in the face was of someone older. There was something dishevelled, almost wild about his expression. An archetypal Highland face with high cheekbones, a sharp nose, bent where it had been broken more than once. With his red hair and those staring eyes he had the look of an undersized Celtic warrior.

The man started to say something to the detective, but noticed Michael and stared hard at him for a couple of seconds until Michael looked away.

'They're ready for us, for the autopsy.'

Michael felt a moment of relief. That it was them not him who'd be there for it. He wouldn't have to see them pulling that sheet all the way back and cutting into the boy's body. He watched as she nodded to the man, who Michael now presumed was also a detective. They both turned, standing together. She was almost a foot taller than him; from a distance they could easily be mistaken for a mother and son. They both looked again at Michael for a moment then the woman nodded a quick thanks at him before the two went back inside to the morgue.

Chapter 5

Monica put the empty cardboard cup down on the metal worktop, her head buzzing from caffeine. She thought back to the call that had come in just as she was about to take Lucy into the cinema. They'd been standing in the lobby choosing a film, her little girl bouncing from heel to heel in excitement. It was going to be their little slice of time together.

Then, of course, her phone rang. For a moment she'd considered letting the smell of popcorn steal her away from the job. She could easily have taken Lucy's hand and walked her to the ticket counter, then on to the pick 'n' mix and the cushioned theatre seats. All the way to her profound apologies three hours later to her boss. It was at moments like this that Monica wished she was a different person: a better mother and shittier police detective. Because when her mobile phone rang she had let go of Lucy's hand and taken the call.

Instead of the buzz of sugar and a film, she was left with the stabbing look of disappointment on her child's face as she tried to explain that work had called and Granny would come over to the flat and watch a DVD with her instead. They could go to the cinema tomorrow. Maybe. Monica glanced up at the clock on the wall of the morgue. Almost 10 p.m. on Saturday night. Unless the killer miraculously handed himself in in the next couple of hours there wasn't much chance of that happening now.

She shook her head to dismiss the useless thought, stepped closer to the body. So close she could have reached down and touched the dark marks on the boy's neck, the purple stains of settled blood on his legs and stomach. The electric light flickered above her head. Why always in a basement with no windows? She'd googled this once: 'Why are hospital morgues located in basements?' The consensus was that back before electricity being underground helped keep the bodies cooler so less likely to rot. But she liked to think that maybe in the middle of the nineteenth century when they were building the first public morgues they'd put them underground because the builders knew that we all end up in the ground eventually, one way or the other. That the ground is the correct place for the dead.

The pathologist turned to face Monica. It was the first time they'd met, but he didn't offer a greeting. Instead he nodded at the body lying between them as if it was nothing more than a dead animal laid on a butcher's block.

'You've witnessed an autopsy before?'

She nodded but didn't reply. How many had she seen? More than she could remember.

'It's a difficult thing for some people, seeing how simple we really are under the skin, all these simple horrors. Your forensic boys have done what they needed to?'

She stared at him. 'Forensic girls. The team's led by Gemma Gunn, a woman. They've examined him at the scene, and earlier tonight.'

'Of course they have. We do things by the book though, don't we, Christian?' Raising his voice and addressing the nurse typing on a computer behind him. 'What did they find?'

Isn't that what you're supposed to tell me? Monica thought, but didn't say. The doctor was in his late fifties or early sixties. Thin with shaved grey hair visible under his standard hospital head covering, blue eyes and an accent she couldn't place. English or maybe something else.

When she didn't reply he tried again. 'I heard there were marks on the boy's back?' he said slowly with a thin smile. Monica understood then that the new pathologist was trying to test or intimidate her. To establish his authority.

'They could be bite marks,' Monica said. 'The forensics team told me informally that they were bigger than any human bite they'd seen though.'

'A monster then?' he said with a chortle.

Monica stared at him, ignored his unworthy laugh. 'They swabbed for any traces of saliva at the scene before they moved him. But they suggested that it could have been an animal skull or a model of a jaw.'

He nodded slowly, face falling back to blank. Perhaps a little disappointed that Monica didn't seem rattled by the bite marks. He turned and looked at a computer screen, began reading off the preliminary results of the forensics report in a low voice.

'Dirt under his fingernails. No defence wounds. Cuts on his wrists and ankles suggesting he was restrained. Probably with plastic cable ties. Multiple bruises around his neck. He was choked repeatedly before he died. Cuts and bruises across his body, series of shallow puncture wounds low on his back.' The doctor laid a knife on the slab, metal ringing on metal. 'It's an awful thing to do to someone.' Monica took a deep breath and wondered exactly which 'thing' he was referring to.

'We're ready to go, Dr Dolohov,' the nurse said, stepping away from his computer. An audio recorder was held in the nurse's gloved hand.

26

'Maybe we can find a little more,' Dolohov said, half a smile at Monica before he pulled the white mask tight across his face and picked the knife up again.

When she was younger Monica had believed she would never get used to seeing a blade cut into the skin and flesh of a human body. Yet after five years working murder cases in Glasgow, ten in London and now here, back where she started life, seeing men, women, children opened up on slabs like this one felt horribly close to 'normal'. She watched as the pathologist made a cut on each side from armpit to sternum and one from sternum to groin forming a Y down the boy's body.

Dolohov laid the knife on the table, used his hands to fold the skin back, exposing intestines and internal organs. All the sacred things, the things that were never meant to see the light of day. The sacrificial parts.

She watched out of a sense of duty to the boy as much as anything. A boy who might have had family, might have had friends who cared about him, but was at least the most important person in his own life. She watched the doctor cut his rib and chest plate away and remove the organs. Cutting them free piece by piece with practised movements, like a hunter butchering an animal.

The boy had been tortured and killed. Savaged by a monster. But he had then been posed in a particular way. Pointed to the west, almost like he was praying, almost like a message. A message for who though?

Dolohov wiped blood off the pink lining of the boy's stomach with a towel, then ran the knife across the organ and slid a gloved finger into the cut. He'd done this before, lots of times, she could tell. The way his fingers moved and his hands followed, slowly, slowly, as he opened the stomach out.

'Empty. Either he hadn't eaten for a while or probably he vomited everything back up during his ordeal,' the doctor said into the recorder being held by the nurse.

The smell caught her then. Even though the body had been refrigerated, there was still that iron smell of blood, meat, mixed with traces of digesting food escaping from what was left of his stomach.

'I don't see anything caught in his teeth. It's possible he was cleaned by his killer before he was dumped,' Dolohov continued. Monica nodded at this information, stored it in her brain.

The door creaked open and DC Crawford stepped into the room. Monica glanced at him and caught the expression on his face; the tightness in his jaw told her exactly why he'd needed to visit the toilet before the autopsy began.

'I now move to his throat,' Dolohov dictated as he stretched the boy's head back. There was a grim click as he realigned a bone in his own neck.

He reached in again, made cuts, worked the tube of the boy's windpipe loose and laid it on the slab.

'You can see where it was traumatised, then crushed. Someone strong. Probably he was choked unconscious, then revived. The toxicology report will tell us more.' He used his knife to point out the injuries. 'He bit his tongue almost off. Or else it was bitten by his attacker. Monstrous.' He turned to the nurse. 'Take a picture of the wound. We can check it against the marks on his back.' The nurse nodded and reached for the camera on the worktop.

When he'd finished, the doctor ran his fingers down the bloody windpipe again, paused, and then repeated the action.

'Funny,' he said, his face blank. 'There's something lodged in the pipe.' He cut it lengthways, opened it out and held something up for Monica to see.

She snapped a glove onto a hand and took the thing from him, shook her head in disbelief and whispered the name that immediately came into her head: 'Michael Bach.'

Sunday

Chapter 6

Monica took a deep breath of the cold night air. Pleased to be outside again after the hours underground in the morgue with the organic smells of the opened body hanging in the air.

She glanced over to the main entrance of the hospital. The Saturday night casualties were beginning to roll in to the emergency department. Monica watched as an ambulance pulled up, a man stretchered out, blood down the front of his shirt, head bandaged like a wounded soldier. The compact city centre of Inverness seemed to specialise in its own vision of hell at the weekends.

'Do you want a lift?' Crawford asked.

She turned at the sound of his voice. She had almost forgotten he was walking beside her she was so intent on driving home, crawling into bed for a few hours at least before they went to speak to Michael Bach in the morning. She remembered then that she'd left the Volvo over at police headquarters, but it was only a five-minute walk away from Raigmore Hospital across the roundabout.

She checked the time on her phone. After 1 a.m. She opened her mouth to refuse his offer. The old habit: never owe anyone anything. Then she reminded herself that it was only a lift, that if they were going to work together she was going to have to get used to him at some point.

'Sure, thanks.'

Crawford nodded, gestured over to the Audi. 'It still bothers me when they cut them open ... I suppose I'll get used to it eventually.'

Monica looked at him, surprised he'd been so open. But why would you want to get used to the smell of a decomposing corpse? Why would anyone? It was a question she'd asked herself more than once over the years.

Monica climbed into the Audi beside him and slid the seat back almost as far as it would go to fit her legs in. She would be home to make breakfast for her daughter anyway. It was something, even if the rest of the weekend had gone to shit.

She felt the phone vibrate in her pocket. *Mum?* She could already picture her mother's expectant face. Could imagine just how excited she'd be about the high-profile case her daughter was in charge of. Desperate to offer her own opinion on the murder. Angela Kennedy had hoards of 'information' gleaned from reading crime websites and watching television shows.

It wasn't Monica's mum though. With a sinking feeling she answered the call.

'DI Kennedy?' The echoes of a call centre in the background.

'That's right.'

'You put out a call for missing persons – young males?'

I did, didn't I? That sinking feeling growing all the time.

'We've just had a call come in. A man named Steven Wright has just reported his son missing.' Monica stared out at the rain, which had started up again. Watched it land on the windscreen and blur the wall of white lights from the hospital building.

'Where do they live?' Monica asked, feeling Crawford's eyes on her.

'That's the thing, they're over in Wester Ross. In the mountains. Only about twenty miles from Gairloch, where the body was discovered.'

Monica clicked the phone off.

'What is it?' Crawford asked, the excitement in his voice barely contained.

'A possible ID on the victim,' Monica said. She felt the phone vibrate as the address came through. Near Achnasheen, in the mountains just off the main road to the west coast.

'We should go then, shouldn't we?' Crawford asked, seeming to hesitate. Perhaps surprised by her lack of enthusiasm.

Yes, we should, shouldn't we? Monica thought. She pictured Lucy waking up, wondering where her mummy was again. Maybe it could wait – they could visit Steven Wright first thing in the morning. What difference would it make anyway? She imagined asking the question of her boss, Detective Superintendent Fred Hately. Could almost hear his response: *You're the senior investigating officer, DI Kennedy. It's your call, your responsibility.*

She stared out of the windscreen at the mist and the rain again, coming on heavier now. Just as thick and dark as the guilt that was hanging over her, which seemed inevitable whichever way she turned.

Chapter 7

Connor Crawford pulled the Audi to a stop in front of the row of darkened houses. The steep black of the mountains rose up behind them like a vision of impending doom. Ready to collapse on those homes, on the lives of the residents.

Well it's coming for all of us eventually, Monica thought. She climbed out of the car and felt the rain, falling more as mountain mist now, hitting her face. The scattered lights from the row of houses, the smell of coal smoke hanging in the air, gave the place a strangely medieval feel. The hamlet that was safe, self-contained, until one day an unexpected horror came into its midst. Or from its midst more likely. If you wanted to bet on it, then it was probable that whoever killed the boy had known him. Far more likely than being murdered by a stranger.

'It must be that one,' Crawford said, stating the obvious as he pointed to the only house with all its lights on. A marked police Vauxhall parked outside. Monica nodded. Crawford had drunk off a can of Red Bull before they left the hospital car park. Another one at the turn-off after Garve. He'd tried to make small talk, speculating about the case as she'd typed out a text message to her mother to explain that she wouldn't be home.

After a while Crawford had given up and they'd completed the forty-minute drive through the dark night, among the mountains, in silence. To take her mind off the journey she tried to flesh out a profile of her new colleague. She noted the neatness of his vehicle's interior. The cables of muscle and vein on his forearms when he'd rolled up his shirtsleeves to drive. He seemed to carry almost all of his muscle across his narrow shoulders and his neck, which was almost as thick as his head. Like a tom cat's. She'd noticed his misshapen nose, concluded it could be from boxing. Some kind of martial-arts training would fit with that insecurity he seemed to wear like a jacket.

She followed Crawford up the path to the front door of the house, let him go in first. On a night like this it was only right to spare the father the extra shock of a giant woman showing up at his door out of the darkness.

Monica clocked the garage to the right of the house. A small untended garden sat scruffy in the light coming from over the door: a square of grass that hadn't been cut, flower pots overtaken by weeds. Just too busy to deal with these little jobs or some kind of stress in the household? The kind of stress that would lead a kid to run away, to find himself in a nightmare? The kind of stress that could make a father kill his son, stage it to look like something else?

She remembered the body. Posed in that particular position, the traumatised windpipe. What kind of father could do that to his son? And the unpalatable answer that her mind served up for her: some. More than you might think, given the right circumstances.

She dipped her head to go inside when a uniformed police officer answered Crawford's brisk knock. The officer – PC Carol Stewart, Monica recalled with a hint of satisfaction – led them into the hallway.

Monica noticed that Stewart had a pistol strapped to her belt. The Highlands were the only part of Scotland where armed police regularly responded to non-emergency call-outs. Something Monica still wasn't used to. She couldn't help thinking of the Police Scotland motto – 'Keeping people safe.' That and occasionally shooting them if necessary.

Monica caught Stewart's arm and spoke under her breath. She wanted to know for certain before she faced the father: 'Do you have a photo of Robert?'

Stewart – neat short hair, thick-framed glasses – looked down at Monica's hand on her arm, then nodded to a pinboard behind her on the wall.

Monica scanned the collage of family life: suntanned faces on holiday somewhere. A birthday meal at a restaurant and a boy she knew. One she'd met not long before in the morgue. The same short dark hair, the same scraps of facial hair, worn with adolescent pride. A smile that looked intelligent, a kid you could imagine on a school quiz panel. Monica felt a mix of emotions rising. Satisfaction that they were making progress in the investigation, a familiar dull horror at the conversation she was about to have.

PC Stewart led them into the small living room. A gas fire was burning blue; a landscape print hung above the mantelpiece. The lights overhead were switched on bright, as if they might somehow ward off the night out there and all of the terror. Because in Monica's experience most parents would do anything to convince themselves that it wasn't their child. That it was the wrong door, the wrong name.

She watched Steven Wright's face closely as he looked up from the untouched mug of tea in front of him. Greying hair, a thin care-worn face. He was wearing blue jeans and a checked shirt that somehow gave him an air of vulnerability. The poor soul who was underdressed for the party. Her initial instinct was that whatever had happened to his son, he wasn't involved. Well, instincts could be wrong; a lot of the time they were.

Monica sat down opposite on the sofa, asked herself whether she should take him to the station to interview him. Something told her not to. Until the body was formally identified it was still a missing-person inquiry. Steven's memory might be clearer while there was hope his son was alive. Harsh as it sounded.

'When did you last see Robert?' Monica asked. She watched Steven Wright's expression change as he formulated the response, flicked his eyes up to the left. According to some online experts this meant that he was telling the truth, accessing a memory rather than inventing a new story. But only if the person is right-handed, if they're left-handed it's the opposite. And what if the person's remembering a lie?

'It was Friday ... late. I'd been sitting down here—'

'What were you doing?' Crawford asked, cutting in.

Monica glanced at him, a little annoyed that he'd interrupted. But she was interested to see how Steven Wright responded. His eyes flicked from Crawford to Monica. 'I was watching TV. The news at ten o'clock. There was a story about a pilot whale being beached near Inverness. I remember the time because Robert still wasn't home and I was worried – he hadn't called.'

'Is it normal for him to come home late like that?' Monica said.

'It ...' His eyes darted around the room. 'It's been difficult. His mother left. She walked out, six weeks ago. Since then he's been ... It's been difficult for both of us.'

'Where did his mother go?' Monica imagined the darkest answers: into a hole in the back garden, into a ditch. She watched closely as Steven Wright's hand went to his mouth and his eyes went up to the left again.

'I don't know. She said she needed to be on her own, needed time to think.'

'To think about what?' Crawford asked.

Steven Wright shook his head quickly, as if warding off an attack. 'She's got nothing to do with this. My son's missing—'

'Have you heard from your wife? Since then?' Monica asked.

Steven Wright stared at her for long seconds. He seemed confused that she was asking about his wife when it was his son who was missing.

'Not directly,' he said finally. 'She called her mum, two weeks ago. Just to say she was safe.'

Monica made a note to have someone check with the woman's mother, to track her down as quickly as possible. At the least to save her from finding out from a news report that while she was away finding herself her son had been brutally murdered.

'So he came home after ten? You checked on him?' Monica said.

'That's right, half an hour later. Something like that. He was fine. Lying on his bed, half asleep. I had to get up early the next morning. I drive a truck, doing industrial deliveries across the Highlands. I've tried not to be away at the weekends, but it's difficult. I've got to work.'

'So Robert was safe in his room at ten thirty on Friday night. What about the next morning?' Monica asked.

'I didn't want to wake him. It's important he gets his rest. He's got exams this year – he has to do well in them if he's going to go to university. He needs to study hard, stick in ...'

'It's just the two of you now? He doesn't have any brothers or sisters?' Monica asked.

'That's right, just me, Robert and Ellie – our dog – since Amanda left.'

Monica looked up at this. 'Where's Ellie now?'

Steven looked around the room. A look of panic crossed his face – a sudden realisation that Ellie might be missing too. He stood up from his chair, shouted, 'Ellie! El!'

There was a low sound from upstairs, a door scraping over carpet. A few seconds later Monica watched as a grey shaggy-haired old dog came slowly to stand on the upstairs landing. She looked down at them through the bannisters briefly before turning and wandering back in where she'd come from.

Steven Wright sat slowly back down again. Grateful for the moment of relief in the chaos of uncertainty he found himself in.

'So Robert was in bed safe on the Friday night,' Monica said, working out the times in her head. Robert's body was found in the early afternoon. Saturday, around 1 p.m. Assuming Steven was telling the truth, that gave a window of about thirteen hours from when Robert was last seen to when his body was discovered. Although she struggled to believe that even the boldest murderer would have dumped the body on that open croft land in broad daylight. 'What were his plans for today? What were his routines for a normal Saturday?'

'I don't know. Occasionally he takes the bus to Inverness with his friends. He likes to read books, the Internet. Just the normal things that kids do up here. Moan about having nothing to do. He's been going out on his mountain bike a lot.'

'Have you checked if his bike's still here?' Monica asked.

Steven Wright looked up at that, a pitiful moment of hope crossing his face. Maybe Robert had fallen off his bike somewhere. Sustained a slight injury, but otherwise was fine. 'I haven't checked. He keeps it in the garage.' Steven gestured out to the front of the house.

They followed Steven Wright as he led them back out into the night, over to the garage. The twin doors were open a crack. 'Is it normal to leave it unlocked?' Crawford asked as he pushed the door further open with his foot.

'No one locks their doors up here – who would steal something?' Steven said. Managing to sound appalled by the idea.

Who indeed? Monica thought as she followed Crawford and peered over the top of his head into the shadowy garage. She saw the bike illuminated by the torch on Crawford's phone. It was propped just inside the door.

'Is that his bike?' Crawford asked.

Steven looked past them, desperate hope lingering. 'That's it. That's his bike.'

'Did he have a mobile phone? A laptop?' Monica asked.

Steven Wright glanced between them as she spoke. The panic seemed to rise like a tide now. She noticed that his hands were shaking, as the realisation built. 'Of course he's got a bloody phone. I've spent all night trying to call—'

'And a laptop?'

'He keeps it in his room, in the desk.' Steven gestured back into the house. Arms folded across his chest now. An attempt at self-comfort as the cold mountain mist settled on his face and worked its way through that thin shirt and into his bones, where it would stay.

'Who are Robert's friends? Does he have a girlfriend? Anyone he would have sneaked out last night to meet?' Monica asked.

'Sneak out?' Steven Wright looked horrified at the idea. 'Why would he sneak out? He's got friends at school but none nearby. They're all spread out. It's a rural area, too far to cycle to—'

'And none of them have cars?' Crawford asked.

'Why are you asking about cars?' Something clicked in Steven Wright's mind then. Something that had been on the verge of his conscious thoughts but been held back by a dam of denial. 'Why are you asking about cars?' He repeated the words slowly as if they had some kind of deep significance. 'On the radio, this afternoon, when I was driving home they said that they'd found a boy. He'd been murdered in Gairloch. They said that ...' his voice broke then, his whole body shaking at the words he was about to say '... they said he'd been tortured. It isn't Robert, is it? It can't be. He was upstairs in bed. It isn't Robert, is it?'

His eyes went up to Monica's, then down to Crawford's and back again, the desperation rendering him somehow less than human. *It is Robert*, Monica thought, and you'll come to know that well.

'Robert fits the description,' Monica said finally. What else could she say? She watched the disbelief on the man's face and the shadows growing deeper. 'I think it's him. I'm really sorry.' Her words came out almost mechanically. Who would ever have thought that those words could come so easily.

She watched as he bent forward, head still shaking. The uniformed officer – PC Stewart – stepped towards Steven Wright and put an arm round his shoulders.

Monica turned to look down at Crawford.

Strangely, it was at that terrible moment she noticed for the first time just how green Crawford's eyes were when they caught in the lights above the door. Green like he could be wearing coloured contact lenses. A look of horror was frozen on his face and she wondered just how much he was enjoying his first murder investigation.

'We'll have to take him to Inverness to identify the body,' Monica said. She was leaning to whisper into Crawford's ear. 'And we'll need forensics in here. Make sure that no one touches the garage door or the kid's bike. Get DC Fisher on the phone, tell him that we're going to need to track Robert's phone and get his laptop fast-tracked by Digital Forensics today. There's bound to be something on there. Maybe he arranged to meet someone.'

Chapter 8

Michael sat bolt upright in bed, soaked in sweat and in the darkness. In his dream Nichol had been standing outside his window, staring in. Not moving but with his laptop bag over his shoulder. Rubbing that stone over his mouth and shouting, 'What happened to him, Michael? Why did you leave him?'

Michael wiped the sweat off his face. He tried to slow his breathing as he looked around the bedroom and fumbled for a cigarette with his shaking hands. He remembered that he'd lost them somewhere between the morgue and home. He leaned across to flick on the lamp and check the time: 4 a.m. The dark hours, the lonely hours. He blew pretend smoke into the air, whispered, 'Shut the fuck up.'

At the end of the bed Colonel Mustard, one of three semi-feral cats that had taken up residence in the house, lifted his head at the sound of Michael's voice. The cat stretched his legs out into points and glanced over for a moment as if to say, *Is it time for food?*

Michael closed his eyes in reply, but then the marks on the boy's face filled his mind. All he could smell was the stench from the morgue. He swung his legs out of bed. He knew he needed to do something to find Nichol. To take action. That had been his father's answer to everything, until Joseph hadn't ever come back.

For a second Michael was eight years old again, sitting on the stairs crying while the adults stood in the corridor below, talking in low voices. He took a deep breath – knew he needed a cigarette more than oxygen – then pushed the memory down into a hole with the others as he went through to his kitchen.

The house stood on a moor close to Ullapool. He'd bought it a couple of years previously, not long before his father got ill. They were going to share it. Michael would keep his flat in Inverness and come to visit at weekends. It hadn't worked out like that.

The cats followed him down the hall, Colonel Mustard in the lead, shrieking and crossing his path until Michael opened a can of meat and split it into three bowls. He watched them devour it as he waited for the kettle to boil and tried to work out what he'd done with his cigarettes.

A squall battered at the window, and as he started at the unexpected sound his dream came back to him, and an almost panicked impulse: *You need to look for Nichol; you need to find him.* He remembered the boy staring in through the window, the bag over his shoulder, holding that stone up in front of his mouth. A gesture that was somehow obscene.

Michael forced the image out of his mind and went back to searching for his cigarettes. Eventually he found them in the lining of the down jacket – they must have escaped through a hole in the pocket.

He lit one off the gas stove then went out into the storm anyway, just to check. There were no traces of his dream, of course: no footprints in the mud, no message. Just the mist and the rain. Safe inside, Colonel Mustard jumped up onto the window ledge and settled down to stare out at Michael through the dirty glass. *What are you going to do about it?*

Chapter 9

Monica stopped at the top of the stairs. Under the normal smells of an unfamiliar house there was a faint hint of an odour. Almost a perfume. She paused, glanced downstairs then pulled the forensics suit on, followed by the gloves and the shoe covers. There was a strip of ghostly pale flesh between where the suit ended and the gloves began, and she tugged harder at the materials, forcing them to meet. Experience told her it was improbable that Robert's room would be a murder scene, but experience also told her to never feel safe because of knowledge. She pushed the door slowly open. The sound as the wood scraped over the carpet was loud and intrusive in the silent space.

She clicked the light on and scanned the unfamiliar room, took in the empty bed. A desk with a half-drunk mug of something still standing on it. Robert had been out on his bike and come home late. Where had he been? Monica tried to sense his mood as she looked for tiny details and any signs of what the boy had been feeling and thinking when he was last in the room. The bed was still made but with the top sheets slightly ruffled. She glanced at his pile of dirty laundry over by the window and wondered if he'd changed his clothes when he came in. Had he planned to go out again? To meet someone? She made a mental note to ask Steven Wright to go through his son's clothes and look for anything missing. If Robert had put his best clothes on maybe it was some kind of romantic meeting gone wrong? Gone very wrong. Someone he had met online? Or some kind of jealousy that led to murder?

The tentative theories drifted up and away as Monica leaned closer to the desk. She noticed the pile of school books. History, astronomy, maths. A few postcards Blu-tacked up beside a timetable, the stub of a ticket to a gig in Inverness. The little fragments of a life, of an identity being formed.

Had he sneaked out to meet someone once his father was asleep? That's why Steven had seen him lying on top of the covers? Pretending to be asleep? Friends or a girlfriend that he hadn't told his father about? A boyfriend?

But the bike. The kid was too young to drive. He went everywhere on his bike, and it was still there in the garage. So someone picked him up? Then what? An argument? Suddenly finding himself well out of his depth?

Monica thought back to the way the body was laid out precisely on the croft land near the sea. Those strange bite marks on Robert's back. The repeated trauma to his windpipe. The injuries all seemed to point to someone who enjoyed what they were doing. Someone of considerable physical strength – almost certainly a man – who wanted to prolong the act.

She looked around the room again, hoping that Steven Wright was wrong and that Robert had conveniently left his phone for her to find. Because if he had met someone then there had to be something – a message, a call, a contact name. Monica knew how many apps immediately deleted messages you might want hidden, but there had to be some trace.

For a fleeting second she thought of Michael Bach and his lost boy. Nichol Morgan. The name was somehow familiar. She pushed the thought away as quickly as it had come.

She crouched by the bed, used a pen to carefully open the drawers of Robert's desk. Inside was the laptop that Steven Wright had mentioned. She lifted it out and slid it into a clear plastic evidence bag. So far it was their best bet – the most obvious chance of finding a clue that would lead them to the identity of Robert's killer.

A sound from the back of the room caught Monica off guard. Wood on wood. She turned quickly to face the noise, the surprise making the breath catch in her throat.

The dog that Steven Wright had called earlier tilted her head to look up at Monica. It was partially obscured by the curtains so she hadn't seen it when she'd come into the room. Monica let out a deep breath and took a step closer. The dog lifted a paw and again ran it over the wood panel beneath the window. The sound Monica had heard.

'You miss your friend, don't you,' she said as she crouched beside the big dog – a Scottish deerhound, she thought. Like a greyhound, only bigger and with a thick shaggy coat. The dog's back end was pushed up uncomfortably against the pile of washing.

'Just like me, too big for normal things,' Monica whispered as she ran a hand through the dog's soft downy fur. 'I wish you could speak; you'd make my job so much easier.' Ellie slapped her long tail on the carpet and pawed at the window again.

Monica stood up and looked out through the glass at the night outside. It was lit by a bright chunk of the moon now. Outside the window was the flat roof of the garage. If Robert had wanted to sneak out without waking his father he could easily have climbed out onto the roof then pulled the window closed behind him. At the end of the garden there was a commercial pine forest. Planted in straight lines and dense so the sun would never touch the ground. Beyond the forest she could see the steepening slopes of those dark mountains.

What had drawn him back out there? What was so tempting that he'd leave the warmth of his bed? Monica wished she could ask Robert Wright himself. She felt the tiredness gathering; it was after 4 a.m. now. Lucy would be in a deep sleep. In a different world Monica would be lying there beside her. Enjoying the warmth and comfort of those blankets, and all of Sunday to look forward to with her daughter when they finally did wake up. Wouldn't life be simpler like that? Without that obsessive need to know – that need to identify some kind of meaning behind the chaos of a terrible crime.

She glanced back down at the dog, who was curled up as tight as its large frame would allow. She contemplated her actual Sunday. Like it or not, there was no way she could take a break while the investigation was at such a vital early phase. There would be another trip to the mortuary. With Steven Wright this time for the formal identification of Robert's body. Then the interview with Steven and a visit to Michael Bach's house. Who knew what else would come up in between?

Chapter 10

Michael spent almost ten minutes wandering around outside the house in the early morning. Looking for ghosts from his dreams up here on the moor? Maybe he really was going mad this time. He lit a cigarette. It was still dark, and the distant mountains across the water to the north and south were only visible as heavy black walls.

He took a deep draw from the cigarette, realised that he was standing in front of the small byre at the end of the house. His dad had renovated it not long before he'd died. He had been strong right up until near the end. Almost like he could fight off the cancer through force of will alone. Part of Michael still couldn't believe that anything could have made his father as weak as he was in those final days. It seemed almost to violate a law of nature.

He couldn't make himself go inside the byre. Go through his father's things like he'd asked. Instead he turned and walked down through the dark of the early morning towards the beach. He felt the icy bog water run into his shoes. The fetid smell of the bog followed, but thankfully no cloud of midges; it was too late in the year for them now.

At the shoreline Michael sat down on a rock. He stared out across the water, smoking as the dawn broke. The sea was flat calm this morning, slack and thick and dark like wine. Almost purple: the colour of bruises, the colour of love bites on a body.

He remembered the boy's face, pale white on that slab. He tried hard to put it out of his mind, but it was only replaced by a memory of the dream, of those dark corridors. Of Nichol standing at the window, staring in, and the feeling that he had somehow brought with him to Michael. The panic of grief, of loss, of needing to look for someone but having no idea where to start.

The dark water spread to the horizon. To the edges of the primordial mountainous landscape. There were times when Michael thought it was the most beautiful place imaginable. This morning it couldn't have felt more bleak, magnifying his insignificance and the pointlessness of it all.

Impulsively he stood up and stripped his clothes off then walked out into the cold water until it burned his skin and took his breath away. Dad would have admired this at least, he thought as he trod water and tried to slow his breathing. Something brushed his leg and made him wonder: was there any truth in the story that great white sharks occasionally ventured into these cold waters? Could there really be a monster down there in the dark? He ducked his head under. Tasted the salt and let the bitter cold take away all the thoughts, for a moment at least.

When his teeth were chattering he swam back to the shore and dried himself off as best he could with his T-shirt. He pulled his clothes back on then struggled to get the lighter to spark with shaking hands. Like a shipwreck survivor desperate to start a fire, he thought as the cigarette finally caught.

He pushed the lighter back into his pocket and felt his phone beside it. It made him wonder if the police would contact him if they heard anything about Nichol. Probably not. It wasn't like he was next of kin. He flicked through the messages on the phone to check anyway and found himself stopping on that last one from Nichol again: 'The future is in the stars.' It still didn't make any sense. There had to be someone who knew where he'd gone. Someone who knew Nichol better than he did.

It occurred then to Michael just how little he actually knew about the kid's life. He knew that Nichol's mother was dead and that he'd never met his father. But what about his friends and his extended family? Michael had never met any of them, had barely even spoken to Nichol about them. He hadn't even gone to the boy's accommodation with him that time he'd asked. Just dropped him off in the street outside and driven on to another appointment.

With bubbling guilt Michael recalled Nichol's face that day as he had turned away from the Land Rover towards the double doors of that grim 'house of multiple occupancy' – a hostel by any other name – on Union Street in Inverness. An expression that was hard to pin down. Was it disappointment? Resentment?

'Well what can I do about it now? Fucking hell!' Michael stared up and down the lonely beach, vaguely startled by the sound of his own frustrated and guilty voice. But unexpectedly an answer came into his head: *Go to Inverness. Look for him.* Suddenly it even seemed obvious.

It was still early when Michael set off to drive east through the mountains, past Beinn Dearg and then Ben Wyvis, standing alone like a worn-down tooth, back towards Inverness. The deer had come down from the hills and gathered by the sides of the road, drawn to the heat of the tarmac as the cold autumn nights grew longer.

Michael lit another cigarette and turned up the heater to dry his clothes, which were still damp from the seawater.

Colonel Mustard lifted his head at the welcome heat. The warm air from the heater fan ruffled his fur where he lay on the dashboard. He stretched his ginger paws out in contentment so his toe pads splayed open showing the soft downy fur between.

The cat had barged his way into the Land Rover when Michael had made the mistake of starting the engine with the door still open. The sound of the motor was a signal to Colonel Mustard that there was warmth on offer, and he had dug his claws into the dash when Michael tried to remove him. Finally Michael had given up, not for the first time, and let Colonel Mustard come along for the journey.

Part of Michael was secretly glad of the company. He reached through the steering wheel and ruffled the fur on the cat's head. In response Colonel Mustard stared at him for a moment then closed his eyes and stretched out further.

Michael shook his head and pushed a CD into the player, *Trojan Rastafari Box Set (Disc 3)*. The sound of the Caribbean filled the vehicle, and Michael stared out at the long thin clouds hanging among the mountains. He'd found that reggae suited the Highland landscape much better than the awful 1970s folk music his dad had insisted on playing any time they were in the car together.

The thought triggered a memory. One that seemed to belong to someone else: Michael and a brother in the back of a car. A brown interior. It must have been the days before seat belts because the two boys had climbed over into the boot together. They were waving at the cars following them on the motorway.

Two boys laughing, smiling.

Michael wiped a hand across his face as he suppressed the memory. *Jesus*, he thought, *what's going on with me today?*

He pulled up outside the hostel on Union Street. Took in the Victorian buildings from a time when the architecture of Inverness had been some kind of Walter Scott Highland fantasy. It was rough at the edges now though. More than at the edges, Michael thought, glancing up and down the street. His eyes landed on a patch of blood on the pavement and a matching spray of vomit against a wall. Just another Saturday night.

The double doors of the hostel were propped open with an empty beer crate. Michael stepped over it and caught the smells of smoke and dust in the dark lobby. He glanced around the shadowy space then moved towards the staircase.

'Ho!'

Michael jumped at the shout, turned and realised that there was a small office at the opposite end of the lobby. A counter barred the doorway, and a man was on a seat behind it, legs propped up on a table. 'You don't just wander in off the street, gudgie.'

Michael stepped closer and took the man in: long greasy hair, dark stubble spattered across a suspicious face. A guitar balanced on his legs. He stared at Michael with an accusatory expression.

'The door was open,' Michael said.

'Yeah, well there's a buzzer. And you come to the office; you don't just walk up the stairs.'

Michael stared over the counter at the mess surrounding the man in his 'office'. Stacks of old newspapers and a row of dirty mugs with cigarette ash in them. Even after more than a decade as a social worker, Michael was surprised how some people would clutch at any crumb of power.

'Sorry. I didn't realise.'

The man shrugged. 'Well you'll know for next time. What do you want anyway?'

Michael forced a smile, thinking, *There won't be a next time, believe me.* 'I'm a social worker. One of my clients was in temporary accommodation here. He went missing. I spoke to someone ...' Michael searched for the name but his mind was blank '... on the phone last week?'

The man's eyes dropped to the floor, suddenly shifty. 'I don't know anything about that; I'm just the manager.'

'He was seen getting on a train,' Michael said. 'I just want to know where he's gone. His name was Nichol Morgan. You must have seen him.' The man's eyes flicked around the office as if deciding on the best lie to tell. Michael leaned on the counter. 'I need to know. It's really important.'

'I probably saw him,' the man said finally, realising that Michael wasn't about to leave. 'There's loads of them in here, they come and go ...'

'What about friends?'

The man shrugged. 'He kept himself to himself, just came to his room to sleep. They're transient, these kids. From all over the Highlands. Congregate in the city for a free doss — that's why the centre of town's the way it is now. Fights. Junkies. Just last week one of them woke up, decides to throw himself off the top of Rose Street Car Park. Splat. A nice mess for them to scrape up.' The man laughed at that, lit a cigarette, patted his greasy hair down at the back. 'Probably your boy just wanted a change of scene. It's a free country, isn't it? Have you never thought about just packing up and heading off somewhere else, gudgie? To Rose Street Car Park even.' The man's face came alive, but his laugh drifted a long way from anything funny.

Michael leaned further over the counter and for half a second found himself reaching out to grab the collar of the man's shirt, imagining himself pulling him over the counter and shaking him. He managed to stop himself and found he was patting the man's shoulder instead. A strange and threatening gesture. The man looked down at Michael's hand and tried to brush it away, clearly unnerved.

Michael took a step back. Unnerved himself by what he'd done. But the thought from his subconscious rose to the surface: *How have you put up with these horrible people – for ten years, for longer? Maybe you should just drag him over the counter and strangle him. You'd be doing everyone a favour.*

Michael patted himself down for a cigarette. His hand was shaking when he found the damp packet in his pocket and lit up. Then he looked back at the man across the counter, who was now eyeing him differently. He looked frightened.

'Did Nichol leave anything in his room?' Michael asked finally. Repressing the urge to apologise to the man for his aggression.

'Someone else is in it now. We have to turn the rooms over quickly when someone leaves, it's the only way we make money,' the man said, his tone almost apologetic now. He glanced beyond Michael as if checking for a potential escape route. 'The police came for his things when he was declared missing the other day. I saw them take everything out. There wasn't much: some books, his laptop—'

'Wait, his laptop?'

The man nodded. 'That's right, I saw them carrying it out.' Michael remembered his dream, Nichol standing at the window with the laptop bag over his shoulder. He could barely remember seeing the kid without the thing. It was probably his only valuable possession. There was no way he would have left without it unless something had gone seriously wrong.

Chapter 11

All through the drive home Michael turned over what the man at the hostel had told him. It made no sense. If Nichol had gone and left the laptop then there had to be a good reason. He had to be in danger. *He came to you for help*, Michael thought, *and you let him down*. Just like before. Just like with Joseph.

Michael gripped the steering wheel a little harder and tried to ignore the thought.

As if trying to provide a visual distraction, Colonel Mustard chose that moment to stand up on the dashboard and stretch, blocking Michael's view of the road ahead. Michael swore as the Land Rover swerved across the middle white line. He tilted his head so he could at least see the reflective snow poles that marked the edge of the carriageway. Then he reached to push Colonel Mustard to the other side of the dashboard before he caused an accident.

The cat hissed in outrage and jumped down onto Michael's lap. Michael swore again as Colonel Mustard scrambled up his jumper onto his shoulder, the cat using his claws indiscriminately as crampons. Finally he settled down across Michael's shoulders like a heavy living fox fur. Purring gently in Michael's ear, completely content with his new bed.

Michael thought about trying to shift the cat, whose body heat was already causing a patina of sweat to mix with the damp of the saltwater on his jumper collar. Finally he decided against it and looked out at the landscape instead. The morning was edging into afternoon now. The thin clouds that had drifted among the mountains earlier had coalesced into a thick blanket across the sky. It made the day feel prematurely dark and gloomy. In the autumn and winter these days in the Highlands could feel like the sun had never really risen. That the night never really ended.

Well that's the oldest story there is, isn't it? Michael thought. The question of what keeps the world turning, what holds back the darkness. He bent his head carefully to light another cigarette. Maybe his twentieth of the day already.

Finally he took the turn-off for the long driveway that led up to the croft.

When he reached the brow of the hill Michael saw that there was a car parked outside the croft. A dark-coloured Volvo. Two people were standing at his front door, one tall in a black coat, the other small and thin. Together, silhouetted against the horizon, they looked like characters from a Nordic fairy tale. The giant and the goblin.

Michael stepped awkwardly out of the Land Rover, transferring Colonel Mustard from his neck into his hands. The cat shook his head then jumped out of Michael's arms, ran past the two people and into the house through the makeshift cat flap Michael had cut in the door.

Michael walked towards the two detectives from the morgue. They watched as he approached, then held out IDs that were unreadable in the gloomy overcast day.

Without thinking to ask why they were waiting for him, Michael pushed the unlocked front door open and led them inside past the kitchen and into the living room. He watched as the woman stooped to fit through the low doorway. She glanced around, seeming to take in the battered leather sofa, the worn rugs and the untidy piles of books, then they both sat down and she turned to Michael. 'Why do you think we're here?'

'Nichol?' Michael tensed as he said it, thinking again about the abandoned laptop. It could only mean that something terrible had happened. It was the only explanation that made any sense. The premature evening was shyly starting to drift in through the windows, and he wondered if they'd found another one. Another body, one with a name this time.

Neither of the police officers answered. Instead the male detective leaned forward in his chair, his wild green eyes fixed on Michael. The detectives let the silence fill the room. The woman with her pale face and dark hair tied back in an untidy bun. She really was as large as she'd seemed in that corridor at the hospital when Michael had thought for a moment that he was facing an apparition.

'When we spoke last night at the morgue you mentioned that your client Nichol Morgan was carrying a stone around with him. Before he went missing?' the woman said finally.

Michael nodded slowly, confused. 'Sorry, what did you say your names were?' He asked the question to buy a moment of time to think as much as anything.

The woman dug methodically in her pocket then held out her warrant card again. 'I'm Detective Inspector Monica Kennedy. This is Detective Constable Connor Crawford. We're investigating a murder.' She folded the ID away again. Her eyes never leaving Michael's face. 'Like I said, Nichol had this rock he carried round with him.' Michael hesitated, a moment of discomfort at what he was about to share. As if he were being disloyal, highlighting something of the kid's vulnerability. 'He used to ... to kiss it. The piece of rock – he'd hold it up to his face.'

'And you don't think that's a strange thing to comment on?' Crawford asked this time. His eyes hard on Michael's face. Michael stared back at him. Took the man in, his dark red hair and thin face. There was something of an air of tragedy about him. His staring eyes were like old photographs Michael had seen of doomed Confederate soldiers in the American Civil War.

Michael cleared his throat. 'I told you yesterday.' His eyes went to DI Kennedy. 'It was something new. I thought it was ...' His hand reached into his pocket for a cigarette but found his lighter instead. He turned it over in his fingers.

'It was what?' she asked.

'Strange.'

DC Crawford glanced at Kennedy. She nodded and the detective reached into his inside pocket. He pulled something out and slid it across the table to Michael. It was a photograph of a dark piece of rock with a mobile phone lying beside it for scale.

'This rock was removed from the victim's throat during the autopsy.'

'From his throat?' Michael picked the photo up. He felt his body instinctively imagining the rock lodged in his own throat, imagined the suffocating pressure. 'Was the boy – was he alive when it happened?'

'Maybe you can tell us?' DC Crawford said, again leaning forward as he spoke.

Michael frowned, and then snorted as if he were about to laugh. Both detectives stared at him, DI Kennedy's eyes unblinking and almost black.

'Sorry, but you think I did this?' His voice was rising and he swallowed to calm himself. He realised it now: of course they thought he killed the boy, or why else would they be here?

'Who's saying that?' DC Crawford let his words hang in the shadowy room. 'We're just asking questions.'

'Did you give that stone to Nichol? Is it the same one?' DI Kennedy spoke this time.

Michael stared at the photograph. He remembered the dead boy's face and that patch of blood against the white of his dead eye. 'Nichol's one was bigger. It was a different shape, and I've told you, I've no idea where he got it from.'

He slid the photograph across the table towards the female detective.

'You live here alone, no wife or anything?' she asked, glancing round the room again.

'That's right. My father bought it. He ... got ill, passed away,' Michael said. He felt the spark of anger in his stomach when he realised that he'd justified himself to them.

'It must be lonely living up here, in the middle of nowhere,' DC Crawford said this time. 'And a career in social work. It's a difficult job from what I've heard. Soul-destroying seeing the mess some people's lives are. Then coming home here, no one waiting for you, no one to talk it all over with. It must be hard.'

Michael looked down at the table. He lit a cigarette then looked up at the male detective again but didn't reply.

'Just for the record,' DI Kennedy said, still watching Michael closely. 'Where were you the morning you were supposed to meet Nichol? And this Friday night through to Saturday before you came to the morgue?'

'I was working. Visiting clients.'

'On both occasions? That's kind of vague.' Her dark hair was still wet against her forehead, and he watched as a drop of rain rolled past her left eyebrow.

'You're a detective, see if you can figure it out,' Michael said. His frustration began to feel alive under his skin. He knew that he needed to curb it before he allowed that anger from earlier in the day to take hold. 'What are you doing to find Nichol – surely that's the priority now? It's an obvious connection.'

'You don't have to worry about that,' she said.

'But surely ...' Then the dream again, echoing through his mind. 'Listen. Nichol had a laptop. I went to his accommodation earlier today; the manager said that he left it in his room. The police took it when I reported him missing. There's no way he would have just left it unless he was in trouble. There has to be information on it, something that might say where he's—'

'We'll keep that in mind,' DC Crawford interrupted.

'If you're not going to bother looking at it, Jesus Christ! Give me the laptop – I'll look through it.'

'We're taking this seriously,' Crawford said. 'We're taking everything you say seriously.'

Michael examined the two detectives again. He took in their tired faces, their matching staring eyes. They probably didn't even realise how similar their fixed expressions were. 'Take this seriously then: get the fuck out of my house,' he said softly.

He took another draw on his cigarette. It tasted dirty. Outside the window it was grey now. The storm clouds covering the horizon and hiding whatever else might be out there. Dead boys and the people who killed them.

Chapter 12

DC Crawford stopped their car at the end of the track and waited for a string of vehicles stuck behind a lorry on the narrow road to pass. Spray rose off the wet tarmac behind them. He glanced at DI Kennedy. 'Do you think Michael Bach knows something?'

Monica watched the beads of rain hitting the windscreen as Crawford pulled out into the road. The mountains ahead of them were obscured by the clouds now. She checked the time on the car radio: 14:00 on a Sunday. That made it well over twenty-four hours without sleep now.

After they had finished at the Wrights' house there was the early-morning drive back to Inverness and police headquarters to take Steven Wright's official statement, where he repeated more or less what he'd told them in the living room of his house. But before that they'd been back to Raigmore Hospital. To the morgue, where Steven confirmed that the body lying dead in that fridge was Robert Wright. His only son. His only child.

Monica glanced at Crawford and realised that she still hadn't answered his question. With the exhaustion she wasn't sure what she knew.

'I think that he seems genuinely concerned about his client. You saw his house. It was a mess, disorganised,' she said finally.

'So?' As if mirroring her own tiredness Crawford reached into the door pocket and opened one of the Red Bulls that he seemed to exist on. He offered a can to her. She hesitated then took it and took a deep pull on the sickly-sweet drink. It tasted like the medicine she gave to Lucy when the kid had a bug. She immediately repressed the thought. She hated even letting her daughter appear in her imagination alongside the horrible crimes she investigated. It was like proximity to her work tainted Lucy somehow.

'I'm not sure,' she said. Choosing her words carefully, uncertain how much she should share with him. Would he fixate on a theory and ignore contrary evidence? Or perhaps more likely try to bulldoze through any tentative theory to demonstrate his powers of critical thinking? 'I think our killer planned it out,' she said finally. 'I think he spent a lot of time on it. I think he lured Robert outside somehow. Hopefully we'll know more from his laptop, but I think there was a logic to what the killer did. I think it was someone methodical. I think there was a logic to where the killer put Robert.'

'A logic behind strangling someone, torturing them? Dumping them? You saw how angry Michael Bach got when we pressed him. He had access didn't he? To kids, vulnerable boys? And the stone, that's a coincidence is it? A fucking big coincidence.'

Monica didn't reply. Instead she fished in her pocket for her mobile phone and put in a call to headquarters. They were approaching the Braemore junction and she knew that once they turned off into the steep mountainous landscape to the south the reception would disappear. 'I need you to check an alibi with the Highland Social Work Department asap – there'll be an emergency skeleton staff in, even on a Sunday. The name's Michael Bach. He said that he was working away on Friday evening and Saturday morning.' When the call was finished she glanced over at Crawford. 'When we hear back we'll know one way or the other whether he's a suspect.'

They followed the long road south to Gairloch, through Dundonnell, under the bulk of An Teallach and skirting Fisherfield Forest, an ancient hunting ground. These were the most remote mountains in Britain. The gloomy shadows they cast were broken only by an occasional distant pillar of heavenly sunlight cutting through the clouds among the hills and lochs far off to the side of the road; a Romantic oil painting, a scene from the Ossian myths brought to life.

Monica stared out of the window thinking what a strange parody of a Sunday drive it was. Touring the scenic west coast with a virtual stranger, looking for a killer somewhere in that wide landscape.

The tiny Gairloch police station was on a road close to the sea. Crawford pulled the Volvo over, climbed out slowly and stretched. Above the water, thick clouds were obscuring the slowly setting sun.

Monica's eyes fell on an orange shop sign further down the road: OPEN. Crawford looked in the same direction. 'My grandad would have marched into that shop and told them they should be closed on the Sabbath,' he said with a laugh.

'Your family are Wee Free?' Monica asked. Referring to the strict Scottish Presbyterian Free Church.

Crawford nodded. 'That's right. Me and Mum lived with them when I was a kid. On a Sunday you were supposed to sit and read your Bible, a proper day of rest.'

'I bet that was fun.' Monica watched Crawford's eyes narrow as he turned to look out at the water. She resisted the urge to ask more: why they'd had to live there? Why just him and his mother? What about a father?

He shrugged. 'I quite liked the Old Testament. Cain and Abel, the story of every murder boiled down into a few paragraphs. The Bible feels more serious if you read it literally. My grandad did and he met the devil.'

Monica turned to look down at Crawford. 'He really said that?' Crawford glanced up, ran a comb through his hair and bent to check it in the wing mirror of the Volvo.

'I think he believed it too. He said that when he was a young man he'd been tempted by gambling, by ... fornication he called it.' Crawford shrugged. 'He said that the devil came and whispered to him in his bedroom, outside his window.'

'What did the devil look like?' Monica asked. She was intrigued by the stories people told themselves. By what they could actually believe.

'Just like a man, he said. But different, more real than a man. That part gave me nightmares.' Crawford laughed then put the comb into his jacket pocket. 'There's still a little bit of me that believes it. Even after all these years. Sometimes I wonder if he'll come for me. What that would feel like. Anyway.' He nodded at the small police station stuck on the end of a row of terraced houses. '"Nothing good ever came of a job begun on the Sabbath," he'd say.'

Monica looked down at him again and thought, *You're not a bad man, Crawford. Not as bad as I thought.*

DC Ben Fisher was already waiting for them in the small office when Monica opened the door. She looked around, taking in a couple of posters tacked to the walls: one warning of the dangers of speeding, the other reminding tourists to keep their possessions hidden from view. *Well, if they've ended up in the police station it's probably too late for that advice*, Monica thought as she nodded to Fisher.

Fisher looked up from the laptop he was working at and adjusted his glasses. He was still only twenty-six, more or less straight out of university. The youngest member of the Major Investigations Team, younger even than DC Crawford (who was twenty-nine, Monica knew from his file), Fisher had already managed to alienate himself from some of the older detectives with his references to formal best practice and with the Blackstone's *Senior Investigating Officers' Handbook* he carried around with him, his aspirations laid out for all to see.

Monica's boss, Detective Superintendent Fred Hately, had assigned Fisher to coordinate the house-to-house inquiries and sift through the local calls coming in. The young detective's black hair was combed in a precise side parting and he was wearing a white shirt under a dark blue suit. Neat and precise too, and when his hand went up to adjust his glasses for a second time Monica was struck with the thought: *He's putting on a show.* Demonstrating to the boss how deeply he's concentrating on the investigation.

She sat down across the desk from him and wondered dimly when she had become so cynical. Crawford gave Fisher a hard stare, as if he were laying down some kind of challenge that Fisher gave the impression of being oblivious to, and was certainly uninterested in. Crawford picked up a seat, still staring at Fisher. For a second Monica thought he was actually going to turn it around and straddle it. Instead he set it down and went over to the coffee maker.

'I bought sandwiches; I thought you might not have had a chance to eat,' Fisher said, pointing to a small fridge in the corner of the room. Another nugget from the *SIO Handbook*:

'Practical approaches to addressing welfare; proper food and drink are a necessity.'

Generally Monica found it easier just to go without eating in the midst of an investigation. Something that her mum seemed to find infinitely baffling. It wasn't unusual for Monica to come home from an investigation in the early hours of the morning, desperate to sleep, only to be met with the smell of roasting potatoes or a thick Scotch broth bubbling on the hob. Her mother insisting that she eat something: 'At least a wee bit. You'll waste away otherwise, a big girl like you.'

'What's come in so far from the house-to-house inquiries?' Monica asked, pushing the irritating memory away and glancing at the window; outside a thick sea mist was moving in off the Minch. Just the three of them, here at the edge of the world, Monica thought. As far from a glamorous investigation, from busy offices with banks of monitors and endlessly ringing phones, as it was possible to get.

Fisher glanced over the notes on his laptop as if there might be something important that he'd somehow forgotten.

'So far there's nothing that I'd consider to be of obvious significance. It's slow going because so many of the houses are detached with long driveways. Everyone seems to know everyone here and they all want to talk, but in terms of important sightings or names of potential suspects, there's nothing that really stands out.'

Monica nodded. It was a little over twenty-four hours since the body had been discovered, although it seemed like days already.

'There's one thing that could be important. It came from a crofter out on the peninsula, just before the turn-off to the dump site. He says that he saw a white Maestro van, one he didn't recognise. It was early on Saturday morning – he was out all night tending to a sick cow,' Fisher said. 'The road's a dead end, so the van must have been heading in the direction of the dump site.'

'I take it he didn't get the registration number?' Monica asked. That would just be too much to hope for.

Fisher shook his head. Monica considered it for a moment. 'If the kid went missing some time after 10.30 p.m. on the Friday and we work on the theory that his body was dumped before it got light on the Saturday morning, that gives us a relatively small time frame. There wouldn't have been many cars on the road at that time of the night. There's only one obvious route that leads from the Wrights' house near Achnasheen over the mountain pass above Loch Maree to Gairloch. Unless the killer took a much longer roundabout way. There are a couple of garages and a few hotels close to the road. I wonder if any of them had CCTV that we could pull a registration plate from? Can you look into it? And ask the service provider for a list of mobile phone numbers that pinged the tower that serves the area around the dump site. We can use it against any potential suspects if they were stupid enough to leave their phone switched on.'

Fisher nodded quickly, his face set in a diligent mask as he typed out a note to himself. His overeagerness should have been annoying, if it wasn't so unusual these days. *I'll take overeager and diligent any day of the week*, Monica thought as she glanced between the two junior detectives.

'What about the kid's laptop? That's the main thing we should be talking about here, isn't it? That's what's going to crack this case open,' Crawford said. His tone was accusatory. As if any delay in Digital Forensics sifting through the mass of potential information on the computer was somehow Fisher's fault.

'They're starting with the obvious places,' Fisher said. He seemed to take Crawford's question at face value and ignore the implication of blame. 'Social media, emails, forums. His laptop wasn't password protected, his dad wouldn't let him. So that's saved a lot of time. But ...' he shrugged '... everyone's laptop's like a labyrinth. It could take a while to find that tiny piece of evidence.'

'Meanwhile we do nothing?' Crawford said, his voice rising with frustration. Monica glanced over at him, irritated by his tone. She watched as he ran a hand over his red hair and stood up to pour himself another long black coffee.

She felt a momentary impulse to pull him up. To tell him to wind his neck in. She hesitated then decided against it for now. It was his first murder investigation; he was probably struggling to deal with the emotional impact. It was difficult for some people.

You get a pass this time, she thought as she cleared her throat and reached across the desk to the file of photos from the dump site. She flicked through them. Considered the way the body had been folded forward. The fact that no DNA evidence had been recovered from the scene.

'I don't think this is our killer's first murder,' she said. Almost thinking out loud. 'I think he's done this before. Maybe more than once. He's spent a lot of time thinking and fantasising about it. Planning it out thoroughly.' She lifted her head from the photo of Robert's pale back against the grass of the field and caught the subtle look that passed between Crawford and Fisher.

Were they excited? Afraid?

The smell of coffee drifted in the room. It mixed with the corrosive taste of the sea mist in the air, which was edging its way off the beach and in through the closed front door of the station.

'We need to start looking into sexual offenders in the area. Particularly anyone with a history of sadistic violence. I think he'll do it again. Maybe soon.'

Chapter 13

The Watcher

The moth twisted and turned, threw her wings out sporadically as the silk web was wound expertly and cruelly around her. By the light on his phone he watched her writhe, desperately jerking against the reality of her situation – against the reality of nature. And the rush of adrenaline hit his veins in those final moments as the moth gave up and lay still.

He took a deep breath and forced his heart rate down.

The stars stared back at him from the black sky and told him that it wasn't quite time yet. The excitement was building though, even as he felt the bruises and lingering tightness in his honed muscles from the exertions with Robert.

From his place among the trees he stared at the light of the kitchen window in the isolated house. Watched it flicker as the boy, Paul, passed across it. Pretending not to feel the eyes on him. Pretending that he hadn't already agreed to everything.

Soon, but not yet.

To slow things down he cast his mind back to the first time. Back to a different house. Another doorway. The first sign he'd received. Almost thirty years before with the old woman.

She had fallen at the entrance to her house, in the porch. And she was swearing. Words that he had only heard from adults in whispers.

They were on their way to the park. Him and George. Pushing their BMXs. It was sunny even though it must have been winter because he was wearing his favourite childhood gloves and that hat. The quiet crescent of modern houses, cars in driveways and red stone chips. The strangeness of all those unnecessary rules that the other children seemed to need.

George's father was gone, and his mother liked nothing better than to drink and get what attention she could from men. The parade of men through that small house made George flighty and nervous, which went with his bookish intelligence. He was wearing a sweatshirt, no jacket or hat. A pair of old gloves. No hat meant he heard it first, that swearing from the porch.

'Do you hear that?' George said. Always looking for affirmation, unable even to trust his own senses. His companion didn't reply. He liked it better that way. There was a high fence at the front of the house, blocking sight of it from the road. In these suburban places young mothers drove, fathers went out to work. An old person was something of a rarity back then on those new estates.

He remembered how he had propped his bike against the fence and pushed the gate slowly open and then heard the shouting again.

'Help me. Fucking help me!'

The old woman had fallen in the porch, and with her useless old limbs didn't have the strength to get herself up. He stepped closer down the paved pathway, feeling a strange surge of excitement. She was wedged by the half-opened door, almost straddling it with a leg folded back at an awkward angle.

He stepped a little closer, feeling his pulse rise. Intrigued by how she would react to his presence. Her hair was grey and thinning, her bare legs were swollen, marked with bruises and varicose veins. Her wool skirt hitched up above her waist. It seemed a strange spectacle, her lying there like that.

'What should we do?'

The old woman looked up at the sound of George's voice. Her panicked eyes flickered between them. He stepped a little closer and turned to look at George, who was hanging back by the gate. He couldn't understand why George wasn't interested.

'Help me. I fell.' The panic in her voice had shifted to something else. Relief, shame. He stepped closer again and saw the letters that she must have been leaning over for. Saw that she had made a mess of herself, down her skirt. Spread around the place.

He looked over his shoulder to George again. At his wide eyes and that permanent line of snot down to his lip.

'You have to get someone. I need help. Please, I'm cold.' He noticed that her voice was strange. Different from the way an adult would normally talk to a child. That was exciting too. He stood looking down at her for a long moment. The blossoms of their breath in the cold air.

He stepped closer again. The woman reached out a hand to him, but he ignored it and stepped over her legs to get past. Careful to avoid the mess. She was shouting something, but he ignored her and went inside to look around.

The house carried a smell that was new to him. Though he couldn't have described it as such then, he would think of it later as the smell of neglect. Similar to George's bedroom. But far more pronounced. Unmistakable. Of food gone bad. Mould and corruption and helplessness.

He liked that too.

In the lounge there was a mantelpiece with photographs on it. They were black and white mostly. Pictures of a wedding, a man in uniform, a young woman smiling. More photographs: of school children, people in strange cloaks, like vampires, another wedding.

Beside the mantelpiece was a glass-fronted cabinet. There were objects inside. Porcelain and metal, nothing of interest. But on the bottom shelf there was a cardboard box, opened up to display its contents. A printed label glued to the lid read: VISITORS FROM SPACE. He reached in and picked them up. They were heavy, stones; there was something about them he liked.

Hours later, when the police came and their questions started, it was so easy for him to pretend. To stare down at the floor and to whisper, 'It was George. He told me to go into the house. When I came out he was standing over the lady. I think he dropped something on her ...' So easy for them to put the pieces together. The poor boy with the awful mother and the neglected home. So easy to let George take the blame.

Back in the present he blinked and turned back to look at the stars. They had inched through the sky. Into the correct position. He took a deep breath and felt the darkness enter his body. Another deep breath, then he began to move towards the house.

Chapter 14

By the time they'd finished their meeting the sun was dipping down far out over the Minch, the gloomy Highland day finally admitting defeat and slouching into the grave. Monica looked up and down the quiet road. In the summer this place would be crowded with tourists and rows of cars on the newly christened North Coast 500. When her grandparents had spoken about doing the same route by bicycle sixty years before they'd just called it 'cycling round the top of Scotland'.

Monica ran both hands through her hair and patted herself down for the car key, realised she'd given it to Crawford to drive when they'd left headquarters that morning. She hadn't felt like driving after the interview with Steven Wright and found herself wondering how he was now. How he was coping after providing a list of people who could verify his movements on the morning that his dead son had been dumped after being abducted and tortured. Having to provide evidence that he hadn't murdered his own son, his most basic role as a parent, as a protector, stripped away from him.

For a moment Monica allowed herself to taste his grief. To imagine it was Lucy in that refrigerator. Her little body broken and folded up on that patch of barren ground, a piece of rock lodged in her throat. Monica almost gagged at the echoes of horror and panic, and she stuffed the idea away as quickly as she could.

You get to go home now, she reminded herself. You get to see your daughter, to hold her close and to smell her hair. To see how annoyed she still is about the cinema. Monica pictured the kid with her face in a book. Her glasses balanced on the end of her small nose. The kid glancing up at Monica with a conflicted expression. Half of her still wanting to punish Monica, while the other half was desperate to share her excitement over whatever new picture or story had captivated her.

Monica had tried repeatedly to steer the kid towards sports and games and general light-heartedness. Worried that Lucy would follow her own lonely path through childhood and adolescence: always on the outside looking in. But already, aged only four, Lucy was drawn to letters and numbers rather than people. She loved making up words on the fridge from the magnetic alphabet that she'd insisted Granny buy her. Otherwise her head was rarely out of a book.

'Lucy's her mother's daughter,' Monica's own mother liked to say. 'One hundred per cent. Like a clone.' Ignoring the contradictory facts of the kid's appearance: her curly blonde hair, the welcome fact that she was far from being the tallest little girl at the playgroup or Sunday school. Facts that suggested at least fifty per cent of her DNA came from a different source.

Monica turned at the sound of the Volvo's doors bleeping as they unlocked. Crawford crossed the road behind her, his arms held out from his body to broaden his slight frame. He went to open the driver's door.

'No,' Monica heard herself saying. She opened the door herself and sat down in the driver's seat, sliding it most of the way back. 'You go with Fisher and start working through the sexual offenders' cases. I think our killer will be in his mid-twenties at least, maybe older. Use that as a guide for now.'

Crawford glanced back down the road to where Fisher was carrying his laptop bag and a box of files from the office to his red Volkswagen Polo. Then he looked back at her, his face set hard now. 'Why? Where are you going?'

In reply Monica held her hand out for the key. She took it and started the engine.

The gloom only seemed to deepen on the lonely road to the peninsula. The Torridon mountains that dominated the view from Gairloch on a clear day were at Monica's back now as she drove north. Just the boggy croft land and the big sky, thick with cloud, ahead of her. The edge of the world.

She turned off down the single-track road. The same route the murderer would have taken, the lights from the few houses spread out wide over the land. *Why here?* she wondered; there were a million spots across the Highlands to dump a body, to pose it in a particular position. Did the killer know this area well? Was it someone who lived nearby? The received wisdom was that a murderer would dispose of a body in an area they were familiar with. Monica found her thoughts drifting to the infamous Moors Murders. Those shallow graves on the empty moorland. The meaning of the murders mapped only on to the dark voids in the killers' minds.

But those bodies had been hidden. Here it was left on display. Almost as if it were a message in itself. Monica stared at the flat land on either side of the road. There were sheep in most of the drystone-walled fields, long-horned cows in one of the others. The beasts were standing watch in the gloaming like strange silent judges of everything that passed this way.

The dump site was close to where the road ended, the field still marked off with crime-scene tape. Monica stopped the car, killed the engine and switched off the lights. She felt the first buffets of a breeze from far out over the North Atlantic hit the car windows. An early distant warning that another change in the weather was coming soon.

She got out, pulling her dark Harris tweed coat on over the thin shirt she was wearing. She felt the wind fight her for it as she buttoned the coat and turned the collar up against the cold. The familiar smell of oily wool was comforting against her face as she thought back to the trip with her mum to a 'Traditional Highland Tailors' in the town of Beauly near Inverness. She remembered how they'd picked out the dark herringbone tweed from the reams of different colours and patterns. The feeling of the pristine handwoven wool under her fingers and the anticipation a couple of weeks later when they'd driven back to collect the finished item. The package wrapped in brown paper and the feeling when she'd pulled it on: the satisfaction of finally having a beautiful coat that actually fitted properly. She still loved it, even though it was almost worn through at the elbows and two of the buttons were missing.

She allowed herself half a smile at the memory. Maybe they could take Lucy to the shop to choose a jacket herself one day. Maybe when she was eighteen and ready to take on the world like Monica had been. That would be a nice tradition.

Monica glanced over to the marked police car parked just off the road by the gate. She realised that its occupants were staring out at her through the windscreen. This pair had drawn the short straw. Tasked with spending the night watching the crime scene and ensuring that no ghouls, no journalists too eager for a closer look at the site, crossed the tape. No doubt they were now wondering why the tall detective was standing with an odd grin on her face at the edge of their crime scene.

81

Monica walked over to the car, reaching into her pocket for her warrant card just in case. She searched for a throwaway jokey line that might make the officers feel like they were all part of the same team.

'I take it they don't deliver pizza out—' she started to say, but stopped as the window was wound down and she caught the scowling face staring out at her. The man had pale cheeks and a sullen mouth, the corners folded down into lines of permanent resentment.

PC Duncan Gregg. He'd been on the force since before Monica joined over twenty years previously. There had been whispers about him even then: that he liked to drink and gamble, which wasn't exactly unusual. But that he'd also do things to supplement his police wages: underhand favours, passing on information. The type of low-level corruption that was almost impossible to prove.

Monica met his gaze, noticing the hint of jaundiced yellow around the whites of his eyes in the interior car light.

'Back for another look, is it?' PC Gregg said as he handed her the clipboard to sign. 'Got anyone for it yet? It was a bad one from what the lads were saying.'

Monica cleared her throat. Reminded herself that rumours were just that; there were people on the force who used to whisper about her too. Probably they still did.

'It's still early days. You know what it's like,' she said non-committally as she wrote her name and handed the clipboard back through the open window. She forced a smile. 'Have a safe night. I'll bring takeaway next time. I promise.'

Monica wiped a hand over her face then pulled her dark hair back out of her eyes and dug in her pocket for one of the red elastic bands that the postie left conveniently scattered in the corridor outside her flat. She found one and tied her hair up in a loose bun. The spits of rain and the icy breeze off the ocean were welcome after the long hours without sleep.

When she was younger she'd lived for the thrill of a call coming in. Preferably at 3 a.m. to break up those night-time thoughts. A door opening into another reality where mundane life and the unchangeable past could all be forgotten. She could focus everything on the challenge of solving the crime. Restoring order, bringing some kind of justice.

It was more difficult now, with Lucy. Monica had always prided herself on being harder than the world – but what about Lucy? Could she handle something happening to her daughter? The horrible vulnerability of having someone in the world that she cared about much more than herself. Imagining what it would be like if Lucy was the victim of one of the crimes she investigated.

She shook her head to dismiss the thought and followed the fence round the field away from the police car until she could look back over to where the body had been folded up in that precise way. Why bring the kid – nothing more than an object to the killer – here to this lonely corner?

Monica closed her eyes and felt the cold sea air, the darkness creeping in, and she imagined a man. Driving down that same road, stopping his car there by that fence. Was he alone or had he been with someone else? An accomplice? Monica watched as he glanced around, a final check before he went to the boot of the car and pulled it open. He crouched to lift the thing out. Is it wrapped in plastic? Monica thought so. She pictured him leaning in to pick up that thin body: tortured and broken, with a peculiar black stone pushed deep into its throat. Did that somehow change the body in some special way? The man stepped over the wire fence, moving across the croft land to the place that he'd chosen. He laid the corpse on the ground and knelt beside it to fold it forward. To position it in a certain way. Almost like it was praying ...

Monica lifted her head and opened her eyes. She was facing the same direction that the body had been positioned in. Far out over the sea the thick clouds were beginning to break, and in the darkening sky the first scattered stars were just becoming visible. Monica stared at them, there above the ocean. They stared back, almost like they had seen it all two nights before. And if such a thing wasn't so plainly ridiculous she would have said they knew she was standing there watching them. That they were watching her back.

Chapter 15

Monica paused in the corridor outside her flat and checked the time on her phone. Almost 10 p.m. on Sunday night. She tilted her head to listen through the door. There was no sound from the TV, which meant it was possible her mum was already in bed. She felt a pang of guilt – it seemed unkind to hope that her mother was asleep so she didn't have to speak to her, especially given how often her mum abandoned her own house and stayed over at Monica's flat to look after Lucy – but Monica could easily imagine her excitement about the murder. How desperate she would be to discuss what she'd read online. She had probably already informed half of Facebook that it was her super-bright daughter heading up the investigation.

Monica cringed at the idea and listened for a moment longer. Still no sound from inside the flat so she crouched down and unfastened the buckles and zips on her flat-heeled boots and pulled. The relief as the pressure on her feet was finally released was beautiful, a feeling of such pleasure she allowed her eyes to momentarily close. Size 9s. By rights the boots were at least a size too small. But size 9 seemed bearable. Once you started getting up into the double figures it just became inhumane, as ridiculous as it sounded. Feet were feet after all. What difference did it make if they were big?

She stood up and set her boots by the side of the mat then turned the door handle as quietly as she could. The unlocked door swung open into the flat. Leaving doors unlocked was another one of her mother's hallmarks. It was like she couldn't fathom why anyone might want to enter someone else's home illegally. As if crimes and robberies were things that only ever happened to other people and were best thought of as light entertainment on TV.

Monica swallowed her irritation and gently pushed the door closed behind her. The flat was cosy and filled with a comforting aroma of home cooking.

Monica's mum looked up from where she was sitting in the corner of the sofa by the window. She was holding a tablet on her lap. *That's why the TV's off*, Monica thought with a sinking feeling as she prepared for a barrage of questions.

Angela Kennedy lifted her head and smiled. Her hair was thick like Monica's but far more silver than black now. She was almost a foot shorter than her daughter, whose size had come from her father's side of the family.

'You look tired, Monica,' she said as she tilted her head to take her daughter in. 'I made you lentil soup. Your favourite with the tatties cooked until they go crumbly. There's garlic croutons to go with it.'

She stood up and pushed past Monica to reach the stove, stirred the hot soup then ladled some into a bowl and sprinkled the croutons on top. Finally she ground black pepper over it. Just the way Monica liked it.

'How's Lucy?' Monica asked as she sat on the stool at the kitchen island.

'Oh she's fine, she's sleeping.' Her mum set the soup bowl down in front of Monica and handed her a spoon. 'She was being a bit silly yesterday and this morning. Making a big fuss about not getting to see her film.'

'She's got a right to be angry, Mum,' Monica said, reaching for the salt.

'You should taste it first before you add salt. That's what the doctors say,' Angela said before sliding the salt cellar to Monica. 'Anyway. I told her that Mummy's job's very important. That it could be one of her friends who was in trouble and then she'd want Mummy to help them.'

'You shouldn't have said that,' Monica said. She tasted the soup, which was hot and delicious.

'Well the world doesn't revolve around her.' Angela paused and looked Monica up and down again. Her eyes landed on Monica's stockinged feet and she tilted her head. 'Why did you take your boots off out in the hall?' she asked, eyeing Monica suspiciously.

Monica cleared her throat and glanced up to the right. 'They were a bit clarty. I didn't want to make a mess of the floor.'

'I'll give them a clean for you,' Angela said.

Monica caught her arm. 'It's fine. I'll probably have to go back to the dump site tomorrow morning.'

Her mother's eyes widened in excitement, sensing this was permission to talk about the murder. 'They said on the Internet that it was a bad one. It's been all over the news. Everyone was talking about it after church.'

Monica nodded, thinking back over the unpleasant events of the previous two days. 'It's … difficult,' she said. 'You know I can't speak about it.'

Angela nodded gravely and rolled up the sleeves of the thick grey jumper she was wearing. Her wide handsome face suddenly serious and earnest.

'I bought you some wine.' She reached under the counter for the bottle. 'I know it's easy to end up taking to the drink in your job, but you need something to help you relax. Especially in a case like this. Or there's whisky – do you want a wee dram?'

'The wine's fine ... thanks,' Monica said uncertainly. At times she suspected that her mum was a little disappointed that she showed no signs of being even mildly alcohol dependent, unlike the heroes in her favourite detective books and TV shows. 'The soup's delicious,' Monica said. Partly to dispel the slightly unpleasant thought as her mum opened the red wine and poured her a large glass.

Angela nodded with satisfaction as she screwed the lid back on to the bottle. 'The potatoes are Golden Wonders,' she said. 'And a good tattie makes a big difference with soup.' She picked up a dishcloth and wiped it needlessly across the clean counter. Then she looked up again, her eyes lighting up. 'What about your new colleague? Crawford. Your partner?' She said the word like it had almost mystical qualities. 'What's he like? Does he have a bad attitude because you're a woman telling him what to do? Did you have to put him in his place? Show him that he couldn't mess you around?'

Monica shook her head; sometimes her mum was unbelievable. 'He's OK. He seems to want to do a good job. He's probably had ten different female bosses since he joined the force. It's not going to be new to him having a woman telling him what to do.'

Angela's face fell with disappointment. She tilted her head to look at Monica. 'What does he look like? Is he a rough diamond sort of guy? Probably he drinks too much, does he?'

For once Monica's mum seemed to understand how much pressure her daughter was under. After Monica had batted away her questions about Crawford she managed to keep the rest of her queries about the case relatively subtle, eventually taking herself off to bed with her tablet.

No doubt to read more about the case online. She's probably commenting on stories about it, Monica thought with another pang of guilt at how judgemental she was being after all her mum's kindness.

She went over to the window and peeped out through the gap in the curtains at the dark road and the pools of orange street light reflected off the black tarmac. The pavement was plastered with damp autumn leaves. For a moment she savoured the feeling of being safe and warm inside.

After a minute Monica let the curtains close and sat back on the sofa. She looked over at the time flashing red on the oven display: 22:38. It seemed to be a twisted law of nature. When you've been desperate to sleep all day you find yourself wide awake the moment you can actually lie down. She shook her head and splashed more of the red wine into her glass. Hoping it might nudge her brain down a few notches and let her relax enough to feel sleepy again.

She reached over and selected one of the records from her father's collection of country music. Harsh as it sounded, it might be the only thing she remembered liking about him. She pictured him in his prison officer's uniform with his hard words and hard hands. Taller even than she was, a flinty man who was cold and thrawn.

Monica put the record on the turntable and plugged the big headphones in, watched as the vinyl started spinning slowly in the dark of the room. The crackle before the music started, somehow like life sparking up. Or life ebbing away. She closed her eyes and listened to John Prine sing about the 'Speed of the Sound of Loneliness'. About how 'Some Humans Ain't Human'.

Ain't that right? Monica thought as she sat up and looked around for the bottle of wine again. Her eyes landed on the painting taped to the fridge beside the magnetic letters instead.

Monica took the headphones off. She stood up and walked over to look at the picture. Bright orange streaks spread across what looked like a dark sky. A four-year-old's attempt at a sky anyway.

'Those are stars. Sometimes they fall out of the sky.'

Monica turned at the sound of her daughter's voice. 'Shh. Granny'll be annoyed if she knows you're up.'

'Shh. Granny'll be annoyed,' Lucy repeated back to her. She twisted her head of curly blonde hair to the side, as if what she'd just said was the funniest joke. Monica couldn't help smiling. She was relieved that the kid seemed to have forgotten her hurt and upset over their ruined trip to the cinema. The 'silliness' that Monica's mum had dismissively referred to.

She reached down to pick her daughter up.

'It's late. You should be asleep,' Monica said. She carried Lucy over to the sofa. Trying to disguise how pleased she was that the kid had woken up.

'I was too hot.'

Monica squeezed her tighter and quickly leaned forward to close the murder file that she'd laid open on the coffee table. Hiding the photos of the body before Lucy could see them. She'd have no chance of sleeping then, no chance at all. The thought of her daughter seeing the pictures or even being near them made Monica feel sick.

She slid the file under the table and sat down on the sofa. 'Did you do the painting at Sunday school?' Monica asked.

'I was with the big boys and girls. The man showed us a video of shooting stars. They're coming soon and sometimes there are fairies in them,' Lucy said.

Monica felt herself tighten up. She struggled to keep her voice level. 'What man is that?'

'He was nice, he gave us stickers.'

'That was nice of him.' Monica took a breath and reminded herself that her mother was in the next room while Lucy was at Sunday school. That she had already asked about the Sunday school's vetting procedures and that anyone dealing with the kids had to have been through the enhanced disclosure process. Sometimes it was hard for Monica to keep her alertness from turning into paranoia. She ran a hand through Lucy's hair. 'Close your eyes, you'll feel sleepy again in a minute.'

'I won't. I never feel sleepy.'

Monica looked down at her daughter. At the line of her mouth and the shape of her face. The little marks on her nose from where her glasses sat. Sometimes the strength of her feeling towards the kid frightened her. The risk of something happening to her. That eventually the kid would have to go out there into that cold world on her own.

She remembered Steven Wright's face. The horror in his eyes at the morgue. Could there be anything worse than losing a child in that way? She hugged Lucy close and kissed her on the forehead. The child stirred and closed her eyes. Already she was almost asleep again.

Monica carried Lucy back through to bed and laid her gently down. The kid might be asleep but Monica felt more awake than ever now. She went back through to the sofa and slid the file out from under the table.

Her phone started vibrating on the table beside her.

'DI Kennedy?' The man's voice sounded nervous.

'That's right,' Monica said.

'It's PC Innes MacBean – you called earlier. I was about to go off shift. Sorry to call so late but you did say asap. I wasn't sure how important it was ...' She could hear the wariness in his voice now.

Monica didn't even try to keep the annoyance out of her voice. 'It's fine. If my phone's on then it means I'm working. What is it?'

'You asked about a social worker. Michael Bach? I managed to track down his alibis. His office confirmed that he was scheduled to have three appointments. Two on Friday afternoon. One on Saturday morning up in Durness. He was staying at a hotel up there. He was in the bar until it closed after midnight on the Friday then checked out early on Saturday morning. I could ask to contact his clients, but the office said I'd have to send a request in writing.'

'That's fine. Thanks.' Monica rang off. Durness was on the far north coast. At least a three-hour drive from where the body was discovered above Gairloch. It seemed to confirm what her instincts told her. That Michael Bach wasn't involved in Robert Wright's murder. That he was genuine in his desire to find his missing client, Nichol. Nichol Morgan. The name edged at something again. A hint of something familiar. She shook her head. On long days like these without sleep everything could start to feel strange. Somehow squeezed and warped. She thought back to the interview with the social worker. What was it he'd said: 'Give me the laptop – I'll look through it.'

As if that was going to happen.

She took another mouthful of the wine and leaned over to the record player. She lifted the needle to play the record again.

The crackle off the vinyl sparked a memory. Coming back at her from years before. Like a fist hitting her in the stomach. A dark secret from the past that could maybe just destroy those little fragments that were good in her life. It seemed incredible that her subconscious mind had been blocking it the whole long day, then suddenly laid it bare for her. The voice just as clear as if the words were being spoken into her ear: 'Chris has had her baby. A boy. She's calling him Nichol. Nichol Morgan it'll be.'

Chapter 16

Paul MacKay swallowed the last mouthful of the can. Budweiser. It was better than those horrible yellow cans of Tennent's that the plebs up here drank. He dropped the empty into the bin. If his mum was here she'd start complaining round about now – *You're only seventeen, Paul – one's enough.*

'Well Mum's not here,' Paul said out loud, savouring the teenage thrill of being home alone as he opened another beer. Ice-cold from the fridge, just like in an advert.

He glanced at his reflection in the dark window. His short brown hair was looking decent though his arms were still not ideal – far too skinny. But at least he was starting to get some muscle from the work he'd been doing. Helping Don Cameron up at the Americans' hunting lodge. Building fences, cutting grass. It wasn't the best, but it was an improvement on school, and he had some money now.

Out beyond his reflection the night seemed particularly dark. For some reason he found himself wary of those wide black spaces outside the small detached house, which was set alone, well back from the road. There could be anything out there, animal or human, staring in from the dark.

Paul shrugged the thought away. It was like Mum losing her shit when it came on the news about that boy's body. As if suddenly there were beasts and 'strangers' everywhere. He put the beer down on the kitchen table and shook his head at how naive, how stupid people could be. *The boy — what was his name? Robert, Robert Wright? Probably he'd done something stupid. How dumb would you have to be to go wandering out at night alone?* He went through to the living room and settled down on the sofa to light a cigarette, but a low sound startled him. It came from the back of the house, from his bedroom, just audible under the music on the stereo.

Paul reached over to turn the music down and tilted his head to listen. *Like someone taking a gulp of air, breathing heavily?* For long moments he didn't move as he felt the hair on his arms stand up.

But the sound was gone and eventually he shook his head, turned the song back up — The Knife, 'Pass This On' — and forced out a laugh at the moment of paranoia. He picked up the battered book, *Deep Space Nebulae*, flicked through the familiar images of distant corners of the universe. They were unbelievably beautiful, made up of millions of galaxies. But he couldn't shake the disquiet and eventually had to turn and look at the kitchen, half expecting something to be waiting there. Staring back at him.

There was nothing of course. Just the can of beer, standing lonely on the kitchen table. He turned the music off and went through to take a mouthful. There was a hint of a taste to the beer. Of something slightly off. Paul tilted the can to check the best-before date. Still a year away. He shrugged and finished the rest of the can in one long drink.

It was then he caught the smell of incense, drifting into the kitchen from the corridor. Paul looked up and noticed that his bedroom door was standing slightly ajar. He was sure he remembered pushing the door to and hearing it click shut. He stepped towards it and watched as a vague fold of dark smoke drifted out from the gap. Slow and lazy. Impulsively he reached for the bedroom door handle. But something stopped him from pushing it open. Something deep and primitive inside told him to turn away. To run.

Paul dismissed the idea. It could be a fire; he had to check. He pushed the door open and stepped into the room, lit only by the hall light behind him. His hand went to the light switch and he clicked it on. Nothing happened, *The bulb must have blown*, he decided. Maybe that explained the smoke somehow?

He blinked and the smell came to him again. One of those incense sticks that his mum liked was burning in a stand on his bedside table. Smoke spiralling towards the ceiling from the red dot of heat at the stick's tip. He looked fearfully around the familiar room, over to the window; closed tight. He could just make out the shape of the handle, it was locked down. *What then? You lit the incense stick and forgot somehow? Or someone's playing a weird joke on you?* He set the beer down on the table and reached to switch on the bedside lamp.

Something strange happened with his hand. It fell short, missing its target by several inches. He stared down at his fingers. They were suddenly different, somehow alien. Every line, every shape on his hands was suddenly vivid, even in the poor light. The folds of his knuckles and the white scar where he'd caught his finger in the car door. As if he were seeing those hands for the very first time.

Paul's knees felt weak. He tried to sit down on the bed, but found himself falling backwards instead. He went to put out an arm to break his fall, but his hand wouldn't respond to the command. It wouldn't even move, and panic washed over him. He landed on his back with his head on the pillow, his legs hanging off awkwardly to the side.

His whole body locked up and with a feeling of sheer terror Paul understood that he was completely paralysed.

He tried to control his breathing. To make some kind of sense of what was happening to him. *You're going to be OK, you're going to be OK*, he repeated internally. It was a seizure, something like epilepsy. It would pass though, everything passed.

For half a moment the idea made sense.

Then he remembered the strange taste in his mouth from the beer, and the incense. Someone had put it there beside his bed. They had to have. Didn't they?

As Paul's eyes adjusted to the dark they fell on the shadowy shape in the corner of the room for the first time. Like a patch of black that was somehow different from the darkness. For long moments he stared at the shape, his mind desperately hoping, trying to make sense of it.

Then the noise started. The breathing again, the sound of someone hyperventilating.

Paul screamed. He felt his bladder go as he strained every sinew, every essence of his being to force his body to move. To get up and run. But his screams were like whispers, and his arms and legs barely stirred.

The black shape moved. It came closer and closer still. Then it leaned in until its face became clear in the low light from the doorway. With a sense of horror Paul saw the pale face of a man. The face was familiar. He knew this man, but he was somehow different, was somehow changed.

Paul tried to plead. Tried to say the man's name. The words came out as a dribble down his chin as the man leaned in closer. He spoke, and his voice was like something from a nightmare.

'Don't worry. I know you wanted me to come. I'm here now, and we've got a long time. We've got as long as we need.'

Monday

Chapter 17

The next morning Michael woke early. The house felt damp and cold as autumn started to move into the ground around the building. But his bed had never felt so warm. So still and cosy with the cats piled on the end of it like a stack of living hot-water bottles. Michael found a cigarette, lit it and crawled out of bed to put the kettle on.

Despite the cold he felt brighter than he had in days as he made his coffee in the little pot and went to stand at the open front door. Still in his boxer shorts, he looked out over the wide landscape, the infinite sea and the rows of mountains fading into the distance. They were dusted with the first snow of the autumn and looked rich and golden under the pale boreal light. Michael tried to recall the Japanese word that meant something like 'beauty of transient imperfection'. He shrugged when he couldn't remember it but thought: *This is why I live here.*

The feeling of contentedness persisted during the long drive to work through the mountains. A buoyancy that was in truth almost manic. The memories from the weekend – of the body and the police visit – buried under positive energy. It lasted until Michael pulled into the car park at his office on the hill above Inverness. He lit a cigarette and didn't notice the black car pull up beside him until he turned to get out. The driver climbed out into the morning, dark hair framing her pale white face.

The detective. DI Kennedy. She took a step forward. Her face was grave and he felt a moment of panic rise from his stomach as he thought: *This is when she arrests you.*

'You said you'd help? Finding the Morgan boy?' Her voice was clipped and awkward. Not at all the commanding tone of the day before in the living room when she'd been questioning him. 'Did you mean it? You've seen how it could end.'

Michael stared back at her in shocked silence. She meant that Nichol could be tortured like that boy on the autopsy table. He felt his hand tighten into a fist as it all came back to him: the boy's pale skin, pale like the detective's. Michael realised that his sleep had been far from dreamless, that the kid had visited him the night before. Standing just outside his bedroom door. Dead but upright and walking, carrying that smell of the morgue. Someone else had been there with him too. Someone Michael had known once. Someone younger.

You're the detective. Why do you need my help? There's nothing I can do. But the words never came out, and Michael realised that he was staring into her eyes and nodding.

She reached back into her car then held something out towards him. With a start Michael recognised Nichol's laptop bag. She made a strange gesture towards her chest. A sacrificial dagger to the heart. 'If anyone finds out I gave this to you ...'

She's setting you up, framing you. Michael hesitated and tilted his head to look past her into the empty car. 'Why?'

DI Kennedy's gaze skipped around the car park, an angry gesture. 'It's password protected. I can't get into it. You knew the kid ...'

'But you must have technicians. Experts who can analyse it?'

She glanced around again and for a moment Michael thought that she was going to get back into her car. 'We're investigating a murder. There are other priorities. It might be weeks before anyone's able to go through it.'

Michael stared hard at her because really it didn't make any sense. 'Why do you care now? You didn't seem bothered when we spoke about him yesterday.'

She ran a hand down her coat, which Michael could see now was worn and almost threadbare in places. Her long white fingers on the dark material, as if she were wiping off an unpleasant stain. As if she was disgusted by the idea of asking for help. 'Do you want to find him or not?' she said finally, and the anger was clear in her voice this time.

Michael stared back at her. *Fuck you. After the way you spoke to me yesterday. Now you act like I should just roll over and put myself at risk.* But he reached out and took the bag anyway. She must have read him and known that he would.

DI Kennedy pushed a card into his other hand. There was an address written on it.

'I need it back by the end of today.' Her words were a command this time.

Michael opened his mouth to ask a question but she had already climbed into the car. He stared dumbly at the car's red tail lights as they moved off into the gloomy morning. If it hadn't been for the bag in his hand he might not have believed that the strange interaction had even happened.

When Michael walked into the open-plan office he saw with a sinking feeling that his colleague James Clarke was already in. He was standing over Michael's desk with a mug of coffee in his hands. Probably poised to deliver some wisdom from the weekend, Michael thought. Why selfish drivers who abused the family parking spaces at Tesco should be fined.

Or a story about his two young sons that drew attention to his exemplary parenting.

Instead he nodded a greeting and looked down at the bag Michael was carrying. 'Got yourself a new laptop finally?'

Michael followed his colleague's eyes and cursed himself for not leaving it in the Land Rover. 'I'm just checking something on it for a friend.'

James lifted his eyebrows until they met the thick curls of his brown hair. Michael read the expression: *But you don't have any friends.* He watched as James tried to cover it up.

'Another woman is it?'

Michael forced a non-committal smile.

'You're such a dark horse, Michael. There's always something new about you that I don't believe. Honestly.' James watched as Michael shook his jacket off and dumped it over a chair. 'I heard about that boy – it must have been quite a shock for you. What they said online – that he was tortured – was it really true?' His voice was low and conspiratorial in the grey social services department office. A place where some days the paranoia hung low like smoke.

'I don't know. I only saw his face,' Michael said.

'Of course. There was an expert on the news who said it could have been a creature, a big cat even. They said that he'd been mutilated.' James's expression changed as realisation dawned. 'Your brother. Sorry, Michael. I'd forgotten.'

'It doesn't matter.'

James coughed and wiped a hand over his red face. He forced out a laugh and lowered his voice even further. 'Anita was in earlier. What have you done to piss her off this time?'

'Piss her off? There's nothing I can think of. Is she still around?' Michael asked. Wondering whether he had done something to annoy their boss or if James was simply looking to put him on the back foot after his own faux pas.

'She's on her way to Glasgow for a meeting.' James took a step closer. 'Just so you know. She was asking questions.'

'What kind of questions?' Michael couldn't help taking the bait.

James took another step closer so he could speak into Michael's ear, his eagerness making it plain that he was pleased to have piqued Michael's interest. 'About Nichol Morgan. Why you're so interested in him. Why you were asking so many questions last week when he disappeared.'

Michael edged away from the unpleasant sensation of James's damp-coffee breath on his ear. He turned to face him. 'And you really believe that Nichol would have just gone off without telling anyone?'

James tilted his head. He glanced at the laptop bag again then back to Michael. 'I think ...' He was speaking slowly. Making a show of measuring his words. 'I think Nichol was capable of a lot more than you think. You had a positive influence on him. But how well do you really know him? He'd been in trouble before. So what's to say he isn't up to no good somewhere?'

'Have you always been this cynical?' Michael heard the spite in his own voice, but James shrugged it off.

'We can't all be on a crusade, Michael. It doesn't always turn out that well in the end. I think we both know that you've got some experience there.' James stared at him, something like satisfaction spreading from the folds of skin at the corner of his eyes.

Michael dropped his eyes to the desk. He knew what his colleague was referring to: a disciplinary hearing from the year before. A couple who had made a formal complaint against him.

'They left their five-year-old daughter wandering in a park at night. Alone while they were virtually unconscious, drinking wine. She could have been run over or abducted. Anything could have happened.'

'So you turn up unannounced at their house. You lay hands on Daddy. You threaten to assault him—'

'I only grabbed him by the collar. I never threatened him. If that had been a poor family from down in the Marsh—'

'But it wasn't.' James was speaking precisely and clearly enjoying himself. 'It was a family with money. A family who knew how to play "blame the social worker". It was a final written warning they gave you in the end, wasn't it?'

Michael stared at his colleague but didn't reply.

James shrugged and folded his hands across his belly. He glanced at the laptop bag once more. His eyes lingering suspiciously on it this time. 'All I'm saying, Michael, is that sometimes in this job it's better to keep a distance. Whatever it is you're thinking about getting caught up in. Don't.'

Chapter 18

Crawford glanced at Monica as he drove across the bridge into Rapinch. The Marsh. A part of the city that people didn't want their kids visiting. She kept her eyes on the road. The metal bridge with the strange low pavements that had always seemed like you were walking in the road. The railway bridge running parallel that the boys at school claimed they jumped off when the tide was high. The harbour with its huge ships that could be from anywhere in the world. Ben Wyvis, that scoured mountain dusted with autumn snow in the far distance. All of it together under the grey morning sky.

'You're from Rapinch originally, aren't you?' Crawford said.

Monica turned her head to look out at the Chinese launderette, the newsagent under the shadows of the blocks of flats, the shop on the corner that sold everything.

'My mum still lives here,' she said finally.

Crawford probably wanted to make one of those hilarious jokes about the place: junkies, teenage mothers – something like that. Or to ask an awkward question. Something he'd heard about her: *Didn't you used to know people from down here? People who ended up in jail?* All those old things. Those mistakes that still haunted her.

Instead he said, 'Is it true they still speak an old version of Gaelic here? Some of them?' Monica didn't reply. She reached down for the file Crawford had been holding when she'd arrived in the major incident room in Inverness. She had still been too distracted by the conversation with Michael Bach – by what she had done – to properly take in what he'd told her about the suspect.

'What do we know about this guy again?' She checked the name on the file. 'Owen MacLennan.'

Crawford shrugged, seemed to accept that she didn't feel like making small talk.

'He's the best match so far. A sadist and a sexual predator. Aged thirty-five. He got started early when he worked on his grandad's pig farm on the Black Isle. He spent his leisure time having a bit of fun with the pigs. Torturing them. He says he liked using a hammer best, if you're interested. When he was fourteen he was up at the Children's Panel for abduction and sexual assault. He got a kid drunk and tied him up, kept him like that for two days. The boy said he thought MacLennan was going to kill him.'

Crawford pulled across the road into a space outside a block of modern tenement flats. Not far from where India Street met Jamaica Street. More names from the past. Names Monica had tried to avoid in the four years since she'd moved back north to Inverness to be near her mum when she had Lucy. It had felt like a mistake then and it felt even more like a mistake now.

'Here's the clincher though,' Crawford said. 'He served five years in jail for manslaughter. He took a man back to his flat in Aberdeen and strangled him to death. The only reason he didn't get life for premeditated murder was because they couldn't disprove his story. He claimed self-defence.' Crawford leaned across to pull some photographs from the file. The first showed a bed stained black with blood. The second showed a torso with stab wounds clearly visible on the chest and stomach.

'That's MacLennan. He had defence wounds on his hands and arms too. The prosecution strongly suspected he'd inflicted them himself.'

'But there was reasonable doubt,' Monica said. It was the type of story that she'd heard before. What detective hadn't?

'Would you try to convince a jury that someone was stupid enough to cut themselves up like that? He lost three pints of blood. "Substantial degree of provocation." Four to nine years. He claimed it was a consensual S and M session, but the victim freaked out and attacked him. He said he was just defending himself.'

Monica held the photo up. The splashes up the white wall and the bloody bed.

'Here's the best bit,' Crawford said. He turned to face Monica, his green eyes shining with excitement despite the dark rings that surrounded them. 'I checked his address for vehicles registered to him. What do you think I came up with?'

'A white van?' She felt a flutter of excitement herself as she remembered the report that Fisher had highlighted. Maybe they could find the killer quickly and prove that Nichol Morgan at least was safe from him.

'A white Maestro van. MacLennan's only been out of jail for three months. He bought the van a couple of months ago,' Crawford said as he climbed out of the car.

Monica followed him out and checked up and down the street, wary as she recalled that strange moment from the night before. When the music had triggered her memory: Nichol Morgan. Charlie Bartle's nephew. How could she forget?

She tried to suppress the thought and followed Crawford across the road and through the door into the close.

'I'll lead the questioning,' Monica said. She let the silence in the communal stairwell fill in the rest. Crawford nodded, although something like disappointment flashed across his face. *Well*, Monica thought, *there'll be plenty of monsters for you to test yourself against over the years, Crawford. More than enough.*

She followed him up the stairs, caught the smells of fried food. The sounds of breakfast television leaking through doors. Under them that stillness, that dry musty smell that every tenement building seemed to share.

OWEN MACLENNAN. Stamped on a nameplate attached to a blue door. Monica took a breath and caught Crawford's eye: *Remember I'm doing the talking.* She hit the door.

Monica asked the question again. 'What were you doing on Friday?'

Owen MacLennan smiled and held his hands up. They were big and strong. Strong enough to strangle, to kill. 'I've not done anything. This is fucking harassment.'

'I'm asking you because you're on the sex offenders register. A van just like yours was seen up there. So we want to know where you were.'

'My excitement comes to me. I don't need to go looking for it,' MacLennan said. A smile edging his mouth as one of his thick hands went to his bleached-blonde hair. Monica noticed his long fingernails. They were yellowed at the ends.

'I heard that boy was all opened up,' he said. His voice had gone soft. 'They're saying it was a beast. A monster. If you've got any pictures, give me a look and I'll give you my opinion on the type you might be looking for.'

'Why don't you start by telling me where you were on Friday?' Monica said. Staring hard at him as she spoke.

'You're persistent.' His voice was like gravel now as he caught smoke in his throat. He pursed his thick lips and blew it across the room in a filthy kiss. He smiled again. Monica felt the skin on her arms crawl. 'I think I've seen you before,' MacLennan said. Speaking down the length of his cigarette to her.

'You must be bright. You noticed the tall woman,' Monica said without breaking eye contact. The response she'd given a thousand times. To drunks in the street in her uniformed days. To every type of stupid comment or attempted intimidation.

'Nah ... not that.' He wagged his cigarette at her. 'From when I was younger. When you were younger. Not that I want to say it in a bad way, but maybe before you had any wee ones? Before you stretched that belly out.' He arched his neck and pushed his head back then gave a throaty laugh.

On the wall behind him there was a strange print of Jesus on what looked like a different planet emerging from his tomb. A green desert with the earth as a speck in the distance. A long-tailed star was passing across the sky.

Monica leaned forward. She was about to speak when Crawford cut in.

'Strange picture for someone like you to have on your wall.'

Monica tried to catch Crawford's eye. He was leaning forward with his arms on his knees. His handsome face was twisted up. Monica was over six feet herself but Owen MacLennan dwarfed her in the small room.

'How so, big man?' MacLennan said as he turned to face Crawford, a wide smile across his cold face.

'You think this is funny?' Crawford said.

'I've spent my time on the cross, son. This is my resurrection.'

Crawford snorted but didn't reply.

'What? You were born perfect?' MacLennan sounded almost perplexed.

'I've seen your file. I know what you've done,' Crawford said.

MacLennan ran hard fingers across his jaw, ruffled his bleached hair. *sweet meat* was carved in blue ink on his thick forearm. 'Maybe I should ask one of my associates to take a look in *your* file then, son. Find out what you've got at home. Anyone of interest we should know about.' MacLennan's blue eyes were like ice. 'You've seen my file, wee man. Do you think I'm joking?'

The tendons on Crawford's neck had gone tight and his mouth twitched.

'You want to go back to jail, Owen? Is that what this is?' Monica said. 'Making threats when you're five minutes back on the streets?'

MacLennan's face changed. His eyebrows folded up in rage as he jumped to his feet, filling the room. His cigarette hit the wall behind them in an explosion of red sparks.

'And who the fuck are you? Coming into my own fucking home?' His wild eyes flitting between them like he might just launch himself at them. 'Walking in here asking me fucking questions?'

Monica felt the familiar adrenaline dump but kept her face straight. 'Sit down, Owen.' She knew how to deal with an aggressive bully. She'd had enough experience over the years. More than enough. 'Fucking sit down, now!'

MacLennan slumped back in his seat and smiled like an actor coming out of character at the end of a play. There was no trace of anger left on his face as he reached for another cigarette. He turned to Crawford. 'Sorry, mate. It's my fucking temper. I was joking there. But the game we're in? You like to know where I live and what I'm up to. It's the same the other way too. I like to know a bit about you, about where you live.' He exhaled smoke and let his smile spread like something rotting.

'Are you finished?' Monica said.

MacLennan stared back at her. His wide smile didn't touch his eyes. 'I do know you, sweetheart. Don't I?'

'What were you doing in Gairloch?'

'That's right. Monica Kennedy. I told you I knew your face. You were mixed in with Charlie Bartle's crew. Weren't you, doll? Friends with his bird, weren't you?'

Monica's stomach lurched and the ground dropped away. *Charlie Bartle.* A name that she hadn't heard out loud in over ten years. But here it was, just the day after his nephew had turned up in a missing person's report. Almost like it was inevitable.

'That must have been a funny one,' MacLennan continued. 'You ending up police. Him ending up inside. Almost like it was connected. Who'd have thought it? Drugs they got him for, wasn't it? They always said it was a strange one. Him getting caught like that when he was always so careful.'

Monica stared back. Her mind gone suddenly blank.

'It must be hard for the other police to trust you. Them knowing about the sort you've been connected with. How you treat your so-called friends.' His voice was rich as butter.

Beside her Crawford tilted his head so his eyes pointed to the floor. Clearly he'd heard stories about her too. Obviously someone still remembered them, even though she'd been away from the Highlands for fifteen years.

'What? You don't want to ask your questions now, darling?'

Monica swallowed. Her throat had gone dry. She found herself standing up. Her hands were shaking as she stepped forward with a mad impulse to hit him across the face. Instead she leaned in close to him. Close enough to smell the cigarette smoke on his breath.

'You think I don't still know people around here?' Her voice was barely a whisper in his ear. 'People who would do me a favour. A police detective? Especially if it meant they could lay hands on someone like you.' She stood back and stared down at him. Her hand was still shaking and she was almost as surprised as he was by what she'd just said. She pushed her hand into her coat pocket. 'Do we understand each other, Owen?'

He stared up at her and started to speak. Stopped.

'What? You've got something to tell me now?'

MacLennan swallowed. His thick Adam's apple sliding up his throat. He held his hands up. 'Fair enough. We've had our bit of fun. I was here in my flat on Friday. All of the day and all of the night.' He turned away from Monica and forced out a laugh. Then he lit another cigarette. 'You happy with that?'

Before she could answer he stood up. He was taller than her by several inches and much heavier. He looked down at her and pursed his thick lips. His voice was low and grimy. 'You know. I've got a feeling in my gut. Something that tells me that poor boy, he wasn't the last. That maybe there's another poor boy.'

'What are you talking about?' Monica asked.

MacLennan shrugged his shoulders as his wide smile spread back across his face. 'Just ... What would you call it? An intuition. Don't forget that I've still got my friends too, angel. The next time we speak –' his cold blue eyes cut into her '– it's not going to be friendly like this was.'

Chapter 19

The laptop bag lay untouched on Michael's desk for the rest of the morning. He tried to ignore it and focus on his work. Resolved to listen to James's advice this time, he would call the detective and drop it off at the address she'd left him. Looking for the kid was one thing, but getting involved in a murder investigation when the police had already questioned him – had implied that he was a suspect – was insanely stupid.

He should have listened to his instincts that morning and never even touched the thing. Michael glanced over to James and felt a layer of sweat beginning to stand out on his back. The laptop bag was lying right there on his desk for anyone to see. For anyone in the office to notice: 'Isn't that Nichol Morgan's bag? I thought the police had taken it?' What were the chances that anyone would believe a detective had just given it to him?

Michael repressed the urge to grab the bag off the desk and stuff it into the filing cabinet by his knees. He glanced at James again, who lifted his head and smiled. 'Are you all right? You look like –' *you've seen a ghost*; he stopped himself '– like you're exhausted.'

Michael fought to keep his eyes off the bag. 'I didn't sleep well.'

James seemed to accept that. He stood up. 'Yes, well I'm not surprised. Anyway.' He reached for his waxed coat. 'I'd better go. I've got a client visit. I'll be back later.'

Michael watched as James pulled his coat on then spent an agonising minute adjusting the collar before he finally turned and walked away down the corridor. Michael took a breath. *Wait five minutes to be sure he doesn't come back*, he told himself. After two minutes he punched DI Kennedy's number into his phone. It rang then went through to voicemail: 'This is Detective Inspector Monica Kennedy—'

Michael swore under his breath and hung up, suddenly paranoid that by leaving a message he could be providing evidence against himself. It would be better to put the laptop bag in the Land Rover now, then drop it off at the detective's house at the end of the day. He would apologise to her. He could even lie and say that he couldn't open it – that he couldn't crack the password. How would she know the difference?

That's right, the voice at the back of Michael's head piped up. *Lie. Hide. Pretend that it's not your problem. It's how you like to do things. Isn't it? Just like when you were a kid.*

The dream came back to him then, the feeling of it more than anything. Those long corridors laid out almost like a maze. Somewhere deep down, somewhere hidden. There was someone down there too. Michael could tell. They were lost and desperate for help. They were desperate to be found.

Almost without thinking, Michael pulled the laptop out of its bag and set it down on his desk. Right there for anyone to see. He took a breath and wiped a hand over his face, resisting the guilty urge to look around the office. The laptop was a MacBook Pro. An expensive machine. This raised a question before he had even started: where had Nichol got the money for it? The unpalatable answer: what if it had come from a predator? That was how they operated with vulnerable kids: giving them gifts, giving them attention.

Michael pulled the sleeve of his jumper over his finger, paranoid this was some kind of set-up to get his prints on the machine, and switched the computer on. He watched as the password screen appeared. Forgetting his momentary paranoia he tried a couple of obvious passwords: nicholmorgan, nicholmorgan2001. Both of them were wrong.

Michael squeezed his brain. What would the kid have used? He knew Nichol was interested in literature and philosophy. He'd been carrying a stack of books the last time they'd met. *Beyond Good and Evil* by Nietzsche on top of the pile. Michael tried them both: Nietzsche. Beyondgoodandevil. Neither worked.

He leaned back in his chair, feeling a sense of relief that the task was impossible. The idea that he might be able to hack the password was ridiculous in itself. Nichol was computer savvy. There was no way he would have set a password that you could guess in five minutes.

Michael pushed the laptop closed, slid it back into the bag and stood up. Immediately feeling lighter. He crossed the office to the empty staffroom. He could drop the laptop off that evening and then it was over. At least he'd tried. No one can say that he hadn't. Michael hit the button on the coffee machine and watched the superheated liquid splash into his mug.

The phone in his pocket vibrated. It was a text message from a client he was due to visit that afternoon. He began to type a reply when the answer came to him: *The future is in the stars*. The last text message Nichol had sent him.

Michael hurried across the office and pulled the laptop out of the bag. He typed the words in then watched with a strange mixture of excitement and horror as the computer accepted the password. The screen lit up. Michael hesitated then clicked open the email program. He noticed that his hand was shaking.

'Come on. Where are you, Nichol?' he whispered under his breath.

Michael was quickly disappointed. Nichol had obviously never synced his email accounts with the mail program on the machine. He tried in the web browsers, hoping that Nichol had stayed signed in to his accounts online, but the sites he tried, Gmail, Yahoo, MSN, asked for an email address and password.

He checked the web browsing history. Timetables? Hotels? But it had been cleared. *Why the text message then?* He must have known Michael would work it out. There had to be something.

Michael started to work through the files. There were school things, folders organised by subject: 'Maths', 'English', 'History'. Michael clicked through them, increasingly frantic that there was nothing to find. The folders only seemed to contain school work. Finally he clicked on the last folder without much hope: 'Untitled'.

Inside it there was a single document: 'Melissa'. Michael clicked it open. The file was an image of Nichol holding an ice cream. He had a wide smile on his face, and a girl was standing beside him. She had blonde hair, and they looked about the same age.

Michael looked around the room then back at the picture. It was a recent photo. Nichol had his arm round the girl's shoulder.

'Melissa?' Michael stared at the screen. All the fear and reticence that he'd felt was momentarily forgotten. 'What do you know?'

Chapter 20

Monica pulled up in the police headquarters car park. The sounds from the busy roundabout nearby echoed off the tarmac. Raigmore Hospital was visible across the road with its lights on against the grey morning sky. She felt Crawford's eyes on her and turned to stare down at him.

'I specifically told you I was questioning MacLennan,' Monica said. She found herself wishing again that they would just let her work on her own. Things would be so much easier that way.

'I was fucking backing you up, Monica. Like we're supposed to,' Crawford said. One of his hands went up to wipe his forehead.

She shook her head in disbelief. 'Don't you fucking swear at me! You end up in tears in front of MacLennan, practically and you're backing *me* up? I should have brought Fisher with me instead. At least he can keep his mouth shut.'

Crawford looked down into the footwell. That quiff of red hair fell forward over his eyes.

'What did you say to MacLennan anyway?' he said as he lifted his head. The anger rising in his voice. An obvious desire to hit back at her. 'Where were you this morning? They said you were in early looking at evidence, then went out again?'

'That's got nothing to do with you,' Monica said. 'I'm running this investigation.'

He shook his head and put his hand up to fix his hair, a distraction tactic if there ever was one. 'We're supposed to work together,' he said.

'We don't have time for this shit now, Crawford. Fucking suck it up,' Monica said. 'You've seen the state that kid was in. We need to catch whoever did it. Not sit moaning about how we do it.'

'I'm not—'

Monica cut him off before he could continue. 'MacLennan knows something. I'm sure of it. You heard what he said – he was taunting us. We need to get him under surveillance. I'll call Detective Superintendent Hately to speak about getting more bodies in to help. You start going through the CCTV footage. See if we can get a registration plate to confirm the van seen up there was MacLennan's.'

Crawford nodded slowly. 'Fine.'

'A possible sighting came in this morning,' she continued. 'Someone says they saw Robert on the Friday night before he was murdered. I'm going to follow up on it then speak to his friends, see if any of them know anything.'

'OK. Fine,' Crawford said again, without meeting her eye this time.

She watched as he climbed out of the car. He had left a half-full can of his sickly energy drink in the cup holder. She took a mouthful of it and stared at herself in the rear-view mirror. Those old names MacLennan had uttered, the ones she'd tried to leave behind, rose to the surface again. She pushed them back down as far as she could and resolved to keep them there.

An hour later Monica took a left at the lonely roundabout outside Achnasheen. Virtually the only rural roundabout anywhere in the north-west Highlands. In a place where there was no obvious need for one. Someone somewhere had had a budget to use up.

For a few seconds a train ran alongside her on the railway line that went through the mountains to Kyle of Lochalsh opposite the Isle of Skye on the west coast. The sleeper train from London to Inverness, then on to the west: Mallaig, Glenfinnan Viaduct, Fort William. It was supposed to be one of the most picturesque railway journeys in the world. She glanced at the carriages and wondered if the passengers visible at the windows were having a better morning than she was.

Up ahead the signpost for the Glens Hotel rose into view, and she turned into the long driveway. The place nestled in the mountains about fifteen miles south-east of Gairloch and the moorland where Robert's body was found. The Victorian building appeared at the end of the track, its grey granite emerging from white mist.

Dark windows looked down on her as she crossed the empty car park. She checked her phone: 'No Service'. Inside the heavy double doors the foyer was deserted apart from an ancient stuffed bear that stared at Monica with sad glass eyes. Moth-eaten patches on his face and one paw held up as if he were guarding the plate-glass doors beside him that opened on to a ballroom. The place had a musty smell of faded glamour. A long time faded, Monica thought as she tried the reception bell.

A distant voice responded to the sound. Monica followed it into the ballroom. At the far end there was a bar draped in red and gold with a man standing behind it, holding a crate of beer.

'Muir Maitland?' Monica's voice echoed off the high ceiling. The man was in his fifties with a red face – red from the drink,

Monica guessed. He was dressed smartly in a green tweed jacket, matching waistcoat and a red tartan tie.

'That's right. You're a detective then? They said someone would be coming in this morning.' He looked her up and down taking in her unusual size with unembarrassed curiosity written over his face.

Monica introduced herself and handed her ID to him. Then she took the smiling photo of Robert Wright from her pocket and placed it on the counter. She watched as Muir's hand went to his forehead, damp from the exertion of shifting crates of beer.

'Is this the boy you saw on Friday?' she asked. Her eyes went past him to the rows of whisky bottles glowing golden in the bar lights over his shoulder. He took a dirty-looking dishcloth out from under the bar and used it to dry the sweat off his forehead.

'That's him. I'm good with faces. When you work in the hotel business, people want you to remember them. You know? I'll always remember your face now. Even in five years. And your height. It's not exactly hard to miss you.' He gave a strange puffy laugh.

Monica ignored his comment. 'Where did you see him exactly?'

'It was up on the road to the Americans' place,' Muir said. 'That's the hunting lodge down the side glen a mile down the road. I was making a delivery, late on the Friday night. The lad was stood by the side of the track holding a bike. You'll see folks up that way all the time in the summer. The path goes through the mountains. All the way to the west. There's always cyclists, backpackers and the like—'

'You were delivering ...?' Monica said, cutting him off.

'Well. I was collecting actually. Sometimes the Americans ...
Not that I want to gossip, but they're rich. Billionaires.
Sometimes they turn up at unusual times and ask for catering
to be brought in. It's always the best. Your wild salmon, your
malt whisky. They were here the week before, so I had to collect
the big pan carriers we'd left up there.'

'The Americans, are they gone by now? Or are they still
there?' Monica asked.

'They'd left before I saw him, the boy. It was just a flying
visit. The shooting for a week then on to somewhere else.'

'What time did you see Robert Wright?'

'Maybe nine. Half past nine. Something like that?' Muir
said. His red face folding up in concentration as he considered
it.

'And you saw him by the track?'

'That's right. He was on his bike. Just near the entrance gate.
That's where the path through the mountains crosses the track.
I gave him a wee wave but he didn't wave back. He just stared.'

'Stared at you?'

'Like a dirty look. It didn't bother me – I mean you know
what boys are like.'

Monica slowly pulled a bar stool out and sat, her feet only
a few inches off the ground, her eyes not leaving Muir's face.
'What are boys like?'

Muir ran a hand over his head again as he considered the
question. 'You know. They're angry, morose. Always on
the Internet or playing those online games.'

Monica thought about it for a moment. Had there been
something on Robert's mind other than everything with his
mum? Did he decide to go for a bike ride to clear his head?
Did he go home to get something then sneak back out again?

'He was on his own?' Monica asked.

'That's right. God knows why anyone would want to go out in the dark. But I suppose some people just have their own habits. Don't they? Especially up here. I never thought anything of it until I saw it on the television last night.'

'Did he look lost? Or frightened?' Monica asked.

Muir shook his head. 'No, not so I noticed anyway. He had a head torch on, lights on his bike. That's what I spotted first. He looked well prepared enough.'

'And did you see anyone else up that way? Anyone at all?'

'Just the boy. It's quiet up there now that the tourist season's over.'

A stout woman with grey hair wearing a cleaner's tabard came into the ballroom and started pushing a brush around the floor.

Monica glanced over to her then thanked Muir for his help. She had already turned to leave when a question occurred to her. 'You didn't see another van up there? Anywhere round here in the last week or so? A white van. A Maestro?'

Muir shook his head slowly. 'None that stood out anyway. There's always folks going up and down the main road here, but there was nothing out of the ordinary.'

'And the name Owen MacLennan. Does that mean anything to you?'

'I can't say it does. Betty?' He shouted over to the cleaner. 'You don't know an Owen MacLennan, do you?'

The cleaner straightened up and leaned on her broom. 'No one I can think of.'

'You could ask Don Cameron,' Muir said. His voice perking up at the idea.

'Don Cameron?'

'Yes. Don works up at the Americans' sometimes as a gamekeeper. He cuts the grass as well. He would probably recognise the vans that the local workers use.' Muir dabbed at his red forehead with a handkerchief this time. 'He might even have spotted the lad?'

Betty snorted a laugh. Monica caught the end of the fierce look that Muir turned on her.

'Am I missing something?' Monica asked, her eyes going between the two of them.

'No ... It's ...' Muir stammered.

'It's more likely Don Cameron had something to do with that boy than anything,' said the woman.

'That's just gossip,' Muir said.

'Well my mother used to say that the Camerons were mixed up in things. Back in the 1970s and 80s,' Betty said.

'What kind of things?' Monica asked.

'It's just stupid gossip,' Muir said, cutting in before Betty could reply. His face had gone a darker shade of red. 'Don's the strong and silent type. A gamekeeper, you know?'

'You said it yourself!' Betty said, the indignation clear in her voice. 'That you wouldn't be surprised if he had done something to that lad.'

'I never meant it – it was a joke!' Muir said, guilt twitching all over his face.

'Serious jokes to make when a boy's been murdered,' Monica said. She watched as the cleaner stared down at the broom she was holding. Probably she was realising for the first time that the strange tall woman was a detective. That there might be consequences to what she said.

'It wasn't ...' Betty's words faltered.

'People make jokes sometimes,' Muir said, speaking quickly, dark sweat patches visible under his armpits. 'There's nothing serious in it. It's just something we'd say: "I'll get Don Cameron to collect that twenty-quid tab you owe me." That kind of thing.'

Folk psychology. Blame the loner, the outsider. From Monica's experience it was the natural human response to murder. And sometimes it was the right one.

'You think Don Cameron could be up at the Americans' now?' Monica asked. She looked from Betty to Muir.

Muir nodded without looking up, his face still burning. 'It's possible. Or over at his croft.'

Chapter 21

The turn-off that led to the Americans' hunting lodge was a narrow track up into the hills. Trees from the forest overhung the road on either side and scraped the roof of the car like ghostly fingers emerging from the thick mountain mist that had descended.

Monica clicked the radio on. The voices that filled the car were speaking Gaelic. They drifted in and out of focus for several minutes before two new voices in English became audible between the bursts of static.

The disjointed voices made the road feel lonely, disjointed from reality, and for a moment Monica wondered if she'd messed up and taken a wrong turning, but just as she was thinking of turning back she left the folds of mist behind and the lodge became visible in the distance. It was at the head of a long loch with slate-dark mountains rising steep on either side, powdered high up with the first autumn snows. The lodge itself was a Victorian building, similar to Balmoral, grey against the water.

She parked at the gate and climbed out of the Volvo, felt the cold coming down off the mountains, even through her thick coat. She tried to imagine Robert on his bike. *Why did he come up here alone in the dark?* She took the photograph of his smiling face out of her pocket.

She remembered the bruises on his body. The bite marks. The way that he had been positioned, pointed to the west. Did that have some kind of significance? She shivered at the idea, then followed the path away from the house as it rose.

From the top of the hill she could see down into the next valley. There was more dark pine forest and a distant road with a row of buildings alongside it. Then more mountains on the horizon. Slowly Monica realised that she was staring down at the back of Robert Wright's house. A branch of the path must cut through the forest.

Could someone have seen him up here? Could they have followed him home and lured him out of the house somehow? Owen MacLennan? Or the other man that Muir had mentioned, Don Cameron? It was a horrible thought. But something had made Robert leave the house.

Monica stared down at the gloomy woods. The kid must have gone through those trees at night. The proposal to reintroduce wolves and even bears to this barren landscape hadn't gained much traction in the Highlands so far, but the fear of predators seemed so deeply imbedded – especially after dark – wouldn't a teenage boy alone have been scared? So why do it?

She racked her brain for an answer. Robert's mother had left. She had split his family – split the foundations of his life. Was that where he was vulnerable to being manipulated somehow? This line of reasoning made Monica fall back on the idea that the killer was someone who knew him.

Owen MacLennan's words from that morning, his hateful mocking expression came back to her then: *I've got a feeling in my gut. Something that tells me that poor boy, he wasn't the last.*

Monica shivered again and felt the damp of the mist seeping through her coat. She turned and walked back towards the hunting lodge. The place was closed up for the winter now, with shutters over the many windows.

At the back of the lodge there was a large garage. The doors were open on one side. A couple of quad bikes and a ride-on lawnmower were parked inside. A good place to bring a kid you wanted to torture. She studied the area as she would study a crime scene. It would be too easy though to find a bloody set of animal's teeth on the workbench, or cable ties and a mattress. She remembered what Dr Dolohov had suggested at the autopsy, that maybe the killer had taken Robert somewhere to clean him after the murder. This would make a nice private place for the job while the owners were away. No one anywhere nearby to interrupt or to hear a sound.

Monica looked around for a little longer but there was nothing, of course. No sign of Don Cameron, or anyone else for that matter. She tucked one of her cards beside the light switch at the entrance and wondered for a moment if it would sit there until the spring. Then she turned and walked back up the track to her car.

As she climbed behind the wheel Monica heard the phone start ringing in her pocket as it picked up a signal again.

'DI Kennedy? It's Detective Superintendent Hately.'

'I need more officers for a surveillance operation on Owen MacLennan,' Monica said. Getting her request in before Hately had a chance to deny her out of hand. 'I've put DC Fisher on it for now but I'm going to need help. At least until we can get a warrant to search his flat and vehicle.'

There was a long pause on the other end of the line. As if her boss hadn't quite understood what she'd said.

'That's not why I'm calling,' he said finally. 'They've just found another body. It's laid out in the same way as Robert Wright.'

Monica stared down into the forest. The tendrils of mist spreading among the treetops. Of course there was another one – it made sense that there would be. Hearing the news made her exhale heavily because she wasn't even surprised.

Chapter 22

Michael parked outside the school gates and lit a cigarette as he crossed the empty tarmac of the playground. It was a large school with a central four-storey building with windows looking down from three sides.

A strange childlike anxiety crept over him and several old scenes ran through his mind: the kids who had a hard time, the bullying and the cruelty – all the little everyday horrors. He'd avoided the worst of it. His father's anachronistic philosophy of toughness had made the other boys wary of him. *That and there was no sport in it with you, was there?* Not after everything with your brother. Michael took a long draw on the cigarette until the smoke scorched his lungs and burned the memories away.

He started at the distantly familiar sound of the school bell ringing for the end of the day. It echoed off the red-brick walls as the kids poured out, emptying across the playground, some running in groups, others alone with their heads down through the chill of the early-evening air. Each in their own world. Creating their own story. So vulnerable, so easily damaged, so easily destroyed.

Michael took another deep draw on the cigarette. At the entrance he discovered that they don't put cigarette bins outside schools any more. He took a heroic last draw then extinguished the cigarette and put it in his jacket pocket. He turned back to find the glass door already open.

'Michael Bach.' It was a statement, not a question.

The man standing in the dark foyer was younger than Michael had expected. He had dark hair with a neat side parting and he was wearing a black headmaster's gown over a grey suit.

'Mr Ward? Thanks for seeing me.'

He must have read something on Michael's face because he smiled. 'This?' He tugged the lapels of the gown. 'The school council decided I have to wear it to set an example to the kids with their uniforms. It is a bit fancy dress, isn't it? I'm sure some of the first years think I'm a wizard or something.'

Michael found himself smiling back. 'Sorry, it wasn't that. I just imagined you as older.'

'Well. Usually I feel older if that makes a difference?' Ward said, smiling again.

Michael followed him down the corridor to his office. There were educational posters on the walls: MATHEMATICS IS SPOKEN HERE, ENGLISH SKILLS. His desk was of dark wood as were the seats. There was a large metal cupboard standing in the corner.

'Nichol was a bright boy. I didn't know him well of course. Unfortunately with the school being the largest in the Highlands I don't have the opportunity to get to know all my pupils as well as I might. But I did meet him in passing. He had some problems when he was younger but had been doing better recently. He was interested in computing if I recall?'

'That's right,' Michael said. As he spoke he wondered again about the laptop: how could Nichol have afforded it? 'He did quite well in the computing exam too. He's hoping to study it at college.'

Mr Ward nodded. 'I got the basics when you called earlier, but I wanted to hear it directly from you.' He sat down on the other side of the desk, his smile replaced with an authoritative expression. *You must have to use that expression a lot as a teacher,* Michael thought.

'Nichol fitted the description of the victim. The boy was murdered over in Gairloch. You probably heard about it. They asked me to identify him.'

'I read about it, of course. It's been a huge event for the local media. It was mentioned on the national news also, I believe.' Ward formed his fingers into a steeple as he spoke. 'They say the boy was in a terrible state. It must have been difficult for you. Seeing what had been done to him.'

Michael remembered the body lying on the slab. The ghost of the boy walking, standing just outside his bedroom door at the croft. For the first time he clearly remembered those dream words, spoken as the boy's neck twisted back. Back further than a neck should twist. With staring eyes: *You've seen what he does. When he gets us alone.*

He shivered at the sudden recollection and felt Ward's searching eyes on his face. 'Anyway,' Michael said finally, 'the police don't seem to think that finding Nichol's a priority. I found this.' He dug in his pocket for the printout of the photo and handed it to Ward. 'I think this girl's name is Melissa. I thought maybe she was a pupil at the school?'

Ward took the picture and stared at it intently. 'You don't have a surname?'

Michael shook his head. 'I'm not even certain that her name's Melissa.'

'I don't recognise her,' Ward said. He tilted his head and stared at the photo. After a moment he turned to the computer on his desk and typed in a password. 'When Nichol went missing I personally spoke to all his classmates. And the police too of course, after you'd filed the missing persons. I always keep a close eye when we have these types of situations arising with pupils or ex-pupils.'

'And you didn't find anything?' Michael asked.

'Well,' Mr Ward said and turned to put his hands flat on either side of the keyboard. Then he paused and smiled again, seeming to enjoy setting the pace of the conversation. 'If I had I would have passed it on to the police. To the social services if it had been appropriate.'

Michael nodded. The proper procedures. 'Sure. Was there ...' Michael thought of the best way to frame the question then decided just to come right out with it. 'Was there anyone that Nichol was spending time with? Anyone who might have been in a position to groom him, or ...'

'*Groom* him?' Ward sounded appalled at the idea.

'Nichol had an expensive laptop. I don't know how he could have afforded it. I thought maybe there was something going on, maybe someone was putting pressure on him?'

Ward looked shocked and he frowned. 'We take the safety of our pupils seriously. Everyone connected with the school has been vetted.' Michael realised that Ward was covering his own back, fearful of a social worker on a crusade, looking to blame the school.

'I didn't mean someone from the school,' Michael said. 'Maybe someone who Nichol had mentioned to other pupils, I thought the girl in the picture might have some idea. I don't know ...' His voice trailed off.

'You do know about Nichol's family, don't you?' Ward said as he leaned forward across his desk.

'What do you mean?' Michael didn't like Ward's conspiratorial tone one bit.

'You know his family. He's a Bartle. They're from the Marsh? You must have heard of them in your work? Actually they're notorious. Drugs. Violence. Criminality. You'll see their names in the court reports on a weekly basis, unfortunately.'

'Of course I know about the Bartles – who doesn't? That doesn't mean Nichol's a criminal.' Michael sounded harsher than he'd intended. Almost like he was an argumentative schoolboy himself. 'I'm sorry. I didn't mean to be rude. Nichol got teased about his family sometimes ...'

'No, it's all right. I didn't intend to imply a flaw in Nichol's character. Just that he lacked a stable home environment. And that unfortunately there are other ways of getting hold of expensive items than buying them.' His tone somehow managed to paint Michael as the naive bleeding-hearted social worker.

Before Michael could reply Ward had already turned back to his computer screen. He opened a spreadsheet. 'I can't see a Melissa in any of Nichol's classes. Nor the year above or below. It's a less popular name now than it once was. It's not so frequently seen. It could be that the girl is in a different school.' Ward glanced at the photograph again. 'They do look happy together, don't they?'

Michael looked at the picture himself. Their wide smiles like the start of a future.

'One of the great tragedies of this job is seeing potential squandered. Every day. Every week. Young people with every-thing ahead of them. But that tragic lack of vision. What they could be. What they could become.' Ward clicked on the screen again. Turned back to Michael. 'Maybe you have the same experiences in your role? We're in similar positions after all. Attempting to guide, to care. Sometimes to save them from themselves. Or to show them what might be better for them.'

'I suppose you're right,' Michael said. 'Although a lot of my clients are struggling just to keep their heads above water. My job can be ...'

'Lonely?'

'I was going to say difficult. But yes, I suppose it can be lonely too. Trying to help when people don't think they need help. When they think you're interfering.' Michael glanced up and met Ward's eyes. He realised that he'd been more open than he intended.

Ward nodded and looked back at his computer screen then peered over Michael's shoulder. He seemed to make up his mind about something. 'Listen. Can I keep this photo? I'll make some enquiries, colleagues in other schools. We have to be careful with this type of thing – the perception of the pupils and their parents? I'm sure you understand? But I want to help. Maybe this girl can provide a clue to Nichol's whereabouts. Could I ask you for your contact details?'

Michael nodded and dug a card out of his pocket, pleased that Ward had agreed to help when he'd seemed to be winding their conversation down. He slid the card across the desk.

'Leave it with me. I'm not promising anything but I'll see what I can do. I'll speak to Nichol's teachers again and see if I can't jog their memories.'

Chapter 23

Monica made it to the top of the narrow footpath, breathing heavily from the steep walk. She stood with her hands on her hips and stared over past Crawford to where the body was now clearly visible.

It looked strangely beautiful in the shallows of the mountain loch. It lay, folded over as if at prayer, as Robert's body was. Close to the steep edge at the front of a huge amphitheatre-shaped corrie that had been carved from the mountain by an ice-age glacier. It was a remote location at the back of Beinn Eighe in Torridon. The water was calm and reflected the body perfectly. White skin on white, and the red marks. The mountains rising steep behind it like stone fortresses in the water, then the infinite grey sky.

'This is fucking crazy,' Crawford said under his breath. 'Why bring a body all the way up here?'

Monica glanced at him. The first flecks of snow had landed on his red hair. The steam was rising from his head into the chill mountain air.

'Why would he bring a body up here?' Crawford repeated. Monica shrugged. To her it seemed clear. After where he'd put Robert, he'd want to move things on a step further. Make it a little bit more interesting and exciting. This made her wonder how warped that meant her own mind was – when it seemed so obvious to her.

That's a question for another day. For never, she thought as she took a step closer then glanced past the body to the wide glacier-scoured landscape beneath them. It was a labyrinth of flat rock, moorland and patches of water. Then the ocean. The peninsula where Robert Wright's body had been dumped was just visible in the distance despite the gathering clouds.

'It's another boy? Same as before?' Crawford said, his voice seeming to seek consolation somehow.

'It looks like it. But we'll have to wait until we can move it,' Monica said. She stared at the pale body. *Of course it's a boy,* she thought. That's his thing. Why would he change that now?

She looked behind her to the path where Gemma Gunn and the rest of the forensics team had been dropped off by the mountain rescue quad bikes and were now changing into their white suits. They would have to work quickly because it would be dark soon, and Monica could already feel the change in the weather. Flecks of snow were beginning to spiral across the rocks: harbingers of the storm that was due to come crashing in off the North Atlantic and rip through this exposed location.

Monica turned back to the body. It looked like a sculpture, white marble against the water. She remembered what Hately had told her earlier on the phone: 'It was found by three guys working on a path. They've been up there every day for the past two weeks. They say it definitely wasn't there when they finished last night. They thought it was a mountain rescue dummy until they got close enough to see the –' he'd paused then, obviously feeling around for the right words '– the marks.'

Monica stared at the body from the shore. After a moment she couldn't help stepping into the shallows for a closer look.

The ice-cold mountain water seeped into her boots as she splashed over to the body.

She leaned in close, taking care not to disturb any possible evidence. It was definitely a boy. He was slim with short dark hair. There were puncture wounds on his back and on his neck too this time; no doubt that would add fuel to the nonsense in the press about some mysterious wild animal being responsible. But Monica had no doubt the killer was human, a man enjoying himself. Enjoying pushing everything just a bit further than the last time.

She crouched, not noticing the hem of her coat dipping into the water, and stared down at the dead boy's face. It was twisted to the side with mouth open and white teeth scraping at the rock. As if he were drinking from the icy water. She could see the downy stubble on his cheek.

One of his dead eyes was staring out into infinity. Somehow it was marked with those last moments of pain, of terror. Monica resisted the human impulse to reach her hand out and slide his eyelid closed.

That little detail – that the man who had done this had chosen to leave the boy's eyes open after everything that he'd done to him – told Monica something about the killer.

She stared into the boy's visible eye. *Well, it's over now. For you at least. Like it will be for all of us*, Monica thought. She straightened up and felt the tightness of her boots. They were more uncomfortable than ever now, soaked with the icy water.

She sloshed over to where Crawford was still standing watching her from the shore and stepped out of the loch. For what it was worth, she didn't think this body was Nichol Morgan, or if it was him then he didn't look much like his missing person's photograph.

'What are we dealing with here? A serial murderer?' Crawford asked.

Well, what do you think? Monica thought. Two boys dead, folded up ten miles apart in the Scottish Highlands within four days of each other and it's a coincidence? 'It's the same killer,' she said finally. 'To give them the label of serial we need a third body.'

Crawford ignored this last comment. He fixed his eyes on the loch behind her. 'Why here? It must have taken hours to bring him here. Can you imagine?' Crawford held out his hand to the wide rocky landscape below them. Streaked with low-level storm clouds now.

'His body's directed towards the horizon – maybe towards the rising stars,' Monica said, thinking out loud as she remembered the night sky and the stars above the first dump site. 'The same as Robert. I think that could be a big part of it for him.'

'Why?' Crawford asked. He shivered and zipped up the orange Gore-Tex jacket he'd pulled on, turned up the collar against the cold mountain wind, which was becoming more insistent as the storm gathered.

Monica turned the collar up on her own thick coat and pulled it tight at her waist. She shook her head slowly.

'I don't know.' She wondered about those strange internal maps, the strange cold byways of insanity that the human mind could go down. 'Maybe he doesn't either.'

'MacLennan told us there would be another body. Another boy killed. He must know something. We have to bring him in now, surely?' Crawford said. The outrage was clear in his voice as it came out in icy clouds.

'He hinted at it,' Monica said. She stared back over at the boy's dead eye. 'We need to keep MacLennan under surveillance. We need to keep looking for something solid to build a case around. You saw what he was like at his flat. He'd actually enjoy it if we brought him in for an interview with nothing concrete against him.'

The radio Crawford was holding made a noise. He stepped away to answer it, and Monica watched as the forensics team moved in to surround the body. In their white overalls and rubber boots they looked like pagans around a sacrifice in the dark water. Behind them, further out on the loch, the water kicked up in a white spray as the wind came on stronger. The start of the gale.

She felt Crawford's hand on her elbow. He spoke quietly: 'That was Hately. We've got a possible ID on the victim.'

'What's the name?'

'A woman called Lisa MacKay. Her son Paul's seventeen. She's on holiday in France. Paul was home alone. She's been trying to contact him since last night.'

Chapter 24

Michael parked the Land Rover in the street outside his flat in Inverness. His phone had already rung ten times before he located it among the mess of papers in his bag.

'The Internet's gone off again. You said to call if it went off for three hours. You were supposed to be here this morning!' Michael realised with a surge of guilt that it was Henry, a client he was supposed to have visited that morning. Henry's routines were important to him.

'I'm sorry, Henry – something came up that I couldn't get out of,' Michael said. He hated the sound of his voice as he made the excuse.

'Yes. But the Internet's gone off! Do you think someone could be targeting me? Do you think it's the government again?' Several years previously the American government had attempted to extradite Henry for hacking into an FBI database.

'I'm sure it's not that, Henry. You don't do that type of thing any more. It's all in the past now.' Michael located his keys and patted himself down for a cigarette. He felt the first flecks of icy rain on his face as the coming storm from the west edged its way over Inverness.

Henry came back on the line, more frantic than ever: 'It's what they did last time though. I think it could be the same again!'

'Have you phoned the Internet company?' Michael knew what the answer would be already. Henry hated talking to strangers. Michael lit the cigarette and ran a hand over his face. 'Listen. I'll come over this evening, OK? Phone me if the Internet comes back on, though.'

Michael pushed the door of the flat open and was met with the smell of empty rooms and bad memories. He'd bought the place five years earlier when he moved north from Edinburgh with Alice, his ex-girlfriend. The relationship hadn't survived their second winter in the Highlands.

He took a draw on the cigarette and glanced round the living room. It was gloomy in the autumn evening. Everything looking just a notch shabbier and more depressing. The fading paint that they had chosen together. Michael couldn't help remembering the first night they had spent there, sitting on the carpet, still waiting for the furniture to arrive. They'd eaten Chinese takeaway from the cartons. What was that old line his grandmother used to use: *If walls could speak. What would they remember here?* Michael wondered. Laughter and plans for the future? Probably they'd remember the arguments, the hard words.

You're never present, Michael. You said it would be different up here … If you're not working then you're off somewhere in your head. You haven't dealt with things. Things from your childhood. I think you should speak to someone. I think you need help.

Why don't you fuck off then? If it's so bad living with me. Why don't you just go?

Alice had eventually gone, as he'd suggested, and he'd lived in the flat alone until his dad died. He'd intended to sell it and move to the croft – it wasn't like he could afford to run two homes – but six months later he somehow hadn't got round to putting the place on the market.

He threw his damp jacket across the kitchen table. It was the only piece of furniture other than a mattress in the bedroom. The milk in the fridge had gone off, so Michael took his instant coffee black and went to stand on the balcony. The weather was grey. Dirty and old-fashioned and medieval. Medieval like a boy tortured to death, like another boy missing.

He went back in, reached over and clicked the radio on just in time to catch the local news on BBC Scotland. He lit another cigarette and watched the lights of the city below flick on. The lights on Kessock Bridge in the distance were flashing red against the darkening sky. He was barely listening to the presenter's voice until her words cut through: 'Police are refusing to confirm that the body, reported to be that of local teenager Paul MacKay, was the victim of murder. The discovery of the body earlier today, the second to be found in similar circumstances in just three days, has sparked alarm.'

Michael turned to the radio in horror. He was hardly able to believe what he was hearing. The implications if another boy was dead: that there might be a serial killer out there and he was personally involved in the case. With a shaking hand he picked up his phone and read through the news reports online, pressing Refresh repeatedly in case a new development emerged. When he'd read everything he could find he dropped the phone back onto the table and lit yet another cigarette. It meant that Nichol really could be dead but not yet found.

He flinched at the sound of his phone buzzing with a message, suddenly edgy and fearful. He stubbed out the cigarette and went to pick up the phone, hoping it was Henry saying his Internet was fixed.

But the message was from a number Michael didn't recognise: 'I saw you at school today. I know Nichol. Meet me under the bridge across from Rapinch in 30 minutes.'

Michael looked out of the open window at the night outside, at the empty street and the lights from other windows. A paranoid idea began to form: *Someone could be watching you. They could be playing with you. Trying to get you alone? It can't be a coincidence – the message coming in right after what you heard on the radio.*

He forced out a laugh and tried to shrug off the absurd idea. 'Jesus. You're really starting to sound like one of your clients now,' he said out loud.

Michael read the message again. He called the number, but it went straight to voicemail. He stared at the message, trying to decide what to do. It seemed obvious: pass the information to the police. There was a murderer out there. He lit another cigarette. Listened to the rain hitting the window and the sounds of the evening traffic drifting in from outside.

You really think waiting for the police to do something is an option? the harsh voice at the back of Michael's head piped up. *When they have a new body and nobody to blame yet. You want all their attention focused on you? You can go, or you can let Nichol down again. It's up to you.*

Chapter 25

The underpass was ghostly. Cold and crypt-like with concrete posts and metal railings lit by white electric light against the dark. In the distance a man dressed in a tracksuit with his hood up was strolling in the opposite direction through the evening, a pair of Rottweilers bouncing along beside him. They were off the leash and their shadows danced under the lights. Their intimidating throaty barks echoed back down the riverside to where Michael was standing.

Just keep going, buddy. Keep your dogs away from me too, Michael thought as he glanced up and down the path. He zipped his dad's old down jacket against the damp air and the cold that seemed to be creeping off the water of the River Ness up through the pillars of the bridge and into his flesh and bones.

It was cold like the grave, like the morgue. He found his thoughts drifting again to the boy lying in that mortuary, to the report on the radio and the coincidence of the text message coming straight afterwards. He squeezed the phone in his hand and tried to ignore the idea that they were all connected. Peered at the darkness by the sides of the bridge, those strange urban pockets of thick undergrowth with broken glass trodden into the dirt. He stepped towards the shadows and caught the edge of a smell. It was almost like perfume in the evening air. Close to a perfume, but subtle. More like incense.

He flicked the cigarette and took a step closer. A chip of glass cracked beneath his foot. The sound was loud under the bridge against the muffled noises of cars passing overhead. *Why would someone burn incense out here? It had to be something else.* He peered into the shadows. There were shapes beginning to form as he stared and his eyes became more accustomed to the dark. There was a feeling beginning to form too. A strange sense of horror.

It was similar to how he'd felt back at the morgue. Just before he'd met DI Kennedy. As if an unwanted door was opening. A strange hidden space that could lead down into any kind of hellish underworld.

Michael jerked round as a sound echoed under the bridge. Wood screeching against wood. There was a gap in the fence further down the path, and someone standing by it, eerily still under the street lamp. Michael turned away from the smell and walked hesitantly towards the hooded figure. He realised that it was a girl and made the obvious guess: 'Melissa?'

Her face glowed pale in the dark.

'I'm sorry.' She turned and started walking, almost running along the path towards the centre of town.

Without thinking Michael ran after her and grabbed for her arm, harder than he'd intended. It was thin like it could break.

'Where is he?'

'I shouldn't have texted you, I'm sorry.' She glanced back towards the bridge. 'A man was following me.'

'Are you sure?' Michael turned to look back down the path. It looked dark and empty. But the smell, where had it come from? Before Michael had a chance to consider that, Melissa continued down the path, walking fast with her head down.

'It's OK. There's no one there!' Beside them the river moved, quick and black like oil. Dark as the uncertain future. 'Did you see who it was?'

The girl didn't reply but grabbed Michael's arm and led him down a narrow path between some houses. She stopped then turned to him. 'My name's not Melissa. That's just what Nichol called me.' Her hands were moving, folding in on themselves. 'It was stupid. We should have met somewhere else!'

'Just take a breath.' Michael tried again: 'Do you know where he is? Something happened. What was it?'

'Nichol gave me your card ages ago. It had your number on it. I saw you today. I thought you could help – he said you were good to him.'

'I want to help.'

'I can't handle thinking about it,' she hissed.

Michael glanced over her shoulder, down the path between the houses to the river. Was there really a man? Or was it just anxiety? Anxiety strong enough to make her think someone was watching her?

'Thinking about what? When did you last see him?'

'Just before he disappeared.'

'Where did he go?'

'I don't know. He never told me. He was like a big brother. We'd known each other since we were kids. I think he was trying to protect me.'

'From what?'

She looked around but didn't reply.

'You heard about that boy who was killed over in Gairloch? The police found a stone in—' Michael managed to stop himself. Sharing the full horror of what the police had told him about the stone being forced into the boy's throat would do her no good. 'The stone was ... close to his body. It was similar to the one Nichol used to carry. Do you know where he got it?'

She shook her head as if trying to shake the connection with the murdered boy out of her mind. 'Nichol's alive. I'm sure of it.'

'Who was he afraid of?' Michael caught her arm again. 'I can't help Nichol if you won't tell me.'

'A couple of weeks ago. Before he disappeared we were at his uncle's flat. I'd asked Nichol to help me with some school work.'

'His uncle's?' Michael was sure he'd never heard Nichol mention an uncle.

'Eddie. He's a great-uncle or something. Everyone knows him. I never liked him but Nichol ... I don't know. He stayed there sometimes when he didn't want to go back to the hostel.'

Michael nodded and looked at the ground.

'You know what he's like? He always had things under control. Like he knew more than everyone else?'

Michael nodded again. It tied in with what he knew about the kid.

'This time he was quiet. Just in his own head. He was turning that stone over and over in his hand. Holding it up to his mouth in that weird way and not answering me. Then ... It just wasn't like him at all ...'

'What? You had an argument or something?' Michael asked.

'Nichol has this way of always noticing things. Like he knows when something's bothering you. Like once I dyed my hair silver and it looked horrible so I had to dye it again to cover it up. But he took a photo and kept showing people. Like he knows when you feel weird about something and sees it as a way of teasing you or something.'

'He makes things into a joke?' Michael said. He was trying to keep the growing impatience out of his voice. Wishing she would get to the point.

She nodded slowly, swallowing a breath. 'I suppose so.'

'But he went too far this time?'

'No, it wasn't like that …' Her face crumpled. For a second Michael thought she was going to start crying. 'I think maybe it was my fault. Maybe I scared him …'

'What happened?' Michael asked. They were walking along Friars' Street heading towards the Old High Church, getting closer to the centre of town.

'We were at Eddie's. Nichol had gone to get a drink. He had this bag of clothes he kept there. I wasn't being sneaky – I just wanted to borrow a jumper because I was cold. I found this phone in there. It was one I hadn't seen before.' Melissa stared at the ground. 'I guessed the passcode – it was his date of birth. I was only going to take a selfie on it, set it as a screensaver – as a joke.' She wiped her face with her sleeve. 'He started shouting at me like he was going to hit me. I'd never seen him that angry before. We'd had fights, but—'

'What was on the phone?' Michael asked.

'There was just a message. There was no name or anything. It was just a message from a number. It was someone asking Nichol to meet them.'

Chapter 26

The Watcher

He held the lock of Paul MacKay's hair close to his nose and took a deep breath. Enjoying the smell – shampoo (*Head & Shoulders*) and under that sweat, blood – and the fresh memories from the evening before that it triggered. Memories that he could lose a lifetime in.

After long minutes of contemplation he reluctantly folded the lock into his wallet and turned back to the TV.

The news report detailed the frantic efforts of the police. The reporter was dressed in a pristine anorak and standing by the side of the snow-blasted road, clearly delighted by all the excitement. Police officers were trudging back to their vehicles. The strange large woman detective. He noticed the way she moved – courting attention somehow.

And as he watched he turned the stone over in his hand and found his mind wandering back to the time after the old woman. Things had been awkward for him. More attention paid by his parents and a series of psychologists. With George locked up he was alone with his imagination.

Two years after that first incident – when the adults' interest finally began to subside – he was able to walk alone to the park near the old woman's house. To finally retrieve the box of stones from where he had buried it. At night he would turn those stones over in his hot hands. Almost feverish as he watched the dark sky. The celestial bodies. Venus, Mars, Jupiter – and of course Saturn, the most important of them all. The black star.

Slowly he had discovered that if he let those black stones speak to him, he could divine some meaning from them.

They showed him George. Hanging, slumped, from the bunk in his cell. Long before his mother came into his bedroom and quietly told him the *horrible news* that after being bullied terribly in the juvenile prison, George, racked with remorse and self-hatred, had taken his own life. She saw the look of shock on his face and readily interpreted it as sadness. Which it was, in a way. He'd always imagined that George would come back into his orbit eventually – that they would be reunited. But it was the proof of the stones' power that had shocked him. Almost as much as his response in the days that followed surprised him.

The feeling of satisfaction.

He knew that he'd done the old woman a favour. What was the point of another useless old person taking up space?

But George was different. He was young, with a whole life ahead of him.

He had extinguished all of George's potential. Edged him into non-existence and changed the very fabric of the universe. What was more, George had slipped into that non-existence willingly.

Chapter 27

It was almost fully dark by the time Monica and Crawford arrived back in Inverness. The storm had followed them east as a blizzard over the high pass after Kinlochewe and along the long road through the mountains. They'd left as a yellow Sea King search and rescue helicopter had flown into the remote snow-blasted corrie, arriving like a screaming beast from above and taking the body and the forensics team back to Inverness before the gale-force winds made it impossible.

Monica glanced at the time on the dashboard. It was just after 6 p.m. and for a moment she allowed herself to imagine being at home in the warm flat with Lucy. Safely locked away from the night outside and hearing what new excitements the kid had discovered today, what new details about the world had drawn her fascinated attention.

Well, today Mummy found another dead body. He was mutilated and tortured, so she's going to have to watch his autopsy. An autopsy's when you cut someone's body open and take all their insides out to find out how they died. Then Mummy's going to have to visit the dead boy's house. So she won't be home any time soon.

'Should I come to the autopsy?' Crawford asked.

Monica glanced over at him.

'I guess it'll be this evening?' he said.

Monica thought about it for a second, wondered if he was asking because he was squeamish. Or was it because he was nervous after their disagreement that morning? He had to have overheard her on the phone just half an hour ago discussing the arrangements with Hately.

'No. Go back to the incident room and find out where we're up to with Robert's laptop and tracking his phone. We need to rule Owen MacLennan out or in. Things are going to get more complicated with a second body to investigate – Hately will want to expand the team probably.' When did more numbers, more opinions ever make anything run more smoothly?

She pulled into the car park and watched as Crawford climbed out of the Volvo, crossing to the headquarters building with his thin arms out wide away from his body, Scottish hard-man style.

Monica shook her head. She reversed to turn the car and drove the short distance across the busy road to Raigmore Hospital.

Dr Dolohov looked up from the laptop in front of him when Monica walked into the morgue. 'Our second meeting in three days. I think you really like me, no?'

She looked back at him without returning his smile, then took a step closer to the body lying between them on the slab.

'We three have been waiting for you.' Dolohov nodded to the nurse standing at the far end of the room dressed in surgical scrubs. Then to the body. 'How did a dead boy outrun the detective on her way to the mortuary? It's like a riddle. The one about the man who tried to outrun death. You remember?'

Monica tried very hard to ignore him and stared down at the boy. Now she could see his face properly, he looked a little older than Robert Wright. But similar. The same type: dark hair and white skin. There were the same marks around his neck where he'd been strangled and cuts on his wrists from ligatures. From thick plastic cable ties, she'd guess.

For a fleeting moment Monica remembered the afternoon she had spent teaching herself how to break fastened cable ties off her wrists. It was after visiting a murder scene. A woman had been starved to death in an oil tank, her hands fastened behind her back with cable ties. The tank was only six feet deep. If she had been able to free her hands, she could have reached up and pulled herself out.

That had been a bad one.

Monica shook her head to dismiss the memory, opened the photograph on her phone. She compared the boy's dead face to the smiling, living one. A smile that no longer existed. Just like that.

Dr Dolohov stood with his hands on his hips watching her. 'Do you have a name for this one at least?' he said finally.

'We think he's called Paul. Paul MacKay. His mother's out of the country. She's about to fly home to this.' Monica gestured at the body. 'She sent us these photos.' Monica held the phone out for him to see. 'It looks like it's him. The first thing she did last night when the kid didn't reply to her was put a post out on Facebook asking if anyone had seen him. It got shared all over the place and the media picked up on it. They put two and two together when the report about the body came in. But we'll have to wait for her to formally ID him.'

The doctor nodded and ran a hand over his bald head. He tied the mask tight behind his neck and pulled a somewhat unnecessary hair cover on.

She cleared her throat. 'The boy's mother, Lisa MacKay, she asked one of the officers that she spoke to if someone would hold the kid's hand during the autopsy.' *It'll make a big differ-ence, won't it. To a cold dead body*, Monica told herself harshly, attempting to create some emotional distance from the woman's pain.

Dr Dolohov shrugged and glanced over to the nurse. If either of them was surprised by the request they didn't show it. 'Why not? Maybe a little kindness from a stranger will help this tortured boy to pass over,' he said, his voice was muffled by the mask. 'What more can any of us ask for when it's our turn?'

Dolohov checked the fastenings on the mask behind his neck again. He glanced over Monica's shoulder as the door slowly opened and her boss, Detective Superintendent Hately, stepped in. She looked at him, took in his regular Glaswegian-Italian features. He had dark eyes and short dark hair flecked with grey that somehow managed to look like it had cost a lot to style and was entirely uncared-for at the same time. He was a couple of inches shorter than Monica and was wearing a well-cut suit. He smelled of aftershave. He fitted the profile of what they used to call a media-savvy politician – in the days before social media and Internet news became twin hydras that no one in a public position could seem savvy in front of.

His hand went to his tie as he nodded to the doctor, then at Monica. His eyes landed on the body: vulnerable and exposed in front of them.

When was the last time you came down to witness an autopsy? Monica wondered. This confirmed what she already knew – that the media were going to be all over the case. There was going to be interest and pressure from higher up the chain of command. More interference.

'We begin,' Dr Dolohov said finally. Breaking the silence that had fallen over the morgue.

Monica pulled a single surgical glove on, stepped closer and awkwardly laid her own long fingers over the boy's cold dead hand. She looked at the strange asymmetrical bite marks on his arms and on his neck, watched Dolohov turn over the knife in his hand. He stared down the length of the blade as if checking its edge, then slowly cut into Paul MacKay's chest. As close to tender with the knife as it was possible to be.

Then the familiar ritual. The funereal rites of rationality. The opening out of the body. The removal of the organs. Piece by piece, weighing them, peeling the skin back from the boy's face. The sound of metal on bone as Dr Dolohov cut through the skull. A thin line of sweat appeared on his forehead from the exertion. He wiped it away with the back of his arm, smearing his gown pink as the sweat mixed with pinprick splashes of blood.

He separated the brain from the webbed fibres and cut it from the spinal column. Then he weighed it and held it up in one hand to the light, like a botanist examining a particularly unusual bloom.

'Funny,' he said as he slipped the brain back inside its empty skull, 'how a whole person, a whole personality exists in that thing. The most complex object in the known universe.' He cracked his own neck to the side. Shook his head and pulled the skin back over the boy's head.

Finally he opened the crushed remnants of the windpipe out and held up the piece of black stone between two fingers for Monica and Hately to see.

'In case anyone thought it wasn't the same man.' He pointed to the flecks of red blood on the black stone. 'Oxygenated. It looks like this boy was still alive when the killer forced it down his throat too.'

Hately shifted beside her and cleared his throat. Dr Dolohov dropped the stone into a plastic evidence container.

'We'll need to have the stone analysed, fast-tracked. It's clearly significant to the killer. We need to find out where it came from and if it matches the first one,' Monica said.

When the autopsy was over she was impatient to get back over to the office, but Hately stopped her in the corridor outside the morgue. They stood there facing each other under flickering electric lights, surrounded by the pungent smell of hospital floor cleaner and a hint of something under it. Something going bad.

Monica knew what was coming, more or less.

'We'll bring in more support for you first thing tomorrow. More officers to deal with the calls coming in and help with the house-to-house inquiries.' Hately's hand went to the lapel of his jacket, and a little tic at the corner of his eye went off. The one that meant he was under pressure.

Monica nodded, hoping it was the end of the conversation but knowing that it wasn't.

'I've spoken with senior management. This is a high-profile investigation. It's essential that we deal with it effectively.'

'I understand that, sir,' Monica said. Because of course she'd rather deal with it ineffectively.

'We feel that it's important to use the full range of support available to us. Especially in a situation like this. With a major public-interest factor.'

'Fine. I'll keep that in mind,' Monica said. She turned to go.

The door at the far end of the corridor swung open on its hinges, the sound loud and invasive in the quiet space. The man who was standing in the doorway was small and neat with a shock of thick white hair. He was dressed in a grey three-piece suit.

'Ah, good timing. This is Dr Hamish Lees,' Hately said, his eyes momentarily avoiding Monica's. 'He's a criminal psychologist. He's lectured all over the world and advised on a number of high-profile murder cases similar to this one. We're lucky that he's volunteered to come in and advise on the investigation.'

Dr Lees looked Monica up and down, his head tilted to the side as if she was a curiosity. Roll up, roll up. Here she is, the giant woman with her gangly limbs and wide shoulders. Her strange pale skin and her damp, too-small boots pinching her feet. A knowing little smile crossed his face, as if he could somehow taste her insecurities and self-doubts, as if they were amusing to him.

She felt an immediate dislike. One that for some reason she felt no compulsion to disguise. 'I see,' Monica said. She stared down at Lees, taking pleasure from the fact that he was forced to look up to her. She then turned to Hately. 'I take it I don't have a say in this? I've worked with psychologists in the past. I would have consulted one of them when I needed to.'

Hately started to speak, but Lees held a hand up to stop him.

'You're DI Kennedy. The SIO?' Monica didn't reply. She let the awkward silence fill the hallway until finally Lees went on anyway. 'And what? You think I'm going to tread on your toes? You think that you're handling things so well that there's nothing an outside expert can contribute to the investigation?' His voice was strangely gravelly but high-pitched at the same time.

'I think that we'll catch the murderer by being thorough and focused with our investigative work. I think that our killer plans his actions carefully. I think that he's killed before—'

'Ah,' Lees said. Half a smile spread across his suntanned face. 'I see. You're the amateur psychologist. You're going to get inside the killer's head and outsmart him on your own.' He chuckled. 'Well. I'm here now. So obviously your superiors don't agree with that approach.' He smiled up at her as he said it. An oddly boyish and antagonistic gesture considering he must have been in his late fifties at least.

Monica continued to glare down at him. She didn't reply, but she could feel the sweat standing up on her back and her face flushing with anger.

'Dr Lees has requested to see the bodies,' Hately said. He glanced between the two of them.

'And I'll need copies of the files. The crime scene photographs and the autopsy reports,' Lees said. 'Just as soon as you can get them to me.'

She didn't reply and for long seconds none of them spoke. Finally Hately cleared his throat again and led Lees through the double doors and into the morgue.

Chapter 28

Monica stepped into the canteen at the Inverness office. For a moment she was surprised to find the place deserted until she reminded herself that it was 8 p.m. on a Monday. The canteen closed at five. All the sensible people had gone home hours ago – as she should have done. To tuck Lucy into bed and read her a story rather than wish her a hurried goodnight over the phone with more promises of the good times they were going to have. Just as soon as Mummy's important case was resolved ...

Monica wondered whether any of her male colleagues ever felt as guilty when they had to disappoint their young children. She had considered asking Hately once – she knew he had two teenage sons – but had dismissed the idea. He would probably have seen it as weakness. She swallowed the feeling of guilt over Lucy, reminded herself that this was her job, it paid the bills. When Lucy was older she'd understand.

She glanced at the rows of empty Formica-topped tables with matching chairs bolted to the floor. The migraine-inducing overhead strip lights. She spotted Crawford at the far end of the room and felt a momentary flash of anger that he'd asked to meet her here instead of in the incident room.

Crawford's shirtsleeves were rolled up past the elbow and his dark tie was loosened. He was alone at a table staring at a laptop and looked up at the curious squelching sound of Monica's footsteps on the linoleum floor.

'What's wrong with meeting at the office?' Monica asked. Letting her irritation at Hately and Dr Lees – at her own inadequacies as a mother – leach into her voice.

Crawford shrugged, surprised at her tone. 'I don't know – it's quieter, I suppose.'

'Where are you up to with Robert's laptop? His phone?'

'His phone?' Crawford shook his head. 'Still no trace. The killer must have ditched it. There's nothing significant on the laptop. No strange forums or unusual pornography.' He was talking quickly and tapping his foot on the ground, clearly impatient to get on to something else. Probably to tell her whatever it was that had made him drag her here.

'What about gay porn?' Monica asked. Interrupting him and taking pleasure from delaying him when he'd insisted she walk all the way down here in her wet boots rather than describe what he'd found over the phone. 'I'd wondered about an older boyfriend? Maybe someone Robert met online and kept secret?'

Crawford shook his head.

'No. There's nothing like that. It's vanilla heterosexual porn and very few sites. But listen.' The impatience mounting in his voice. 'You need to see this.'

He gestured to the laptop then clicked the screen. 'I lit a fucking fire under the uniform boys over in Gairloch this morning. Told them to get their arses back out and do follow-ups to track down anyone who could ID the van.'

'And?' Monica sat down beside him. Her knees jabbing the metal bar under the table, making her wince but feel alive for the first time in hours. As she stretched out a wave of pleasure matched the pain, and she allowed her eyes to close for a moment as some of the pressure was released from her feet.

'A video,' he said, folding his arms in and leaning over the laptop.

She sighed and then matched his stance.

'Was it from one of the garages' CCTV? Or a hotel?'

'Neither. They all came back either blank or they didn't face the road. This was from someone's house. From their living-room window. They're in dispute with the council about something – got their son to set up a camera to watch their driveway.'

Despite her tiredness and the pain in her feet, Monica felt a prickle of adrenaline and leaned in closer to Crawford.

He hit Play, and on the screen a van pulled into the picture. There was a man in the front seat, obscured by shadows. He climbed out then walked round to the back of the van. He seemed to check something with the rear door, then turned back to the driver's side. The man was tall but his face was indistinct with a beanie hat pulled down low on his forehead. Up to that point the van had been parked side on to the camera, the number plate hidden. As the van turned towards the screen, Crawford hit Pause and held his notebook up.

The registration number written in Crawford's careful block capitals matched the numbers on the screen. It was Owen MacLennan's van.

'This is from early Saturday morning. Just after 1 a.m. It puts MacLennan right in the frame as Robert's killer.'

Monica leaned in closer again, feeling that growing sense of excitement. 'Can we zoom in and ID his face for certain?'

Crawford clicked the screen to expand the image. The face was lost in the shadows. 'I guess we can try to enhance it, but ...' He shrugged his shoulders.

'We need to bring MacLennan in and search his van,' Monica said.

'I just called to check up on DC Fisher. He's watching MacLennan now. He says he's still at his flat. He's been there since this morning apart from a trip round the corner to the newsagent's for fags.'

Monica nodded, the pain from her soaked boots and broken promises to Lucy forgotten for now. She couldn't wait to see MacLennan's response when they confronted him with his lies. How his glib facade held up under real pressure.

She leaned past Crawford and ran the video back again for a third time.

'Can you slow it down?' Monica asked.

Crawford leaned in beside her. 'What are you seeing?'

'Just play it to the end,' Monica said.

They watched as the van pulled out. Monica hit the Pause button. For a split second as the van turned, the window at its rear faced the camera. It was momentarily bright under the electric street lamp.

Monica felt the chill run up her back and the hair on her arms stood on end. Crawford leaned over and zoomed in again. From the window of the van a face looked out towards the camera. It was blurred but distinctive. The face of a young man.

Chapter 29

Monica stared up at the block of light that came from Owen MacLennan's kitchen. Bright against the black of the building and the dark nine o'clock sky beyond it.

She flexed her toes inside her tight, damp boots, craving to drag off the hateful things.

'Shouldn't they be in by now?' DC Fisher piped up from the rear of the car. Monica and Fisher were watching the back entrance of the flats. Safe inside the Volvo while Crawford and two uniformed officers went in through the front door to make the arrest.

Monica glanced at Fisher in the mirror. She noticed what he was wearing for the first time. A fleece over a white polo shirt. His dark hair in its usual side parting. She also noticed how similar his hair was to Hately's. *Not a bad idea*, she thought. Copy the boss closely enough and eventually you might be the boss.

'It always feels longer when you're waiting at this end,' she said finally. Even though she wasn't sure if it was true. At least at this end you weren't running the risk of being shot or stabbed. Unless things went ugly wrong.

'Of course. I'd never thought of it that way,' Fisher said dutifully. As if she'd offered some radical new perspective. Monica blinked, trying to shake off the growing sense of dislike she was feeling for her younger colleague.

An indistinct voice echoed over the radio. The voice was followed by the sound of an impact: the team smashing at the door with a battering ram. The radio crackled. 'It's a reinforced door. We're almost through.'

Another impact, then shouting as they finally burst into the flat. Monica watched the light from the kitchen window. *If he's coming it'll be now.*

Long seconds passed. Then Crawford's voice came over on the radio again: 'He's not fucking here – the place is empty.'

'But I saw him with my own eyes fifteen minutes ago. He never left the building. How can he be gone?' Indignation in Fisher's voice masking the fear that he'd fucked up somehow, been spotted by MacLennan.

Monica felt her old friend the spike of adrenaline as she climbed out of the car. She crossed the street and stepped through the gate into the paved area at the back of the flats. Darkness all around beyond the glow of the light.

This is things going wrong, Monica thought as she tried the door handle. It was locked tight. Through the reinforced glass she could see one of the uniformed officers checking the corridor inside. The officer held her hands up when she saw Monica's face: *he's not here.*

'He can't have just vanished?' Monica turned at the sound of Fisher's voice. She felt her own frustration and disbelief mounting to match his. How could MacLennan have just walked right out from under them?

She grabbed Fisher's radio. 'Are you certain he's not in the flat somewhere?'

Crawford's voice came back at her: 'Of course I'm certain. Fucking hell. We're trying the other flats. Someone must have seen him.'

Monica pushed the radio back into Fisher's hands and gestured to the right. 'Check that way.'

Without waiting for his reply, Monica turned and ran round the other side of the building to the narrow alley that separated it from the next block. Silent pools of orange light reflected off the black tarmac. In that moment it felt like no living thing had ever walked down that path. Rain started falling gently.

Where was he? They couldn't have just let a murderer disappear. Monica took a deep breath. She tried to control the tide of frustration as she ran a hand over her face. She looked up and down the alleyway again. This time she spotted a small ground-floor window that overlooked the path. Did he go through the neighbour's flat? Then crawl out of that window?

Monica ran to the other end of the alley, which opened on to a small car park. MacLennan's van was still there, alone in the dark. She hesitated then walked slowly towards it. *This is when the lights come on*, she thought. *The engine fires up and he drives straight at me.*

But as she moved closer Monica saw that the van was empty. Where the hell was he?

She glanced around again. The only other exit from the walled-in car park was at the far end. But she could see the lights of the police van. He couldn't have gone that way; they would have seen him.

MacLennan's van was parked beside the high wall that surrounded the car park. Monica looked up at the wall. From the roof of the van it would be possible for a tall man to reach the top.

You'd better get help. You can't follow him alone, Monica thought. There was no sign of Fisher or the others. Her hand went to her phone, but there was no time. Every second she wasted now was a chance for MacLennan to get further away.

Instead she climbed up on to the bonnet, then the roof of the van. She felt the thin metal creak under her weight as she reached for the wall and scrambled up.

The space on the other side of the wall was black, covered by the night. MacLennan could be hiding down there. He could be waiting for her. Monica swallowed and stared down into the dark.

This could be a mistake. This could be the biggest mistake she'd ever make. But if she didn't follow him now he would escape, he would kill again, and it would be her fault.

Monica jumped down into the blackness. She hit the uneven ground hard and her knee buckled beneath her. She swore under her breath and gritted her teeth against the pain, then lay still for a moment and struggled to quiet her breathing, blinked as her eyes adjusted to the dark.

She knew he could be right there beside her. They'd never hear her once he'd covered her mouth. Once his thick hands tightened around her throat, she'd be finished.

Monica felt around on the wet grass. She was crouched in what felt like an abandoned garden turned to wasteland: a mess of thick weeds, rubbish and what looked like the rotting remains of a piece of furniture. She blinked again, willing her eyes to read more into the shapes. Opposite her a wall was lit by the creepy hue of a street lamp, allowing her to get her bearings. It was then that Monica realised there was a figure in the shadows.

She froze, reluctant even to breathe as the shape moved. She had been stupid to take the bait; to follow him on her own. The rain hit Monica's face and she caught the smell of dirt and abandoned places. The smell of dying alone.

Owen MacLennan turned and stared in her direction. Monica bit her lip and dropped her face to the ground until she tasted dirt. She held her breath. She knew in every cell of her body that he'd kill her if he saw her. Nature taught that a cornered predator would strike to kill, and MacLennan was a human predator, a base creature, when all his talk and attempts at diversion were stripped away.

Finally, agonisingly slowly, Monica heard the sound of feet scrabbling on stone. She looked up to see MacLennan reach for the top of the wall then pull himself up and over. Monica rolled on to her back and took a deep breath. Offered up a prayer of thanks to all the gods above as she dug in her pocket for her phone then dialled Crawford's number.

He answered instantly. 'DI Kennedy? Where the fuck are you? We can't find him anywhere.' His voice was horribly loud in the silence of the night and she cringed.

'I'm following him. He went over the wall in the car park,' Monica whispered as she unfolded slowly to her feet. She tested her knee and felt the pain, then bit her lip and tried again. The pain was still there but the knee held her weight. It couldn't be that bad.

'You need to cut him off,' she hissed.

'We're coming. Don't try to stop him on your own,' Crawford replied, and Monica cancelled the call.

She ran at the wall and grabbed for the top. Her foot slipped on the sheer surface but she managed to catch herself before she fell back. She reached again and pulled herself up. On the other side there was another car park, smaller than the one behind her containing MacLennan's van. It was enclosed on three sides. He was there, hunched over against the rain, working at the lock of a car.

Monica took a deep breath. Her heart and lungs fighting like they would burst. She peered back across the abandoned garden. *Come on, Crawford. Where the fuck is he?* She lowered herself down the wall, digging her toes in to grip the wet stone. She slipped again but caught herself, then felt her foot touch the ground.

She hardly dared to breathe as she turned towards MacLennan. The back of his hoody read ANGEL OF DEATH. There was a wing on either side of the writing and they stretched tight across his broad back. He hadn't heard her, or perhaps he was pretending, tempting her to come closer.

Monica looked around for a weapon, a rock or a stick. But the ground was fallow. The car door clicked open and Owen MacLennan straightened up. He was about to get in and drive away. And as it always felt, she was on her own.

'You're under arrest, Owen.' Monica stepped forward and reached for his arm.

He twisted away and spun around. The look of surprise that spread across his face shifted into a smile when he saw her.

'I could tell you wanted it. From the moment I saw you,' MacLennan said as he took a step towards her. 'And I told you that I'd see you again.' That wide smile was fixed and cold with no trace of humour.

'You want to think about what you do next,' Monica said.

'But I thought I was under arrest?' He took a step closer and held his wide hands up. 'You know what? I think that theoretically a man like me could just tear a woman like you open.' He stared with those blue eyes as he stepped closer still. Almost close enough to touch her. Monica stared back at him. *Come on, Crawford. Where are you?*

MacLennan reached a hand towards her face. 'And I bet you'd taste sweet inside.'

The sound of the sirens came then. Echoing off the walls as they moved in their direction through the night. Monica glanced away at the sound, felt a flood of relief.

MacLennan smirked when she turned back to him.

'What? You think they'd stop me?' he said, then dropped his hands in front of him and held them up for her to cuff. 'But I'm not that stupid. I've got things to look forward to.'

Monica caught the look of glee that crossed his face. 'What are you talking about?'

'Maybe you'll find out. Maybe we'll find out together. Me, you … Lucy?'

Monica felt her stomach dropping, her blood turn gangrenous.

'What the fuck did you say?' The sirens were drawing closer.

'A sweet little thing from what I hear,' MacLennan said. That smile so wide across his face. 'Daddy unknown. So she's looking around for a father figure. Someone she can learn from. A man who'll teach her about the world.'

Monica hit him hard across the jaw. He took a step back and shook his head, and she felt drops of rain spray off his bleached-blonde hair onto her cheeks. A line of blood was running down his lip, but he was still smiling as the rain continued to fall under the street lights.

'I enjoyed that. But it's still assault, darling,' MacLennan said.

The flashing lights and the sirens were almost upon them.

He winked at her then held his arms up for the other officers to see as they blocked off the car park exit and climbed out of the marked vehicles. He smiled again. 'We'll just keep that between us until next time.'

Chapter 30

Michael walked across the metal bridge into Rapinch. He was still trying to process what Melissa had told him: someone had wanted to meet Nichol. They'd given him a phone. Someone Nichol was afraid of, who'd frightened him so much he'd run away.

Michael had fallen into walking with his head down, the paranoid feeling of being watched by a demon on his back. Melissa's anxiety had made his own fear into something real. Something creeping in the shadows behind him. He moved quickly past two men dressed in dark bomber jackets who stood smoking outside a bookie's and then crossed the street past an abandoned pub with shuttered windows and peeling green paint.

He found the block of flats that Melissa had described and stopped. The feeling of paranoia knocked around his mind and he took a long breath of night air, catching the smell from the fish and chip shop on Grant Street that seemed to always hang over this part of the town in the evenings. He tried to shrug off his fear – he'd visited Rapinch hundreds of times and who would be watching him? He reached for another cigarette but found the pack empty.

Instead he watched the entrance and without realising it pulled the collar of his jacket tight until it was almost hiding his face. Michael remembered then that he'd been to the block before, visiting a previous client who had in the end been swept up by the sad and twisted expectations of the life he'd been born into and was currently serving time in Polmont. Michael had never known Nichol had a link to this place, though. His Uncle Eddie's place. He was sure he'd never heard Nichol say the man's name. That was another secret. Another thing he hadn't revealed.

A woman and two men were talking loudly outside the block. Their clothes and faces were hidden by the shadows but the sound of the woman's voice was slurred with alcohol and unmistakably argumentative as she berated one of the men: '... and you never give me a penny and you expect me to just fork out from what I've got and then go asking for more ...'

Michael tensed as he walked closer, expecting them to challenge him. But they were intent on their disagreement and the bottle they were passing between them and didn't even look up. Inside the block smelled stale, of fading cigarette smoke and cooking oil. Melissa had told him that Eddie's place was on the fifth floor.

Michael found it at the end of a dark corridor. He hesitated on the doorstep. Nervous that Melissa had been lying to him, making up stories, but somehow even more nervous that she was telling the truth. He knocked on the door.

Finally, just as he was about to walk away, it slowly opened a crack. The smell that leaked out into the corridor was one of decomposition, and he took a horrified step back as the face of a corpse appeared in the doorway. It stared malevolently out at him, sallow cheeks and thin grey hair plastered to yellowing skin.

'You must be thon Michael Bach. Thon boy from the social?'

Michael felt that impulse to turn and run away. The same one he'd felt at the morgue.

Eddie must have caught Michael's expression because he smiled. Almost as if he was enjoying the disturbing effect his appearance induced.

'Don't worry, son. I might look frightening but I'm not half as scary as I used to be. My fighting days are long gone.' He ran a hand over his emaciated face. 'Nichol mentioned you, that's all. I heard about that boy over in Gairloch. Another one this afternoon too, they're saying. Another young lad. Death has a way of sharpening folks' minds.'

Michael nodded slowly and tried to hide his reaction to the man's appearance. 'I'm sorry to bother you. I heard that Nichol left some things here?'

'You heard?' Eddie's voice had gone suspicious and mocking. 'Who'd you hear from?'

'Someone called me from his accommodation. They said some of his things were missing.' Michael's hand went to his face as he told the lie. 'I'm supposed to collect them.'

Eddie stared at him a moment longer then his smile widened into an expression that Michael knew well: take the piss out of the social worker. 'Fair enough, son. Better out of my fucking road anyway.' Slowly he turned and started to shuffle back down the hallway, his slippers making a rubbing sound on the worn carpet floor. Michael stood on the doorstep for a moment longer, surprised that Eddie had so readily allowed him in. Finally he followed him down the hall.

'In there,' Eddie said. He'd stopped at the open door to a bedroom. The lights of the city outside were visible beyond the window. Eddie gestured at a duffel bag on the floor. 'He's always leaving shit lying about. Fucking expects me to clean up. Your job now, I suppose, just like you're his mam. Fill your boots.' His voice turned into a hacking laugh as he left Michael and went into the living room.

Michael glanced around the small room, still surprised by how easily Eddie had let him in. He knelt, feeling a moment of discomfort that he was about to go through the kid's belongings without permission.

Eddie's voice echoed through from the living room. 'Who was it you said you spoke to at the hostel? Funny they didn't come over themselves.'

Michael forced himself to open the bag, and emptied it out on to the floor. There were clothes and a couple of school books but no sign of the phone. He went through the bag's pockets and the lining: still no sign. His frustration mounted as he looked around the room. Something, some kind of intuition, told him that the phone had to be nearby. Nichol wanted Michael to look for him. Why else would he have texted the laptop password. He must have left the phone here. He must have known Melissa would tell him about it.

The room was small, just a bed and a chest of drawers. He tried under the bed and down the side of the mattress. Then the chest of drawers. Still there was nothing. Where could it be? The answer sprang into his mind: Eddie had taken it. He'd been through Nichol's bag already. Of course he had. Why else would he just let Michael come in and root about?

Eddie looked up as Michael came into the living room. He sucked on the oxygen canister propped by his chair. Then he sat back, took a mouthful from a can of lager and lit a cigarette.

'You took your time, son.'

Michael looked down at the bag he'd carried through from the bedroom and nodded.

'Something on your mind? You've got that look,' Eddie said. A smile was playing around his mouth, narrow dried-out lips like scraps of leather. The yellowed teeth behind them. He took a deep draw on the cigarette and offered Michael the packet. 'State my lungs are in, I might as well get the pleasure of a smoke. Yours might be worth saving though, eh?'

Michael accepted the offer, a flash of nicotine-dependent gratitude making him smile, and lit up, blowing smoke across the stuffy room at Eddie.

'Did Nichol leave anything else here?' he said.

Eddie's eyes danced up the wall and finally landed on Michael's face. His grin growing wider. 'Just that bag you're carrying. That's your lot.'

'It's important. He could be in danger. There was a phone.'

'Nichol'll be fine. The boy's resourceful. You'd have to be, growing up with his family.'

'He's only seventeen.'

'Only seventeen? My father killed his first German when he was sixteen. If Nichol's old enough to cross Charlie Bartle, then he's old enough to deal with the consequences.'

'What are you talking about?'

'Wee Charlie. The man's an animal. Just like his dad. No fucking Mensa membership for guessing *his* name either, Big Charlie. He gave me this. More than thirty years ago now.' Eddie pushed the fringe of his thin grey hair to the side of his forehead and pointed to a long scar that ran down the hairline towards his ear. It was faded but still visible on his waxy skin. 'Yeah. That's why I fucked off down the road for twenty years. I took the consequences. He'd battered my sister

Jean, knocked half her teeth out, so she came hiding round to my mam's house. Charlie puts his foot through the door and gives me this with a golf club. He dragged her back down the street by the hair with folk standing watching outside the pub. She came round two days later with a face like a football. I says to her, "Jean, if you don't come with me he'll put you in the ground."' Eddie paused. 'You know what she said? "That's my husband you're talking about."' Eddie started coughing then hacked and spat into a wad of tissues.

'You still haven't answered my question. Did you take the phone?'

'Fucking phones. That's all you hear now. I'm getting there, son. Did you never learn the benefit of manners? A bit of sympathy? What I'm saying is that the Bartles are Nichol's family. Big Charlie's dead now. Thankfully. His sons carry the torch though. All of them have done time over the years, or should have.' Eddie leaned forward. His eyes were suddenly bright in his skeletal face, as if he were going to lay down a handful of aces. 'Charlie Bartle Junior's not long out of prison.'

He sat back heavily in his chair and folded his arms, staring at Michael. The room was uncomfortably hot with both bars of the electric fire burning red in the shadows.

'What does that have to do with Nichol's disappearance?' Michael asked. Intrigued despite the feeling that Eddie was laughing at him.

'Nichol's mother. Chris. She was a cousin with the Bartles. A bit older than young Charlie. She liked a drink. Do anything for a drink.' His smile widening again. 'It's no fun having a mother who likes a bottle more than she does you. Just ask young Nichol. His wee face when he was chasing after her: *Mummy, Mummy . . .*' Eddie broke into another hacking laugh. Michael watched him and felt his hand tense into a fist. Dislike mingling with disgust. 'Charlie went down for drugs. It was a big haul. Chris went down at the same time – she got caught up in it. You know what happened after that?'

Michael didn't reply, Eddie leaned forward again. Intense like an Internet conspiracy theorist. 'Nichol got taken away by the social.'

'So?'

'So maybe he blamed Charlie Bartle for what happened? Tried to even things out? Revenge is the biggest motivator, isn't it?'

It sounded improbable to Michael. But maybe there was a connection to Bartle. Maybe he'd given Nichol the phone and the laptop? Maybe got him involved in something. If so how would it connect to the murdered boys? Unless Nichol's disappearance was completely unrelated. It sounded plausible until, with a sinking feeling, Michael remembered the black stone Nichol had carried with him. It was a clear connection to the boys, it had to be. Could Bartle be involved in the murders?

'You know Nichol,' Eddie said, interrupting Michael's thoughts. 'The boy's sharp. And there's plenty from up here who ended up in a barrel of cement at the bottom of the firth. Nichol knew that. It's hard to speak with your throat filled out with cement. Keep asking questions, you might find out for yourself.'

'Or we could go and speak to the police now,' Michael said.

'Sit the fuck down, mister social worker. You think I'm fucking stupid. Going to the police with a story about the Bartles? I'm just having fun here, son. I like my life. As much as it's existing in a fucking rubbish dump.' The man's beady red-rimmed eyes danced around the room as he spoke. It felt like the most truthful thing he'd said since Michael arrived.

'Where's the phone? You still haven't told me.'

Eddie held his skeletal arms out wide. 'That's because I don't fucking know. The kid left that bag, that's all.'

'You don't give a fuck about Nichol, do you?'

'That's the social for you. You're all the same. Telling people how they should be living their lives. What they should think.' He coughed into his arm and looked up at Michael again, his amusement at playing take the piss out of the social worker clearly at an end. 'Now why don't you be a good boy and fuck off back to whatever it is you've got at home. Leave playing in the Marsh to the people who belong here.' He held his own phone out for Michael to see. 'Or you could wait for these boys to come and have a chat with you. Let you know what they think of the social?'

Michael stared at him for a second. He felt a crazy impulse to push Eddie out of the way. To go through his pockets and through the cupboards in the room. Instead he turned to leave then stopped at the door and swivelled back. 'I'm going to speak to the police. I'm going to tell them about the phone.'

Eddie shrugged. 'I'm sure they'll be falling over themselves to get round here. There'll be teams working round the clock looking for a boy like Nichol.'

Michael stared at Eddie for a moment then shook his head and pulled the living room door closed behind him. He was glad to be out of that room. Away from the smell of decomposition, from Eddie's lies and his staring eyes.

In truth a part of him was even relieved he'd hit a dead end. He could drop the laptop off at DI Kennedy's house, legitimately tell her he'd tried everything. Had gone further than he probably should have; no one could say that he hadn't.

He reached for the front door and turned the handle, felt that welcome cold breeze from outside after the stifling heat and smell inside the flat. It was then that he remembered Eddie's face. Those beady eyes dancing up the wall over Michael's shoulder in the living room. The way they seemed to go there almost involuntarily.

Michael pushed the front door closed and walked back down the corridor to the living room.

Eddie looked up from his can of lager. 'That was quick. Forget your fucking sanitary towels here, did you?'

Michael ignored him and looked at the wall. There was a shelf there with a framed photograph of a younger Eddie on it: dressed in a bad 1980s suit outside a church. Michael pushed the picture to the side. Behind it there was a row of books.

'Nichol left these, didn't he?'

'They're mine. They've got nothing to do with Nichol.' Eddie's voice rose in panic. He climbed slowly out of his chair.

'Just sit down,' Michael said as he pulled the books off the shelf. They were philosophy and maths textbooks and included *Beyond Good and Evil* by Nietzsche. Michael held the book in his hand. There was something strange about the way it felt. Like the weight was off. Michael turned the book on its edge, realised that it was glued shut and secured roughly with grey duct tape. He dug his thumb into it and peeled the tape off. The book fell open.

'What is it? It's mine.' Michael felt Eddie's weak hand reaching for the book. He easily shrugged him away. There was a hole cut into the pages at the back of the book. Inside it something was wrapped in plastic. Michael pushed the book into his jacket pocket and peeled the plastic off. His disbelief and excitement grew as he saw the black phone inside.

'Ten years ago. Ten years ago ...' Michael looked up at the sound of Eddie's voice. Eddie was staring at him with sheer hatred in his eyes. 'You better hope those boys don't get a hold of you while I'm around, son. You better fucking hope,' he said as he tensed and untensed his fists.

Michael stuffed the phone into his pocket beside the book and pushed past Eddie.

Out in the hall Eddie's hacking voice followed him to the front door. 'You better fucking hope I'm not around when you get yours, boy. I'll be first in line for my fucking swing. You're out your depth here, son. Nichol doesn't want anyone to find him.'

Michael ran down the stairs and out into the evening rain. He felt confident that Eddie was bluffing about the *boys* on their way over, but he wasn't keen to find out either way. He felt the phone in his pocket again and walked a little faster. He couldn't quite believe that he'd actually found it; that what Melissa had told him was the truth.

As he was stepping back onto the metal bridge two police cars came blasting over it, their lights flashing and sirens screaming in the night. The cars passed so close that the disturbed air ruffled Michael's clothes. He jerked back, startled out of his cycle of thought. In the distance he could hear the sound of more sirens, all screeching in the same direction.

Michael watched the lights disappear and wondered who was having a bad night of it. In that moment of distraction he didn't hear the car pulling to a stop beside him. By the time he noticed, the car door was open and the driver had stepped onto the pavement and was already reaching for him.

Chapter 31

Monica turned the phone over in her hand, resisted the urge to call her mother for a third time to check that Lucy was OK. She felt sick playing MacLennan's words back over in her head – just imagining him being anywhere near her daughter.

Detective Superintendent Hately shifted on the seat next to her as on the screen MacLennan was led into the interview room. He sat down, dwarfing the lawyer beside him. Usually a suspect appeared reduced when you watched them being interviewed. With MacLennan it was the opposite: he actually seemed larger.

DC Crawford and DC Fisher sat down across the table from him. The words *lambs to the slaughter* came into Monica's head. The protocol was that as the arresting officer she shouldn't lead the interview. She'd had to be content with briefing the two detective constables on the kind of questions to ask. It wasn't the same as digging into MacLennan's lies herself, not by a long way.

The door behind Monica opened and Dr Lees entered. He nodded at Hately, then at Monica before crouching by the monitor. Hands folded into a steeple, head tilted slightly to the side, playing the role of genius intrigued doctor beautifully. He really was a wee prick.

'You'll have enjoyed that tonight. Chasing someone down? Nothing better, is there?' MacLennan's voice echoed through the speakers.

'You shouldn't have started running and we wouldn't have had to stop you,' Fisher replied.

'You stopped me, did you, son?' MacLennan said. His big hands flat on the table, a trickle of blood down the front of his T-shirt. 'I call it police harassment.' He smiled and tousled his bleached hair. His finger went up to his mouth and found a tooth loose where Monica had hit him. He pushed on it with his thumb. Monica flinched as it moved inward slightly.

'You enjoy playing games, don't you, Owen? You enjoy talking, telling stories? Is that fair to say?' Fisher said, following the directions Monica had given him.

MacLennan's blue eyes fixed on him. 'You're new at this, aren't you, son? You look about twelve. Just a wee virgin. In the interrogation room, I mean – I'm sure you've been fucked before. Probably by him.' MacLennan tilted his head towards Crawford, who stared fiercely back but managed to keep his mouth shut.

Fisher kept talking, and Monica felt stupidly proud that he was ignoring MacLennan's attempts at diversion: 'You like telling stories, but ultimately you're a fantasist. Do you know what that means, Owen? It means you don't know the difference between the truth and what you've made up.'

'What makes you say nasty things like that about me, detective? Detective-defective. That's you pair, isn't it? Defective detectives?' MacLennan smiled as he spoke and took hold of the loose tooth between two fingers and rocked it gently.

'We've got video evidence that you were in Gairloch. We've got video evidence that you had a boy in the van with you. Right now your van and your computer are being stripped down. It's all coming together, and it's going to lead us to you and Robert Wright,' Crawford said. He leaned across the table as he spoke.

MacLennan leaned across the table himself so that his face was inches from Crawford's. 'Is it?'

'You're looking at life for murder, Owen. I think you need to accept that you're going back to jail. What you need to think about now is how long that's going to be for. If you help us fill in some of the blanks it'll look better for you,' Crawford said.

The lawyer beside him started to say something, but MacLennan held up his hand to silence him. He stared down at the desk. For once he seemed not to have a glib response to hand.

'How did you choose Robert? What led you to him?' Fisher continued.

MacLennan raised his eyes for a second. Something passed across his face. If Monica hadn't known better she would have called it fear.

'We found another body today. A young man called Paul MacKay. What do you know about him?' Crawford said. This time MacLennan's eyes didn't move from the desk. The detectives seemed to be finding their mark.

Monica leaned in to the screen.

'Last Friday night. You were driving to Gairloch. What happened? Where did you meet Robert?' Crawford asked.

'Last Friday?' MacLennan ran a hand across his face. 'Friday. That was Gairloch. There was a boy ...' Monica glanced at Hately: *He's going to admit it.* Relief. Lucy was safe; she could forget MacLennan's hideous threats.

'What happened, Owen. With the boy?'

MacLennan's hand went to the tooth. He pushed it back, then forward again. Finally he gripped it and pulled hard. Monica flinched as the tooth came away slowly in his hand.

He put it carefully down on the edge of the desk. 'There was a boy.'

'Tell us what happened,' Crawford said. His voice alive with excitement now, and Monica willed him to pull back, to not be overconfident with a born liar like MacLennan.

Slowly MacLennan lifted his head. He glanced between the two detectives. An expression on his face – with horror Monica realised that it was close to glee.

'There was a boy. But I'm confused,' he said.

Monica heard Hately's phone buzz. He ignored it.

'Why are you confused, Owen?' Uncertainty crept into Fisher's voice.

Hately's phone buzzed again, then there was a rushed knock at the door.

'I'm confused because you keep asking me about a boy in Gairloch. But which boy are you asking about?'

There was another knock on the door. It opened and a uniformed officer stepped into the room. He had an expression that said, *This is urgent, sir.* Hately stood up.

'We're talking about Robert Wright. You know that,' Crawford said, shifting in his seat.

MacLennan let the smile sit on his face for a few seconds without speaking. 'See I wasn't sure if you were talking about the boy I was driving with. Or that poor dead boy they found over there in Gairloch.'

Hately stepped out into the corridor then looked back over his shoulder at Monica.

'What are you saying?'

'He's quite slow, this one, isn't he?' MacLennan gestured at Crawford then turned to stare at the camera. 'Are you there, detective Monica? These boys are a bit slow so I'll explain it to you. If you ask me nicely I might tell you about the boy I drove to Gairloch with. But if it's poor dead Robert Wright you're asking me about then ...' He held his arms out wide.

Monica stepped out into the corridor. Hately was standing with two uniformed officers and a woman with an anxious expression and permed grey hair. She was holding a handbag across her chest like a piece of body armour. Behind her there was a teenage boy with short dark hair. He had a familiar face. A face that Monica might just have seen before on video.

'This is Owen MacLennan's neighbour Anne Wilson and her grandson Rory. He's staying with her just now. Rory says he drove up to Gairloch with Owen MacLennan last Friday night.'

Monica turned and looked back into the room. Dr Lees was looking up at her with something between surprise and a hint of detached amusement on his face. On the screen beside him MacLennan's eyes were fixed on the camera. Almost as if he could see into the room, and his wide smile was all for her.

'We can't just let him go,' Monica said. She was aware that her voice was rising in the busy incident room. That people were looking at her.

'The kid says he was in the van with him,' Hately said, struggling to keep his tone level, authoritative. He put his hands on his hips spreading his suit jacket wide, folded his dark eyebrows together in his best macho Glaswegian expression and stared at Monica.

'How do we know the kid's not lying?' Crawford hissed and ran a hand through his red hair. He stood up at his desk, the crown of his head jostling the shoulders of Monica and their boss. Dr Lees had stepped away from the group as a child does away from blame.

'You saw the video footage from Gairloch. It's not exactly fucking HD! He could easily just be telling us what MacLennan told him to.' The dark circles standing out under Crawford's eyes almost pulsated with his anger.

'Unfortunately. Logically. If we apply the same standard then there's no way we can say that the video is of Robert Wright,' Dr Lees said, unnecessarily loud so his words bounced around the room. 'This young man claims he was in the van with MacLennan.'

'Why was the kid in the back of the van and not the passenger seat?' Crawford said. 'That seems a bit fucking weird. Wouldn't you say?'

'Just watch yourself, detective,' Hately said, his voice slowing ominously as he stared down at Crawford. 'I understand you're frustrated. We all want to solve these crimes. But if the kid says he doesn't remember, we can't force him to remember.' His eyes shifted to Monica, and she knew he was telling her to keep Crawford on a tighter lead. She met his stare but didn't say a word to Crawford. Instead she leaned back against a desk and crossed her arms.

'I told you that MacLennan threatened my daughter,' she said, staring directly into Hately's eyes. Daring him to belittle Lucy's importance. 'He knows her name. He knows things about … her father.'

'And he claims that you assaulted him as he tried to give himself up,' Dr Lees piped up. His voice was smooth and precise. 'It isn't uncommon for this type of offender to seek to intimi-date. It must be upsetting for you, but really the chance of him actually attempting to harm your daughter is minimal. When this type of personality makes a threat it's actually less likely that they'll carry it out. If he had any real intention against her he would have kept it secret rather than warn you about it.'

Monica turned. She stared down at him, her eyebrows raised. She wouldn't let him see a glimmer of what she felt inside: the nasty mixture of fear, hurt and rage. Under her crossed arms she grabbed a pinch of stomach skin through her shirt and twisted it until the pain dampened the feelings down. She spoke slowly and carefully, as if to a child: 'He knew my daughter's name, Dr Lees. Legitimate intention aside, his intention was threat.'

'Monica,' Hately warned, and she knew he meant it, because he never used her first name. In fact she was certain this was the first time he'd even acknowledged she had an identity aside from her police rank and surname. His voice was still slow. 'I'm sorry, DI Kennedy, but you know how easy it is to find information online these days. MacLennan could have seen a photo of your daughter on Facebook. A friend of a friend of a friend. That kind of thing. It's your word against his.' He cautioned her with his eyes. 'Think about this rationally. Do you want some assault investigation hanging over you? We've got no evidence. There's nothing we can keep him in for. We have to let him go.'

Chapter 32

'Everyone hates us. We're like bankers, but with shit pay,' said Anita Patel, Michael's boss, as he passed her a glass of red wine and put his own gin and tonic on the table. 'It's always been that way, Michael. What's new this time?' She pushed a strand of brown hair back behind her ear, then took a sip of the wine, leaving a smudge of pink lipstick on the glass.

Michael felt Nichol's phone in his pocket and wished again that Anita hadn't seen him. If he'd walked on to the bridge thirty seconds later he would have missed her.

'It's nothing. It's just a difficult case.' He took a mouthful of his drink and glanced around the pub. They were in the Black Isle Bar on Church Street. One of the nicer establishments in Inverness. Although not a long way in distance from the bridge that led across the river to Rapinch, it was miles away in privilege. Outside, the black rain reflected off the cobbles under the street lights.

Anita took a draw on her electronic cigarette. The tip lit up blue in the gloom of the bar. 'It's that kid Nichol Morgan again, isn't it?'

'Has James been speaking to you?'

'You ask pretty much everyone in the department about him last week. Then today you disappear without bothering to cancel your clients ... James didn't have to say anything.'

'I was supposed to meet Nichol. I let him down.'

'You have to keep things professional, Michael. No one wants the media or the complaints department all over them. I certainly don't. You're already sitting on a final written warning. You've been distracted since everything with your dad.' She held up a hand to silence him as he tried to cut in. 'Which is *totally* understandable. But it's the truth.'

'I'm fine.'

She leaned in so her hazel eyes were close to his. 'Michael. I know you. This isn't really about this kid. You're chasing your brother – can't you see that your father's death has brought it all up again?'

'Anita –' Michael tried to keep his voice calm '– none of your *analysis* changes the fact that one of my clients is missing.'

'But you're taking your work home with you. You're asking questions that could breach confidentiality.'

'You want me to pretend nothing's happening? Pretend that two kids haven't been murdered?' He put a cigarette in his mouth and almost lit it before he remembered.

'This is the Highlands, Michael. People still think about Orkney. Believe me, you don't want to be the social worker on a crusade.'

The Orkney witch cult, 1991, the nadir of social work in Scotland. Child abuse. Black magic and devil worship. Children taken from their homes. Families broken up over a satanist cult that existed only in the minds of the investigating social workers.

Anita shook her head. 'You still get people who think we encourage kids to tell lies about their parents. That we try to break up families ...' She held her hands out with her palms up like a bringer of knowledge. The other message was unspoken: *If you fuck up, you're on your own.*

Behind her at one of the tables in the back corner of the pub there were two men with hoods pulled down, partially hiding their faces. Michael realised that they were staring over at him. He blinked and they looked away.

Anita dropped her hands back onto the table. One on either side of her wine glass so the tips of her painted fingernails were almost touching.

He looked over at the two men again. They were talking now. 'Did you ever meet him? Nichol, I mean?'

Anita sighed, picked up her wine and finished it in one long swallow. 'Listen to me, Michael. You need to leave this.' She slid the empty glass across the table. It made a noise like a Ouija board pointer. 'I've seen his file. The kid's been in trouble in the past. You need to accept that it's possible he got mixed up in something. That he just decided to go.' She stared at him. When he didn't reply she said, 'I'd better go. Jamie already thinks I'm having an affair with someone from the office. If I'm late home he'll probably leave again, and that would be a problem, especially with the kids.' She stood up and fastened the buttons on her coat. She clocked the look on Michael's face. 'I was joking, Michael. About him leaving. But don't worry, he knows I'm not having an affair with you.'

Michael watched her cross the pub, push through the glass doors then walk down Church Street to where she'd parked outside the Old High Church. He waited two minutes, until he saw her car pass the window, then hurried towards the exit himself. On his way out he glanced at the table at the back of the room. This time it was empty.

Chapter 33

Michael shrugged off his wet jacket and held down the power button on the phone. He was desperate to finally see what was on it. The screen stared back, black and empty. The battery was dead.

'Fucking technology,' he said out loud as he looked around the empty flat. He stood up and tried the kitchen drawers and the cupboard under the sink for a charger. Mixed in with a mess of electric cables there were two ancient ones: a Nokia and a Motorola. Neither fitted Nichol's phone, no matter how hard he tried to force the connector.

Great investigating skills. He couldn't even find a way of switching on a phone. His frustration was mounting after the crazy long day. He threw the chargers onto the counter and ran nicotine-stained hands over his face. For a moment he wondered what his dad would have said, seeing his son like this. Then he smiled as he remembered the cheap multi-adapter he'd bought when his father had been ill in hospital and had forgotten the charger for his Kindle. He remembered how he'd put it in his own car along with the Kindle when his dad lost any desire to read.

Michael ran out into the rain across the street to the Land Rover and dug through the detritus strewn over the dashboard. Eventually he found the thing coated in a layer of grease and fluff.

Back in the flat he dusted it off, plugged the USB end into his laptop, found the end that fitted the phone and waited impatiently for it to charge. He lit a cigarette and wondered if the phone would switch on at all. It would be great after everything if the fucking thing didn't actually work. The red light on the phone's base flashed off and on though, seeming to accept the charge.

As he watched the light Michael couldn't help wondering again where the phone had come from. Maybe whoever had killed those two boys had been using it to lure Nichol somewhere alone. Maybe that was the purpose of the message Melissa had read? Maybe Nichol had gone to the meeting and never come back? Maybe he was dead somewhere already?

Horrible thoughts. Michael tried to reassure himself with the reminder that Nichol had purposely left the phone. He had hidden it then tried to contact Michael. Maybe that meant Nichol had never actually gone to meet the person who messaged him? Maybe it meant he was safe?

The phone played a jingle as it came back to life; the black screen turned white and the passcode request came up. Nichol's birthday. Michael realised that he'd forgotten to actually ask Melissa the date. Impatiently he laid the phone down again and logged onto the social services database, searching until he found the file on Nichol. He tensed as he punched the numbers into the phone and waited for it to respond.

Melissa wasn't lying. The phone accepted the number and lit up, a range of apps spread across the wallpaper.

'Come on, who were you messaging? Who wanted to meet you?' Michael whispered. He fiddled with the unfamiliar operating system until he eventually found the app for text messages and clicked Open.

But the messages had been deleted. Whatever Melissa had seen had been wiped from the phone. Michael swore and threw his head back with frustration. *Why would Nichol delete the messages?* He checked the call register. Then the contacts list and the voicemail. They were all empty too. Why wipe everything but leave the phone hidden? It didn't make any sense.

With a mounting sense of desperation he tapped the Photos icon. There was only one file saved in it. A video. *One file – just like the laptop*, he thought. He went to open the file but hesitated and lit a cigarette instead.

He remembered the first dead boy. Lying on that slab in the morgue. Another one down there beside him now. And he wondered just what might be on the video, just what the kid might have seen. Something bad enough to make Nichol decide to take off. Leave his laptop and the rest of his things and just go. Or something so bad that someone had to be sure Nichol never had the chance to tell anyone what he'd seen.

Again Michael went to open the video. Again he hesitated then stood up. He reached for the cheap bottle of Co-op own-brand whisky he had found in a cupboard and splashed a good three fingers into a glass. He took a long swallow then picked up the phone and hit Play.

Nichol's face filled the screen. The camera panned round to show another boy. His face was hidden. He was crouched on the grass; behind him there were green leaves. It must have been taken in spring or summer.

The recording stopped, then started again. The boy was kneeling now. With a growing sense of discomfort Michael realised that he was crouched beside a gravestone. The shot zoomed in closer to the boy. Behind his shoulder Michael could see a name on the headstone: ALEXANDER ALLEN 1890–1915.

The shot moved to the boy's hands. He was holding a box. Slowly he leaned forward and pushed it into a shallow hole.

The shot moved closer. It showed a hand pick up a pile of dirt then throw it onto the box. *Earth to earth. Ashes to ashes.* The camera panned away, caught a flash of blue sky and another gravestone. Then the video ended. Michael stared at the screen, more confused than ever.

He took a breath. He was actually relieved that there was nothing horrible on the recording. He hit Play again. There was no sound and the recording was slow and jerky, giving it an eerie quality.

As he played the video for a third time he realised that the final frame didn't show another gravestone. It was actually a monument. One that Michael had seen before somewhere. It was distinctive – a cross with a sword. A First World War memorial. He felt a burst of excitement as he realised he knew where the monument was.

Tomnahurich Cemetery. A large Victorian graveyard that wasn't far from his office.

Michael thought about it for a few seconds then checked the time. It was nearly eleven. Long after the cemetery would be closed. But he knew where the grave was. He could go now and find it, dig up that box and discover what was in it while the night and darkness were on his side. He had to do it. He owed Nichol that much.

Chapter 34

The cemetery gates were closed and chained shut, black and forbidding set against the shadows stretching to the trees. Michael followed the iron railings away from the gate as he searched for some way in, perhaps a gap in the fence that he could squeeze through. The thoughts that he'd tried so hard to ignore came rolling back in: two dead boys now. Beneath his own selfish fear was the sense that really he could be making a huge mistake. He could be opening a door to something that might not just end up fucking up his job this time. This could end up being something far worse.

Under the street lights and the low-hanging branches a story about the place came back to him. With it a sense of unease he remembered that it was actually Nichol who had told it to him. A folk tale about two men who went into the cemetery. They met the fairies who live inside the hill, in the underworld. Spent an evening dancing with the little people, and when they returned to the real world a hundred years had passed.

Michael tried to put the story – the strange coincidence that it came from Nichol – out of his mind. He stepped off the pavement and followed the railings further across the wet grass. Finally the fence met a wall and Michael was able to shin his way up and over. He jumped down inside the cemetery. Within the burial place the sounds of nearby cars became strangely distant. As if muffled by some curious barrier between life and death that hung among the trees and the rain falling almost as a mist now.

Michael crossed the grass to the path that led up the hillside to the war memorial. It took a rambling route among Victorian crypts dug into the slope, trees and fallen gravestones, all the time the smell of rotting leaves and wet earth. Michael heard a stick snap behind him. He whipped round and stared into the night for any sign of movement but saw nothing.

He took a breath and tried to shake off the oppressive sense of being followed that had been with him all evening. He continued up the path illuminated only by the dull moonlight. But his mind wouldn't stop recalling Melissa's terrified face, Eddie's warnings and those pathways and corridors in his dreams. Who was to say he wasn't dreaming right now? All of it could be a dream, and maybe these were the places he belonged now: in morgues and ghostly corners.

The sweat mixed with rain on his back, uncomfortably hot in his dad's down jacket, but he hurried on up the path to the top of the hill anyway. Thankfully it didn't take long to find the distinctive white memorial from the video. Standing on the far end of the narrow hilltop. He walked over to it and squinted at the nearby gravestones.

He cast the dim light from his phone over the names on the headstones until finally the light hit on the engraved letters: ALEXANDER ALLEN, 1890–1915. Michael ran his fingers over the cold stone to check that the words were really there – that his mind wasn't playing games.

Without stopping to think, he crouched by the grave and picked away the dead leaves plastered over the grass. Beneath them he could see where the ground had been disturbed, and patchy grass had started to grow back. He stared down at the ground for a few moments. That morning he had been in his office at the start of another work week; now he was on his knees with his bare hands on the earth covering an unknown dead man. He started to dig.

The box was not more than six inches deep. Michael felt his fingernail hit wood and bend back painfully. Carefully he shifted more of the dirt until he was able to fit his hand down the side of the box and prise it out.

He set it down on the wet grass and turned it over. It was small, about half the size of a shoebox. He felt around for a catch but couldn't find one. Finally he realised that it was the kind where the top slid off. He leaned his phone against his knees, the torch light switched to bright, and pushed at the box's top edge.

Inside was a packet of cigarettes, Marlboro Reds still in their cellophane wrapper. There was a can of strong cider and a plastic figurine of a Japanese manga character. There was also a plastic lighter and a small model car. At the bottom of the box, wrapped in cellophane, was a photograph. Michael pulled it out and held it up to the light.

Three faces looked back at him: Nichol as a younger teenager with two other boys about the same age. Maybe a little older. The three boys were leaning across the bonnet of a car, Nichol and one boy on one side, the third boy on the other side. Michael recognised the badge on the car. It was an Alfa Romeo, half of its number plate obscured.

Carefully he put the things back into the box and slid the lid closed. The rain fell a little harder in the darkness. If anyone was watching from the shadows, they kept their silence.

Tuesday

Chapter 35

Monica stopped in the corridor outside her flat – no sound from the other apartments in the block now that it was well after midnight – and took a deep breath. The last thing she wanted was for her mum to see how rattled she was. With an exhale she reached for the door handle. It was unlocked, as she'd known it would be. *For fuck's sake.*

Monica pushed the door closed behind her. She turned the key then slid the deadbolt and the chain home. Angela Kennedy looked up from where she was sitting on the couch.

'Is that you, Monica? I made you turnips and roasters. I thought you'd need something hot after everything. I heard about that boy – it must have been terrible.' She caught sight of Monica's face for the first time. 'Is everything OK?'

'Where's Lucy?' Monica said. She didn't even try to keep the harshness out of her voice.

'She's in bed. I told you on the phone,' Angela said. The concern written plain across her face.

Monica turned her back on her mother and pushed the bedroom door open. She pulled the covers back and reached for the kid, squeezed Lucy tight and took a breath of her hair. Felt that small warm body. Lucy opened her eyes. She was still almost asleep as Monica laid her back down and pulled the covers up over her before retreating.

'What's the matter, Monica? Has something happened?'

'I told you to lock the front door when you're here with Lucy. I must have told you a hundred fucking times. Anyone could just walk in off the street.'

Her mother stared back at Monica. Her wide handsome face confused and upset. 'I'm sorry ... I thought ... I was sitting right here.'

On any other night Monica would have laughed at such a justification. The idea that a woman in her late sixties would be any obstacle to someone with intent.

'You thought you would ignore me?' Monica stared down at her, rage heating her skin. 'You thought you knew better than me? About how to look after my fucking daughter?'

'Everyone seems really nice here. I'm sorry ...'

Monica could see that her mum was close to tears. She took a deep breath and counted to five.

'Listen.' She tried to keep her voice level despite the image of MacLennan's hateful mocking face forcing its way into her mind. 'I really appreciate everything you do with Lucy. But I need you to promise me that you'll lock the door when you're at home with her.'

'Of course, Monica. I'm sorry.' For a horrible moment Monica thought her mum's voice was going to break and she was going to start crying. Monica's harsh inner voice wanted to shout at her, yell that she'd be crying a lot more if it was Owen MacLennan who had come through that unlocked door.

'You know what I'm like,' Angela said finally. 'I'd forget my head if it wasn't screwed on. I'll keep the door locked from now on. I promise.'

Chapter 36

The Watcher

He turned the card over again. Read the name and then laid it down precisely on the car seat beside those special objects. The wire and the open razor.

Through the windscreen the lights in the flat were visible against the sky, crowding out the stars. The street was empty now after the excitement with the police, after they'd finished wasting their time chasing Owen MacLennan. As if he were capable of anything, of the planning and self-discipline required. As if he ever had a meaningful thought.

MacLennan's face appeared at the window again. Ugly and pitiful with his fearful eyes darting out into the darkness. *MacLennan must suspect by now, bless him.* But he must have known it would end this way. Or why else would he have responded when they first met? He had been just out of prison then – not even three months ago – confused and in need of guidance.

'Why did you do it, Owen? Why would you want to hurt someone?' A question asked in the tone of every wimpish helper. But with the little flag left hanging. The wrinkle of amusement at the corner of the mouth. The coldness in the eye when it met Owen's as the big man shrugged.

'What was it like, Owen? When he knew that you were going to finish him off? I bet it was memorable?' Then the meeting of eyes again as Owen looked up in surprise – the flash of shared excitement. Finally Owen had found someone to respect, someone to admire.

When he looked up again at the window it was empty. Owen had retreated inside – to wait? To hope? The excitement hummed through his body. But he was very much in control this time. This was strictly business.

Chapter 37

It was after 1 a.m. when Monica got into the shower and turned the water up as hot as she could stand it. She washed the dirt off her skin and tried to wash the memories away. Those dead bodies. MacLennan's expression when he'd mentioned Lucy's name. The way he drank in Monica's hurt, the way he had enjoyed that little taste. The thought of what he could do to Lucy if he got to her.

What were Lees's condescending reassurances worth? Nothing. Less than nothing, because he hadn't looked into MacLennan's eyes. He hadn't seen what Monica had seen. He didn't know what it meant: that she could never leave her daughter alone while MacLennan was out on the streets. She could never sleep knowing that he was out there.

She turned off the shower and tested her knee. It was still painful where she'd jarred it. She tapped out two ibuprofen and dry-swallowed them.

Monica stared at her long body in the mirror, lit white in the eerie bathroom light. She glanced down at her big feet, which were rubbed red raw and blistered from those ridiculous boots.

'Jesus Christ, you're pathetic,' Monica whispered as she stared at her reflection. Then looked over her naked body again and for the first time in a long time really let the poison flow: *Man-ica, gangly, saggy, disgusting.* Monica shook her head and wiped her eyes. *Monica the man, grotesque, horse-legs.*

She forced her mind to come back with the rebuttals she'd taught herself. All those years ago as a teenager when it was getting so that she wouldn't undress to bathe without turning the lights off: 'Strong, statuesque.' And she added some new ones: 'Life-giving, nurturing.' Her voice wasn't much more than a whisper but it was some kind of psychic defence. She found herself thinking back to Miss Bennington, the classics teacher at school who used to call her Athena. In a strange way it had made her feel better because Miss Bennington genuinely seemed to revel in Monica's size. Maybe behind the teacher's heavy glasses and thick red lipstick, in her antiquated mind, she really did think Monica carried some little spark of the divine. She remembered the time Miss Bennington had run after her to push a battered green Loeb edition of Marcus Aurelius' *Meditations* into her hands at the end of another day of casual taunts and comments in the school corridors. She'd felt special then. Funny how a little thing like that from an adult could make you feel noticed.

Monica finished drying herself and tapped out two codeine tablets to go with the ibuprofen. In the living room she swallowed them with a mouthful of red wine and picked up the case file again. There had to be something: some way to prove that MacLennan was involved.

She stared at the photographs of those bite marks on the bodies. The pieces of rock forced down their throats while they were still alive.

She picked up her phone and called Fisher, only realising when it started ringing that it was already well after midnight. The call went through to voicemail. 'I forgot to ask about the stone earlier. Have we heard anything back yet? And the bite marks on the bodies – are we any further on with the jaw reconstruction?'

She hung up and put the phone on the table, made herself shut the file and lay back on the couch. The idea of actually sleeping now seemed impossible despite the days without rest, and after a minute she sat up and opened the blind a crack to look out at the street below. Just to check. Her eyes reacted to a hint of movement and with a sinking feeling she realised it was a man. Staring up at her window. MacLennan? He'd come to intimidate her, and what could she do about it?

On the table her phone started to ring: 'Unknown number' flashed across the screen.

'Sorry for calling so late.' It was a man's voice.

Monica stared down. The man's face was partially lit by the phone he was holding. 'Who is this?'

'I've got the laptop. I got caught up ... I didn't want to—'

Monica stood up and opened the blind for a better view of the street. This time the social worker gave an awkward wave up at her. Michael Bach. She'd almost forgotten about him. Had almost succeeded in blocking out the whole unpleasant thing; Marcus Aurelius would be proud. She hit the buzzer and stepped into jeans and a jumper while he was climbing the stairs.

'I wasn't sure if you would be here,' he said when Monica opened the door to him. 'I heard about the second body. They were talking about it on the radio, and I thought at first that it might be Nichol ...'

Monica took him in. He was wearing the same faded mountaineering jacket he'd had on at the hospital. She noticed one of the seams was held together with duct tape. He looked dishevelled: a few days without shaving, short untidy brown hair sticking up at wild angles, dirt on his hands and packed under his fingernails. He was clutching a plastic 'bag for life' like his own life depended on it. A faint smell of sweat mixed with the damp of the outdoors overlaid by the stink of cigarette smoke drifted off him. In a strange way it all seemed to convey some kind of honesty, of straightforwardness. She had the odd impulse to confide in him what Owen MacLennan had said about Lucy. To share the fear that bubbled beneath her skin.

Monica ignored the impulse. 'The investigation's progressing,' she said and gestured for him to come in. 'We'll have to keep our voices down. My mum's staying.' As Monica said this she pictured her mum's excited face. She would be thrilled at the idea of Monica going off-piste and roping an outsider into one of her investigations. She felt a pang of affection towards her mum, mixed with sadness over how she'd spoken to her earlier. She hadn't even thanked her for cooking the mashed turnips and the potatoes that lay untouched in the roasting tin.

Michael nodded awkwardly then stepped into the kitchen and sat down on one of the stools. He glanced at the food, then at Lucy's painting, which was still taped to the fridge.

'Do you have any idea ... I mean, are you close to finding someone?'

'We're following up several lines of inquiry,' Monica said. 'It's still early in the investigation.' *Plus our main suspect has an alibi. He seems to know a lot about me though. A lot about my daughter.* She cleared her throat. 'Anyway,' she said. Making her voice firm and professional. 'What did you find on the laptop?'

'There's virtually nothing on it,' Michael said, a dirty hand going up to his unkempt hair. 'I found a picture of a girl, it's the only thing still on there. It was like Nichol wanted me to find it. I went to his school to try and find the girl. She must have seen me, and Nichol had given her my number.' He was rambling now.

'How did you get into the laptop?'

Michael paused. 'Nichol texted me the password.'

'Texted it?'

'It was the last thing he sent me. I thought it was some cryptic ...' He shrugged then dug in his pocket for his phone. He flicked through the messages and held it up for her to see.

'The future is in the stars.' She remembered the open sky above each of the dead boys, the way it had made her feel so small. *Did Nichol Morgan really know something?*

'What is it?' Michael asked. He tilted his head. 'Have you heard that phrase before?'

Monica shook her head. She realised then that he was perceptive, sharp despite his distracted air. 'It just sounded odd. What did the girl say?'

Michael stared at her for a moment. Clearly unsatisfied by her response. 'She was frightened,' he said. 'I don't know – paranoid. She thought someone was following her. She gave me an address. A guy called Eddie who was related to Nichol. It seemed like he was the only semi-reliable person in Nichol's family.' Michael's hand went to his face and left a smear of mud on his cheek. She wondered exactly what he'd been doing to turn up here filthy with his hands covered in dirt.

'He'd never told you about this guy before?'

'I thought ... well I hoped he would have told me something like that. But he never did.' Michael dipped his head. 'Anyway. Nichol had left another phone there. He'd hidden it. There was nothing on it except a video of him and some other kids burying something in a graveyard.' His eyes went to the plastic bag he'd laid on the worktop.

'And you dug it up?' Monica asked, for the first time feeling a hint of admiration for him.

Michael nodded then reached into the bag and pulled out a wooden box stained dark with dirt. 'I think Nichol knows something. Maybe something to do with the murders, maybe something else. Eddie was talking about this guy called Charlie Bartle. He had some story about a vendetta, about Bartle getting out of jail ...'

Monica swallowed the shot of adrenaline. Thankfully Michael was looking down at the box and missed the flicker of panic that crossed her face before she was able to stop it.

'It sounds unlikely but maybe there's some element of truth to it? What do you think? Does that name mean anything to you?'

That name. The bad memories that went with it. The second time she'd heard it in one day after all those years.

Michael looked up at her. *Tell him*, a voice in her head whispered. *Why don't you?* For a crazy moment she was going to, but instead she shrugged. 'I know the name. The Bartles, but ...' Her throat was dry and her voice was a whisper. She held her hands out, shrugged again and watched thankfully as Michael nodded and seemed to accept her reply. 'What's in the box?' she asked.

Michael slid it open and handed her a photograph. 'This one is Nichol. I think this boy was in the video with him. If I can find out who they are ... I thought maybe Nichol's staying with them.'

'Did you speak to the girl? Maybe she'd recognise them,' Monica said, staring at the three boys leaning over the front of the car. A white Alfa Romeo. A relatively unusual vehicle. She clocked the first four digits of the obscured number plate.

'I've texted her and tried calling. I think she's frightened,' Michael said.

Monica nodded slowly then reached for her own phone. She took a picture of the photograph and dialled Crawford's number this time. If she sent him the photo he might be able to identify the model of the car and narrow down the search, it seemed like the kind of thing he would know. Again she reached an answerphone. She wasn't sure if she should be angry or glad that both her young oh-so-eager protégés were getting some sleep.

'I want you to run a registration for me. I'm sending a photo now. We've only got the first four digits. It's a white Alfa Romeo. I'm not sure of the model. There can't be that many of them. Thanks.' She hung up and laid the phone on the counter, waiting to see if the call had woken him and he would phone back.

'The man who did them. The murders. Do you think he's done it before?' Michael asked.

Monica watched his face and tried to read him. Was he a typical social worker? Thinks he's the first to realise that the world's a fucked-up place; doesn't understand that some people have known it since before they were born. She noticed a scar running across the knuckles of his right hand.

'There's no evidence to suggest that.'

'But you do? Why else would you have taken the risk of giving me the laptop?'

The silence drifted between them. She felt his eyes watching her face. Ready to judge her response. Again she couldn't believe she'd taken the risk of giving him the laptop. Passing evidence to a civilian, someone she didn't even know.

As she hunted around for words to placate him her phone buzzed on the counter. *Saved by the bell.* She picked it up and read the text from Crawford. She wrote three addresses down in her notebook, hoping Michael would forget that he was waiting for an answer.

Finally she stood up. If they could find Nichol Morgan and prove he was safe then at least she could forget about Charlie Bartle. The kid might even know something. 'Here.' She held the page from her notebook out to him.

'What?' He stared down at the scrap of paper like it might be contagious.

'Visit these houses. Find out if any of them are the boys in the photo. Start with this one.' She pointed to an address. 'It seems the most likely. Registered to a man called Alan Gentle, age nineteen, in Lossiemouth. He's had two speeding tickets in the last two years.'

Michael stood up. A look of outrage was spreading across his face. 'What the hell are you talking about? Surely you can handle it now?'

'We've got two dead bodies. Two murders to contend with. The team's stretched to breaking point just trying to deal with them.' She stepped towards the door, needing him to just take the piece of paper and go. 'Do you want to find Nichol or not? You said yourself that you'd let him down.'

Michael shook his head slowly then felt his jacket pockets and took out a cigarette. He looked like he was going to start arguing.

Monica heard her phone buzz again. She glanced at it, about to switch it to silent, but then saw Crawford's name on the screen.

When Monica answered, she could hear Crawford's words, but they made absolutely no sense. 'It's MacLennan. He's dead. He killed himself.'

Chapter 38

Monica left Michael standing on the pavement. She drove too fast down the deserted roads painted black in the rain, her mind awash with confusion. The expression on MacLennan's face when he'd threatened Lucy. *Why would he have killed himself?* It didn't make any sense.

There were the other feelings mixed in. Relief that her daughter was safe now. And darker, unworthy ones. Sheer pleasure that the man was dead, that she had lived to dance on his grave.

Monica accelerated over the bridge. A pair of drunks slouching home along the railings looked up as she gunned the engine. She turned hard right through the red light and on to Huntly Street by the river, driving the wrong way down the one-way road because she had to get to the flat. She had to see if it was true with her own eyes. She turned left at the end of the road. Then straight across the roundabout and another hard right, thinking, *We should have kept him in. Maybe if we'd pushed him harder he would have told us something – he might even have confessed.*

She could hear the sound of the sirens in front of her now and followed them down the narrow street until the dark walls were illuminated with flashing blue lights. Neighbours' faces appearing at windows. Scared and sinister.

Monica pulled up hard behind the marked cars. She took a breath to compose herself as she held up her ID for the uniformed officer covering the front door to see.

It looked like the patched-up door to MacLennan's flat had been broken open for the second time in one night; there were splinters of wood on the floor. As Monica stepped over the threshold, she caught the smells of the creature's den. Smoke, chemical cleaner, food going bad. The lights inside the flat were switched off, but in the light from the stairwell she recognised Crawford's narrow but muscled shoulders at the living-room door.

Monica went to stand beside him, pushed the door open wider.

Owen MacLennan's body was swinging just a few inches above the ground. He was hanging from a length of wire that was looped over a hook drilled into the ceiling. He was naked and both his wrists were cut. His hands were palm out. Blood black against the white of his body. The wire had cut deep into his neck, the flesh bulging all round it. He swung gently.

Monica took a step past Crawford, closer to the body. She heard a clicking sound as he tried the lights. 'The fuse has gone, or he removed the bulb,' Crawford said.

The room was cast in an orange glow from the street light outside, mixed with the blue police lights flashing against the curtains. A straight-edged razor was laid neatly on the mantelpiece, and spurts of arterial blood rose up the wall above it.

She reached for MacLennan's wrist, felt for the pulse that she knew was long gone.

'Christ, Monica ...'

She glanced back at the sound of Crawford's voice. 'If no one's checked then he could still be alive,' she said as she leaned in to avoid stepping on the thick blood on the carpet. She looked up at MacLennan's face.

'So he knew what was coming, decided to take the easy way out?'

Monica didn't reply. MacLennan's mouth hung open, his tongue a piece of meat. There were human smells of sweat, blood and something else. Garlic. She realised she was smelling Owen MacLennan's last supper.

She stepped back and looked around the room again, squinting in the orange half-light. Her eyes went back to the blood-soaked razor. *So he cuts his wrists, then loops the wire around his neck? But there would be blood all over his face and the wire.* She saw the small stool kicked across the room to the window. *He loops the wire around his neck first. Cuts his wrists then drops the razor onto the mantelpiece – that would explain the spurts of blood up the wall – and kicks the stool away leaving himself hanging as a final display of contempt for the world.* That made a kind of sense, in the twisted mind of someone like MacLennan. But the bigger part of Monica couldn't believe that it was true, that he'd done it to himself.

She looked back at the body again. The mark still on his lip where she'd hit him. The feeling of relief washed over her for a second time. Lucy was safe; did she really care if justice was served? Monica closed her eyes, *because that's how every tyranny starts.*

She looked back at the razor and realised that there was something beside it. Laid out so that it was impossible for them to miss.

'Shouldn't we go?' Crawford said. 'Won't we contaminate the scene?'

Monica ignored him, dug in her pocket for a pen and carefully flipped the leather wallet open. By the light from her phone she could see that inside there was a clutch of cards. A coffee shop loyalty card. A driving licence. A bank card. She read the name on the driving licence, visible through the clear plastic, out loud: 'Paul William MacKay.'

Crawford blew air through his teeth as Monica took a photo of the licence with her phone then flipped the wallet closed again.

'Who called it in?' Monica asked as she turned back to face him.

'The neighbours. The ones from earlier. The ceilings are thin here apparently. Blood was soaking through their ceiling light fitting. The grandmother couldn't sleep after everything. She was watching TV when the blood started dripping down right in front of her. She must have thought she was in a fucking horror movie – collapsed with chest pains. I gave the kid my card last night. He was too scared to call 999 but he texted me of all things. It's lucky I was still awake. They're up at the hospital now.'

Monica nodded and watched the body swing slowly on the wire. She heard a creaking sound as it moved.

'When you came in, was the door—'

'It was locked from the inside. I had to tell the lads to batter it down. Anyway ...' Crawford nodded at MacLennan, hanging there in the dark, the thick muscles on his chest and arms standing out even in the gloom. 'Can you imagine someone being able to do that to him and no one hearing? We've got Paul's wallet. I think we'll find more. I think he knew it was a matter of time and took the easy way out. Maybe the wallet lying there is his way of laughing at us – showing that he got away with it in the end.' Crawford cleared his throat. 'So the kid, Rory, was lying then? About going with MacLennan on Friday?'

'I guess we'd better find out,' Monica said.

Chapter 39

Michael watched the Volvo accelerate away. He looked down at the note DI Kennedy had stuffed into his hand before scrunching it into a ball and throwing it into the gutter.

He lit a cigarette and blew smoke into the cold morning air, shook his tired head at the memory of the detective's arrogant expression when she'd handed him the note. Like she could order him about. Even after he'd spent all day and night running around for her.

He crossed the car park to the Land Rover, found his keys and realised that he was still carrying the laptop bag slung over his shoulder. As he opened the driver's door and went to lay the bag on the back seat the sound of a siren echoed in the distance. *That explains why she took off like that*, Michael thought. Other thoughts followed immediately. *Is there another body? Maybe Nichol this time? If not then he knows something. He's afraid.* Like Michael's brother must have been afraid all those years ago.

Almost without thinking about it he turned back to where he'd thrown the scrap of paper into the gutter.

He was already on the outskirts of Inverness, heading east towards Lossiemouth, when his phone started ringing.

He answered, squeezing the phone between his shoulder and his cheek.

'Michael? Michael? Is that you?' He recognised the panicked voice immediately. It was Henry. 'Are you on your way yet? The Internet's still off. You said you'd come.'

'Listen, Henry. It's difficult right now,' Michael said. Feeling the guilt beginning to well up. Once again he'd completely forgotten about his client.

'You're coming though, aren't you? You said you would.'

Michael glanced at the time: 4.30 a.m. Henry must have been up all night waiting for him. He swore and then reluctantly hit the indicator before slowing for the next right turn off the A96.

'I'm on my way, Henry. I'll be there in thirty minutes.'

The dilapidated manse sat in the foothills of the Cairngorm mountains. The black sky overhead was thick with the streaked Milky Way as Michael parked and let himself in. He found Henry in his usual space upstairs in front of the computer. The room was lit only by the weak light coming off the multiple screens.

'It's still not working. It must be the government again.' Henry was rocking in his seat.

'I'm sorry that I wasn't here sooner, Henry. I'm really sorry. Do you have a contact for your service provider? A bill or something with a number on?' Michael went to put his hand on Henry's shoulder to comfort him, stopped when he remembered that his client hated being touched.

'What kind of bill? I don't know about that.'

What was the name of his carer again? Michael tried to remember. Gordon? Greg? He took a stab: 'When Greg comes to help you he opens the mail for you. Does he have somewhere he normally puts it?'

'I called Greg but he didn't answer. That's why I tried you, Michael. I knew you'd come.'

'When he does come, does he have somewhere specific that he puts the envelopes for you?'

'I hate envelopes. You never know what's going to come in them.' Henry's rocking intensified.

'I'll be back in a minute.'

Michael wandered around the dark manse. The musty smell of ancient wooden floorboards that creaked as he walked. The rows of dusty old books. The cupboards full of dried noodles, biscuits and crisps. Finally he found a drawer full of service bills in a cupboard in the upstairs hall. Michael was about to dial the number when he heard Henry's voice: 'It's come back on.'

Michael dug around in the kitchen until he found an old jar of instant coffee. It had almost turned to rock, but he dug some out and made himself a mug anyway, his desire for caffeine outweighing any squeamishness, and waited for twenty minutes. Henry's anxiety receded with every successful click and page load. Finally Michael pulled his jacket on.

'OK, Henry. I'm going to head off now,' he said. He was met with a blank expression. 'I'm going to leave. OK?'

'OK.' Henry turned back to the screen.

Michael nodded at it. 'What's that?'

'It's a video I made,' Henry said.

'Do you know a lot about videos?'

'Yes.'

Michael felt for Nichol's phone in his pocket. 'What about phones? Do you know anything about recovering data from phones? Deleted messages or videos? That kind of thing?'

'Yes,' Henry said. Still not looking away from the screen.

'If I left this with you,' Michael held the phone out, 'would you be able to have a look at it? Find out if there's anything hidden on it?'

'Yes.' Henry took the phone and laid it on his desk.

Chapter 40

The first light of dawn was breaking as Monica and Crawford crossed the car park to the large hospital building. The third time she'd been there in four days. That had to be unlucky, some kind of bad omen. But Monica still couldn't suppress her need to smile. She tried to force an appropriate sombreness into her mood. It seemed perverse that a dead man – hanging there soaked in blood like a sow at slaughter – could feel like such a weight removed from her body.

She glanced down at Crawford and noticed his red-rimmed eyes. He reached for the packet of mints in his pocket and stuffed another two into his mouth. She'd noted the mixed smells of whisky, cheap perfume and something else she didn't have time to think about, let alone do, seep off him in the Volvo and realised why he'd unexpectedly asked her to drive. Turned out he hadn't been sleeping after all, well not in the slumber sense. Probably he was still more drunk than sober.

In the grey morning sky above the hospital a plane passed, descending towards the airport out at Dalcross. Another omen, Monica thought. Lisa MacKay might well be on that plane – back today to see the remains of her only son.

Would MacLennan's hanging corpse, that unlucky tarot card Lisa had turned over to define the rest of her life, would it give her any comfort? Somehow Monica doubted it.

'The kid says they're waiting in the cafe for a taxi. His gran's fine, probably a panic attack,' Crawford said as they passed through the automatic doors then turned left down the wide corridor to the empty canteen area.

Monica immediately recognised Rory and his grandmother from the night before at the police station. They were sitting together silently at a table by the window. Somehow he looked younger now. Skinny and staring resolutely at the phone in his hands. Understandably she looked older, with deep worry lines on her forehead and hands folded tight around an inhaler. Neither of them looked up or gave any indication they had noticed the strange couple: the tall woman who looked like a corpse and the small red-eyed man who smelled of cheap whisky and sex.

'You're feeling better now, Anne?' Crawford asked. 'We just want to ask a few questions about what happened.'

The woman nodded, her face slack with shock.

'You said there was blood coming through into the living room, Anne? Did you hear anything from upstairs? Anything before you saw the blood?' Monica asked.

Anne shook her head in a panicky motion. 'There was nothing like that. I was just watching TV. I was all stressed way after going up to the police station. I couldn't sleep ...'

Monica looked from Anne to Rory, then back again. The kid kept his head down. Still staring straight at the phone, pretending he was deaf to what they were saying right beside him.

'Rory?' Monica said. 'Did you hear anything from upstairs?' The kid glanced up and shook his head then dropped his eyes quickly. 'You spend time with Owen sometimes?'

Rory looked up at her again but refused eye contact. 'Owen's always nice to me. He lets me use his broadband. We watch films sometimes at his place. Just the two of us.'

'Sort of like a friend? Or an uncle?' Monica asked, her skin crawling at the thought.

The kid dropped his eyes again and nodded.

'It's been hard for him.' Anne spoke fast, as if needing to justify her ignorance of MacLennan's criminal record. 'Not having his mum or dad around.'

'I understand what it's like,' Monica said. She turned to Rory again. 'You said you went with him in the van.'

'He said that I'd never be safe again,' Rory said, staring at his phone as he spoke. The Lego-themed pyjamas he was still wearing under his coat hung off his skinny teenage legs. 'He said that there was a man who tells you to go with him and you do it. That he'd ask boys to do things. Use them for whatever he wanted. That if I didn't say I'd been with him in the van, if I didn't lie about it ...'

'Did he tell you anything else about this man? Did he tell you his name?' Monica asked. She was struggling to process what the kid had just told her. If it wasn't Rory in the van with MacLennan then was it Robert? And who was this *man*, the accomplice?

Rory shook his head slowly. 'Just that I should be afraid of him. That everyone should be afraid of him.'

Chapter 41

Michael arrived in Lossiemouth as the grey clouds coming off the sea began to spit out sleet. The entrance to the flat was by the side of a shop, a blue door with no name on it. Michael rang the bell and waited. After a long pause the door buzzed open and Michael climbed the musty stairs inside to the first floor.

The young man standing at the door at the end of the short landing was tall and skinny with tattoos weaving all the way up both of his bare arms.

'Alan Gentle?' Michael asked.

He tilted his chin. 'What do you want?'

'I'm here about Nichol.'

Alan's face changed, teenage arrogance falling away as his eyes darted in panic. He tried to slam the door but Michael managed to catch it on his arm, alarmed by the kid's sudden agitation.

'Is Nichol here? I just want to know he's safe.'

'How did you get my address? He's not here. I don't know anything.' Alan's voice rose as he backed away.

Michael hesitated then stepped inside the flat, holding his hands up. 'I'm not here to cause trouble.' He dug in his pocket for the photograph. 'I found this picture. It's your car, isn't it?'

'Where did you get this from? I thought ...' Alan's voice died away.

'You thought it was buried?'

Alan nodded slowly and took the photograph from Michael's hand. When he looked up again his eyes were wet, like he might actually be about to cry.

'First Zandy. Then Nichol. I thought –' he forced out a bitter laugh '– maybe you'd come to ... How did you get my address?' His voice suddenly panicked again.

Michael reached slowly into his wallet for his ID. 'My name's Michael – I'm working with the police. You're not in any trouble.' Partly true at least. 'I'm Nichol's social worker. He might have mentioned me?'

Alan took the ID with a shaking hand. Then nodded slowly. 'I remember. You've got a Land Rover? A red one? Short wheelbase.'

'That's right,' Michael said. The relief of recognition as he pointed back to the street. 'It's right out there.'

Alan didn't turn but reached for a cigarette instead. 'Come in,' he said, as if Michael wasn't already inside the flat. Michael nodded awkwardly, pushed the door closed behind him and followed Alan into the living room.

He took in the three-piece suite and polished wooden floor, three walls painted white and the fourth plum purple – straight from an interior design website. The place was surprisingly neat and coordinated compared to its scruffy exterior.

Alan sat down slowly, still holding the photograph. 'Me, Nichol, Zandy,' he said, pointing to their faces in turn. His hand was shaking harder now.

'Nichol and Zandy went somewhere together?' Michael felt a moment of hope, but it was quickly squashed.

'Zandy's dead. Fuck knows where Nichol is.'

Dead. Another one. As easy as that. Somehow those dead boys were orbiting closer.

'That was your funeral for him? When you buried the photo?' Michael asked.

'His mum didn't want us at the real funeral. The service or anything. She blamed us for what happened. His proper name was Alexander Allen. The same as the one on that gravestone. We used to joke about it, you know?'

'How did he die?' Michael heard the tremor in his own voice.

'Killed himself. That's what they say anyway. The river ...' Alan mouthed the words rather than spoke them.

'He jumped?'

'One of the bridges in Inverness.' Alan stubbed his cigarette out but lit another one immediately. 'His mum was ... fucking pissed off, you know? Like we'd killed him. Me and Nichol went to the door. She was screaming at us. We'd led him astray ...'

'She wanted someone to blame?'

Alan nodded frantically, a drowning man reaching for a raft. 'That's right. Scapegoats or something.'

'What actually happened?'

'Nothing. It was just normal – a warm day. A Saturday. Me, Nichol and Zandy. Just driving about. My dad got me the car for my birthday. I still came back through to Inverness most weekends then, you know? We stopped off, had a few cans. A smoke. They made out that he'd been totally going mental with it, but it wasn't like that.' He looked up at Michael again, the guilt and shame on his face painful to see. 'We were just heading home. Nichol went one way. I went the other way. Zandy went another ...' Alan's voice trailed off. 'The next morning I start getting calls from his mum. There's stuff all over Facebook.

About how he got home safe and went to his bed, but he wasn't there in the morning. They said he must have been on something, legal highs or drugs. He must have gone wandering. Everyone was out looking for him. They'd been going right past but no one noticed. He was caught up in the weir. Under the water. He was all swollen up, they said. Like ... like he wasn't even a human any more. I can't believe he jumped. He wouldn't have jumped!'

'What do you think happened to him?' Michael said. His voice low in the still room.

Alan looked up slowly. The cigarette smoke rising by his hand in a slow blue cloud. 'This is about the man at his window. Isn't it?'

'The man at his window?' Michael repeated. The fear in the boy's voice was infectious.

Alan swallowed. 'It was the day we had the ...' he searched for the right word '... the funeral for Zandy. At the graveyard.' The box in the shallow grave. The green grass and the trees. 'It was stupid – just like saying goodbye, you know?'

Michael nodded.

'It was after that. We were just sitting, talking about Zandy and some of the things we'd done. The times we'd been out drinking together, stupid things he'd said or whatever.'

Michael nodded again.

'You know what Nichol's like. Like he's a friend, but there's a part of him – he says things that are hurtful, like on purpose sometimes. Like he wants to hurt your feelings or something? Like people have a dark sense of humour, you know?'

'What did he say?'

'He was joking about. He said that he'd seen someone going into Zandy's house. The night he died.'

'He saw someone going into Zandy's house? On the night that Zandy killed himself?' Michael couldn't believe what he was hearing.

'That's what he said. I was totally, like … shocked or whatever. It was like he was joking, but we're talking about our friend who fucking killed himself. I was, like, *come on, Nichol …*'

'What did he say?'

'He kind of laughed. Like I was overreacting to a joke or something.'

'He didn't say anything else?' Michael watched Alan's face change. Fear. Denial. 'What did he say?'

Alan reached for another cigarette. His hand was still shaking. 'He said that he knew who Zandy had gone with.'

'He knew him?'

Alan nodded slowly. Hesitated as he caught Michael's eye. Fear passing over his face.

'Did he give you a name? Say what he looked like? This is really important.'

'No. Nothing like that – I told you. It was more like he was joking. Then I heard he was missing …' Alan's hands went to his head, reliving the moment.

'Then you realised he might have been telling the truth?'

'I don't know. I didn't want to think about it. How could I have known …' Alan's voice trailed off.

'Do you have any idea who he might have been talking about? Anyone he mentioned?'

Alan looked up at him again. The suspicion and hesitancy written plain on his face. 'No. I've got no idea. You know what he was like? He kept a lot of things to himself. I never even knew he had a fucking social worker until we saw you driving past one day. It's like …' He searched around for another example. His eyes lit up. 'Like the laptop. One week he's got this old piece of shit; the next he's got a fucking MacBook Pro. He comes out with a story about how he got it—'

'What was the story?'

Alan paused. His face froze like he might have said too much. 'You know?' he said slowly. 'The social worker?'

'The social worker?'

'His other one. You know. Annemarie or Amy or ...'

Michael felt the chill as the shock ran up his back. 'Anita?'

Chapter 42

Monica took a mouthful of the coffee, almost gagged at how sweet Crawford had made it. The hospital cafeteria was starting to fill up with outpatients now. The mix of emotions in the air was almost palpable. The death sentences handed out to some. The heavenly light of reprieve to others: the lump is benign; the cancer is responding well to treatment.

She tried another sip of the coffee and replayed her own moment of reprieve. Owen's body swinging from the hook on the ceiling. The monster was dead, and order could be restored to the village. Or maybe only halfway restored, Monica thought. Because the fear in Rory's voice wasn't something that you could fake.

Why would MacLennan kill himself when he was enjoying it all so much? The question niggled at her like a stone in the shoe. It seemed impossible, but what if Rory was right? What if there was a second killer out there? More cunning and sophisticated than MacLennan.

Monica moved her toes as if there really was a stone in there, glanced down at her black trainers. Mercifully comfortable after the hideous damp boots and bought from a European website – EU size 44.5 so they didn't count as 10s. She shook her head at the ridiculous sleight of hand and looked up to see Crawford walking back into the cafeteria, arms out to the side, little chest pushed out. She clocked his body language straight away: *I can't wait to tell you what I've just discovered.*

'I wasn't sure if you'd still be here,' he said as he jogged the last few steps towards her.

'Lisa MacKay's almost here. I thought I'd wait for her.'

Crawford's face fell. 'Right. I'd forgotten.'

'You have news?'

Crawford ran a hand over his dishevelled quiff, obviously enjoying the moment of suspense. 'Toxicology,' he said finally.

'From Paul MacKay?' Monica knew that the preliminary results from Robert Wright's blood and urine had come back clear. It could take weeks before they had the full results from his brain and organs.

Crawford nodded slowly. 'GHB. Gamma-hydroxybutyric acid.'

'So MacLennan drugged him?'

'That's what it looks like. GHB leaves the system rapidly though. After about four hours you can't detect it,' Crawford said. 'It's possible that Robert was drugged as well, but that he was alive for long enough after so that it cleared his system.'

Monica considered this for a moment. She remembered how thin both Paul and Robert had been on the slab. Especially compared to the thick ropes of muscle on MacLennan's naked body. It didn't seem to quite fit.

'We know how strong MacLennan was. Why would he need to drug them? He could have just grabbed them and strangled them unconscious. He would have preferred that – for them to know exactly what was happening.'

'Maybe he intended to hide the cause of their deaths?' Crawford said, his hand massaging the back of his neck.

'But why would he leave them on display then?' Monica said.

'I don't know.' Crawford shrugged. 'I mean killing someone isn't exactly a logical thing to do anyway, is it?'

Monica looked around the cafe at all the faces. The bustle of voices. The sounds of trays clattering on tabletops. She wondered how many of them would agree. How many of them had given serious consideration to killing someone for one reason or another.

'It depends whose logic you're judging things by,' Monica said finally.

But Crawford wasn't listening. His eyes had gone past Monica to the car park outside the window. She turned to follow his gaze and immediately understood why.

There was a woman walking across the car park towards the hospital entrance. She was wearing a long brown coat and her eyes were covered in sunglasses. But even then, with her short dark hair and slim build Lisa MacKay bore an uncanny resemblance to her dead son lying refrigerated beneath their feet.

Chapter 43

Michael watched as Anita came through the revolving door and glanced over to where he was sitting at a corner table. It was a different pub to the one they'd been in the night before. The kind of place to drink alone.

He caught the sound of her heels clicking off the dirty wooden floor. *She looks out of place here*, Michael thought. With her neat shoulder-length hair, make-up, nails and raincoat tied at the waist. Not like him. He fitted right in with the daytime drinkers.

Anita checked the table for spilled drinks then set her expensive-looking yellow handbag down. She turned to say something, but her face froze when she caught Michael's expression. For an uncomfortably long time neither of them spoke. Over her shoulder the barman was serving another early-afternoon drink to a man who'd already had too many. Probably a lifetime too many.

'It's true. Isn't it?' he said finally. 'You did know Nichol. You bought that laptop for him. You tried to stop me from looking for him?'

Anita stared back, and the panic in her hazel eyes shifted to something like terror.

'You heard about the boy they found yesterday?' Michael said, struggling to keep his voice down. 'What the fuck happened?' Anita's hands were shaking. Michael reached out and gripped her arm. 'Do you have any idea how serious this is? He might have been murdered.'

'I wish I'd never seen him.'

'But you did see him. Then you lied to me about it.'

Anita stared back at him, anger and hatred finally edging out the fear in her voice. 'This is your fault, Michael. You used me. You got me into bed, then you acted like I'd asked you to marry me. I just needed support. My mum was ill—'

'We're both adults. It was a mistake. It's got nothing to do with this,' Michael said, but the sense of shame at what she was saying blossomed. Even through the anger.

'Oh it does though,' Anita said. 'That's when I met him. I'd come to your flat. I just needed to talk. Do you remember? You said you couldn't handle it. I don't think I've ever been more vulnerable.' She shook her head. 'What does it say about me that I wanted to be with someone like you?'

Michael stared at the table. The righteous anger that he'd been nursing drained away as he recalled the tawdry scene he'd tried so hard to blank out.

'What? You've got nothing to say now you're not playing the rescuer?' She shook her head. 'Nichol was outside – almost like he was waiting for me. He saw that I was crying and we started talking. We ended up driving around, talking. That was it. I know you won't believe me but he was the one in control that night, not me. I let my guard down. No one was listening to me, and this attractive kid was interested. It's pathetic. It turns out he was just using me.'

'What are you talking about?'

'I met him again. To apologise, make sure he'd keep his mouth shut or whatever. He started talking about how he needed a laptop. He knew I'd just bought one.'

'Wait. You're telling me that he blackmailed you?'

'You've got this thing about you, Michael. Because you make excuses for yourself when you hurt people, you do the same for everyone else.' She shook her head again. 'He knew that I regretted spending time with him. He saw the opportunity—'

'You could have spoken to me, Anita. I would have talked to him.'

She laughed, not even forcing it. 'That's funny, Michael. Jesus. Whatever Nichol is, he's more honest with himself than you'll ever be.'

'We had a good time at least, didn't we?' Michael said.

'I can't believe you just said that. You know, one day you're going to look around and you're going to see that people have stopped chasing after you.'

He avoided Anita's eyes and looked past her to the lonely bar. He wondered how things had ended up like this. With Anita, with Alice, with Nichol.

'Listen. I'm sorry. I let you down. I let myself down, but there are two kids who are dead. Someone murdered them. Whatever Nichol is or isn't, I just need to know that he's safe.'

'And I've got no idea where he is! Believe me. If I thought I could have avoided this—'

'Did he mention any names? Zandy Allen? Charlie Bartle?' Michael caught the change on Anita's face. 'What did he say about him? It's important.'

She stared at him for a moment. 'Last week before he went missing. I hadn't seen him in months. I'd almost forgotten – almost let myself pretend it had never happened. He was standing by my car. He asked if I'd give him a lift.'

'Where did you take him?'

'I dropped him where he asked. In Rapinch, behind an old pub. He said he was going to speak to someone. One of the Bartles – a guy called Charlie Bartle.'

Chapter 44

'I know he was involved. I haven't stopped thinking about it,' Lisa MacKay said. She was staring fixedly down at the mug in front of her. 'I *know* he was involved.'

An hour earlier Lisa had crumpled to the floor of the mortuary after Monica had led her down to view the remains of a boy who looked so like her that it would be hard for Lisa to look in the mirror again and not see Paul looking back at her. The boy who was made of the flesh from her womb, of the milk from her breasts. And all of the darkest things were creeping, creeping for her.

Monica had knelt beside her and put one of her long hands on Lisa's head. Like maybe she could hold the darkness away. But there was no comfort. There was nothing.

'Who are you talking about exactly?' Crawford said from beside Monica. Monica could have asked the question more delicately, but it would have amounted to the same thing.

'Don Cameron did it. I know it. I've seen the way he looks at Paul,' Lisa said. Her eyes were locked on Monica's face.

Don Cameron. The name chimed for Monica: the game-keeper that Muir Maitland at the hotel had spoken about. The man he had inadvertently named as a potential suspect. Cameron worked exactly where Muir had seen Robert Wright the night he was murdered. A connection between the victims opening right up for them. Could Don Cameron have helped Owen MacLennan somehow?

'How do you know Don Cameron?' Monica asked. She tried to keep her voice level as she watched Lisa stare around the interview room. The woman was clearly dazed. Still deep in shock. *How many years do you have left after this day?* Monica wondered as she reached across the desk and put a hand on Lisa's shoulder. *How many years after the weight of this world has crushed you down?*

It was five minutes before Lisa could speak again.

Finally she said, 'Paul works with him sometimes. He helps him to cut the grass at the lodge. Things like that. He –' she put a hand to her chest then dropped it to the desk '– he must have convinced Paul to stay at home while I went on holiday. He must have planned it.'

'Why do you say that?' Monica asked.

'Paul was going to come with me on holiday. One day he just changed his mind. He said that he needed money. Don needed his help on a job. Don must have planned it, convinced him to stay ... I was angry. I told Paul I'd wasted money on him. But in the end I thought it was better to just shut up and let him make his own decisions.' Her hand fluttered up to her mouth, back down to the table.

'I can't imagine how difficult this must be for you, Lisa. But we need you to tell us as much as possible about Don Cameron,' Monica said.

'He hardly speaks. That's what Paul likes about him – that he's the opposite of me. He's in his fifties, I suppose. Lives with his father still. He works as a gamekeeper. Paul goes on about the guns he has. He's clever – he'll fix things for you: cars, central heating, all sorts of things. You know at first I thought it was good – Paul having him around, a fucking father figure. I'll never forgive myself for that.'

When they finally finished the interview, Monica found Hately waiting for her in the corridor outside. The look of satisfaction was clear on his face – it meant good news. *If you can say any news in a double murder investigation is good*, Monica thought. She gestured for Crawford to wait for her in the incident room and followed Hately into his office.

'I thought you'd want to know that forensics have just called from MacLennan's flat. They've found a T-shirt that matches one Stephen Wright said was missing from Robert's room.' Hately was speaking quickly, his excitement bubbling in a way that was unusual for him. A sign of just how serious the case was. But still the contrast with Lisa MacKay's horrified face just moments before felt particularly stark. 'It's splattered in blood that we can test for DNA. That's clear evidence linking both victims with Owen MacLennan.'

Monica nodded. Somehow she wasn't even surprised. Everything seemed to fit neatly to prove that MacLennan was the killer. Too neatly, if you asked her, like paint-by-number policing.

'We've finally managed to track down Robert Wright's mother too,' Hately continued. 'She's been on a meditation retreat down in the borders for about six weeks. She's in a state of shock obviously, but she says she doesn't know anything.' He shrugged. More *good news*.

Monica cleared her throat, aware that she was about to ruin the rest of Hately's afternoon.

'I'm going to need an armed response team to bring someone in for questioning. It's a gamekeeper. He's got certificates for multiple firearms.'

'DI Kennedy, I've just told you that we have found Robert's T-shirt at MacLennan's flat. You saw Paul's wallet there earlier. Digital Forensics say MacLennan's computer's at least fifty per cent sadistic pornography. Every snuff film you can find on the Internet.'

'Lisa MacKay doesn't know about MacLennan yet. She just named a man called Don Cameron as a potential suspect. He was previously named to me as a potential suspect by another witness. He employed Paul MacKay and works about a mile from Robert Wright's house.'

'Haven't you heard what I said?' Hately said, and Monica watched the tic go off at the side of his eye. 'We've got evidence linking both of the victims with MacLennan.'

'I think he might have had an accomplice. I think it's possible it was Don Cameron.'

'Do you have any evidence for this?' Hately asked, his voice rising. 'Beyond hearsay.'

Monica cleared her throat. 'The kid, Rory Wilson, said that MacLennan had threatened him—'

'The same kid who lied about being in the van with MacLennan? Who could have caused this investigation to fall apart.'

'He was terrified,' Monica said, her voice rising to match Hately's. 'If we don't at least follow it up we're giving Don Cameron time to destroy evidence.'

Chapter 45

The Watcher

The waitress came to take his order. He met her question silently and watched as her hands went to the pouch on her apron, then back up to her hair. Her nervousness interested him.

'Just a tea,' he said finally, watching her shaky fingers scribble the order. He glanced around the cafe. It sat in a corner of an industrial estate with trucks outside the window. The smell of fried food. The handful of customers looked fat and docile to him. He stretched his back. His body felt beaten up after all the exertions of the past few days but good because of it.

The waitress brought his tea. He waited for her to go, then his hand dropped to his pocket and he turned the lock of hair over between his fingers. Lifted it out and passed it quickly under his nose, taking a deep, satisfying breath, then dropped it back in his pocket and took the phone out. He hit Play and moved the timer to his favourite part of the video again. The sound was turned down, but he already knew the words off by heart.

Paul woke up. The bright electric light in his face. He tried to move on the mattress then felt the restriction on his arms and remembered that he was tied down. For a full minute Paul writhed and screamed there on the mattress. It was beautiful to watch.

He stared around the cafe at the customers and the waitresses. It would be funny if they could see why he was smiling so widely.

Finally Paul stopped moving. 'I feel really ill.' He mouthed the words along with Paul. 'I feel really ill.' Paul was playing his part well. The regret. The hope.

The bell rang as the cafe door swung open. He clicked the video off and slid the phone into his pocket as the police officer stood in the open doorway. He glanced suspiciously around the room as if there might be some crime taking place, as if the need to be vigilant had never been higher.

Finally the police officer – PC Duncan Gregg – walked over and sat down at the table.

The waitress came with Gregg's usual white coffee, and he hunched over it, weakness and suspicion somehow evident in his body language, in his folded mouth, his yellowing teeth and his grey skin.

'What do you want anyway?' Gregg asked. His tone defensive.

'I told you,' the man sitting opposite him replied. 'I've got information. A name that's come to me. I need you to pass it on.'

'I'm not ...' Gregg looked around the room. 'I'm not doing anything that hurts anyone.'

'What about when you haven't been able to pay the mortgage because you've gambled it on horse racing? I think your wife and your daughter might disagree.'

Gregg's face went red. Clearly he wanted to stand up and storm off. The thoughts played out in his yellowing eyes: *The money would sort his problems out this time; it would all be different.*

'Don't – don't you mention them. They've got nothing to do with this,' Gregg said.

'Of course they don't.' He slid the envelope across the table to Gregg. Then a piece of paper with a name and address on it. 'You said you know Don Cameron?'

Don Cameron's unexpected and hidden affection for Paul MacKay, which had almost ruined everything with the boy. He smiled at the idea of the man lusting after his teenage acquaintance. Doing nothing about it, but watching him. Then attempting to intervene, almost ruining everything.

Gregg nodded and looked around again, a look of fear on his face. 'That's right. I used to anyway.'

He nodded at the piece of paper. 'That's someone who harmed a friend of Don's. A dangerous person, believe me. I think your friend will be pleased to get that name.'

Gregg picked up the envelope and slipped it into his pocket. 'I wouldn't be doing this if it was going to hurt someone who didn't deserve it.'

'Of course not.' He reached into his pocket and felt for that lock of hair again. Let the sharper tips where it had been cut rub against the end of his thumb. 'Oh, the detective who's leading the murder investigation. DI Kennedy. What do you know about her?'

PC Gregg tilted his head, a look that said, *Why would you want to know that?* But then he shrugged. *What was a bit of gossip after all?*

'Big Monica the man?' Gregg laughed dismissively. 'Just what I told you: she's a loner. Got herself knocked up somehow though. Braver man than me. I think her wee girl's called Lucy.'

Chapter 46

Michael left Anita sitting at the table in the pub. He walked quickly through the rain, which was falling heavily now. A superstitious feeling seemed to hurry him on: *If you don't find Nichol now maybe you never will.*

He tried to battle the feeling. *You should call the detective and pass the information to her*, he told himself. It was the sensible thing to do. He could clearly remember what Eddie had said about how dangerous Charlie Bartle and his gang were, but for some reason Michael couldn't stop himself from walking all the way down Church Street. Then on across the metal bridge into Rapinch.

He found the place Anita had described easily. So easily that it almost felt like he was meant to go there. The old pub was virtually in the shadow of Eddie's flat. The afternoon was coming to a dank and premature end when Michael walked round to the back of the building and stood outside a metal door. No cars parked outside and no light from any of the shuttered windows. The rain came down harder still. Filling the blocked gutters on the building to overflowing until the water spilled over into dark smears down the stone exterior.

Michael hesitated then pushed on the door and watched as it swung all the way open. The pub had looked desolate and shut down the night before, but it seemed looks could be deceiving. The sound of distorted music echoed down the corridor. Every instinct told him to walk away. To call DI Kennedy and come back with the police. Instead he dropped his cigarette on the ground and stepped into the dark corridor. It smelled of damp. Of aftershave and smoke, and beer gone stale. He followed the music – 1920s jazz of all things – towards a second door. He could hear voices behind it.

Michael pushed it slowly open. The room was eerie, lit only by candlelight. The music came in bursts from an out-of-tune radio. Two men were standing by a pool table. There were another two at the bar and three more sitting around a table. On it was a laptop and a pile of papers.

'This is a private club,' said one of them as they all turned at the sound of the door. 'Members only, mate.' The man who spoke had short blonde hair brushed forward above hard eyes.

'I'm looking for Charlie Bartle,' Michael said. Everyone turned to one of the men at the table. He was broad-shouldered with dark hair and a face that knew violence. 'I need your help,' Michael said.

Charlie Bartle lifted his chin and stared at Michael for a moment, taking him in. Then he turned and nodded slowly to one of the men at the bar, who stood up.

'I'm trying to find Nichol Morgan. I'm his social worker. He came here to meet you just before he went missing,' Michael said.

Silence. Then from over his shoulder Michael heard the sound of a metal bolt sliding home. He realised that he'd made a mistake, realised that he'd known it all along.

'I haven't spoken to the police yet.'

'Fucking right you haven't spoken to the police,' the man who'd spoken before cut in.

Charlie Bartle held up a hand. Silence filled the room again. A story that everyone knew well but couldn't quite recall the ending of as they sat waiting in the room.

A story of violence and time slowing down.

'I know who you are. My mother told me you were coming today. She always said she was fucking psychic. I never believed her.' Bartle reached into his jacket pocket and put a butterfly knife on the table. 'The thing is, what if Nichol's not safe? What are you going to do then?'

Michael felt the hand on his shoulder. Somehow the violence seemed inevitable and instinctively he threw an elbow back, felt it hit the man's face. He turned. *Left hook. Cross.* From a lifetime ago. A boxing coach shouting in his ear and the stink of sweaty old gloves. The man fell back with both his hands on his broken nose.

Michael saw the glass launched at his face. He managed to slip to the side so it bounced off his shoulder. He hit the man who'd thrown it and watched as he collapsed back into the table. The laptop, the knife and the pile of papers fell to the floor beside him.

Bartle ducked for the knife. Michael kicked it away and grabbed Bartle's throat. 'Where the fuck is Nichol?'

A light flashed at the side of Michael's face. Then he was on the dirty wooden floorboards. *Get up. Keep fighting.* Michael tried to stand, but the floor sloped away at an angle. He stumbled a few paces until he hit the bar and slumped back down, his hand at his face as he felt something hot run down his wrist. He saw the blood splattered across the floor. He heard the shouts that didn't seem to mean anything as the thrill of violence filled the air. This was what some men lived for.

Michael's head rocked back from the first stamp. White light from his forehead. Then the next. *This is what it feels like to be kicked to death* was the cold realisation as his arm blocked the third stamp. He saw the trainers and tracksuit bottoms this time.

There was shouting and more movement as Michael tried to push himself up. But the bar just kept tilting away from him.

Charlie Bartle bent down so his eyes were level with Michael's. Michael could feel the blood soaking into his collar and the deep pain of bone grating against bone.

Michael tried to say something to those blue eyes, but the pain came on stronger. Bartle reached for Michael's hand and pulled it away from his face to reveal the injury behind.

'Oh he's fucked,' someone said with laughter in his voice as the light from a mobile phone shone on Michael's face. 'He's fucked.' Other voices joined in with the laughter.

'Where's Nichol?' Michael tried to say, but the words came out wrong. The men laughed harder at him. Charlie Bartle stood up and said something. Someone else replied and reached over the bar to grab something. It was a baseball bat. *This is how you die*, Michael thought. On a dirty floor in a dirty old pub.

He tried to move again but his hands wouldn't work properly. *Try your phone. Get help*. Michael went for his pocket. The man who'd spoken first knelt in front of him with a wide cruel smile. The kind of smile you only know when you're at your most vulnerable. He pulled Michael's hand easily away and shook his head. Even in his disorientated state Michael could see how much the man was enjoying himself. He patted Michael down. Opened his wallet then took something else from Michael's pocket and handed it to Bartle.

Bartle said something then. Words that didn't make any sense. He knelt closer so his face was level with Michael's and said the words again. Michael slowly understood what they'd taken from his pocket. It was a business card. The words that Bartle was saying, when you fitted them together made a name. A name Michael knew: 'Monica Kennedy.'

Chapter 47

Monica pulled into the petrol station on Longman Road. It sat unsure at the edge of the grim industrial estate that was the first thing to greet visitors from the south driving down off the moor and into the capital of the Highlands.

She filled the Volvo then went inside and stuffed an armful of Marks & Spencer ready meals into a basket. It still seemed strange to find a branch of this smart shop anywhere near the roughneck side of Inverness. 'Fancy that,' her mum had said when Monica had first arrived home with a load of meals in the store's crisp white bag. Thinking of her mum made her feel guilty for shouting the previous night. It had all been for nothing after all, with MacLennan now no longer part of this world.

She balanced the basket against her thigh and reached for a few cans of Crawford's energy drink, pausing and choosing instead the sugar-free version. She then added a large bag of salted popcorn for the kid.

It was only when she dumped the bags of shopping into the back of the car and saw the contents spill out over the seats that she realised that she'd started using food as a way of expressing her affection. She was becoming her mother, she thought, with an odd mix of interest and disquiet as she pulled back out on to the dual carriageway. The rain had come on stronger, and the dreary afternoon light was fading into evening.

Hately had reluctantly agreed to her request to bring Don Cameron in for questioning, although it would now be the next morning before the armed unit went in for him. Time stretched uncomfortably between now and then, but there was little she could do. Hately had hoops to jump his suited arse through after all. She should go home and pick up Lucy, hold her tight. Monica stared at the white lights of Rose Street Car Park, beyond them a beautiful panorama of the city.

She gripped the steering wheel a little harder. Lisa MacKay wasn't ever going to be able to go home to her son again. Wasn't going to pass another day without thinking about him. Monica sighed and tried to dislodge the horror of Lisa's interview earlier. To focus instead on the specifics of the case. Like a puzzle. She ran back over the investigation in her mind.

It was the drug, the GHB, that wouldn't stop niggling. *Why would MacLennan have needed his victims to be incapacitated?* She recalled that look of sheer pleasure when he'd taken a deep breath of her fear for Lucy. Why would he have missed out on the delight of that first moment, the thrill of his victims' terror?

Maybe that was where an accomplice came in? Don Cameron? Maybe his impulses – what he needed from the victims – were different to the straightforward sadism that drove MacLennan? Maybe, maybe, maybe.

Monica hesitated at the roundabout then switched lanes at the last moment. Instead of taking the exit for her flat she found herself taking the road that led over the river and west alongside the Beauly Firth. Through the gloomy mountains.

After an hour's fast drive she found the entrance to the track. The trees were hanging low in the dark, surrounding the lonely house. Monica switched the car engine off then killed the headlights and climbed out.

It was a clear autumn night now that the rain had stopped. Icy cold with billions of stars overhead. Monica peered at the shadows among the trees. It felt almost as if someone was watching her; those little prickles of primal intuition. She shivered at the idea and buttoned up her coat. Sometimes it was hard to keep paranoia at bay in this job.

The MacKays' house was small. A single storey crouched among the pine trees with empty dark windows. Monica knew that Lisa was still in Inverness staying with friends. Of course she was – how could she ever come back?

Everything had happened so quickly with the discovery of Paul's body and then Owen MacLennan that Monica hadn't had the chance to investigate how Paul had met his killer. Whether he'd known MacLennan, or been ambushed somehow.

Monica looked around again as her eyes adjusted to the dark. She caught the edge of an outline in front of the house. The shape of a car. She stepped closer. A blue Volkswagen Golf, the driver's door unlocked, and she shone the light from her phone inside. CDs and food wrappers were strewn over the passenger seat.

So Paul could drive, Monica thought. *Had his own car, but didn't take it out the night he was abducted. Had Don Cameron lured him out? Got him somewhere quiet where MacLennan would meet them? That would make sense if Cameron was involved.*

She walked over to the front door of the house. It was locked. She dug in her pocket for the key that Lisa had given her but it wouldn't fit in the lock. Maybe she'd handed over the wrong one in her distressed state.

Monica walked round to the back door. Locked too. Bolted from the inside. *It would be typical to come all this way and not even make it into the house.* She stared across the overgrown garden to the thick forest of plantation trees beyond it. In the distance she caught a flicker of light among the trees. Will-o'-the-wisp? She peered closer, trying to make out any shapes among the densely planted forest. Finally she gave up and turned back to the house. Around the corner she found the bathroom window had been left open a crack.

'You've come all this way,' she whispered.

By the light of her phone she was able to unlatch the window, and with hands, then arms, then her shoulders twisted until they screeched in pain, she rolled awkwardly in.

Monica took in the smells of an unfamiliar house waiting like the ghosts of the recently murdered. Cheap aftershave and cigarette smoke. Monica clicked on the hall light and looked around the small house. Just a kitchen, a living room, two bedrooms and a bathroom.

It was obvious which door led to Paul's room: the one with the poster of a woman in a bikini. Monica pushed the door open. The smell of aftershave was stronger in here, but there was another smell beneath it.

With a feeling of déjà vu Monica recognised incense. There had been exactly the same smell in Robert Wright's bedroom. One teenage boy burning joss sticks felt plausible, but Paul had been all about lager and girls in swimwear. Not the kind to visit New Age shops.

If the boys didn't burn incense, maybe their killer did? Had they been looking at the whole thing back to front? Maybe the boys hadn't gone out to meet their deaths; they'd met their killer at home first. But then she thought of MacLennan and his filthy-smelling room. There had been no signs he'd ever burned incense. So was this where Don Cameron came in?

She tried the bedroom light, it clicked but the room remained dark. Monica shone her phone's torch at the ceiling light. The bulb had been removed. *Just the same as MacLennan's flat.* Another coincidence, or something else? She reached to switch on the bedside lamp instead and studied the room: a packet of cigarettes destined never to be smoked, a tobacco tin, Rizla papers and a lighter beside them. She glanced at the window. The curtains were open to the dark night outside. Monica stepped closer to the window. It was pulled closed but not snibbed. She turned and looked at the room again. It was more disordered than Robert Wright's. More the typical unruly teenager's with posters and scattered clothes, whereas Robert's space had been neat and contained.

'You would have been more fun at a party, Paul,' Monica whispered. 'I would have chosen Robert for the pub quiz though. No offence.'

Her eyes fell on the can by the bed. Budweiser. She pulled on a glove and picked it up. There was still some left at the bottom.

As she set it back down a memory chimed. In Robert Wright's bedroom there had been that distinctive mug by the bed. Still half full. She felt the hairs of the back of her neck begin to stand. *The GHB. They were drugged in their houses. They weren't lured out at all.*

Monica walked quickly out into the hall, down the corridor to the front door. The key was still in the lock. That's why she couldn't open it. And the back door was bolted from the inside. *He came in through the window. Like a monster from a fairy tale. He drugged them and took them away.*

Monica unlocked the front door and strode back out into the cold night air. It had stopped raining now, the air clean and fresh after the smells in the house. She went to the Volvo for a proper police torch, and then to the outside of Paul's bedroom window. Under the bright light scratch marks were visible on the wooden frame where the old white paint had cracked off. As if someone had prised the window open enough to unfasten it as she'd done in the bathroom.

She flashed the torch down at the ground and saw fragments of white paint on the stones. Monica remembered the dog in Robert's bedroom. Ellie – she had been scratching at the window. *Could one man have got the boy down out of the window and off the flat roof? Even one as strong as MacLennan? Did Don Cameron help him?* That made a lot more sense. One in the bedroom passing the paralysed body out to the other waiting on the roof, with Robert's father asleep mere yards away. She recalled a video she'd seen of a firefighter carrying an unconscious victim over his shoulder from a burning building. There was no doubt it was possible. A simple collapsible ladder would have made the whole job even easier.

Monica turned and shone the light towards the pine forest at the end of the garden. From there it would have been easy to see into the bedroom window. Easy to move right up to the window without being seen.

So Don Cameron sneaked in and drugged the kid while MacLennan waited somewhere with the van? But Paul was alone. Why not just go to the door, offer him a beer and wait until he passed out? Of that Monica wasn't sure.

She walked towards the forest and found a rough track through the mossy trees. There was the faint sound of a car passing in the distance on the main road, and it was somehow comforting. There in that dark place. The path led her over a small hill, then down the other side to a clearing in the trees. The place was spooky, dominated by tall pines. She picked her way by the light of the torch, roots and pine needles visible in its beam, then gravel. There were tyre tracks filled with rain-water. It wasn't just a clearing, she realised; it was a lay-by off the main road.

So they carried Paul here. Did they kill him here too, in the van? Or out in the open? Or did they take him somewhere else? The place where they cleaned the bodies up and made the bite marks in their flesh?

With the smell of rotting leaves and damp earth rising around her, she pulled out her phone to call Hately. They needed to get to Cameron before he got wind of them coming. As her phone searched for a connection she walked across the lay-by, her eyes skimming the ground, and it was then that she saw it: a single footprint. Unexceptional except that it was at the edge of the clearing, where the gravel met the dirt of the forest floor. She leaned in closer, tucking her still-silent phone between ear and shoulder, and examined where the earth was dry despite the volume of rain they'd seen for days now. She dusted the pine needles away and as the torch jumped a few steps away a flash of red caught the light. She reached into her pocket for a glove and stretched over the footprint to pick the thing up. A used shotgun shell. The plastic was still bright red, unfaded by weather. She cancelled her attempt to connect to Hately and instead used the phone's camera function to photograph where she had found the shell. She then dropped it into an evidence bag and kept searching. There was another shell, this one lodged in the mud a few feet away.

So someone had stood on the edge of the clearing. Fired a shotgun. Was that a coincidence? Or had Paul tried to run?

The drug was wearing off, so Cameron had fired a warning shot?

Another car passed on the road, its lights and engine muffled by the thick trees. It was a lonely spot, despite how close to the road it was. An uncomfortable feeling washed over her, as if she was being observed. She clicked off the light and stared into the darkness.

'Hello?' Her voice echoed back to her. Drowning in the rain.

She turned and walked back to the centre of the clearing. Switched the light on and cast it over the ground until the beam hit something else. She stopped and knelt in the damp gravel by a tiny cube of glass. From a smashed windscreen?

Monica glanced back to the edge of the clearing. Panned the torch. There were a few more fragments of glass. Beyond the glass there were tyre tracks, deep like a driver had gunned an engine. *They got Paul into a vehicle, but someone else was watching. Someone who tried to stop them. Who shot out part of their windscreen?* This scenario raised more questions than answers, though. *Why would someone be watching? Why didn't they call the police?*

A sound echoed around the clearing. Monica jumped. Almost dropped the torch. Her heart in her mouth before she realised that her phone was ringing. The volume turned up to max. *Bloody thing.* She took a breath, annoyed by her reaction. She pulled the phone out of her pocket. *Michael Bach?*

It was DC Fisher.

'DI Kennedy?' It was a weak signal. 'I just got the results on the piece of rock back.' There was a pause before she caught the words: 'I thought you'd want to know.'

'Where does it come from?' Monica asked, scrunching her face against the sound of the wind and rain and trees around her.

'It's a compound made up of various elements – iron, nickel, garium, calcium ...'

'So it's mostly metal?' She was shouting now.

'That's right. I've—' Fisher cut out.

'What is it, Fisher? Just tell me.' Her voice echoed back to her from the trees.

'Well, it's sort of an outside interest—'

Monica jabbed at the volume button on her phone and moved to the centre of the lay-by, where the rain fell hard. 'Fisher? Repeat that,' she shouted.

His voice was suddenly clear: '– a bit embarrassing, but I've always been interested in physics. Astronomy.'

'And?'

'And the chemical make-up of this rock means that it would fit with what we might expect to see from a space object that had entered the earth's atmosphere.'

Monica tried to work out what he was saying. 'You mean the rock could have come from a meteor?'

The line crackled, and she pushed a finger into her other ear.

'Well technically it would be called a meteorite. Someone picks it up—' Fisher cut out again.

'Can you find out where the meteor landed? Or where it could be bought?' Monica was drenched now, her coat heavy with rain.

'As far as I know, each meteorite has its own mineral finger-print. I should be able to cross-reference this—'

The future is in the stars. The bodies posed under the sky.

She looked around the clearing again. The shadows among the trees, the sound of the falling rain.

'Is there any particular significance of this time of year, Fisher? Astronomically, I mean. I know we're near the autumn equinox.'

She could hear Fisher's breath heavy on the line. 'Well, now you mention it, there are the Taurids.'

The line cut out.

Monica pulled up in front of the Glens Hotel. The place was almost solid black in the darkness, only a couple of rooms in the vast building illuminated.

All through the journey from the MacKays' house to the hotel she'd alternately tried to call Fisher and Hately, with the reception dropping out every time. Finally, her frustration bordering on rage, she'd pulled over when her phone showed a sliver of reception and managed to send a long text message to Hately. She'd requested that they seal off both Paul's and Robert's houses for forensics to conduct a thorough search, test Paul's lager for GHB and begin a search of the woods and lay-by behind Paul's house. All things she was sure Hately would thank her for after her insistence they bring in Don Cameron for questioning.

The main doors to the hotel were still open, and the stuffed bear watched as Monica followed the melancholy sound of traditional Highland fiddle music through the empty ballroom towards the bar.

'Excuse me?' she said.

Muir Maitland turned from his stool. He glanced at the bottle in front of him. Seemed to think for a second about trying to hide it.

'We're closed,' he said finally. Monica caught the slur at the ends of his words. 'Hotel guests only.' He reached for the radio and turned the haunting music down a notch.

'Don't worry. I won't keep you long.'

He blinked, seemed to realise who she was. 'Detective—'

'I take it you heard about Paul MacKay?'

Muir looked back at his glass. In the lights over the bar the whisky was golden like treasure.

'Well. They say what's for you'll not pass you by.' Inevitability. A favourite security blanket against the chaotic nature of existence.

'I doubt Lisa MacKay sees it that way.'

Muir shrugged. 'You wanting a dram?' He reached for his other security blanket. Monica caught his hand before it found the bottle of Royal Lochnagar.

'I'm fine. But you never finished telling me about Don Cameron – gossip, whatever you want to call it?'

Muir's eyes went to the other bottles behind the bar. 'Just that – gossip. What I told you before.' He shook his arm free, searching for the word. 'Jokes. It was jokes. Like people—'

'I know what a joke is. But then two boys are murdered. A man *you* said worked with one of them. And *you* saw the other boy right outside Cameron's work place.'

The colour had drained from Muir's red face. 'I ... just saw that boy. That's all I know,' he said. 'The other stuff, you can ask anyone round here. They'll say the same.'

'I'm asking you though.' Monica leaned in closer. 'You can tell me here, or we can make it formal ...'

Muir ran his hand over his head then wiped it on his knee. He reached for the bottle again. 'My old man told me that the Camerons were involved in things. Back in the 70s, the 80s. Bad things.'

'What kind of bad things?' Monica's voice was low in the wide space of the ballroom. Muir glanced up at her. The words seemed to stick in his throat.

'You've heard of Shona Mackenzie?' Monica nodded. Everyone in the Highlands had. She was a divorcee who had disappeared from a hotel in Aviemore in the 1970s. 'My old man used to work down there, running the hotel. Big parties, celebrities, the skiing. Most glamorous place in the country, they used to say.' Muir went for his glass again. 'Well, my old man, he heard that the Camerons – Don, his father –' Muir looked around the ballroom as if someone might be listening from behind the curtains, and Monica couldn't stop herself from following his eyes '– he heard that it was them who killed her.'

'Why would they kill her?' Monica asked.

Muir rubbed his thumb and forefinger together: *money*. 'Her brother wanted her dead, wanted the family business. Paid them to do it.'

'How did your dad know this?'

He shrugged. 'He knew a lot of people. It used to be that way, the Highlands. Like I say, it's gossip. The old man wasn't a liar though. The way he said it, they'd done other ones too. Some of those unsolved murders you read about.' This time he tapped the side of his head, fingers shaped like a gun. 'Some you don't hear about. The way he told it, they'd done all sorts.' He gestured towards the high windows. The dark miles of mountains and moorlands beyond. 'Lot of places to bury a body out there. Makes you think though.' Monica lifted her head, waiting for him to continue. 'If any of what my old man heard was true, why would Don go leaving those boys out for your lot to find when there's so many good places out in these mountains to put someone when you want them to be forgotten about?'

Wednesday

Chapter 48

Monica watched as the Camerons' croft house in the distance came slowly alive from the dark. Wednesday morning. Five days since Robert's body had been found. Monica tried to calculate how many hours she'd slept since then. Not enough, she decided. *It shows too*, she thought, looking at her reflection in the rearview mirror. The circles under her eyes darker, her skin mottled. Not for the first time Monica found herself asking that uncomfortable early-morning question: why? Why let cases like this one crowd out everything else in her life? Ahead of her own wellbeing – even ahead of Lucy. The unguarded reply her tired mind served up: *Because they mean something, because they're important. More important than being a good mum?*

Monica dismissed the unpleasant thoughts – reminded herself that someone had to do the job, someone had to catch the murderers, the rapists and criminals – and glanced at her phone. Hately had confirmed that a forensics team was on its way to Paul's house, but she'd heard nothing more from Fisher about the meteor. She wondered why Michael Bach still hadn't returned any of her calls. Probably he'd lost interest. Maybe he never even went to Lossiemouth and had blocked her number. It was possible, but somehow it didn't seem to fit.

'Is everything OK? You keep looking at your phone,' Crawford said. He was tensed forward, closer to the windscreen and, in the distance, the house.

Monica shook her head. She was surprised he'd even noticed in his agitated state.

'It's nothing.' She leaned forward herself to peel off her thick coat, too warm in the heated car interior.

Crawford glanced at her suspiciously, but before he could speak figures from the armed unit fanned out across the croft land surrounding the house. Their black uniforms in the weak dawn light made them look ghostly as they faded against the moor.

Monica watched as three of them reached the front door and entered the house. Light glowed from the open doorway, and Monica tensed, almost expecting the sound of a gun going off. She looked at Crawford. He was still crouched forward in anticipation.

Nothing happened. Then a voice over the radio: 'The house is secure. No sign of the target. But his father's here.'

Monica felt the knot tighten in her stomach. *No sign of the target. Where the hell was he then?*

An armed-response vehicle was blocking the entrance to the driveway, so Monica climbed out of the Volvo and jogged along the track towards the house. Hill fog had drifted down over the moor, fragmenting the shapes of the peat hags and the lines of mountains stretching away to the south.

'Why would he run if he's not involved?' Crawford panted at her elbow. 'We should have gone in last night. Hately should have fucking made it happen.'

Monica glanced down at him. 'Just be careful, Crawford.'

He turned to look up at her. His handsome fox-like face twisted. 'Be careful? Did you not hear what they said? He's gone. Disappeared.' Crawford gestured out across the wide landscape. 'He must have guessed, or seen something. Taken off.'

The officer at the door stared at them as they approached. They looked ridiculous: the tall dark woman and the small red-headed man jogging and arguing as if they were family on a day trip to the country. Monica glared and carried on past the officer as Crawford paused to sign them both into the property.

Inside there was a new carpet in the porch and the smell of cooked bacon coming from the kitchen. Niall Souter, head of the armed unit, stepped into the hall just as Monica arrived. He was speaking into a phone, and Monica could tell he was trying hard to keep his voice calm.

'There's no sign of the suspect. The house is clear. The suspect's father is secure in the kitchen. He's elderly and had to be given oxygen. We're expanding the search on to the moor, sir.'

He covered the phone and turned to Monica. 'Can you stay inside the property for now? We've got the go-ahead to continue the operation south on to the moor. One of the guys stepped on a random cement cap out in the garden.' Souter held his hands out to indicate a width of about two feet. 'It seemed quite freshly laid, like it could be covering something.'

Monica nodded as Souter continued walking away down the hall.

'You think it could be evidence?' Crawford asked.

She shrugged. 'I guess we'll find out later.'

The heavy wooden door into the kitchen scraped the flagstones as she pushed it open.

'You'll be the clever ones then?' Roderick Cameron was sitting in a battered wing chair. 'There's some meat left. I offered it to your other boys but they weren't the sort that were interested.'

Cameron was in his eighties, Monica knew that from their research. He looked older though; he looked like he should be dead.

An oxygen canister was propped beside him and he caught Monica's eye. 'I got a fright. That's all. This lot pointing guns everywhere.' He nodded to the armed officer standing beside the stove, a black cap pulled low over his face.

'That must have been a shock,' Monica said. She looked down at the old man's folded hands and noticed something moving. 'What have you got there?'

'This is foxy,' he said as he held the creature up. 'He's just a baby. I found him wandering about at the bottom of the field. Someone must have got his mother. He'll take a bit of meat if you mash it up now.' The fox's fur was still more grey than red. It pushed its face under Cameron's hand. 'I think he got a fright too.'

Monica crouched to sit on the stool beside Roderick Cameron. The man's eyes were grey. Cloudy, but there was still sharpness. She tried to imagine him forty years younger and forty years stronger.

'Do you know the name Shona Mackenzie?' Monica asked. Something passed across Cameron's face. Recognition, then emptiness.

'Can't say I do,' he said finally.

'No?' Monica stared at him. 'What about Owen MacLennan? Does that name mean anything to you?'

'I knew you were going to ask something like that,' Roderick Cameron said. 'A lassie like you.'

'Like me?'

'That's right. One of those. Asking questions, sticking your beak in.' Monica held his gaze. Watched as his face broke into a smile. 'I'm only joking with you, dear. You're just doing your job.'

'But you didn't answer my question,' Monica said.

'Did I not? I don't remember so well now.'

'You don't?' Monica leaned in closer. 'I think you remember quite well. I think you remember a lot. Do you remember what's buried out in your garden, under that cement?'

If he was surprised by her question Cameron didn't show it. 'Who knows what's buried out in these places? My family's been here since before Culloden, they say. There's a lot been put in the ground over the years.'

'What kinds of things?'

Cameron gazed at her for a moment then blew his cheeks out. He looked past her to Crawford. 'Would you pour me a cup of tea, son? This other lad –' he gestured at the armed officer '– he said he couldn't pour me a cup, but you look a good boy.' Crawford shook his head slowly but found the teapot and topped up Roderick Cameron's cup.

'Thanks for that, son. I'm still strong, but in the mornings it takes me a while to get going.' He took a mouthful of the tea. 'That's nice. A dram would be better, but I'd be pushing my luck at that, wouldn't I?' Cameron gave a wheezy laugh.

'What about your son?' Crawford said. 'Don. Where is he?'

'Don? Well he'll be in the hills now, I should think. He's a good lad. But he always had that funny way about him.'

'Which hills would he have gone to? It's important that we find him quickly,' Monica said.

'Well he wouldn't have told me that. Wouldn't have trusted his da with that.'

'Don worked with a boy called Paul MacKay,' Monica said.

'That's right,' Cameron said. He shifted in his seat to face her. 'Young Paul. I remember him now. A good lad.'

'Paul was murdered. A couple of days ago.' Monica's eyes didn't move from Roderick Cameron's face. 'He was tortured then strangled to death.'

'There's some like that,' Cameron said. He met her gaze with his cold, grey eyes. 'Some who have these strange ways about them.'

'What about Don? Did he have that strange way about him?' The old man didn't reply. 'Did he kill Paul?'

Roderick Cameron laughed. 'Why would Don do that to Paul?' He sounded genuinely perplexed. 'Young Paul was a good lad, like a son to Don. They worked together, you see. It broke Don's heart to hear what happened.'

'Why did Don run then. If he wasn't involved?' Crawford asked.

Cameron looked up at him, stared at Crawford as if he'd just asked the most ridiculous question. 'I should think he's out doing what your lot should be doing. Getting a hold of whatever piece of filth it was did that to young Paul.'

Chapter 49

Monica watched the forensic tent being set up over the cement cap in the garden. The cap seemed to cover a hole that was about the width of the top of a wheelie bin. Wide enough to hide evidence in. Wide enough to cover a buried body.

'What was that about Shona Mackenzie?' Crawford asked. He stepped away from the tent and stared up at her.

'Probably nothing,' Monica said. 'Just gossip I heard from the guy at the hotel.'

'And there was no need to share it with me?'

She glanced down at his flushing face. The spitting rain was already gathering on his red hair, forming fat droplets. 'Everyone in the Highlands has a theory about what happened to her. We're not investigating a historic case; I was just trying to unsettle him.'

'*Very* effective.'

She raised an eyebrow and smiled. 'Petulance doesn't suit you, Crawford.'

He turned away to look out at the moor. They stood in silence as the forensic team worked away.

'Do you think he genuinely believed what he said about Don?' Crawford asked.

'I don't know. And would he really know if Don was involved in the murders?'

'How long will it take to track him down?'

Monica shook her head and looked out into the mist. People went missing in the Scottish Highlands. Went missing and were never found. 'It depends when he left. He's a gamekeeper so he'll know the country well. There are ten thousand square miles in the Highlands. If he left six hours ago and covered three miles an hour that's already eighteen miles in any direction. That's a big circle on a map, and that's assuming he's on foot.'

'What a fucking mess,' Crawford said, hands on hips. 'When the media get hold of this they're going to destroy us. We should have gone in last night – Hately should have demanded it.'

Monica heard the sound of a cough from the open doorway behind them. Crawford spun round, expecting the detective superintendent to be standing there, but although the suit was well cut, inside it was DC Fisher. Staring primly at them from behind his glasses.

'DI Kennedy. There's something you need to see.'

They followed him down the corridor to Don Cameron's bedroom. It was neat like the rest of the house, spartan even. Just a single bed in the corner and a wardrobe. From the corridor Fisher pointed at a red sweatshirt lying folded on the bed.

'I found that tucked underneath the pillow. It matches a sweatshirt Paul was wearing in one of the pictures his mother sent us.' Fisher held up the photo on his phone for them to see.

Monica leaned closer to look at the image. She started to say something. Afterwards she could never remember what, no matter how hard she tried, because at that moment an explosion of gunfire tore through the house.

She rocked forward, instinctively covering her face. Fisher was closest to the kitchen door but Crawford reacted first and pushed past him. He was already in the kitchen doorway as another bang exploded and Monica felt a blow to her face before she fell forward.

Monica tasted blood. She wiped her face and looked at the blood and fragments of bone on the palm of her hand. At first she assumed Roderick Cameron had put a gun to his head and found a way out. But when she looked up he was still sitting very much alive in his seat – with a shotgun pointed at her head.

She then heard the noise and her mind registered that Crawford was screaming.

'Don't!' She held up a hand to Cameron. 'Don't.'

He cocked the shotgun awkwardly with his arthritic hands, but then Fisher landed on him. Their bodies connected with a soft *humph* and the chair fell backwards against the wall. The gun went off again and clumps of ceiling fell with a spray of plaster.

Then there was silence.

Crawford sat half up, his legs bicycling against the stone floor. He looked at her, his face white, his eyes wild. He held up an arm – hanging off at the elbow. Dark blood was pumping out across the floor and the mess of bone, flesh and ceiling debris. Monica moved then. She grabbed his arm and pushed it to his chest, pressing down on the wound to stop the bleeding.

'Don't look at it, Crawford.' She gripped him close, her arm tight round his neck so his face was buried into her armpit. His hot breath pushed through the thin cotton fabric of her shirt. 'You're going to be fine, Crawford. You're going to be fine.'

'You see him?' Roderick Cameron was struggling beneath Fisher's knees, which straddled his chest. 'You see him?' he repeated, nodding at the dead body of the armed officer on the floor. 'That would have been you.' His voice broke into crazy laughter.

'Fucking shut him up, Fisher!'

But the old man's laughter echoed in the blood-stained kitchen.

Chapter 50

Michael fell a long way through the dark night from the top of the Rose Street Car Park. Five storeys to the pavement below. *The man at Nichol's hostel was right*, Michael thought as the cold air rushed past. You were destined to take that fall. He tensed for the impact that would destroy his body.

Instead he woke up.

He was still lying on that wooden floor and still bleeding. He'd been there for days. Centuries. With the sound of the men laughing at him. He tried to move, but the floor was soft and he was sinking into it.

Michael panicked and opened his eyes. He saw that he was in a bed, in a darkened room. The pain went off in his face and he crumpled. Slowly the memory came back to him. *Monica Kennedy?* The expression on Charlie Bartle's face changing to recognition. Then uncertainty.

The next memory was of being dragged across the floor. Then the feel of wet concrete, the rain falling through pink street lights. He remembered hot blood running down his throat and more time passing, then faces, voices.

Kids in blazers. Nichol Morgan. Michael's father. They all watched at the back of the crowd. Solemn in the rain, like mourners at their own funerals. The grey sky gone black, and another boy watching. One without a face. A brother Michael had almost forgotten about. A brother he'd buried deep, deep down.

Dad? Joseph? I'm sorry. He'd tried to stand. He tried to run towards them. The overwhelming feeling of loss and panic when he realised that he couldn't move. That they were drifting away.

Then the sound of an ambulance siren. Nichol. The kid was mouthing something to him. Words and letters that Michael couldn't quite make out. Michael reached out to him. He realised he was back in the hospital bed. *What was he saying?* He reached out again but fell back through the bed and into unconsciousness, where he followed his long-dead brother down corridors, corridors they shouldn't be in, as Nichol watched on.

'You can go in the morning.' The woman's accent was clipped. 'Your eyeball wasn't dislodged, which makes things simpler. We pinned your cheekbone with a plate, but it's important you don't blow your nose hard or apply pressure to your face until it's started healing.' The surgeon spoke like someone who had drilled metal plates into a lot of faces. 'Anything you'd like to ask me?' she added.

Could he smoke? What would happen if he blew his nose hard? But before Michael could form a coherent question the surgeon had smiled and walked away, her rubber shoes squeaking on the polished floor.

Michael pushed himself up against the pillows and looked around the small ward. An old man in the bed opposite stared fixedly at him. The man's skin was tight like a mask. Michael turned away to the window. Outside it was dark, and the lights of the city were burning as a distant, different reality from which he had been removed. The lights slid and blurred. Michael blinked and realised that he was still barely conscious, on his way down to another drugged sleep.

But a fragment of his dream came back to him. Nichol. His mouth moving at a fevered speed. Faster than seemed possible, yet sounds were still coming out somehow. Slowly Michael put the sounds together. They made a name: *Zandy Allen*. Shouted over and over: *Zandy Allen Zandy Allen Zandy Allen Zandy Allen Zandy Allen*. The words seemed to fill the ward. It seemed that the old man on the bed opposite had joined in, the sounds pouring from his mouth: *Zandy Allen Zandy Allen Zandy Allen Zandy Allen*.

Michael remembered the video of the graveyard. The phone that he'd taken from Eddie's flat. Did the dream mean something? In his disorientated state it seemed like it had to have some deep significance.

There's something else on the phone besides the video. The idea came fully formed into Michael's mind with the weight of revelation.

He looked slowly around the ward, attempting to block out the sounds as he tried to recall what he'd done with the phone. A dazed panic rose because he couldn't remember. *Find it!* his internal voice screamed at him. *You have to find it!* There was a cupboard beside his bed. It seemed like the obvious place to look. Michael leaned over and pulled it open roughly, like a drunk in an unfamiliar house. It was empty.

The nausea came on strong then and he thought maybe Bartle had taken it. Michael could remember someone going through the pockets of his jacket but he couldn't remember if Nichol's phone had been taken. He tried to stand, but his feet wouldn't hold him and he slipped and fell back against the bed. Something was pulling at his arm, and he saw a tube sticking out when he looked down. As he pulled it out a buzzer went off somewhere.

'Fucking thing.' He threw it down and blood squirted across the floor. He tried to stand again, but fell on to his hands and knees.

There was shouting now from down the corridor. *Fucking thing.* He realised for the first time that there was a something on his face. He tried to pull it off, and the pain came on like an alarm screaming through his body.

The sound of laughter. Hacking up from broken ribs and rotten mouths. Dark eyes on his back and an open mouth waiting. Michael started laughing himself. He lifted his head and realised there was a plastic bag beside the bed. *My clothes,* he realised slowly.

He dug into it. Ripped it open and pulled the clothes out across the floor. *Where is it?*

'Mr Bach. Michael!' Someone was shouting. The laughter was louder too. Overpoweringly loud.

Michael found his dad's old jacket and went through the pockets like a jealous husband. *Empty, empty, empty, empty.* 'Where the fuck is it?'

He felt the needle going in just as he remembered.

Henry. He'd given the phone to Henry to check. How could he forget? The laughter made more sense now. He tried to hold on to it all: Nichol's words from the dream, Henry and the phone. But it was hard. The noises faded and the colours blurred as Michael slid away from consciousness.

Chapter 51

It was later. Michael slowly became aware of the bed and the rest of the ward. There was something else. Someone sitting beside him. The smell of strong perfume cut through like smelling salts.

He opened his eyes and saw a woman by his bed. She was dressed like a Highland seer in long dark clothes. She had dark hair and dark skin that was prematurely aged yet strangely beautiful. Like a cracked old oil portrait.

A fragment from a dream. She spoke: 'Do you know who I am?'

'You've got the wrong ward,' he replied, but as he was saying the words Michael caught the family resemblance and realised that he did know who the woman was. There was only one person it could be. 'You're Eddie's sister. Charlie's mother. Jean Bartle. Eddie warned you that I'd spoken to him?'

'Eddie's a bastard, but he's still family.' Her voice was worn rough.

'I met your son.' Michael gestured at the dressing on his face. The words came out sounding strangely garbled.

'That wasn't Charlie. You started it. You hit first – those boys are fighters, what did you expect?' Her voice was rising, anger masking fear. Michael sank back on the bed, knowing what she said was true and cursing himself for his stupidity. 'He *saved* you. They would have killed you. If you tell the police it was Charlie, they'll have him back in the jail.'

Michael reached out and caught her thin arm. 'Nichol went to see him. He disappeared the next day.'

'He went to Charlie to ask for money. Charlie gave it to him. A thousand. That was the last he saw of him. You can say what you like about my son, but he's not a liar.'

'He gave Nichol the money, just like that?' Michael said. It seemed unlikely, given everything he knew about Bartle.

She looked down, looked up again. Her dark eyes meeting his. 'Charlie owed Nichol.'

'Why?'

'Christine got the jail because of Charlie. Because she wouldn't turn on him, they both got the jail. She could've spoken to the police. She could've blamed everything on him, but she didn't. Nichol ended up in care because of it.'

Michael looked away. The pain in his cheek and the nausea came on again. The sweat ran across his forehead in prickly drops. *Vomit. Blow your eyeball out across her lap.* He took a deep breath and closed his eyes.

'Charlie never hit you. You know that's true. He gave Nichol the money to help him.' There was a pleading edge to her voice.

'Why did he need the money? What was he running from?'

'He never told Charlie. Sometimes it's better not to know. If Nichol wanted you looking for him he would have told you why he'd gone.'

'You know where he is. Eddie told me you'd know,' Michael said.

'Eddie's a bastard. Just like you're a fucking bastard,' Jean said. Her words loud in the quiet ward.

'What about Nichol. What's he?'

'The boy's alive, I know he's alive.'

'And I should just believe you?' Michael said, still struggling to form his words properly.

She looked over her shoulder at the double doors out of the ward, then leaned closer so her dark eyes were level with his. 'I'll tell you, but if you speak to the police about Charlie it'll come back to you seven times over.'

Michael stared at her face, the deep lines where her brow furrowed. Part of him didn't believe that she was actually there in front of him.

'Swear it,' she hissed. 'Swear it on your father and on your brother. They'll be wandering down those corridors for ever. They'll never find peace if you lie.' Her voice was rough as cracked leather.

'How do you know about my brother?'

She didn't reply but moved closer so her breath was hot on his face. Michael twisted away and the pain returned like pliers on a broken tooth.

'Jesus! I swear.'

She put a hand on his arm. 'They follow me sometimes. They tell me things.'

'What are you talking about?' Michael said as a feeling of panic washed over him.

'They helped me when I was just a wee girl. My brother, Eddie and my dad used to get hold of me. I'd go in my head and they took me away. I could never get them to stop. My dad said that I was that filthy – that inside I'd never be clean. But they came and kept me safe. They took me with them.'

She grabbed Michael's arm again with both her hands this time, gripping hard so her fingernails broke his skin.

'They still show me. The dark one does. I open the door and he's there in the dark waiting. He told me that you were bringing trouble for Charlie. He told me that Nichol's alive. There's two of the boys down there in the fridges. A man's had his hands on them. Down their throats and it's the end of them. But Nichol's still alive.'

She's insane. She's actually insane, Michael thought as Jean Bartle stared at him, her pupils dilated.

'The boy doesn't want to be found. You've had your warnings, and he's watching you now. There'll be enough bad coming your way when you give yourself over. Enough so you wished you'd listened to us.'

For a second neither of them moved. Finally she let go of his arm and stood up.

'They don't lie. If you keep looking for Nichol it'll be the end of you.' She stared at him for a second longer. Then turned and walked out of the ward.

Michael blinked as the room blurred at the edges. He tried to understand what he'd just heard, until he wondered if she'd been there at all. If it hadn't all been a dream inside a dream.

Chapter 52

Even with the drugs Michael couldn't sleep. Thoughts and memories from deep down, from a different life, kept rising up. No matter how hard he tried to stop them. Like some awful leviathan that had been biding its time until he was weak.

His mother's face. *Joseph's still not home. It's not like him. Joseph's still not home. Why did you leave him, Michael? Why?*

Michael squeezed his eyes closed and tried to lose the memory of those words. Of that voice. He heard the sound of feet on the floor again. They hesitated then stopped by his bed. Michael kept his eyes tight shut, afraid that this time it would be his dead mother. This time she would really tell him what she'd always thought: *It's your fault, Michael. It's all your fault.*

'You don't look well.' It was a woman's voice. With a hint of an Inverness accent – the best English in Britain, they used to say. Nothing like his mother's hard Lowland tones.

Michael blinked as his eyes adjusted to the dim light. Time ran strangely in the silent ward. He guessed it was late, or early.

'I thought maybe I was imagining you,' he said slowly.

DI Kennedy sat down on the chair by the bed. 'I'm pretty sure I'm real. Barely.'

He took in her dark hair and pale skin. She was too big for the chair she was sitting in. In a weird way it was good to see her after everything that had happened.

He blinked again. There was a mark on her neck. It almost looked like blood.

'A hospital, and the healthiest drink you can buy is a can of Coke. Did you ever feel sicker from just being in a hospital? That smell?'

She slid a can across the bedside cabinet top towards him. The room was strangely quiet. Just the occasional beep from a heart-rate monitor and the strange intimacy of the hospital ward. Michael opened the can. He was grateful for the cold drink, though he would have preferred a cigarette.

'What happened?' she asked.

'I slipped over in a pub. At least that's what they tell me.'

'An abandoned pub in the Marsh?' DI Kennedy paused and assessed his face. She added two words: 'Charlie Bartle?'

'How did you know?' Michael felt like he should be embarrassed but couldn't seem to gather the emotion through the fug of medication.

'People see things. I know things. You were asking questions about Nichol?'

'Something like that.' Michael tried to tell her what had happened but it wasn't quite coherent. Even in his own mind. 'The box I dug up at the graveyard, it was a kind of funeral for their friend Zandy Allen. Officially he committed suicide. Alan had seen Nichol talking to Charlie Bartle. I put two and two together ...'

'It couldn't have been Bartle. He's a brute, but not in that way.'

'You know him? His mother came here,' Michael said. He was still too disorientated to even be surprised by the idea.

DI Kennedy stared at the ground. Her voice was a monotone. 'One of my friends – an old friend from school – she went out with him. He used to hit her. He almost killed her.' Her hand went to her face then dropped to her lap. 'I set him up. He was in things up to his neck anyway. I just made sure it would stick. I had to sacrifice Bartle, or he would have killed her. Sacrifice myself even because people talk, don't they? Once people hear that kind of thing about you in the force ...' She glanced up at him. 'I never meant for Nichol's mum – Chris – to be there.'

'You never meant for her to go to jail?'

DI Kennedy stared at him but didn't reply.

'That's why you gave me the laptop,' he pushed. 'Because you felt guilty?'

'I gave you the laptop because I wanted to help you find Nichol. I was scared of what was on there. There was a tiny chance that he'd found out about his mum. If anyone could prove what I'd done I'd go to jail. I've got a daughter ... I never knew Chris was in on any of it. She didn't deserve it. No matter what else she'd done.'

'She's done plenty,' Michael said. 'I've heard about it from Nichol. Same as Charlie Bartle has done plenty – by the sound of it.'

Her pale face looked almost grey, with heavy dark circles under her eyes. Her black hair hung untidily down onto her shoulders. She was wearing a fresh white T-shirt with the crease marks from the wrapper still visible down its front.

'I'll have to answer for it some time,' she said finally.

He realised then that her eyes were red, as if she'd been crying.

'Anyway. Fuck it.' She coughed and wiped a hand over her face. 'My colleague, DC Crawford, he got shot today. They're operating on him at the moment, but it looks like he could lose an arm.'

Michael nodded. He could hear the horror in her voice and knew that he should respond in some kind of empathetic way. But the sedatives in his system removed the chance of that connection.

Thankfully she didn't seem to notice and kept talking. 'We found evidence linking another man with one of the victims. It seems like he could be involved somehow. But there was nothing that linked him to Nichol.'

Michael nodded again. He was still trying to form his thoughts into something coherent.

Before he could manage it, DI Kennedy stood up and cleared her throat. Clearing away whatever moment of informality had existed between them.

'I came to tell you to forget about finding Nichol. If Owen MacLennan and Don Cameron took Nichol, then the boy's already dead. If they didn't, then Nichol doesn't want to be found.'

Michael started to say something. About Zandy Allen. About needing to see the results of his autopsy. But she cut him off.

'Believe me, this is going to get messy. The media are all over it already. The last thing anyone needs is you asking questions. You're lucky to be alive.'

Michael tried to speak. But she was already walking away.

Chapter 53

Monica stood at the sink and splashed cold water across her face again. She was sure she could still taste the flesh and bone from Crawford's arm that had sprayed across her face, into her mouth. She gagged when she remembered the room, then dry-heaved, her body needing to expel the memory of Crawford's screaming. The stink of iron and cordite. The sticky blood across the floor.

Finally she wiped her mouth with a shaking hand and stared at herself in the mirror under the flickering fluorescent light of the hospital toilet. A look of stupefied bemusement on her face after a day wandering the hospital's corridors, waiting for news, somehow knowing instinctively it was going to be bad.

A feeling of disgust rose from the pit of her stomach and she turned away. How could she ever look herself in the eye again after she'd been so easily tricked by Roderick Cameron? Playing the couthy old man. *You'll be the clever ones.* Outsmarted by the goblin in the fairy tale, the sawn-off shotgun hidden down the side of his wing chair. A mistake. A fuck-up that had cost one man his life, that had cost her junior colleague too. The one she was supposed to look out for.

She remembered the journey back from the croft in the medical helicopter. Holding Crawford's good hand in hers while the paramedics worked. Saying the same useless words over and over: *You're going to be fine, Connor. Everything's going to be fine.* Words that she didn't even believe herself.

Monica remembered the surgeon's face when she had almost grabbed him by the throat. 'With injuries like this the bone can be obliterated. There's a high risk of infection. Sometimes it's best to remove what's left of the arm and prepare the stump for a prosthetic.' Said with an impassive expression behind his thin glasses. As if he were talking about disposing of some useless household object.

'No!' Monica's voice echoing down the corridor as she'd reached for him. Hately had grabbed at her arm in horror as she screamed at the surgeon, 'You won't prepare it for a prosthetic. You'll fucking fix it – or else you'll get someone in here who can. You're not cutting his arm off.'

She shook her head at the memory of losing control like that. Like Lucy would have done when she was two years old. As if wailing at the unfairness of reality had ever helped anyone.

Monica dried her face then screwed the paper towel into a ball. She walked out of the toilet into the deserted corridor.

She looked up at the sound of a man's footsteps. It took her a moment to realise that she recognised him. Had she somehow wandered down into the morgue?

Dr Dolohov tilted his head. He didn't need to ask the question.

'Roger Martin from the armed response unit died at the scene. DC Crawford survived. It looks like he'll lose his arm.'

'I'm very sorry,' Dolohov said. A moment's silence filled the corridor.

'He's being cared for at least. I suppose that's more than some people have.'

*

The incident room was almost empty. The focus of the investigation had shifted west now, to apprehending Don Cameron.

Fisher was sitting alone at a computer screen. He looked up as Monica approached. It was the first time they'd seen each other since the croft early that morning. He removed his glasses. Without them he seemed older, somehow more intelligent, Monica thought. He had changed out of the light blue shirt he'd been wearing earlier and was now in a standard black police jumper. Presumably his shirt had been sprayed with blood and taken as evidence like Monica's own shirt and trousers.

'How's DC Crawford? I heard they were operating.' He glanced past her. In the distance the lights of the hospital were visible in the grey evening sky.

'You know as much as me then,' Monica said. She shrugged in the badly fitting man's jumper that one of the female officers had bought for her from Primark as a stopgap.

'I didn't think you'd be in. Hately said you'd need some time off,' Fisher said. 'I got one of the guys to bring your car back across. You could go home and I could keep you posted if anything major develops?'

Monica's hand went to her face, still that taste of blood. 'I'm fine.'

'Why don't you spend some time with your daughter. It's Lucy, isn't it?'

'How do you know my daughter's name?' Monica had said it before she could stop herself. The horror over what had happened to Crawford passing so easily to paranoia. She really was close to losing control.

'I'm sorry. I must have heard you say it the other day. I didn't ...' Sudden panic in his voice: your worst nightmare – you've upset the boss.

'It's OK, I didn't mean to say that, Fisher.' She pulled a desk chair out and sat down, her legs and arms heavy, feeling every one of the forty-four years of their lives.

'What happened was … well … I just can't stop playing it over in my head,' Fisher said.

'I'm sorry.'

Fisher coughed and bent to clean his glasses. 'It's OK, I understand.'

Monica spotted the photograph of the black stone on Fisher's desk. She pointed to it, glad to have something else to talk about. To forget that taste in her mouth. Even if it was just for a moment. 'You never finished telling me about the Taurids,' Monica said, referring to their phone conversation of the previous night.

'I didn't, did I,' Fisher said with a forced laugh. 'The Taurids are a meteor stream that pass close to the earth at certain times of the year – right now is one of those times.'

'What about our meteor?' Monica pointed to the photograph again. 'Have you had any luck with the origin?'

'Actually I have. Just this afternoon. I would have called, but …' He shrugged. 'The chemical compound fits with part of a meteorite that entered the earth's atmosphere twenty years ago. It impacted in Australia.'

'Australia?'

'Yes. Parts of it were recovered from the desert there.'

'Do we have a list of buyers?' Monica asked.

'Unfortunately not,' Fisher said. 'It was split up into hundreds of pieces. A lot of them were sold pre-Internet. I'm tracking the online sales, but it seems a lot of the parts were sold unrecorded.'

Monica nodded. 'Where's Hately?'

'Still in a meeting. He was with the families earlier. It sounded ...' Fisher's voice trailed off. 'Anyway. There's a –' he cleared his throat '– crap storm going off. As you can imagine. Don Cameron on the loose. Armed and dangerous ...' A look passed over his face, and Monica knew that he was replaying the scene again in his imagination.

'Have we recovered anything else from the croft?' The first question she could think of to keep the sound of Crawford's screaming out of her mind.

Fisher looked up then shook his head slowly. 'Just the sweater.'

'So nothing solid? No ...' She hesitated and tried to think of a word to describe what could have been used to inflict the bite marks on the boys' bodies. 'No weapons. No DNA evidence?'

'Just the sweater. Paul's mother confirmed it was his,' Fisher replied.

'And Don worked with him. You heard the old man saying how much Don liked Paul. Maybe he had a crush on him and stole it? Or maybe Paul accidentally left the jumper in Don's van?' Monica said, trying out alternative theories to see how they fitted.

'Why would Roderick Cameron kill a man in cold blood if not to protect Don somehow?' Fisher asked.

'I think he did it because he could. He had the gun so he did it. Has the pit under the cement in the garden been excavated yet?' Monica asked.

Fisher shook his head. 'The concrete isn't covering a pit, it's a solid block, only about two feet deep. They think it's been set for a while. Probably too long ago to be connected with Paul or Robert.'

'So all we really have to link Don Cameron to MacLennan, to the murders, is circumstantial evidence,' Monica said, but she thought, *This feels good*. Focusing on the details like a puzzle. Like it's the only thing that matters in the world, and everything else is peripheral.

'That and his father shot two police officers,' Fisher said.

'What about forensics from Paul's house? Do we have anything back yet? Have they checked outside Robert's window for any signs of forced entry or indication that he was carried down?'

Fisher shook his head slowly, but Monica caught the look passing over his face. Realised that there was something he wasn't telling her. 'What is it?'

He hesitated then cleared his throat again. 'I've started going through Paul MacKay's emails,' he said finally. 'There's some weird stuff in there.'

'Weird how?' Monica wondered for a moment why he'd waited until now to tell her this.

'Someone was pretending to be Paul's father. Masquerading, however you want to describe it. He'd set up an email account as William White. That's Paul's dad's name. He'd put up photos, that type of thing. It looked quite legit. He persuaded Paul not to go on holiday with Lisa, said that he wanted Paul to come and live with him again down south. He'd sort Paul out with a job in London. But it was to be *their secret* for now. You know?'

'Manipulating him,' Monica said under her breath. 'Lisa was convinced it was Don who'd persuaded Paul not to go with her. Paul told her he had to stay and work with Don. That must have been an excuse.'

'The last email exchange was the day before Paul disappeared.' Fisher clicked on an email and started reading. '"You know how much I've missed you, Paul. How much I've had to sacrifice for my choices. I want to change things for you. I want to bring you home. I know you want it too."'

'Have you spoken to Paul's real father?' Monica asked.

Fisher nodded. 'He lives in Oxford. He says he hasn't spoken to Paul in weeks. I'm checking his alibis, but he says he was at a work conference over the days Paul went missing, so it should be straightforward to confirm.' He nodded again and then actually had the audacity to smile. Monica stared back at the young detective constable and for a moment felt ice-cold hatred for him. Crawford could have been killed, his arm probably gone, and here Fisher was, smiling like he'd won first fucking prize at his high school computer science club.

Monica swallowed and glanced away, summoning up every ounce of goodwill she could muster to control her anger. She reminded herself that Fisher had been in the room with Roderick Cameron too, that maybe this was his way of coping – by proving he was a competent detective.

'Robert Wright's mother had recently left,' Monica said softly. 'Is there any evidence that Don Cameron could have sent those emails?'

'There's none that shows he couldn't have,' Fisher said, putting his glasses back on.

'That's not what I asked.' Monica closed her eyes and inhaled slowly, wishing for a moment she was anywhere but here with bloody Fisher. She thought of Lucy, of their home, of her small warm body. She exhaled and pushed her hands hard against her eyes.

'There was no laptop or PC at the croft house,' Fisher continued, his voice faltering against her clear anger. 'It's one of the sixteen per cent of UK households without an Internet connection. It doesn't mean he couldn't have taken the laptop with him. Or used a phone to send the emails. You know how difficult it is to pin these things down if people are careful.'

Monica nodded at this. 'It doesn't fit neatly though, does it? With what we know of Don Cameron or Owen MacLennan.'

Fisher glanced around the quiet room then lowered his voice. 'You think Roderick Cameron's telling the truth? That Don Cameron's innocent? That he's gone looking for whoever killed Paul? How could he have known that we were going to arrest him, though? How could he know who killed Paul?'

Monica pictured the dark lay-by. The shotgun shells on the ground. The broken glass. 'It could be a coincidence that Cameron headed off when he did. It's possible he saw what happened to Paul. Maybe he tried to stop it. Maybe he saw the driver of the van and knows who the other killer is?' Even as she was speaking Monica realised how far-fetched it sounded.

Fisher stared at her for a second. 'What if—' But before he could finish the door swung open behind them.

Hately looked crumpled. Both his eyes were fixed on the ground. Slowly he lifted his head and cleared his throat.

'We've been sidelined. We're receiving "assistance with the investigation" from Police Scotland, but they're taking it over.'

The anger that Monica had been resisting finally reared its head. Her body tensed with rage and she stood, so wild and furious for a moment she didn't know what her hands, rolled tight into fists, would do. 'Why? We know the case. It'll take them days to get up to speed!' she shouted.

Hately didn't reply. Instead he laid a tablet down on the desk in front of them. On it was the headline COPS LET KILLER RUN.

'Lisa MacKay went to the media,' he said. 'She blamed us for letting Cameron escape. We've lost the investigation.'

Monica scraped at her hair, unable to believe what she was hearing. She scanned down the webpage. 'This basically says Don Cameron's a murderer. It's prejudicial! Even if he is involved he could claim he's not going to get a fair trial.'

'Forget it, Kennedy,' Hately barked. 'You're off the investigating team.'

'For fuck's sake, sir, we're still gathering new evidence! Focusing everything on Cameron's a mistake. Tell him, Fisher! About those emails ...' She turned to Fisher for support but he stared down at the keyboard in front of him and didn't speak.

'Go home,' Hately said. 'As of now this investigation is about finding Don Cameron. Plain and simple. You're not fit, DI Kennedy, after everything with DC Crawford. It's finished.'

Chapter 54

The Watcher

The pictures on the television showed a croft house on a moor, police cars around the house and grey mountains rising behind. The scene cut to a news conference. A woman who closely resembled her son. She was talking about the police. Crying about how the big woman detective and her team had messed it all up and let the terrible Don Cameron go free.

The man who was watching smiled at that. Seeing the woman make a fool of herself when really it was her fault that anything had happened to her son in the first place. If Paul hadn't drifted into his gravitational pull it would only have been someone else that did it eventually.

He watched a moment longer to see if there was anything more about DI Kennedy – the one who'd come looking for him. But the story ended.

He switched the television off and lay back to stare up through the glass roof to the night. To the stars. He imagined those objects moving through space. Coming closer and closer. Soon they would be here again, drawn to him. He let his mind drift back almost twenty years, to another time when those same objects were approaching. Years after the old woman and George. He had followed the voices from those stones to a desert in a different country, a different continent.

The young man had said something. His arms were propped back behind him and his feet pointed towards the embers of the fire. He spoke again: 'So many stars. The universe.' He nodded to the magnificent night sky above the desert then took another mouthful from the bottle.

The watcher had observed closely how the alcohol affected his companion over their days together. How his movements became jerky. How his accent became rough. He pieced those fragments together. The fractured upbringing. The inter-rupted education. The sectioning for mental health problems. The drug use. A story that would tell itself to any interested party.

He caught that scent of neglect he enjoyed so much. Somehow there again, in that desert. Following on somehow – closer than ever before as he turned the black stone over in his hand.

'Do you think . . .?' The young man glanced over at the *klick whirr* sound as the camera started up.

'Do I think?' replied the watcher, his voice wavering as he felt the beginnings of that excitement. His blood running hot in the cold desert air, the anticipation so thick he could barely speak.

Overhead the first streak of light crossed the night sky. The young man leaned back. He really was quite drunk and didn't notice the beginning of the meteor shower they had come to watch. 'Do you think ... Do you think that the future is in the stars?' As if it were the most profound question. He took another mouthful from the bottle.

Slowly the watcher stood, feeling his legs shake under him. Trying hard to keep his breathing under control as he picked up the small boulder that he'd carefully selected earlier. It was around the size of an old portable television or a microwave.

There was another streak of light, followed by a cluster. The young man shouted, then pointed in childlike delight. 'You're right! I've never seen anything like it!'

The watcher lifted the rock and threw it down on to the young man's head. He fell forward, moaning as his arms and legs spasmed, scraping at the dirt with his fingers. His mouth open in a comical mess.

The watcher might have laughed if it hadn't been so counter to how he had seen this moment play out in all his imaginings. Instead he swore, turned his victim over. The young man's eyes had taken on a strange unfocused glaze and in a ridiculous slurred voice he said, 'What happened?' Holding his arms up in a gesture of resistance.

The watcher quickly retrieved the rock and flung it down again. On to the weak lower part of the face this time.

Finally the young man stopped moving. The watcher glanced over at the camera to check that it was running as he gathered himself and prepared for those special movements.

Chapter 55

Michael swallowed the whisky and wished he had one of the cats with him for company. He resolved to drive up to the croft just as soon as the pain subsided a little. He'd walked out of the hospital some time in the early evening, through the dark city and back to his flat.

The voice of the radio newscaster echoed around the empty room: '… suspect has been named as Donald Cameron. He is considered extremely dangerous and should not be approached.' Michael turned the radio down so it was barely audible. He took another swallow of the whisky and felt it burn his throat as he ran over what Monica Kennedy had told him again: *If Owen MacLennan and Don Cameron took Nichol, then the boy's already dead. If they didn't, then Nichol doesn't want to be found.*

Maybe it was true. Maybe it was as simple as the kid just deciding to go. To try his luck somewhere else. Get on a train and keep going. There wasn't exactly a lot holding him to the world. A few friends, some family who didn't seem too bothered about him.

Not a lot. But more than Michael himself had. He didn't dispute this unpleasant dose of reality, instead he damped it down with another mouthful of the whisky. *What now?* Another thought. Now he had to forget about finding Nichol. Anita was probably right: he was motivated by misplaced guilt. A childhood memory driving him to look for things that weren't there, to invent connections. Michael put a hand to his face. It could have been worse, it could have been a lot worse. He could take this as a wake-up call. He'd had a few difficult years but maybe he could get his life back on track?

An unfamiliar noise echoed through the flat. *The doorbell?* The only person Michael could imagine coming to check on him was James Clarke. He shifted on the mattress. The bell rang again. He knew Michael was there: he'd probably phoned the hospital and discovered he had discharged himself. Michael knew how dogged his colleague could be – could easily imagine James calling the police to open the door.

Reluctantly Michael stood up and slid the bottle of whisky round the side of the mattress. He threw the door open. 'Melissa?'

The girl who wasn't really called Melissa. When he'd met her at the bridge she'd looked different: younger, frightened. She glanced up with wide eyes at the dressing on his face. The cold air from the street hit Michael and he realised how drunk he was.

'It looks worse than it is,' he said. He wasn't sure if that was true because he hadn't looked in a mirror yet.

'It looks awful.'

Michael nodded. 'I'm sorry, I should have called you. I didn't find out anything useful about Nichol.' He was careful with the pronunciation of his words. He shrugged, his legs slightly unsteady, and he hoped she'd leave. She didn't make any sign of going, though, and finally he said, 'Would you like to come in? I was just about to make coffee.'

Melissa turned and looked back down the steps to the road. For a moment Michael thought she was going to walk away, but instead she went past him into the flat.

'Sorry about the state of the place. I'm in the process of selling it.'

Michael made coffee and brought it through to the living room. He noticed that from where she was sitting on the floor the bottle of whisky was visible, tucked at the side of the mattress. He stopped and pointed at the bottle. 'Did you notice that?'

Melissa nodded. 'It doesn't matter, though.'

'I don't normally drink . . .' He pointed to his face then found a cigarette and lit it.

'I like your flat. I'd like somewhere like this,' Melissa said.

'I used to live here with someone, a while ago.' He shrugged again and tipped what was left of the glass of whisky into his coffee. 'It didn't work out. How did you know I was here anyway?'

'I sort of tracked you down. Everyone was saying that someone had killed a social worker. I thought—'

'It's not your fault. I tried to find him, but it seems like he just left.'

Neither of them spoke. The smoke from their cigarettes mixed and lingered like a dirty perfume.

'You never told me your real name,' Michael said.

'I hate my real name. It's really old-fashioned.'

'I won't laugh.'

'It's Margaret.'

'Margaret.' He rolled the name over his tongue. 'It could be worse.'

'"It could be worse!"' She threw her head back. 'That's not empathetic. I read about being a social worker on the careers website. It says you need to have high levels of integrity and empathy.'

Michael splashed more whisky into the mug. 'Sorry. I've hardly slept.'

'Just don't call me Margaret.'

'OK.'

'Why did you decide to be a social worker?' The question hung with the smoke. Michael went looking for an evasion but for once the truth drifted up more easily.

'I had a brother. His name was Joseph.' The word was dry and strange in Michael's mouth. 'He died when I was a kid, and I thought it was my fault. We were walking home from school. There was a river, and we weren't supposed to go there without an adult. He wanted to go anyway. I said I wouldn't so he went on his own.' Michael reached for the bottle. 'He was missing for six weeks. Everyone was looking for him; there were things in the newspapers, the police everywhere. When they found him …' Michael remembered the blue lights of the police cars, the dark skies and the feeling of the world drifting for ever into shadow at the funeral. 'When they found him, his body was … It wasn't him any more. He'd been in the water – you change after that length of time.' Michael glanced at Melissa. She met his eyes. 'Anyway, fuck it. We never spoke about him after that. It sounds … I'd almost forgotten about him. A suppressed memory or something. I can't even remember what he looked like.' For an awful moment Michael thought he was going to break down crying. He took a long pull on his whisky-laced coffee to hush the feeling.

Melissa crossed the room and sat beside him on the mattress. The smell of smoke on her breath.

'I know what it's like to lose someone,' she said softly as she took the cigarette from Michael's mouth and took a drag before blowing the smoke at his chest. She stared into his eyes. 'It feels peaceful here with you.' The radio crackled in the background as the day darkened down.

Melissa put her hand on Michael's neck. The feeling of warm skin on skin. How long since he had last touched someone? He reached for her waist, and her cheap perfume was like a memory from a long time ago, from a different world.

She held him tighter and leaned in to kiss him. Her mouth was soft with lip balm. He ran a hand up her back and felt how thin she was. He reached for the straps of her vest, the warmth of her body pressed close to his. He started to pull the straps down. Felt how thin her arms were. How thin ...

He opened his eyes and drew back. Suddenly horrified with himself. 'This is wrong.' She stared back at him, his horror mirrored in her eyes. 'I'm sorry. It's not your fault. I shouldn't be doing this.'

'I'm eighteen – I'm an adult.'

'You're a friend of Nichol's, he's my client.'

She stood, pulling the straps back up her shoulders. 'I'm not some abused child, just because I come from the Marsh.'

He tried to catch her arm. 'It's nothing to do with where you're from.'

'I thought you liked me, or something.'

Michael glanced round the room. A mattress, a bottle of whisky, a packet of pills, an overflowing ashtray. It told a story.

She picked up her bag.

'Stay, Melissa, please. I need to know you're OK.'

'I'm fine. I shouldn't have come. I just wanted to see if you were all right. To ask if you found that phone. I couldn't stop thinking about it.'

The phone. The dream from the hospital came flooding back to Michael, fully formed from his subconscious. *Nichol. The phone.* Michael had given it to Henry, asked him to analyse it. 'Melissa, wait.'

But the front door was already closing behind her. Michael was too dazed to do anything but let her go. He looked around the room for his own phone then remembered it was still in the pocket of his jacket. He found it and flicked through for Henry's number. There was no answer so he dialled again, then a third time.

'Michael?' Henry's voice finally came on the line. 'The Internet still works.'

'Do you remember I left a phone with you?'

'Yes.'

'Did you get a chance to look at it for me?'

'Yes.'

'But you didn't find anything on it? Apart from the video.'

'I found something. It was hidden in the video.'

Michael stared out of the window in disbelief. 'Why didn't you tell you me?'

'What do you mean?' Henry asked, his voice even. 'You never asked me to tell you what was on it. You asked me to find out if there was anything hidden. I thought you must have known already or why would you have given it to me?'

Michael put a hand to his cheek. He could feel the pulse from the wound. 'What was on it?'

'Another video,' Henry said as if this was the most obvious thing in the world.

Chapter 56

Monica glanced around the dark hospital room then out of the window to the lights of the city. The black spaces beyond. Sometimes it was easy to forget how small the city was in the wide landscape. Water to the north, mountains to the south and west.

She shook her head and looked down at Crawford again, still anaesthetised from the long operation. Lying there with the sheets pulled up to his chest he seemed even smaller than usual. As if the air had been sucked out of him. Whatever product he used in his hair was long gone, and it hung down around his pale face in a red mess. He looked younger too. Much younger.

She should have been more careful. She should have sensed that Roderick Cameron was dangerous. She should have known.

Crawford stirred, and she looked down at him again then out into the empty corridor. The nurses had tried to evict her twice already. Both times Monica had resolved the situation by producing her ID and staring hard at them until they gave up. It confirmed once again her general rule that it was better to ask for forgiveness than permission.

Crawford still had both his arms at least. That had to be something. The mangled one was encased in dressings and held in a kind of scaffolding beside the bed to keep it upright. Monica shuddered at the memory of the injury. The arm hanging down at that hideous unnatural angle. The deep feelings of dread and horror.

She should go home, see Lucy and talk to her mum. It was almost ten at night and she would be desperate to speak to Monica, to know that she was OK. Monica knew that was the right thing to do – it wasn't like Crawford was even aware that she was there – but for some reason she couldn't make herself stand up to go.

She could picture her mum's face already: a mixture of outrage and disappointment on Monica's behalf. Then the inevitable barrage of angry questions. Who? What? When? Why? Searching for someone to blame for her daughter's humiliation.

A noise echoed from the room and down the corridor. With a start Monica realised it was her phone ringing.

'Michael Bach' flashed on the screen. She switched it to silent and laid it on the bed to ring out. Whatever he wanted, she couldn't help him with it. She'd already compromised herself with the laptop, got him beaten up, almost killed.

The phone immediately started ringing again. Monica shook her head but answered this time.

'I need your help.' There was a slight slur to his voice.

'I've been removed from the case,' Monica said. She stared at Crawford's still face as she spoke. He actually looked peaceful despite the tubes in his arm and the cuts where they'd removed pellets and fragments of bone from his face.

'I just need you to drive me somewhere. My face is a mess and I've … had a drink. I think I've found something important.'

Monica pulled up outside the flat and watched Michael Bach come slowly down the stairs to the street. He opened the door and climbed in beside her.

'Thanks for coming. I couldn't think of anyone else,' he said.

Monica caught the smell of whisky on his breath. She took in the stained dressing on his face and wondered just what the hell she was doing there, giving airtime to his crazy theories after what had happened to Crawford. But she put the car into gear anyway. They drove in awkward silence. He seemed as uncomfortable in the forced intimacy of the car as she was. What was there to talk about anyway?

The road through the night led to a house beneath the mountains.

Monica stopped the Volvo in the driveway and glanced across at Michael's bandaged face. 'Are you sure he's home? There are no lights on, no car.' For a moment, there in the dark, she wondered if Michael really was mad. Maybe he was delusional after the blow to his head.

'He'll be here. He never leaves the house,' Michael said.

Monica followed him to the front door and watched as he crouched and found a key under a stone. He groaned as he tried to stand, obviously still in pain from his beating. Monica put a hand under his arm and helped pull him to his feet.

'Thanks. It's my ribs.' She caught that smell of whisky again, mixed with cigarettes, as he went to unlock the door. 'Henry won't answer the bell.'

Monica hesitated then stepped after him into the house. The glow of computer screens was visible on the first-floor landing.

'He wouldn't tell you what he'd found over the phone?'

'He said I needed to see it.' Michael sounded uncertain himself.

A young man was sitting in front of a pair of computer screens in the darkened room. Inexplicably he was wearing a green hi-vis vest over a scruffy black hoody. He had a white bandanna tied around his head, its red disc at the centre of his forehead and Japanese characters on either side. Monica took in the piles of empty food wrappers, the windows covered by heavy shutters.

'This is Henry. Henry this is my friend Monica. She's … an investigator.'

'Police?' Henry's hand shot to his head and he swivelled all the way round in his chair to face them, staring at Monica. He was obviously panicked by this information.

'I'm a detective. I really appreciate the help you're giving us,' Monica said. She dipped her head to try to appear smaller, mindful of how intimidating she could look.

Henry regarded her as you would a dangerous animal. 'Is she OK, Michael?' he asked finally. His eyes never leaving Monica's face. 'Does she have integrity?'

Michael nodded. 'Yes. She does.'

Henry seemed to accept this. His hand moved slowly down from his bandanna to straighten his hi-vis vest and he swivelled back to the keyboard.

'What did you find?' Monica asked. She was keen to get this over with one way or the other.

Henry replied, talking to Michael as if it were him who had asked the question. 'There was a line of code hidden in the video. A link to a site on the dark net.' He opened up a Tor browser then typed something. A page opened. It was black with a single box in the middle of it. Henry hovered the cursor over the box.

'This is another video on the site. The video on the phone was hiding this link,' Henry said, still talking to Michael.

'Can you play it?' Monica asked. She tried to keep the impatience out of her voice.

'Yes.' Henry clicked the video.

Monica watched as it started to play. The recording was jerky. A hand-held camera. After a few seconds 'Zandy Allen, part 1' appeared on the screen.

The video cut to a dark street. A young man, still a teenager, walked past the camera. The video cut again. The same man going into a block of flats. Another cut, then the young man walking down another street. Monica realised with a shiver that it was Inverness High Street. For a second he looked straight into the camera. Another cut. The same teenager walking down a third street.

'This was shot from inside a car,' Monica said to herself as much as anyone else in the room.

The young man drew closer then leaned into the vehicle. A few seconds of silent conversation before he turned and walked on. Another cut. The screen showed the window of a house this time. Lit up against the night. Someone was moving around inside the room. The camera zoomed closer.

'This must have been filmed by the man who took Zandy. Nichol wasn't joking,' Michael said and Monica could hear the disbelief in his voice.

The video cut again and whiteness filled the screen.

The camera panned slowly out. Monica felt the hairs on the back of her neck stand up. The white turned into the pale skin of a face. It was a still shot. Frozen against a dark background.

'Nichol knew that someone took Zandy. He must have been terrified.' The growing horror in Michael's voice 'He came to me for help. That's why he wanted to meet me.'

'Play it again.' Monica moved closer. She tried to work out the implications. If Nichol was telling the truth about the abduction, then maybe he knew who the killer was. 'When did Zandy die?'

'About six months ago. Something like that,' Michael said.

'Owen MacLennan was still in jail six months ago. There's no way this was him.' Monica wasn't sure if this was a good or bad fact. 'You said Zandy committed suicide?'

Michael nodded slowly. 'That was the official story. He threw himself into the river.'

'We need to see the autopsy report.'

'Isn't this evidence that he was murdered?' Michael asked.

'It's a video. We don't know when it was made. We need solid evidence,' Monica said.

'Can't you phone in – ask someone?'

'If I phone in it'll become part of the investigation. It might take them weeks or months to consider it properly. Right now everything's focused on catching Don Cameron.' There was no point pretending otherwise. She turned back to Henry. 'Are there any other videos on that link? This one's part one. Shouldn't there be a part two?'

'Maybe,' Henry said, addressing Michael again. 'But it's not on this site. There's one other video I can access at the moment. Would you like to see it?'

Monica realised after a couple of seconds that he was waiting for an answer. 'Yes.' Then she added a soft, 'Please.'

He clicked through to another page. A video. 'Mark MacArthur part 1' flashed up on the screen.

'Who's Mark MacArthur?' She glanced at Michael. He shook his head slowly, still staring at the screen.

It showed another boy. He was walking along a street in what looked like a small village. Again the video was taken from inside a car. The next shot was the same boy. This time he was sitting in a cafe, the shot taken through the misted-up window. He had dark hair and a pale face.

'He looks like Nichol,' Michael said. The shot changed. A house lit up against the dark. A shape visible at the window.

The next shot was of a boy's face. A close-up. Pale against a dark background. The video ended.

'What the fuck is this? How did Nichol get these recordings?' Michael asked.

Monica said that she didn't know. She glanced at the dark shutters over the window, suddenly claustrophobic. Wished that Henry would switch a lamp on against the oppressive darkness.

Henry turned to Michael for instructions. His face lit up by the screens.

'Can you search for the name online, Henry? Put "Mark MacArthur, Scotland",' Monica asked.

Henry nodded at Michael then turned back to the screen and did as she'd requested.

They scanned down the results. 'Try that one,' Monica said. She could feel her mouth drying in the musty air of the house. Henry clicked open a news story from six months before.

He began to read out loud. His voice was a strange monotone in the quiet room. 'Fears grow for missing teenager Mark MacArthur, who disappeared from his home last Saturday night . . .'

Thursday

Chapter 57

The librarian led Michael into the reading room of the Archive Centre. She glanced at him again as she held the door open. His hand went to his face and he was suddenly conscious of the stained dressing on his cheek, the faint smell of yesterday's whisky.

'The older files are scanned onto microfiche, but the newer ones are only on hard copy,' she said.

'You mean I have to go through them manually?' Michael took in the thick rows of newspapers.

'There are plans for them to all be uploaded to a database, but ...' She gave a bureaucratic shrug – lack of interest or lack of funds. 'Anyway, I'll leave you to get started. Give me a call if you need anything.'

Michael nodded and tapped out two codeine tablets. His face was beginning to throb again. Somehow it had been forgotten through the night as the dawning horror of what they'd found emerged. He remembered DI Kennedy's monotone voice as she'd said, 'So Nichol found the videos. Maybe he hacked someone's computer or a website? He must have been terrified. He was probably wary of the police. Of the system. Of being disbelieved. He hid the phone with the video on it then took off.'

Michael tensed his hand into a fist at the memory. *He came to me for help, and I let him down.* He pushed the thought away and tried to focus. The killer was still out there. He needed to find something – that was the best way to help Nichol.

They had only located one follow-up story about Mark MacArthur's disappearance. Mark was aged eighteen, an ex-pupil of Lochinver High School in the northern Highlands. He'd been drinking on the night he disappeared but arrived home safely. The next morning he was gone. There was nothing else, nothing online anyway.

Monica had dropped Michael outside the Archive Centre half an hour before it opened and driven off before it had occurred to him to ask where she was going.

Michael looked at the rows of newspapers again. He put one of the codeine tablets back in the bottle and dry-swallowed the other. He knelt and found the copy of the *Northern Times* from the week after Mark MacArthur disappeared. It was a broadsheet, a relic. He laid it out on the desk and opened it at the first page.

Chapter 58

Dr Dolohov looked up from his desk. If he was surprised to see Monica it didn't register on his face. His office was small and cramped with textbooks and heaps of antiquated-looking scientific objects. More untidy than she'd expected for a pathologist.

'Inspector Kennedy.' His voice was loud in the confined space. 'You've come to ask me something more about those poor boys? They still haven't caught that man yet. It's a big problem for the police, no?'

Dolohov was holding something close to his chest while he spoke, shielding it from Monica's view. He followed her eyes to his hands and smiled. 'Do you want to see?' There was a strange playfulness in his voice. 'Come in. Close the door.'

Monica stared at him. The way he was half curled over with that smile on his face, like a malignant child in the corner of the playground with some rotten treasure to share.

'What is it?' she asked.

'I told you to come in,' replied Dolohov.

Monica glanced over her shoulder down the empty corridor. She was strangely wary. *Jesus — you really are paranoid this morning*, she thought, then dismissed the feeling and stepped into the office, pulling the door closed behind her.

'What is it then?' Monica asked.

Dolohov smiled then slowly twisted his body to face her. Still shielding his chest.

'Raarrr!'

He moved his hands quickly towards her snapping something together.

'Jesus!' Monica pulled her head back as Dolohov creased up with laughter and held something out for her to see. She resisted the urge to grab him by the neck. 'What is it?' she asked finally.

'The imprints – the bite marks. You remember? On the boys?' He asked the questions like the answer was some obscure piece of trivia.

'Of course I remember. Fucking hell,' Monica said, suddenly angry. 'If you ever try to frighten me like that again you'll regret it.'

Dolohov stared back up at her. 'I'm sorry,' he said finally. Then held up the object again. 'I made this cast from the bite marks on the bodies. It's very strange. I've never seen anything like it.'

Monica took the curious object from Dolohov's hands. It was cast in white plaster. A model of a jaw but longer than any human mouth, with a long row of incisors on both the upper and lower jaws. Mixed in were sharper, canine teeth.

'I take it this isn't some strange animal's jaw?' Monica asked. The thing gave her the creeps, and she was glad when Dolohov took it from her hands.

'These match human teeth.' He pointed to the incisors. 'These seem to be a mix.' He gestured to the sharper teeth. 'I think they could be from a large animal. A tiger or a bear perhaps.' He clacked the model jaw together again. 'He would still have needed a lot of force to break the boys' skin. The bites were deep.'

'So he made a mask or something?' Monica asked. The thing was so idiosyncratic that it was hard to see how it could actually help them find the killer.

'It's possible. He could have used his mouth to generate the force needed. Or some kind of tool – pliers perhaps? The bites were made post-mortem.'

'Almost as if they were separate from the actual torture and murder?' Monica asked. Thinking out loud.

'Or the victims died before the killer had the chance to use it on them,' Dolohov said, looking up again. 'It does seem that the bites were peripheral though. Certainly to the actual cause of death.'

'Christ.' Monica noticed that there was an Orthodox crucifix hanging on the wall behind the doctor. Somehow it made her uncomfortable after seeing that jaw. As if it were another unwelcome symbol of illogicality.

Dolohov caught her glance. 'Don't worry, I won't try to save anyone's soul. My mother likes the cross there. Something from home.' Monica cleared her throat, embarrassed he'd read her so easily. Dolohov laughed. 'You're not the only one. Most people don't like it. I'm actually surprised they haven't made me take it down.'

'You're Russian?' She watched as he put the plaster jaw carefully back into a box.

'My family still live there. Anyway …' He reached for a coffee pot and poured two cups. He handed one to Monica. 'You came here to ask me something?'

She took the cup and swallowed a mouthful, oh so thankful for the hot drink after the long night and those strange videos. 'I need to see an autopsy report. It's a boy who committed suicide six months ago.'

Dolohov stared at her for a second. 'His name?'

'Zandy Allen – Alexander Allen. He was eighteen.'

The doctor turned slowly to the old computer on his desk. 'You think it was the same man?' He nodded to the box with the model jaw in it.

'I don't know. Officially he threw himself into the river,' she said.

Dolohov opened a file on the PC and hit Print. He reached under the desk for the sheets of paper then laid them out in front of him and started to read.

'His body had been in the water for some time so it was damaged by contact with rocks – things like this. Marks on his neck – the official line was: most likely occurred post-mortem or while he was unconscious in the water.'

'Most likely?'

The doctor ignored her question and kept his head down. 'There was no water in his lungs.'

'But I thought he drowned?'

'It's not totally unusual. Occasionally the larynx goes into spasm when water enters the throat. The passage to the lungs is blocked and the victim chokes,' Dolohov said.

'How occasional?'

He shrugged. 'It's difficult to say. Who wants to be a test subject for this? A pathologist will come to a conclusion that a deceased person without water in the lungs has drowned based on other evidence. By finding things: blood in the lungs, objects from the water in the throat.' Dolohov didn't look up as he spoke.

Monica started to say something but he held a hand up as he scanned down the paper.

'The coroner found a stone –' he spoke quietly '– lodged in the boy's throat.'

There it was, the connection she needed, proof that Michael wasn't chasing ghosts. 'The same as the murder victims. Where would the stone be kept?'

'The pathologist concluded that it was death by misadventure – accidental drowning or suicide. The stone would have been disposed of, assumed to have lodged in there while he was underwater.'

'But there must be photographs – a video or something?'

'People are sensitive about their loved ones being videoed undergoing an autopsy. And we have limited resources,' Dolohov said.

'So you're telling me there's no way we can check whether the stone connects the bodies. Who performed the autopsy? I've worked with other pathologists up here before you. I can speak to them. See if they at least remember ...'

Dolohov nodded and flicked through the pages again. Monica caught the change in his expression as his eyebrows folded together.

'What is it?'

'The autopsy was performed by a Dr Munro.'

Monica repeated the name. 'I've been back up here for four years but I don't remember a Munro.'

'No. I've only been here a couple of months but I've heard his name. He only did occasional locum work. Dealing with the remote areas or covering for leave. That kind of thing. But there were ... allegations – problems with the quality of his work. And other things.'

'What other things?'

'He drank too much. Problems in his personal life. I've seen some of his other reports. They're not thorough. He was being investigated for misconduct.'

'*Was* being investigated?'

'He died three months ago. Just before I got here.'

Chapter 59

Michael blinked then watched as the newspaper columns came back into focus. Four hours and so far nothing, the pain behind his eye growing all the time. He decided to go outside to smoke a cigarette.

A storm was gathering from the west. From the long miles of black water on Loch Ness, and before that from the Atlantic Ocean. The ice-cold rain felt like a harbinger. Of what though?

'Of nothing good,' Michael said to himself, if only to dispel the thought.

He gazed around the empty car park, the trees and the mountains beyond. There had to be something he was missing.

Nichol had left – hidden – the phone at Eddie's – Michael knew that much. Then there was the video of Zandy's 'funeral'. Zandy was important. He'd mattered to Nichol. His friendship, his death, his funeral.

It occurred to Michael that Zandy had gone to the same school as Nichol. Had the two other boys gone there too? It didn't add up. DI Kennedy wouldn't have missed a link like that between Robert and Paul, even without Nichol or Zandy being a factor. But there was a connection between Zandy and Nichol. Michael found his phone. There was a sliver of battery left. For a moment he couldn't recall the head teacher's name. He fished around until it came back to him: *Ward, Kyle Ward.*

Michael found the number and pressed Dial, and unexpectedly the receptionist transferred him straight through.

Ward came on the line. 'Michael! I'm sorry I haven't called you yet. This is ... a little embarrassing. Melissa –' Michael cringed at the name '– doesn't seem to exist. Not as far as this school's concerned. I've spoken to some other colleagues—'

Michael cut in. He was too tired and medicated to try to be polite. 'It was actually someone else I wanted to ask you about – an ex-pupil. Alexander Allen, Zandy Allen? I'm afraid he –' Michael cleared his throat '– he committed suicide. Around six months ago. Do you remember him?'

There was a long pause at the other end of the line.

'Of course I remember him. It was awful. Whenever something like that happens it feels like a personal loss. You watch them come to the school as young children. Grow into early adulthood ... He would have been older than Nichol, though?'

'That's right. A couple of years older, but they were friends. I wonder if his ... suicide affected Nichol somehow. I haven't been able to find a contact for his family.'

'His mother. His father wasn't around, as I recall. I attended the funeral of course. Terribly sad. I seem to remember that there was something said. Alexander's mother hadn't wanted some of his friends to attend. I think she held them partly responsible.'

'That's right,' Michael said. He was pleased that Ward's recollection seemed to chime with Alan Gentle's story.

'You don't think that his suicide could be related to Nichol's disappearance? I hadn't connected them in my mind until just now, with Nichol being younger. I hadn't realised they were friends.'

Michael tried to judge Ward's tone. Was it genuine concern? Or a desire to protect the school's reputation?

'I really don't know. I was hoping there might be a connection. Something his mother might remember.'

'I believe that she moved away not long after the tragedy. That may be why you're having difficulty contacting her. She was from the Western Isles originally, I think. I might be able to find a contact for her. If I ...' Ward's voice faded out.

'I wouldn't want to upset her. Just a couple of questions. To see if Nichol had tried to contact her.' *If anything unusual happened before Zandy disappeared. A man following him for example.* But Michael kept these thoughts to himself. There was silence from the other end of the phone. 'I'd really appreciate it if you could help me with this,' Michael pushed.

Finally Ward's voice came back on the line. It sounded far away against the noise of the storm. 'OK. I'll see what I can do for you. I'll call you back. Hopefully I'll have a contact number for you.'

Chapter 60

Monica crossed the hospital car park. Her head down against the weather, the heavy grey skies, the first flecks of icy sleet. She was still trying to make sense of what Dolohov had told her. If Alexander Allen had been murdered back in the summer, then there was no telling how long the killer had been active for. Had Alexander been the first? Or were there others? She found her phone. Hesitated for a moment then dialled Hately's mobile.

He answered after two rings. 'I can't talk now. I'm about to go into a strategy meeting.'

'Wait. This is more important.'

'I doubt that.'

'Listen. I don't think Don Cameron was involved. I've found evidence linking at least two other boys with the same killer. Alexander Allen died six months ago while MacLennan was still in prison, and there's another boy called Mark MacArthur who disappeared. I've got evidence. There could be more,' Monica said. She was struggling to keep her voice level.

She could hear Hately taking a deep breath. 'Dr Lees said this might happen.'

'What does Lees have to do with this?' Monica asked. A flash of annoyance just at the sound of his name.

'He said that you might be traumatised after everything with DC Crawford yesterday. And who can blame—'

'I'm not fucking traumatised.'

'OK,' Hately said slowly. 'Suppose we are looking for someone else. Despite the evidence linking MacLennan and Cameron with the murders. Who is it?'

'I don't know yet,' she said. 'That's why I need you to listen.'

'You need to take a breath, Monica. Think about this.'

'I am thinking about this, believe me.'

'Cameron is armed and dangerous. We need to deal with him as a priority. If what you're saying is true, then the evidence will take us there once we've apprehended him.'

'We might not have a chance to. Cameron might be on his way to kill the murderer. And the killer could be planning to take another boy right now.'

'Lees disagrees. He thinks Cameron will attempt to evade justice. To disappear.'

'He's wrong, sir, with all respect, he's wrong. MacLennan was never in control. I don't even think he was involved in the other murders. The killer used him as a scapegoat.'

'We have solid evidence at his flat linking MacLennan with both murders. The blood results have just come in from MacLennan's autopsy. He'd taken a dose of GHB before he killed himself. The same as Paul MacKay had in his system. Apparently it can be used as a relaxant in smaller doses. And you know yourself that we have circumstantial evidence that Cameron might have been involved.' Monica could hear Hately's hand over the phone and voices in the background. 'I have to go. You need to come in, Monica. Dr Lees has recommended that you and Fisher undergo standard psychiatric trauma evaluations.'

Monica ended the call without waiting to hear what else Hately had to say. She swallowed the ball of outrage building in her throat. She took a breath and tried Michael's mobile number. It went straight to voicemail so she dropped the phone back into her pocket.

As she was opening the door of the Volvo Monica heard her name called. She turned to see DC Fisher walking towards her. Somehow more confident in his movements than usual. With her out the picture, of course, he was one step closer to the boss.

'I didn't expect to see you here,' she said, still angry from the call.

His hand went to his glasses, shielding them from the sleet. 'I saw you pull in earlier.' He gestured towards the police head-quarters building, which was visible beyond the hospital on the other side of the busy road. 'Have you got five minutes?'

Monica gestured for Fisher to get into the passenger side of the car. She climbed in herself and switched the engine on then turned the heating up high.

'What is it, Fisher?'

'I thought ...' He seemed suddenly uncertain. 'I wanted to keep you up to speed with the investigation. Well, some of the results. Everything's focused on finding Don Cameron at the moment. They're talking about bringing special forces in to track him. It's a nightmare, especially with this storm coming in. Looking for an armed man in the mountains when you've got white-outs. Avalanches to contend with ...' Monica nodded. 'He could be hiding up in a snowhole or in a cave. No one would know until they were right on top of him. It's a fucking nightmare.'

She was pretty certain this was the first time she'd heard Fisher swear. He was a curious boy – man – and she realised she'd never asked him anything about his family, his life outside the force. He probably still thought he had a life.

'And ...'

'And no one's looking at the other evidence,' Fisher said.

'You don't think Cameron was involved?'

'We both saw those emails. There has to be a chance someone else did it.'

'Funny that. I never heard you saying that yesterday, when I was trying to get Hately to let me investigate,' Monica said.

He looked away. 'Sorry.'

Monica watched the rain landing on the windscreen and hitting the puddles in the potholed car park. For long moments neither of them spoke. Finally Fisher broke the silence: 'I got the results back on the piece of meteorite recovered from Paul's body. It matches the piece from Robert. They're both from the same fragment of meteor.'

'So it fell in Australia. Twenty years ago. Could it be one of the ...' She couldn't recall the name he had used for them.

'The Taurids? Yes. It's possible. The Taurids orbit the sun.'

'So it's possible part of the meteor that landed twenty years ago is still out there. I mean it could come back?'

'That's right.'

'But we'd know if it had been here before, wouldn't we? All the comets are mapped out in space?'

'No, not at all. Often they're black. Coated in tar so we can't see them. They're difficult to spot, difficult to track. If a comet comes from behind the sun ...'

'What?'

Fisher took a breath, tried to slow down. It was probably the most excited Monica had seen him. 'It's entirely possible that an unknown asteroid – big enough to wipe out human civilisation – could appear tomorrow. Hidden by the light of the sun. An asteroidal impact wiped out the dinosaurs. An asteroidal impact might have melted the icecaps all across the northern hemisphere – Scotland included – ten thousand years ago.'

The reality of his words suddenly felt too much, the ideas too big to even want to try and understand. Lucy was reason enough not to want to ever think about what Fisher was saying. As if the world wasn't hell enough without a sudden meteoritic death punch from space.

'That's interesting, but what does it have to do with our murderer?'

'Well,' he said, almost sounding sniffy, 'we'll soon find out.'

'Sorry. What do you mean?'

'Tomorrow night. The Taurids. It's the peak of the meteor stream. If something's going to happen it would make sense for it to be then.'

Monica stared at her colleague with a prickling horror of realisation. 'Why the hell, Fisher, didn't you just say that at the beginning?'

Chapter 61

Back up in the reading room there was a flask of coffee and a plate of sandwiches on Michael's desk. The sandwiches had the look of leftover conference food, not that beggars could be choosers. He tried to remember the last time he'd eaten, and when no answer came easily to mind he gave up and instead focused on the food and drink.

The door opened and there stood the librarian. 'We ordered too many. I thought you might be hungry?'

Michael nodded and noticed that the woman had an attractive birthmark on her cheek. He tried to smile, but pain shot through his face and he winced. She seemed to get the idea though because she smiled and touched her hand to her cheek as Michael sat back down to go through the next newspaper.

After another hour of flicking through the brittle pages his eyes were swimming. His mind kept wandering off into old memories and alternative versions of reality. Versions where Charlie Bartle hadn't bothered to look at the business card in his pocket. Where they'd dragged him into a shallow grave instead of into the back of an ambulance. In a strange way DI Kennedy had saved his life. He hadn't even told her.

His mind drifted further – into dark alleys and infinite realities. Into a strange distant room with stars on the ceiling and a million different doorways. Michael tilted his head and wondered how he'd come to be trapped in this room. How the corridors had somehow conspired to lead him to this empty place under the stars.

There was sudden pain as his face moved against the palm of his hand. He blinked and realised he'd been on the verge of sleep. He'd been turning the pages over without even registering what was on them. He sat back in the chair and drank off the rest of the mug of cold coffee. The clock on the wall said 4 p.m. Time had taken on a strange dissociative quality for him with the exhaustion, medication, broken routines – the pathway to personality breakdown. Michael refilled the mug and drank it off again.

He looked back down at the page he'd been staring at.

TEEN'S DISAPPEARANCE SPARKS MEMORIES

Michael blinked, not quite trusting his eyes. He looked again. The words stayed the same. He checked the date. Published a month after Mark MacArthur had gone missing in Lochinver. He wiped his eyes and focused on the article.

The recent disappearance of Mark MacArthur (18) has brought back difficult memories for the families of two other young men who also disappeared within days of each other last year. Lewis Fall (19) went missing from his home after a night out with friends in the town of Thurso. Three days earlier Iain Johnston (18) disappeared in Fort William. His family believe that he may have left home early in the morning to go hillwalking, but despite extensive searches by volunteers and the local mountain rescue no trace of him has been discovered.

Michael sat back in his chair and read over the paragraph a second time. *Two more missing boys.* The similarities to what had happened to Mark MacArthur and Zandy Allen were obvious. Not to mention the two murdered boys, Paul MacKay and Robert Wright.

He read on: 'Police are keen to stress that any similarity between the disappearances is coincidental. A spokesperson said, "What this highlights are the dangerous situations that young men often find themselves in. Every year we see tragic cases where young men act impulsively, be that behind the wheel of a motor vehicle, or other risk-taking behaviours."'

Michael noted down the names and dates of the boys' disappearances. He went back to the archives and found the local newspapers from the period. He flicked through for more stories. There wasn't much more information. The boys had been out with friends. Had come home safely, then in the morning they were gone. Just like that. Young men who the police had assumed were suicidal or reckless. There were appeals from family and friends, searches, then nothing.

Michael looked at the list of names he'd compiled. Seven boys, dead or missing. He asked himself: what's the connection? There has to be something. But his internal voice didn't answer. After a minute of staring at the newspaper he stood up, the room felt like it was tilting slightly. He drank another mug of the coffee, trying desperately to ward off the exhaustion that was clouding his thinking.

He looked back down at his notes. Then at the story linking the disappearances. Then it occurred to him to check the journalist's name: Cassandra Harrison. He sat down again and flicked through more papers, looking for anything else she had written.

He was about to give up, go out for another cigarette, when his eyes fell on a story. It was written two months after the first one. DISAPPEARANCES LINKED? Michael read on, a burst of excitement momentarily warding off the exhaustion.

Louise MacArthur (40), whose son Mark went missing three months ago, has appealed for anyone who might have information about her son's disappearance to come forward. She commented, 'Mark's a gentle boy. There seems to be this idea that he's some kind of risk-taker, someone who would have left the house alone in the middle of the night without telling me, but that wasn't him at all. I appreciate everything that everyone has done to try and find Mark, but I don't believe that the police are taking all the evidence into consideration.'

Two previous disappearances of young men that occurred within days of each other in similar circumstances last year have also yet to be resolved. Leaving questions for the families of the missing boys about whether there could be more to the disappearances than the authorities are prepared to accept.

Police Scotland turned down a request for an interview, but a spokesperson issued a statement: 'Unfortunately, despite our best efforts and the huge support and assistance we've received from the public we've so far been unable to resolve these cases. Disappearances are a tragically common occurrence in the Highlands. Although we all enjoy the benefits of our beautiful wilderness, these benefits also come with an element of risk attached. To state that these three disparate disappearances are connected is fanciful. The events occurred in different corners of the Highlands and there is no evidence that would suggest a connection, or any hint of foul play.'

'She's on to it,' Michael whispered and felt his excitement rising. He hurried to the stand and found the papers for the next two weeks. He worked through them quickly but the trail ran cold. There was nothing more by Cassandra Harrison and no mention of the missing boys.

'We're closing in five minutes.' Michael started as he realised that the librarian was standing over his desk. Slowly he packed away his notes and photocopies, then put the newspapers back into the files.

Outside it was almost dark. Sleet was being blown in circles by the storm. He found his phone and looked up DI Kennedy, then watched as the screen went black. Dead battery.

Great timing. For a moment he couldn't even recall where the Land Rover was parked. Finally he remembered that he'd left it in the hotel car park in the centre of Inverness two days before when he'd met Anita. It seemed longer, like weeks.

He turned his collar up against the rain and followed the footpath by the river through Ness Islands and back towards the centre of town, the shadows watching among the trees and the cold end of the day turning to night.

The wind drove the sleet through his trousers and tweed jacket. By the time he made it to the Land Rover, Michael was numb and shivering. He patted himself down for the key, checking each pocket three times before finally accepting that he really didn't have it. In despair at the thought of a long walk to the flat, he tried the door. It was open with the key in the ignition.

'Fucking hell,' he whispered, shaking his head as he switched the engine on. He turned the heating up as high as it would go and carefully spread the damp photocopies over the passenger seat and the dashboard to dry. His eyes fell on the story linking the boys' disappearances. Cassandra Harrison. The journalist from the *Northern Times*.

Michael dug in his pocket for the dead phone. He plugged it into the charger, found the number for the newspaper in his notes and dialled. It was answered after five rings. He could hear the sound of voices in the background.

The man on the other end of the line repeated the name dumbly back to him: 'Cassandra Harrison?'

'That's right,' Michael said.

'OK. Hold on for a moment.' The line bleeped on hold. Michael waited until finally, when he was about to give up, assuming he'd been forgotten, a woman's voice came onto the line.

'Cassandra, Cassandra Harrison?'

'No, I'm sorry, this is the editor.'

'I'm trying to get hold of one of your journalists, Cassandra Harrison?'

'I'm afraid Cassandra no longer works here.' Michael heard a catch in the woman's voice.

'Oh. Do you have a contact number or an email address? She's an old friend. I'm trying to get back in touch with her.' An unlikely story in the days of social media but it was the best Michael's battered mind could come up with.

There was a long pause. When the woman spoke her voice was stilted. 'I'm really sorry to have to tell you, especially over the phone. But I'm afraid Cassandra passed away a few months ago. We were all … She was well liked here. I'm sorry to have to tell you like this.'

'What happened?'

Another long pause. The empty sound of someone looking for the best collection of the worst words. 'I'm sorry. Cassandra committed suicide. She killed herself.'

Chapter 62

Fisher repeated what he'd said. 'Tomorrow night. It's predicted to be unusually active. The peak of the meteor stream.' He took his glasses off. Wiped his face and put them back on. 'It was you who suggested the killer might be working in sync with an astrological event, DI Kennedy. I've just put two and two together.'

Monica thought about the two bodies. Placed in those positions, pointing out to the stars. Like guides, like beacons. Welcoming something from space. She found herself thinking of those dark skies above the ocean at the first dump site. The stars she had stared into, the way they had stared back into her.

'It sounds ...' *What? Far-fetched? Crazy?*

'Doesn't it make sense though?' Fisher said, excitement in his voice. 'The bodies placed where we'd find them? The fragments of meteor in their throats? Like it's building towards ...'

'Something. But what? The murder and torture of two boys feels like a very big something.'

He coughed. 'I suppose that's the million-dollar question. What if he has another boy he's abducted, or ...'

Nichol Morgan.

Monica glanced at Fisher. She needed to speak to Michael.

'It's an interesting idea,' she said finally, expecting Fisher to climb out of the car. 'I'll think about it.' He didn't move though. She turned to face him and he forced a smile.

'How's Lucy? She must be pleased to have you home?'

Her mind and heart paused at that. *Why bring Lucy into it? Why mention her at all?*

'What is it you want to say to me, Fisher? You could have told me this over the phone.'

He looked at the floor of the car. The sound of the rain rattling on the roof continued. Monica had conducted enough interviews with thieves, murderers and rapists to know that it was almost impossible to say when someone was lying. Humans are just so good at it. She'd read that in tests even the best FBI investigators could only identify when someone was telling a lie marginally better than a straight fifty–fifty guess. Monica could tell when someone wanted to talk, though. When there was something they needed to say.

'It's just between us, Fisher. It's better to get it off your chest now.'

'It's …'

Fisher was bowed forward. Almost as if shielding something in his lap. Clearly whatever he'd discovered had rocked him.

'It's better to speak about it now. Secrets eat you up, Fisher. Believe me, it makes things twice as hard if people don't trust you. I'm sure you've heard what they say about me. About my past …'

Fisher looked up at her. 'I answered the phone last night. The information line. I wish I hadn't. There was a guy on the line. He wouldn't give his name but he said he'd seen Don Cameron the day before.'

'The day before the raid?' Monica asked.

'That's right. I thought it was probably a dead end. You know how many of these calls are – false alarms, that kind of thing. But this guy had recognised Don's pickup truck. Said he saw him parked by a payphone in the middle of nowhere about five miles from the Cameron croft.'

'You pulled the phone records on the payphone,' Monica said.

'Of course I did. I got a number with an Inverness area code.' Fisher glanced over his shoulder then lowered his voice in the quiet car. 'I googled the number. Who do you think I got?'

Monica shook her head slowly.

'Inverness police headquarters. It was an incoming call through the switchboard.'

'Who took the call?' Monica asked.

'I don't know. It wasn't recorded. It's one of the general lines so anyone could have answered it and put it through.'

'You think someone on the force warned him that we were coming?'

Fisher nodded, hunched forward.

'I didn't join the police for this sort of thing, ma'am. Why would someone have warned him? A man died. DC Crawford … Either of us could have been killed.'

So it wasn't about Lucy at all; it was about corruption within her second home. 'Who have you told about this?'

'No one. I'm not stupid. I'm only telling you because I know for a fact you were out of the office when the call came in. Why would anyone want to help Don Cameron? It doesn't make any sense.'

Chapter 63

Michael struggled to stay awake on the drive back through the grey-clouded mountains. The long days of broken sleep mixed with his medication taking their toll.

He blinked, slapped his face and pushed one of his reggae CDs into the player. 'Something to keep you awake,' he murmured.

The music filled the car as he drove. The sleety rain off the sea slanted past the snow poles that marked the edge of the road. Tonight the music only seemed to add to his sense of strangeness and disorientation. He clicked the CD off after five minutes.

Just the sound of the car engine. Cigarette smoke and the centre lines on the road. His attention blurred in and out with the realisation that he really shouldn't be driving. Lines on the road, shadows off the mountains and the faces of missing boys. Nichol by the side of the road amid the hypnotic snow flurries. Dressed in his school uniform with a laptop bag over his shoulder. Mouthing something that Michael couldn't quite hear.

Finally he made it to the turn-off for the croft. Pulled the Land Rover up the rough track.

Inside, Monica looked up from the laptop balanced on her knees. Colonel Mustard had worked in close beside her, searching out her body heat in the cold room. He was now nudging his head under her arm.

'You got in then?' Michael glanced around the untidy room. At the piles of books. The worn carpet and the mound of dried cat food. The house felt damp and unwelcoming. He was momentarily self-conscious about the state of the place.

She nodded, then pointed to a pot on the table. 'I made coffee if you want some.'

He shrugged his damp jacket off. He'd left the fire set at least. It was something, even if the rest of the place was a mess. He patted his pockets for his lighter.

'I should have told you to light the fire. Sorry. There's no heating so it gets cold,' Michael said as he crouched down. The kindling caught easily for once. The mix of old newspaper and dried heather that he'd stuffed in burned quickly and sent a reassuring white light twisting around the room.

Michael watched the flames for a minute as they took hold, then stood up. He thought about the coffee then looked past the pot to the cupboard in the corner, the bottle of whisky there. One from his dad's old collection. Ardbeg. Ten years old. Normally Michael wasn't interested in whisky but since his operation he seemed to have acquired the taste.

'You want a dram?' he mumbled as he splashed some into a glass. DI Kennedy didn't seem to hear him. She was still staring at the laptop.

He took a deep pull of the whisky, savouring the taste of lonely winter beaches and smokehouses. He poured some more.

'I found some … disturbing things.' He passed Monica the photocopies and started to tell her what he'd discovered about Mark MacArthur's disappearance. About the two boys who'd gone missing the year before. 'The journalist – her name was Cassandra Harrison – she died.'

'Suddenly?'

Michael nodded slowly. He was glad of the whisky when he saw the expression on Monica's face. 'It was suicide. Her colleagues ... they said that it was totally out of character, that no one saw it coming. How did you know?'

'I checked on Zandy Allen's autopsy. It was botched. There was a black stone found in his throat. It's been destroyed so we can't compare it with the others. The pathologist who performed the autopsy died not long after. So he can't tell us anything either,' Monica said.

'We have to take this to your boss. Someone has to listen now. They have to help us find Nichol. Surely?' Michael said.

Monica glanced up at him. 'I've tried. They're fixated on catching Don Cameron. Have you even looked on a news site today? The media are all over it. No one wants to hear about anything else. My boss certainly doesn't. As far as he's concerned, we can deal with all this next week, or next month. Once we've apprehended Don Cameron.'

'But what if we're right? What if the killer's still out there? What if he's got Nichol?' Michael's voice was rising, loosened by the whisky and the heat from the fire.

'Then we need to find the evidence to prove it. It's the only way Hately will listen just now.' Something crossed Monica's face as she said this. Michael caught the expression and tilted his head.

'What is it?'

She glanced down at the floor then looked up again. 'I think it's possible that someone close to the investigation tipped off Don Cameron before the raid. That they're protecting him somehow.'

'What?' Michael could hardly believe what she was saying. 'You mean someone in the police? Why would they tip Cameron off?'

'I don't know. There are rumours that he did things. Killed people for money, years ago. You've heard of Shona Mackenzie? There were old stories that someone in the police covered up evidence of a murder. Other crimes too. It could be that someone doesn't want Don Cameron brought in. Doesn't want him to reveal what he knows.'

'So if someone's feeding information to Don Cameron, what else could they be doing?' Michael asked. The fear slowly dawning on him as the potential implications stacked up in his mind.

'There's no point thinking about that just now,' DI Kennedy said. Her black hair was tied back in a ponytail. For the first time he noticed the colour of her eyes: dark grey, so dark they were almost black. 'If we can find something that connects the missing boys, something that ties them to Paul and Robert, then Hately will have to listen. And if he doesn't, then plenty of others will ...' She shrugged and reached for her coffee.

Michael understood. *We'll go to the press.* He reached for the whisky again. Despite everything it really was delicious.

'Both of the victims – three if we include Zandy Allen – and Nichol, they're connected by these black stones. They're fragments of meteorites and the key to the murders. To why the killer left his last two victims on display. But if the previous bodies haven't been found, why risk being caught by placing Paul and Robert where they're sure to be discovered?'

'Doesn't that sound insane to you?' Michael said. He was thinking about Nichol holding that rock up to his mouth, kissing it.

'What exactly do you think it's like inside the mind of someone who spends most of their time fantasising about hurting other people? Planning how to actually do it for real?' It was Monica's turn to sound angry. 'Can you imagine strangling someone until they're unconscious then reviving them so you can do it again. Enjoying them begging for their life. Recording it so you can watch it again and plan how you'd do it better next time. What do you think it's like in that person's mind?'

'Like hell,' Michael said. He watched as Monica ran a hand over her face. 'Like the underworld.'

She took a deep breath. 'There's a meteor stream passing close to the earth. It reaches its height tomorrow night. It's possible that the black stones in the boys' throats came from one of those same meteors that landed twenty years ago.'

'And now it's coming back?'

Neither of them spoke. The rain pounded harder on the window, the sound of the storm coming in strong off the sea. Michael took another mouthful of the whisky and listened to the purr of the peat fire in the quiet room. The shifting sense of reality. Of boys killed and fed to the universe.

'So what do we do?' he said finally. 'How does this actually help us find him? He gave that rock to Nichol. We have to find him.'

'The killer chose his victims carefully. He must have known them to get that close. There will be a link somewhere.'

'If only I'd met Nichol when he'd asked—'

'Forget about that,' Monica said. 'We don't have time. If he's planning to kill tomorrow we need to—'

'We have to try the police again. There must be someone who'd listen, surely.'

'How many times do I have to say this?' Monica turned to face him. 'My boss. His bosses. Want to catch Don Cameron, plain and simple. They don't want to hear about new murders. They definitely don't want to hear about some ...' Monica's hand went to her face. She lowered her voice. 'We're going to have to do it on our own.'

Michael stared back at her, at the certainty she seemed to have. He reached for another cigarette and lit it. To hide the expression on his face as much as anything. To hide the fear. And the idea that never left him for a moment that night, even through the whisky. That maybe it would be best if he waited for her to leave then switched his phone off. Booked into a hotel somewhere and never contacted her again.

Chapter 64

The Watcher

The Internet was awash with speculation, reported sightings of Don Cameron from across Scotland and further still: Spain, Portugal, Morocco. The police conveniently focusing everything on their search while he continued his important work, safe in the dark.

He was carefully positioning all the parts. The individuals moving with synchronicity into his field of gravity. That perfect balance between the known and the unknown, the imagined and the real. As the final day approached, Saturn, Mars and Venus were rising, as they had risen over that Australian desert two decades before. The black blood spread wide. Delicate and beautiful.

He remembered how the young man had grunted – his last sound. It was a surprise that he was still alive at all. As the man felt that adrenaline pump through his body he knew intuitively what to do. He knelt beside his younger companion and pushed the fragment of meteor from the old woman's house, the most important piece at that point, deep into his throat. Extending his fingers as far as they would go. Then, when the young man finally stopped moving, he carefully arranged him in the correct position. The first of his offerings to the stars.

*

It was only much later that the missing pieces, the flaws and imperfections, began gathering like a cloud. Somehow the young man's death seemed to lack the significance of George's.

He asked the stones, and slowly he began to understand that what had made George so special lay in destroying his potential. Not in hastening the demise of an already ruined individual. But shaping reality. Turning something good from existence to non-existence. How much more exciting would it be to have a partner like George who would willingly agree to participate? To prolong the act so he could slowly observe as he changed the very nature of reality?

He had listened to the whispers from the stone – speaking to him from deep inside the young man's throat, still posed out there on the desert – and it concurred.

It led him to those boys. Giving themselves willingly to him. What could be better than that?

He stared at the computer screen. All those stories paying tribute to what he'd achieved. He held the stone in his hand, felt the sweat of excitement and asked the question.

The answer came to him. Rising from deep in his subconscious, as if it was what the stones had been working towards all along.

Chapter 65

During the late drive back to Inverness Monica reluctantly called her mum. It was the first time they'd spoken properly since everything at the croft house with Crawford.

'Monica? Are you OK? I've been worried about you.' Her mum's voice was full of such concern it made Monica want to weep.

She stared out through the windscreen at the speeding patch of white light on the tarmac from her headlamps. The flickering snow poles flashing past at the side of the road, almost like bad special effects of a spaceship going into warp speed in an 80s sci-fi movie.

'I'm fine, Mum. Is Lucy OK?' Monica had expected her mother to be disappointed in her somehow, judgemental even. *Probably thinking it's what you deserve – fucking up the only thing you're good at.* Monica cringed when she imagined her mother, her mother's friends, reading the news reports criticising her handling of the investigation. All that pride in her daughter's competence washed away.

'Lucy's asleep now. I'll wake her up if you like? She asked if you'd pick her up from playgroup tomorrow. I've got a hair appointment – I can cancel though.'

'No. Don't wake her up.' Monica glanced at the time. Almost midnight. 'I'll pick her up tomorrow. There are just a couple of things I need to straighten out first.'

'Oh. OK.' She sounded uncertain. A little frightened even. 'Is everything OK, Mum?'

'Everything's fine. It's just ... one of the older kids at playgroup told Lucy about Crawford. She doesn't really understand but she's been having bad dreams. Be careful will you, Monica.'

Friday

Chapter 66

Crawford was sitting propped up on a pile of pillows when Monica walked into the room. She had managed to dodge the nurses in the corridor.

Monica set the tub of hair gel she'd bought on the cabinet top. 'I don't know if it's the right one.' She'd picked up the most expensive from a twenty-four-hour Tesco.

Crawford shrugged his bare white shoulders. 'I use wax from the health-food shop. That stuff's full of parabens. It probably gives you cancer.'

'Right.' Monica couldn't help talking to his injured arm, still in its scaffold. Still attached to his body, though. That was something. 'I'll try to swing by the health-food shop tomorrow.'

She'd meant it as a joke, but he nodded with no humour, his hair hanging forward over his forehead. He looked different like that. Younger and more vulnerable.

'I brought some juice. Energy drinks.' She set the three remaining cans of Red Bull on the cabinet next to the gel. 'Do you want me to open one for you?'

'What?' Crawford sounded angry. The sweat was standing out on his forehead. Clearly he was in pain. He gestured to the clock on the wall with his good arm. 'It's after 1 a.m., boss. Actually I don't want a fucking caffeinated drink.'

'I think he's going to kill again. I think it could be tomorrow.'

'What are you talking about? Hately was in earlier. He said Don Cameron's being tracked all across the Highlands. That it was only a matter of time.'

'I don't think he was involved.'

'Why?' He still sounded angry. But Monica could tell that despite the pain and the medication he was interested. She started to explain.

After an hour they were both still staring at a map of the Highlands attached to the wall with medical tape Monica had found in a storage cupboard in the corridor. She pointed to the locations that the boys had gone missing from, circled in blue marker. The locations where the bodies had been discovered were circled in red.

'They're spread all over the Highlands,' Crawford said. He winced as he reached for the can and took another mouthful of Red Bull.

'No obvious pattern,' Monica said.

'So some of the boys were taken from very rural areas, like Paul and Robert. Some from more urban areas, like Zandy Allen.'

'How's he selecting the victims?' Monica wondered out loud. 'They're all about the same age. Look similar. He knows them well enough to find their weaknesses. But it's over a big geographical area. Could he be tracking them online?'

Crawford shrugged. He looked exhausted. 'Neither Paul nor Robert were that active on social media or forums. Whoever did it must have had personal contact.' He thought for a moment. 'What about the social worker, Michael Bach?'

'What about him?' Monica said. She'd left Michael's involvement out of her explanation to Crawford.

'I don't know. He travels around a lot, has access to boys the same age as the victims. It just seems ...'

'His alibis checked out,' Monica said without meeting Crawford's eye.

'I know.' He closed his eyes and let the medication take away some of the pain. 'If not him then it must be someone similar. Someone who would fit the same profile.'

Monica was halfway across the dark car park when the phone in her pocket started ringing. She'd let Crawford drift off to sleep. Maybe he'd woken up and was wondering where she'd gone.

'Unknown number'. She answered. 'Crawford? Is that you?'

There was no voice on the other end of the line. Just a sound like static. She was about to hang up when someone finally spoke: 'I saw you just the other day, under the pines.' The voice was male, the accent neutral and soft with just a hint of Lowland Scots.

Monica froze. 'Who is this?'

'You know me. You've been following on. Coming closer to me.'

'Like you followed Owen MacLennan?'

'MacLennan.' He said the name like it was a joke. 'A useful idiot to feed to a gang of idiots. It's funny just how incompetent you are. And the other one. Losing his arm. What a shame.'

Monica scanned the dark car park. 'What's your name?'

'Which one?' The sound of a muffled laugh. 'Sometimes I don't even know myself. Which face would you like to see?'

'The face you showed to Robert. To Paul? And those other boys.'

He seemed to hesitate for a second. 'They wanted me to show them. The same as you want me to. Don't you? Why else did you come to look for me?'

Monica glanced back at the dark windows of the hospital. She found herself thinking about the GHB. That faint smell of incense in the boys' houses. Like lambs to the slaughter.

'Why did you drug them if they wanted to go with you? Why did you try to hide it? You didn't want us to know that part, did you?'

Silence. When his voice came back onto the line it was different. Low and horrible and dripping with contempt. 'Those two things came willingly. Just like you'll come willingly.'

Chapter 67

Michael barely slept that night. He lay on the sofa in the living room with the whisky bottle, watching the fire burn down slowly into embers. The darkness outside beyond the windows. The storm battering the glass. He watched the cats as they slept, curled up and peaceful while fears and uncertainties gathered around him.

People gathered with his fears. People who were trapped and lost somewhere. Nichol. Joseph. Neither dead nor fully alive. Watching him from the corner of the room. There among the shadows his father turned to look at him. He'd changed a lot. He had a different, younger face, and a different body, but it was still him. There was a long conversation he wanted to have. A lot of information he wanted to impart, but the walls were already beginning to come down around him. Crushing down.

'Dad!' Michael tried to scream to him, but the word came out as a whisper. And anyway, he could feel fingers – strong fingers – begin to tighten round his throat. The man who was his father looked over as the walls closed in all around and said, 'Let me get that for you.'

Michael sat bolt upright on the sofa. He reached for a cigarette with a shaking hand. It was almost light outside. He stood up and walked out to the Land Rover, got in and started driving.

Chapter 68

Monica stared at the map on her kitchen sideboard until it blurred. She'd tried to fit the fragments together into something coherent. Focusing on the facts of the case whenever her mind tried to drag her back to that phone call. *Had the killer really seen her? Had he been there?* Close by. Watching as she walked alone through the woods behind Paul MacKay's house.

Monica shivered and tried again to dismiss the terrifying idea. She ran a hand through her hair, four days unwashed and lank beneath the grime, grease and, she realised, probably the blood of Crawford and the murdered officer. She wiped her hand on the denim of her jeans and looked back at the lines and points on the map. She had tried cross-referencing locations against known meteor impact sites in the Highlands. Lining them up with the points at which various stars and planets rose above the horizon to see if she could detect a pattern, a clue as to where he might try to abduct his next victim or dump the body. There had to be a pattern. Some reasoning behind where he took them and where he placed the bodies. If she could work it out they might even be able to find Nichol Morgan alive.

Finally she stood up and glanced at the uneaten pile of toast and the pot of coffee her mum had made for her. The little plastic bowl with the cartoon cats on it was lying beside the toast. It was the one Lucy used for those sickly breakfast cereals Monica's mother still insisted on buying. Monica tasted the milk left in the bowl. It was almost as sweet as one of Crawford's energy drinks.

'Fucking hell,' she whispered, making a note to ask her mum to buy the kid something healthier.

It was murky daylight outside now – a lull in the coming storm – and she found herself wondering how Michael was doing up in Lochinver. Hopefully better than her.

Her phone rang on the worktop. It was a local number.

'DI Kennedy?' It took Monica a moment to recognise the accent.

'Dr Dolohov.'

'I got your message. I found the coroner's report you requested. Ms Harrison.'

Monica had called and left a message on her way home from Michael's croft the night before.

'That's right,' she said.

'She killed herself,' Dolohov said. Sounding like this was some great achievement.

'I know that.' Monica made her hand into a fist, tried to keep the irritation out of her voice. 'But what happened?'

'Pain medication. Codeine. Enough to take the edge off. Alcohol. Enough to make the world peaceful, I should imagine. A nice hot bath. And she –'

'– opened her ulnar arteries,' Monica finished, remembering Owen MacLennan hanging in the dark room. The dark blood sprayed up the wall.

'How did you know?' Dolohov asked.

'How much booze and pills were in her system?' Monica asked, ignoring his question.

Dolohov sighed. 'Hold on – I'll look.'

While she waited Monica mulled over what he had already told her. Clearly the murderer had more than one way to kill.

And the bite marks on the boys' bodies when they were already dead – was that just the killer playing games? The main motivation was the teenage boys. Monica felt confident of that. They were roughly the same age with similar looks – pale skin and dark hair. Then there were the stones forced into at least three of their throats. MacLennan had been killed out of necessity, getting rid of an inconvenience. Monica was confident of that too. Was Harrison the same? Had the journalist been close to identifying the killer?

'About twice the legal limit, the old legal limit. A handful of pills,' Dolohov said finally, interrupting her thoughts.

'Were there any signs of violence? Struggle?'

She could hear Dolohov's breath down the phone line as he turned over pages. 'Nothing like that. Door locked from the inside. Good physical health.'

'Physical health?'

'Well. She had recently been referred to a psychiatrist. Prescribed a course of anti-anxiety medication, which would tie in with the timing of the suicide.'

'What was the name of her psychiatrist?' Monica asked.

'Let me see ...' The sound of Dolohov turning more pages. When he came back on the line Monica heard the change in his voice. And she knew the name of the psychiatrist without even having to hear him say it.

Chapter 69

Right up until he took the turn-off for Lochinver – a port village an hour or so north of Ullapool – Michael wasn't certain if he was going to do what Monica had asked. Or if he was going to keep driving towards the mountains in the distance and away from the storm coming in off the Atlantic.

He parked the Land Rover close to the harbour's edge. Colonel Mustard looked up at him from the dashboard, where he'd ensconced himself after chasing Michael out of the croft and barging onboard. For once Michael was pleased of the company. Because as he glanced around outside he wondered if he'd ever felt more tired. More alone. He patted the cat's head then lit a cigarette and realised with a shudder that he was staring at the exact spot where Mark MacArthur had been filmed walking by the pier.

He felt panic wash through his body at the chaos of it. The universe swallowing people. Grinding them into non-existence. It was what had happened to Joseph, his brother. What had happened to his mother and his father. What was happening to him.

An elderly woman was hurrying down the street, trailing a shopping cart behind her.

Michael climbed out of the Land Rover and shouted to her: 'Excuse me, I'm looking for someone!'

She shook her head, barely acknowledging him. Michael stared after her and looked around the street, which was otherwise deserted with the tourist season long over. He tried a newsagent's but it was closed. The only place open was a cafe. Michael ordered a coffee, asked if the man serving knew the MacArthur family. He shook his head dismissively. He'd only been in the village since the summer. He didn't know anyone.

Michael took the scorching mug of coffee the man gave him to a corner seat. He used the cafe's Wi-Fi to search online for an address. Frustration mounting as he watched the phone labouring to load the search screen. How was he going to find a murderer if he couldn't even find a fucking address? He took a mouthful of the coffee. Swore and spat it into a paper napkin as it burned a layer of skin off his tongue.

As he was lifting his eyes from the napkin they landed on a battered, abandoned phone box on the other side of the road. The discomfort on his tongue was forgotten as an idea formed. He left the superheated coffee and crossed the road, trying to remember the last time he'd even been in a phone box. The old familiar smell they all seemed to share. The memories from childhood – phoning friends whose numbers he could probably still remember now, speaking awkwardly to girlfriends' fathers. Something that the kids of today would never have to endure, he thought as he flicked through the phone book. It seemed like another relic. Just like the newspapers in the Archive Centre.

It didn't take long to find the name he was looking for: 'L MacArthur'. There in print.

Michael glanced up and down the street. There was a sense of eyes staring out at him from empty windows, Colonel Mustard watching through the windscreen of the Land Rover. He tore out the page and folded it into his pocket.

*

The house was off a single-track road, surrounded by Scots pine trees. At the side of the building, whipping in the storm gusts, Michael noticed a long-abandoned rope swing.

'I thought maybe you were another journalist. I've been hoping someone would come,' Louise MacArthur said. She set the mug of tea in front of Michael. She had answered the door almost as if she was expecting him. Invited him in before he'd even had the chance to introduce himself.

'What happened to Cassandra Harrison?' Michael asked.

'She killed herself. That's what everyone wants to believe.' Louise MacArthur spoke slowly, without emotion. Michael reached for the mug of tea. He saw the blobs of spoiled milk floating in it.

'But you don't?' he said, pushing the mug away.

'Someone killed her.' Louise's voice was strangely matter of fact – medicated, Michael realised.

'Who?'

'The same person who came for my son. Mark was—' She swallowed her tears. Let the drugs wash them away. Michael glanced around the room. With horror he remembered the video of Mark. Shot through the kid's bedroom window. The killer had been here, watching this very house.

'I've been looking into some other disappearances,' Michael said.

'The same as Cassandra was?'

'We're trying to find a connection. Was there anything different before he disappeared? Anyone who tried to get close to him? Any odd messages?'

She shook her head slowly. 'We went over everything. Emails, Facebook, everything. It was like he evaporated. Like the universe just swallowed him.' Her hand went to her face.

'I heard about those two boys who were murdered. Thinking of Mark like that – how terrified he would have been. He was scared of the dark as a boy. He'd wake up in the night screaming ...'

'Like a night terror?'

'That's right. It was always the same dream. A long corridor with a room at the end. Someone whispering for him to keep walking towards it.'

'I can't imagine how hard it must be.'

'The funny thing was,' she went on, not even seeming to hear Michael, 'he had the same dream the week before he disappeared. The first time in years. I heard the screaming. He told me that it was the old nightmare. A long corridor. Whispering. Almost like he knew what was going to happen.'

'You think he knew? You think someone was following him.'

She shook her head slowly. 'I don't know.'

'Does the name Nichol Morgan mean anything to you?' Michael asked. Louise shook her head again. 'What about Zandy Allen – Alexander Allen? Did Mark have any friends from Inverness? Other parts of the Highlands?'

'No,' Louise said softly. 'He had a few friends here. They've mostly gone off to university now though.'

Michael glanced down at the table, looked up at her. 'Would you mind if I looked in Mark's room?'

It was obviously months since anyone had been in the bedroom. There was a layer of dust over everything. A life frozen at a certain moment. Michael checked the books and posters – nothing obviously unusual – but there had to be something, some clue as to the killer's identity or something that could lead him to Nichol. He tried the drawers and again flicked through the books on the shelf. Philosophy, maths – echoes of Nichol. Then Michael saw it. Right there on the desk. A black stone, just like Nichol's. Had the killer been in here? Inside this room? Michael's skin crawled at the idea. He picked up the stone and felt its coldness in his hand.

The door crept open behind him, dragging across the carpet.

A charge of fear flickered through Michael's body. He whipped round. Louise MacArthur was staring from the open doorway. He held the stone out for her to see, noticing his hand was shaking. 'Do you know where this came from?'

She tilted her head. 'Why do you ask?' Michael heard the catch in her voice.

'Cassandra asked about it too, didn't she?'

Louise looked over his shoulder at the window. Michael couldn't keep himself from following her eyes. As if some horror might be looking back in at them both.

There was nothing of course. Only the rain hitting the glass, beyond it a Scots pine swaying in the storm. When Louise spoke her voice was almost a whisper. 'The week before Cassandra died she came here. She was different – frightened. Up until then she had been so confident. So sure that she could find out what had happened to Mark. To those other boys ...'

Louise turned away and shifted a cabinet from beside the bed. She opened a small cupboard behind it and pulled out a cardboard box.

'Cassandra asked me to keep this for her.' She held the box out. Michael took it. There were stacks of papers inside. 'I couldn't bring myself to ... She told me not to trust anyone.'

'But you're giving it to me?'

'Whatever's in there got Cassandra killed. I thought maybe you had come to kill me for it. Maybe part of me wanted that.' She looked at the floor, then back up at Michael. 'Maybe you can find out what happened to Mark and those other boys. Let them rest.'

Chapter 70

'The hunt for suspected murderer Donald Cameron has been scaled back today as storm-force winds and extreme cold temperatures—'

Monica killed the radio. She glanced up and down the quiet road then over to Lees's office. It was a large Victorian house. The place looked haunted, abandoned. *You should wait*, she thought, *you shouldn't go in alone. Get Michael or Fisher to come with you.*

She dismissed the idea as paranoia and climbed out of the Volvo. As if she couldn't handle Lees – or anyone else for that matter – on her own. She crossed the street, feeling the empty eyes of the house on her as she walked down the grand driveway to the porch. The heavy door swung open at her touch. Almost like it wanted her to go in. She caught the smells in the hallway. Floor polish and a hint under it of incense, somehow bloated and corrupt. It came floating up from deeper in the building.

Was it the same smell as in the boys' bedrooms? Monica felt the hair on her arms stand up as she pushed the door closed behind her. Could Lees really be the killer?

The waiting area was empty, dominated by a strange bronze sculpture with a leather sofa opposite it. Monica knocked gently on the door to Dr Lees's office but there was no reply.

She pushed the door open. The room was grey under the light from a high window. She glanced at the bookcase, the sofa, the desk and a chair. But there was no sign of the psychiatrist. Monica hesitated for a second and caught the sound of voices, echoing from somewhere. She reminded herself that Nichol Morgan was still missing. He could still be alive. If there was a chance of finding him, of proving that Lees was the killer ...

It seemed obvious what she had to do.

She closed the door behind her and pushed the bolt home. There was a filing cabinet by the desk. She pulled on a drawer but it was locked. She turned back to the desk. There had to be a diary, something she could use to work out his movements, Monica told herself. He travelled for his work, consulted all over the Highlands. It gave him the opportunity, just as Crawford had highlighted. He knew how to manipulate people. How to control them. She remembered the way he had casually dismissed her concerns over Lucy.

Monica opened the desk drawer. Pens and notebooks inside, laid out precisely. *There has to be something*, Monica thought as she slid the drawer closed. She tried the next one. Inside there was a piece of slate with words written on it in black ink. She picked it up and held it to the light: 'You must still have chaos in yourself to be able to give birth to a dancing star.'

'What do you think you're doing?'

Monica whipped round. She realised with horror that there was a small door she'd missed on the opposite side of the room. Dr Lees was standing there, staring at her.

He stepped into the room.

'This is a surprise,' he said with a strangely blank expression on his face.

Monica stared back at him. She was still holding the heavy piece of slate in her hands. 'I need to see your diary.'

'My diary?' He made a gentle tutting sound. 'That won't be possible.' He took a step closer.

'I know about Cassandra Harrison.'

A look of uncertainty crossed Lees's face, then recognition. 'The journalist? Ahh, I see.'

'Hately should be arriving any minute. It'll be easier if you cooperate,' Monica said.

'Oh, I doubt that. You see, I speak to your commanding officer regularly. You're on compassionate leave, no longer part of the investigation.' He took another step, staring up at her. She hadn't noticed before how blue his eyes were.

'You treated Cassandra Harrison.'

Half a smile was playing on his lips now. 'I treated her once when she was having anxiety attacks. Do you have any idea how many clients I've dealt with over the years?'

'I know you've dealt with a lot of clients. You've had access to a lot of vulnerable people,' Monica said.

'And you think that means I'm a murderer? We know that Owen MacLennan murdered those two boys, probably assisted by Don Cameron.'

'Where were you on the nights that the boys were abducted?' Monica asked.

Lees shook his head. 'And if I don't tell you, you'll bring violence into this ...' he nodded at the piece of slate she was holding '... situation?' He lowered his voice, his face hard. 'I think part of you would like that. I think you understand violence, criminality. These things attract you. Your *friends* from Rapinch that your colleagues still talk about. The ones that make them wonder about you. And the *unknown* father of your child. I'm sure there's an interesting story there.' He snorted.

Monica dropped her eyes to the carpet. She felt the piece of slate in her hand and a crazy impulse to swing it at his face, but instead raised her eyes back to his. 'You've got no idea what you're talking about. You've got no idea about my life.'

Lees stared back at her and raised his eyebrows. He took another step closer then reached into his pocket for something. He turned and unlocked the filing cabinet, laid his diary down on the desk in front of her.

'You can see that I had clients on both of the evenings that those boys were abducted. If you like you can further violate my clients' confidentiality by contacting them to confirm this. Their details are in the back. Oh, and I have an office assistant too. He can confirm that I was here at those times.' Lees unbuttoned his suit jacket, pushed his hands into his pockets. 'I'll be making a formal complaint about this, of course.'

Monica dropped the slate on the desk beside the diary. She leafed through the pages for the relevant days. There were late appointments for the evenings that Paul MacKay and Robert Wright had been abducted. If it was accurate then he couldn't be the killer.

She pointed to the slate. 'Where did you get that?'

'It was a gift, years ago from a client. A quote from Nietzsche.' He snorted again. 'I suppose that now would be a good time for that other quote of his: "When you fight monsters, take care that you yourself don't become a monster."' He tilted his head back in a dry laugh.

Monica was about to reply when she felt her phone ring in her pocket. 'Michael Bach'. She answered.

'Monica,' his voice shaky over the line, the sounds of a storm around him, 'I think they're coming for us.'

Chapter 71

Michael raced the gathering storm home. By the time he made it back to his house the rain had turned to snow and was whipping over the moorland in stinging clouds.

With Colonel Mustard under one arm, and the box Louise MacArthur had given him under the other, he ran into the house. Once they were inside the cat stretched and jumped onto the sofa, where he sat down and started cleaning himself.

Michael set the box on the coffee table. He hesitated for a moment and thought, *Whatever's in there got Cassandra Harrison killed*, but opened the box anyway. Inside was a mess of newspaper stories, notebooks, printouts, folded and screwed-up pieces of paper. Michael formed an image of Cassandra Harrison: afraid, panicking, pulling things down from where they were pinned on walls, stuffing them into the box. He emptied the papers out across the table and under the smell of ink detected the faintest edge of rose or lavender. The last hint of her perfume.

With a shaking hand Michael flicked through the papers, trying to form something coherent from the mess. He lit a cigarette and picked up his phone. As he flicked through the call register for his last call to Monica his eyes fell on another entry from the day before: 'Highland Academy'.

Kyle Ward. Michael remembered that Ward had agreed to put him in touch with Alexander Allen's mother. Impulsively he dialled the number. The signal was cutting out with the storm, and Michael could hardly hear the receptionist as he asked to speak to Ward. With the phone held to his ear he awkwardly pulled his jacket on then walked outside into the sleet. Up the hill to where the signal was usually clearer.

'That's right. I need to speak to Mr Ward. Yes, it's urgent. It's very important.' He was almost shouting to be heard against the driving wind. Then a beeping sound. On hold.

Finally, after almost five minutes someone came on the line. 'I'm sorry. I can't help you.' It sounded like Ward, but all the confidence, all the institutional authority was gone from his voice.

'Wait! Why?'

'I'm sorry.'

'You found something, didn't you? Nichol's in danger. You have to tell me.'

'There was nothing. Alexander Allen killed himself. That's the sad truth. There's nothing else I can say. I'm sorry.' The line went dead.

Michael dialled straight back. 'I was speaking to Mr Ward just a minute ago, but the line dropped out!' Michael was shouting above the storm.

'I'm afraid Mr Ward isn't free to take any calls now. He's going to be leaving early for the day.'

'We were speaking just a second ago. He's still there, isn't he?'

'I'm sorry. You'll have to call back on Monday.'

The line went dead again. Michael stared at the phone. *What has Ward discovered? Something that frightens him so much that he won't even talk to me?*

The phone buzzed in his hand. Michael felt a surge of hope as he answered, but it was a woman. Slowly he realised that it was Anita. He could hear her words but what she was saying didn't make any sense.

'... serious allegation against you. The police are involved. I can't tell you anything more at this point. I shouldn't even be calling you but I didn't want you to find out by letter.'

'What are you talking about? What am I supposed to have done?'

'You've been all over the place, Michael. I warned you.'

'Listen. Who did this come from? The man who killed those boys – I think he might have Nichol.'

'Can you hear yourself, Michael?'

'It's someone with influence. With connections to the police. Just tell me what they're saying I've done.'

'I have to go. You'll get fair representation, the chance to put your side across. Just ... don't do anything stupid.' The line went dead as the snow whipped in the wind, the moor pale in the claustrophobia of the white-out. He stared at his house, barely visible in the storm. For a moment there was a shape, a shadow by the window. Then it was gone, just a ghost in the snow.

Michael dialled the number and held the phone to his frozen ear.

'Monica, I think they're coming for us. Ward knows something. He's about to leave the school. You have to stop him.'

Chapter 72

Monica was already back at her car by the time she ended the call. She jumped into the Volvo and turned it towards the school. If Ward knew something he might be in danger. She gripped the steering wheel harder as the rain came down heavily, her wipers struggling to cope.

Her phone. *Michael again?*

'Miss Kennedy?' It was a woman's voice. *No, it's DI*, Monica thought. It had been so long since anyone had addressed with a non-police title.

'Listen, if this is a sales—'

'I'm phoning from the nursery. Lucy's still here and she says that you're supposed to pick her up today and not her gran? Is that right or has she got her wee self mixed up?'

A hideous combination of guilt and shame snaked up from Monica's stomach to her throat. It swallowed her voice.

'Miss Kennedy? Are you there?'

'I … No, she's right,' Monica managed to say.

'Oh. OK. It's just that you're almost an hour late.'

Lucy was waiting outside the nursery with the assistant when Monica pulled up. 'I'm so sorry, honey.' But the kid was stiff in her arms, refusing to return her hug. Monica stood up, turned to the nursery worker. 'It won't happen again.'

The woman jerked her head in a terse nod, her arms folded against the rain. 'It's upsetting for the child. If you can at least telephone—'

Monica nodded. 'I'm sorry – I'm in a hurry.' She strapped Lucy into the back seat and pulled out into the road.

Monica raced through the traffic lights as they were turning red, then took a fast right turn at the roundabout. When she was on the straight she tilted the rear-view mirror so she could see Lucy's face.

'I'm sorry I was late, honey.' The kid kept her head down. 'We'll go to Granny's. That'll be nice, won't it?'

Monica accelerated past two cars then pulled in ahead of them, their horns blaring as she went straight on at the next roundabout, her foot barely easing on the accelerator. Past the hospital and the police HQ on towards the Highland Academy.

Monica glanced in the mirror at Lucy again. The kid was holding a book tight in her lap, her head still down. As if she hadn't heard what her mother had said.

Monica turned on to the long road that led past quiet suburban streets up to the school. She stopped at the entrance gates. Had Ward already left? Had she missed him? The play-ground was empty, the pupils already gone for the day. Quickly she pulled up the school's webpage on her phone, clicked on the 'Staff' page and found a photo of Kyle Ward. At least she would know who she was looking for. He had dark hair and was wearing a black academic gown and mortar board. The epitome of a kindly schoolmaster, no wonder he was afraid if he had discovered something about the murders. Monica felt a moment of pity before she reminded herself that he had a duty of care to his pupils. They should be his first priority no matter how frightened he was.

Monica turned to Lucy in the back seat. 'I'm really sorry I was late. We're going to spend a lot more time together. OK?'

The kid glanced up uncertainly. Her glasses balanced on the end of her nose. Monica reached over to touch the soft skin on her cheek. How many times can you break a kid's trust and apologise before broken promises become all they expect from you?

'What have you got there?' She pointed to the book Lucy was holding in her lap.

Lucy moved her arm so Monica could see the cover. 'It's about cats,' she said finally.

'Do you like cats?' Monica asked. Another new interest the kid had discovered while her mother was away. Lucy nodded, the toggles on her little duffel coat shaking with the movement.

'I met a cat yesterday,' Monica found herself saying. 'He was ginger. Maybe you could meet him too?' Monica glanced back out of the windscreen as the front door to the school opened.

A man came out. His face matched the picture Monica had found on the school website. He opened an umbrella and began hurrying across the car park. Monica jumped out of the Volvo and slammed the door behind her. She ran across to cut him off. Shouting his name as he was about to get into a black Range Rover.

He gave her a look, something between mistrust and anger. 'I'm sorry, who are you?'

Monica glanced back at her own car to make sure Lucy was locked safely inside. 'Kyle Ward, I'm DI Monica Kennedy.' She dug her ID out of her pocket. 'I need to ask you a couple of questions about the death of an ex-student of yours. A young man called Alexander Allen.'

'I don't know anything about him. I'm afraid I'm too busy to talk about any of these things.' He climbed behind the steering wheel.

'What things? I never told you what I wanted to ask.'

'Listen. I spoke to the police yesterday. I've told them everything I can.' His jaw was set angrily. This was a man who wasn't used to having his authority questioned. There was something under that, though. Monica wasn't sure what. Was it fear?

'Who did you speak to?'

'He didn't say.'

'What did he want to know?' Ward looked over his shoulder. A hunted gesture. 'Listen, sir,' Monica said. 'I believe that Alexander's death could be linked to other crimes. To abduction, possibly other—'

'I don't know anything about it.' Ward was almost shouting. He glanced around the empty car park and lowered his voice. 'If you're here to warn me again, then don't worry. I've got the message.'

'Warn you? What did he say?'

Ward held her eye for a long moment. She felt the rain on her face, running down her neck. Ward seemed to make up his mind. 'He gave me a name and told me to google it. The implication being that it was a warning.'

'What was the name?'

'Owen MacLennan. He killed himself recently. When I got home, there was a copy of a newspaper article about his death pushed through my letterbox.'

The scene flashed back for Monica. Owen MacLennan hanging in the small room. Blood running down his naked body.

'I'm just a teacher. I have to put on a show of authority for the kids, but ...' He held out his hands. 'This isn't the kind of thing I want to be involved in.'

Ward made to start the engine, but Monica caught his hand. 'You're already involved in it.' She stared at his face. There was something there. Something hidden. 'Something happened today. Didn't it? Something else?'

He looked down then seemed to make a decision. 'I still wasn't sure after the call. I thought it could be a prank. Kids or something. A social worker called Michael Bach – I've been helping him to look for a missing boy. A child called Nichol Morgan. Michael said the boy was in danger so naturally I did everything I could to help.' With a shaking hand he reached for his phone. 'Then, this morning I received an email from Nichol Morgan. He says he's in danger. That Michael Bach ...' His voice faltered. Monica took the phone from his hand and started to read.

Chapter 73

Monica drove, her head spinning. Spiralling was a better description. A mess of churning thoughts fighting for her attention.

Michael Bach – a killer. She didn't believe it. It went against every intuition.

'Where are we going, Mummy?'

Monica glanced in the mirror. She could hear the uncertainty in Lucy's voice. 'We're going to Granny's, honey. I just need to stop at the flat first.'

The email. Supposedly from Nichol Morgan and claiming that Michael was the killer. It was the same pattern as Paul MacKay. Using emails to lure the victim close. Maybe the killer was doing the same thing with Kyle Ward. Bringing him close, isolating him. But Ward was nothing like the profile of the other victims.

She ran back over what Ward had told her. *Someone in the police – could it really be a police officer?* She pulled up outside her flat and turned to unbuckle Lucy from her seat in the back. Then paused. There was no time, and who would be stupid enough to abduct a detective's child from a busy street in the middle of the day? The kid would be fine again in the alarmed car with the doors locked for two minutes. 'I'm just going to grab some things then we'll go to Granny's. Wait here a minute, OK?'

Monica ran to the front door and up the stairs. She stopped dead at the sound of footsteps from the corridor above. Someone was walking towards her flat. Monica moved quietly up the steps. A dark figure was standing outside her door. She heard him try the handle.

With a weird sinking feeling Monica realised it was DC Fisher. He turned slowly towards her. 'Jesus. DI Kennedy, I didn't hear you.'

'What are you doing here?'

He glanced down the corridor. 'Can we go inside? It's about the case.'

She hesitated. 'I think I'm OK out here.'

He tilted his head and gave her a strange look. 'Are you OK? You look sick.'

She didn't reply, and he glanced over his shoulder down the corridor again before taking a step closer. He was dressed in a suit and looked neat and in control. For once he didn't seem stressed.

'The cement block in Cameron's back garden. The forensic team has reported back their initial findings. It's not a grave. There are some personal belongings, but no body parts.'

'Belongings?'

'A purse, a belt. God knows what. But they're old. At least twenty years old. Nothing connected to our murders.'

Monica nodded. Fisher lowered his voice. 'I also have to tell you about the stones. The meteor fragments.'

Monica stared at him. Tried to read his face.

'They're gone,' he said finally.

'But you're the exhibits officer. You'd have to sign them out,' Monica said.

'Someone must have stolen them,' he replied.

Monica stared at him. Was the killer's accomplice right there in front of her? Fisher, with his interest in astronomy and IT. Feeding her information. Hiding behind his geeky persona.

She needed to speak to Kyle Ward. She needed to know what he'd discovered. There could be someone on their way to his house right now, someone who wanted to shut him up.

'I have to go, Fisher. I'm sorry. There's something I have to do.'

He nodded slowly, his eyes never leaving her face. 'Whoever took those fragments was taking a big risk. They must know that we're close.'

She took a step back. Suddenly she wanted to be as far from him as possible.

'Is everything OK. DI Kennedy?'

'Did you do something, Fisher? Did you help to kill those boys?' she said softly.

He stared up at her. For long seconds she couldn't read the expression on his face. Without taking her eyes from him, Monica retreated down the corridor then ran down the stairs and out into the street, climbed into the Volvo and locked the doors again.

'How big was the cat, Mummy? Were you allowed to pet him?' Lucy was staring down at the photographs in her book and thankfully hadn't noticed the panic on her mother's face.

Monica pulled the car away. For several seconds she could hardly breathe, then anger began to rise in her – cold fury – that Fisher might be using his position as a police detective to facilitate murder. Nichol could still be alive, terrified and praying for help. Monica was the only one who could help him now. If she didn't make it to Ward's quickly they might never find him.

She hesitated anyway. Was it worth taking the risk – however small – that something could go wrong while Lucy was in the car with her? She gripped the steering wheel harder. *Be a good mother or be a good detective?* Whatever she did was going to be wrong. She glanced at Lucy's face in the rear-view mirror, not quite able to believe the words she was about to say to her daughter.

'We're just going to help one of Mummy's friends. The man from earlier. He's a teacher. Would you like to help him?'

Chapter 74

Colonel Mustard cut in front of Michael in the corridor. He was meowing loudly and seemed unusually desperate for attention, almost as if he were trying to communicate something.

Michael ignored him and ran through to the living room. He started piling Cassandra Harrison's papers and notebooks back into the box. He glanced at his phone. 'Come on. What does Ward know? What frightened him so much?' Michael whispered under his breath, willing Monica to call him back.

He flicked through the notes as he dropped them into the box. There had to be something there. *There'd better be*, he thought, *because otherwise you're going to lose your job. Probably there'll be a lot of stuff in the press. What'll be left when the tide goes out?*

Michael did his best to ignore the thoughts. He didn't even want to consider what he'd been suspended for. Or who had instigated it. Melissa had probably complained. *What would that be described as? Unethical behaviour? Grooming?* Not to mention Nichol's laptop, which he still illegally possessed. *The laptop*. The dream came shuddering back to him then. Nichol standing outside the window of the house. The laptop bag slung over his shoulder.

Michael ran out to the Land Rover. Nichol's bag was still in the back. He grabbed it and took it into the house. The kid never went anywhere without the bag. Michael had assumed it was something on the laptop, but what about the bag itself?

He'd been so focused on the computer he hadn't thought to go through the pockets on the bag.

'So fucking obvious.' Sleet hammered the window. It was almost dark outside already. As though it was the final day.

Michael pulled the laptop out and ran his hands around the lining of the bag. He checked the front pocket: just a bunch of pens. He opened the front compartment and a manga comic book fell out. There was nothing else. He dropped the bag, swore, then realised that there was a thin zipped compartment at the back. It wasn't hidden but he'd missed it in the low light. With a strange sense of foreboding he unzipped it.

Inside there was a slim A4 workbook produced on a high-quality colour photocopier. Just four or five pages stapled together. On the cover there was an image of a galaxy exploding in beautiful reds and pinks. The words 'Highland Futures Astronomicon' were printed above the image.

Michael gasped. With shaking hands, he went back to the pile of Cassandra's notes. He found the other workbook – Mark's was worn dark, older. His name was written in a child's handwriting on the cover. Michael flicked through the two booklets and tried to work out what 'Highland Futures Astronomicon' was. It seemed to be some kind of Highland-wide schools club. A society for kids with an interest in space and astronomy.

He concentrated on Mark's workbook. In the dim light a name jumped off the page at him. It had been circled in red ink – presumably by Cassandra Harrison. Michael blinked and checked it again. He turned to Nichol's booklet. The same name: *Mr Kyle Ward*. He read the text carefully: 'The president and founder of the Highland Futures Astronomicon is Mr Ward. You can contact him on his club email if you have any questions about club meetings or excursions. A galaxy spiralling into a dark infinity. Michael felt his sense of reality shifting off into a chaotic unknown.

Ward had told Michael that he didn't know Nichol personally – impossible if Nichol was a member of his club. What were the chances that Mark MacArthur had been in it too, even though his school was more than a two-hour drive from Nichol's?

'It's so fucking obvious.' Michael grabbed his phone and searched through the contacts for Melissa. She answered after the first ring.

'I'm sorry. He told me if I didn't he would hurt me. He was waiting outside my house. No one would have believed—'

'You're talking about Ward?'

'He told me to go to your house. Then the social work department came. They made a big thing about it. I never meant to—'

He cut her off: 'It doesn't matter. Ward knew Nichol, didn't he?'

'Of course. Nichol helped with the website. That was ages ago though. He stopped—'

'Six months ago?'

'Maybe, I think so.'

It all fitted together. Nichol had seen Ward abduct his friend Alexander Allen. He found something on the website, something that led him to those videos. He knew he wouldn't be believed so he hid them on the phone.

'Listen, don't go anywhere with Ward. Don't even speak to him.'

'Why? What is it?'

'I'll explain later. Just stay at home.' Michael rang off. The thought came bubbling up straight after: *Monica's with him. She doesn't know.*

With a shaking hand he dialled her number but there was no answer. He stuffed the rest of the papers into the box and looked frantically around for his car keys. He found them and tried Monica again. This time it connected, but the sound was shaky because of the stormy night. 'Can you hear me?'

What if Ward had Nichol? What if that was the culmination of it all? The final killing as the comet passed the earth?

'Michael? I'm ... way to Ward's house.'

'Wait! Listen.'

'... could be Fisher, DC Fisher ...'

'You have to listen. Don't go to Ward's place.'

It was as Michael tried to open his front door to go outside in the hope of finding better reception that he realised something was badly wrong. The door was locked and the key was missing. Michael shook the handle. *What the fuck did I do with the key? I'm going mad!*

'Monica! Do not go to Ward's.' But it was no good. The call had dropped out. He had to get outside; he had to call the police.

He rattled the door and tried his pockets, but still he couldn't find the key. *Where the fuck is it?* He gave up and turned to go out the back way instead. As he did so Michael heard the kitchen door close, and what he saw standing in the hallway, on the dirty old carpet, in his own house, frightened him more than anything he'd seen in his life.

Chapter 75

Michael stared into the black barrels of the shotgun the man was pointing at him.

'Do you know who I am, son?' His voice was quiet. Barely above a whisper.

The shape in the snow. By the window. It was real after all, Michael thought as he took the man in. He wore glasses, had a beard – the face that Michael had seen on the news reports. He was as tall as Michael and broad, wearing a green camo jacket. This was someone in control of a situation, who knew what he was doing.

'You've got this wrong, Don,' Michael said.

'I don't think I do. You killed young Paul. That other lad.'

'Who told you that? Kyle Ward? Someone in the police?'

Cameron stared back, expressionless. Then he reached slowly into his pocket and threw something onto the floor. 'Put them on.' He spoke quietly but with weight like a heavy book hitting a table. 'Fucking put them on now.'

Michael looked down at the handcuffs. *Don't put them on, don't touch them.* 'Who did you speak to? Someone's covering up for the killer. It's a man called Ward. My friend's on her way there right—'

'I'll not ask you again, son. I'm not here to fuck about.' The sound of the gun cocking.

Michael picked up the handcuffs. *Fucking run.* But the door was locked behind him. His hands shook as he closed the cuffs around his wrists, but leaving them loose so he could pull his hands out.

'Close them properly.' Michael had no doubt that Cameron would kill him. He clicked the cuffs closed. 'Put your hands against the door.'

'I never did anything to Paul. I know it wasn't you either,' Michael said. 'This is all wrong. I'm trying to find the man who did it.'

Cameron didn't reply. Just lifted the shotgun so it was pointing at Michael's head. Michael turned to face the door. He had to do something, to move. But then he felt the hand hard on the back of his head, a rag stinking of some sort of chemical in his face. His vision blurring, he swung his arms, tried to turn. But now there was a knee in his back, pressing him down on to the carpet. He was aware of his injured face hitting the floor and a banal thought: *That should hurt*. But it didn't. Everything drifted to black.

Chapter 76

Michael's voice faded out on the other end of the line. Ward's house was fifteen minutes outside Inverness to the west. *Fisher might be on his way there now*, Monica thought. Or maybe he'd called someone else. Maybe they were on their way to silence Ward.

Who should she trust? Michael? Crawford was stuck in a hospital bed. The answer was simple and obvious, same as it always was: she should trust herself and no one else. She accelerated down the road and into the teeth of the storm. Monica checked Lucy in the rear-view mirror.

'What would happen if it never stopped raining, Mummy? They said at the Sunday school that it happened before and that's why there's rainbows.'

'Don't be frightened, sweetheart. I'll look after you. Nothing's going to happen to you while I'm here.'

'There's going to be stars falling out of the sky and there could be fairies in them,' Lucy said in a matter-of-fact voice. One of Monica's favourite things about the kid was the way her attention flicked between different areas, equally intrigued by everything about the world. But right now it only added to the storm of confusion in Monica's own mind.

Up ahead there was a queue of traffic. Monica could see the flashing lights further along. She pulled onto the right-hand lane and drove up to the police car, leaned out of the window.

'You need to let me through. It's urgent.'

The police officer pulled his hood forward to shelter his face from the driving sleet. 'The road's blocked. It's like a bloody river. It's the third time this year.'

'I need to get through. I'm police.' She reached for her warrant card, held it out. 'You need to let me through *now* – it's urgent.'

He looked at Monica, then at Lucy in the back seat. 'It's DI Kennedy, isn't it? I thought you were on leave after everything that happened?' Monica realised that she recognised the police officer. He was the one who'd been guarding the dump site at Gairloch. The one that she'd heard rumours about from the past: Duncan Gregg. Their eyes met, his tightened and suspicious. Something unspoken passed between them.

'Where was it you said you were going? I'm going to have to radio this in,' he said.

Monica didn't wait to hear him finish. Instead she reversed, water spraying up off the road as she swung the car back towards the city. She'd have to take the longer way beside Loch Ness. She swore and pressed down on the accelerator then pulled her phone out again. Maybe Michael could make it to Ward faster if he had already left? But did she really trust him? Monica hesitated for a moment then typed Ward's address into a text message. Hit the Send button.

Chapter 77

From a deep dark hole Michael smelled the petrol, felt it running down his neck and blinked his eyes open. The pain from his cheek was excruciating. He tried to move his arm and realised then that he was tied to a chair in his own living room. The nausea engulfed him, and he tried to vomit, rocked forward as his stomach convulsed.

'It's your choice. You can tell me the truth now and we can end this. Or we can sit here for the rest of the night while I take you apart. I'm a Christian man – I don't enjoy this. But I'll do it.'

Michael's mouth wouldn't form the words. He blinked through the stinging petrol. Cameron was sitting opposite him on the battered leather sofa. The shotgun lying beside him.

'You killed those boys, didn't you? Fucking tortured them.'

Michael shook his head. Tried to think beyond the fear and pain. He moved his hands, his legs, but they were tied tight to the chair.

'Forget about moving, son. Forget about escaping.'

Another wave of nausea. Michael leaned forward, his stomach contracting again. He had to get out of there; Monica was on her way to Ward's right now. He twisted his hand and found there was a millimetre of give in the handcuffs. The petrol was a kind of lubricant. He straightened his fingers, started pulling.

Michael felt Don Cameron's hand on his chin, lifting his head up. He opened his eyes. Cameron was holding a hammer, the kind with a ball on one side of the head.

'You know what I'm going to do with this if you lie to me again?'

'Listen to me. Someone lied to you because they want you to kill me. I've been investigating the murders. Just look in that box.'

Don Cameron stared into Michael's eyes. Held the hammer up in front of his face. Then knelt quickly and smashed it down on to his foot. Michael screamed. Cameron held the hammer up. Blood on the head. Smashed the same broken foot. Bones grinding and turning to pulp.

'Please ...' Michael gritted his teeth. Don Cameron held the hammer up. Smashed it down. The pain was primal and sickening. Michael screamed. 'Please ... Please ...'

Don Cameron dropped the hammer and brought his face level with Michael's.

'I'll be back through with the bolt cutters. We'll start on your other foot.'

Michael clenched his fists, tried to think through the pain. He twisted his hands. He had to escape. He pulled, tried to break the bone in a thumb. It was no use – he couldn't generate the leverage. He jerked forward – maybe he could smash the chair. He twisted and rocked until he toppled over to the side. More sickening pain as his face hit the ground. *Move. Move your legs.*

The door opened and Don Cameron looked down at him. A pair of bolt cutters was hanging from one of his hands. Wordlessly he walked round to the back of the chair and lifted it upright. He sat down on the sofa facing Michael again.

Michael tried to speak but his tongue wouldn't make the words. He tried again. 'I know you were there when he took Paul, but you didn't see the killer clearly, did you? It wasn't me – it was a man called Kyle Ward. You tried to stop him. My friend told me. She knows you didn't kill Paul. DI Monica Kennedy. She's on her way to the killer right now. If we don't go now, he'll kill her too.'

Cameron gazed at Michael for a moment. 'You'd say anything to get me to stop. Same way young Paul would have said anything to get you to stop. It didn't work though. Did it?' He stood up and took a step towards Michael. He crouched down at Michael's feet and started unlacing his shoe.

'Wait! Just fucking wait! I know who killed the boys. I can prove it – just give me five fucking minutes. Please!' He didn't recognise his own voice, and Cameron didn't even look up. 'Someone in the police gave you my name, didn't they? They're trying to get rid of me. Please!'

Cameron pulled Michael's shoe off. Then his sock. He looked up, stared into Michael's eyes and reached for the bolt cutters. He opened their jaws wide then began to close them, halfway up Michael's foot.

'There's a box in the hall. Look at the notes in it. The detective, Monica Kennedy, she's on her way to the killer now. He'll fucking kill her. Like he did Paul MacKay and those other boys. Just fucking read the notes! Please!'

Don Cameron waited patiently for Michael to stop speaking then turned back to the bolt cutters and began to squeeze the handles together.

Chapter 78

The road along the banks of Loch Ness was treacherous at the best of times, narrow and winding. But with the standing water, the driving rain on the car windscreen and the storm-force winds, Monica could barely manage thirty miles an hour. All the time she expected to come across a fallen tree or an accident that would force her to stop.

She'd tried Ward twice on the phone. Both times it had rung out. Maybe someone had got to him already, shut him up before he could show her what he'd found? Finally the turn-off came: a steep road uphill. It was almost like a river with the water coming down it.

In the back Lucy was staring out of the window at the thick plantation forest by the side of the road.

'We're nearly there, sweetheart. We'll go to Granny's after that, OK? Don't be frightened of the storm; you're safe with me.' This time the kid didn't reply.

Monica slowed the car at the top of the hill. The satnav showed the house down a track on the left. She narrowed her eyes, looking for a sign in the dark. There were several tracks leading off through the trees. She knew from experience how often GPS maps were wrong in the rural Highlands.

After thirty minutes of increasingly frantic searching she finally spotted the sign, nailed to a tree: BALNUIT. She turned hard left and accelerated up the track.

Chapter 79

Michael landed hard in the back of his Land Rover. The pain in his broken foot and behind his eye was horrific.

His phone had vibrated with a text message. Don Cameron had put the bolt cutters down. Picked the phone up. He had looked through the notes in the box. Maybe he'd seen the connection. Maybe they were on their way to Ward's. Maybe he was taking Michael somewhere to dispose of him. Somewhere he'd never be found.

Michael gritted his teeth and tried to squeeze one hand out of the cuffs again as Don Cameron climbed into the driver's seat and started the engine.

Chapter 80

Monica pulled up outside the house. The place felt lonely with the pine trees surrounding it and the black sky above. The only light was a vague glow from deep inside the building.

She turned to Lucy in the back seat. The kid was pointing out the window. The sky had cleared and the stars were visible. So bright now that they were away from the lights of the city.

'The shooting stars are coming tonight, Mummy. Do you think we can see them from up here?' The excitement was clear in Lucy's voice.

Monica reached back to touch the kid's face as she felt a surge of love. She thought about unfastening Lucy's seat belt and taking her inside. Decided against it. She would be safer in the locked car. Once she had found Ward she'd drop Lucy at her mum's, take him somewhere to talk. She reached for her phone and opened the Racing Penguin game that Lucy liked, handed it to her. 'I'm just going to be two minutes again. I'll leave the little light on so you know not to be frightened. OK?'

Lucy took the phone and nodded. A picture of childhood innocence with her stuffed rabbit tucked under her arm. Monica leaned over, kissed her quickly on the forehead then clicked the light on, pressed the door closed and locked it.

She turned towards the house. There was a figure visible in the light above the doorway. Ward. He disappeared inside.

Monica heard Lucy say something from inside the car. She looked round but couldn't make out what her daughter was saying through the glass.

She ran towards the house, shouting Ward's name. Clearly he was frightened.

'Ward! Ward! Listen, you'll be safe with me. I can protect you. People are dead, Ward. You need to tell me what you know.' She followed him down a dark corridor towards light shining from under a door. She pushed the door open and stepped in. Caught the smell first. Some kind of incense. There was a bright light in her face. Bright so she had to hold a hand up.

A figure was standing dark against it.

'Ward?' The light clicked off. Sudden darkness and confusion. She realised then that the room was sort of an observatory. Over her head stars were visible in the night sky. One shining brighter than the rest. It was a comet.

'Monica. I told you that you'd come willingly.'

Then horror as she realised what Lucy had been mouthing to her from inside the car: *The man, Mummy. The man who came to the Sunday school.* Horror like her mind was a ball of snakes writhing and breaking apart. She'd brought her child to this man. Like a sacrificial offering. She made to turn away. To run.

She felt the impact on her stomach and the spread of hot blood, although there was no pain as the light came back on and she saw Ward's face. His mad eyes staring into hers as his smile spread wide.

Chapter 81

Pain and fear, and time drifting strangely. Michael realised that he was concussed, or still affected by whatever chemical Don Cameron had shoved in his face.

'Ward! Nichol!' Michael realised that he was shouting. Screaming. The Land Rover stopped. Don Cameron turned, pointed two barrels of a shotgun at him.

'It doesn't mean a thing to me if I kill you and drop you into a ditch. Keep your fucking mouth shut.'

Michael could see over Cameron's shoulder that the storm was clearing. The stars in the sky. The light of a comet. Maybe DI Kennedy and Nichol were already dead. Maybe he'd be dead soon too. He wasn't sure if he cared. If it even meant anything.

The Land Rover started moving again. Who knew for how long, as the pain from his face, his head and his smashed foot settled over him.

The movement of the Land Rover changed. They had pulled on to a track. They slowed, then the vehicle stopped. Michael heard a door open and felt the cold air from outside. He blinked and caught the smell of frost, the smell of the forest. He blinked again, the cold cutting through the fog in his mind.

Strong hands grabbed his legs and pulled him out on to a muddy dirt track. Don Cameron stood him up against the

Land Rover. Michael was barely able to support his own weight and the pain from his smashed foot was horrible. He adjusted his stance, taking his weight on his heel, where it was sickening but bearable.

He blinked again. Don Cameron smelled of sweat. Like a man who'd been moving through the landscape for days; through forests, over mountains.

There were stars above them in the icy night and a dim light in the distance.

'Can you walk?'

Michael nodded. Cameron's dark face was close so Michael could feel the man's breath on his cheek. He turned Michael around. Pushed him against the Land Rover and opened the handcuffs. *Now, hit him. Do something!* But he could barely stand on his heel, let alone fight. Don Cameron had stepped back and was pointing the shotgun at him again anyway. He gestured towards the house.

Michael understood and started moving. Every step was like his foot being broken in a vice, the bones moving where they shouldn't be moving. *She might still be alive.* He had to keep going. He gritted his teeth and tried to hobble faster on his heel.

He saw the car. Monica's Volvo. Realised with horror that it was empty. He put his hand on the bonnet, the engine was cold. Clearly the vehicle had been there for some time. There was a child seat in the back. Michael put more weight on his broken foot and the pain surged in response, obliterating everything else for a few seconds.

He unclenched his eyes. The front door of the house was open. Michael hesitated and looked behind him, there was no sign of Don Cameron. He caught the edge of a sound from inside the house. It was unmistakable: a child crying. Overhead a comet was burning in the cold night sky.

Please no, Michael thought. A useless prayer as he stepped over the threshold then moved down a corridor, leaving a trail of blood from his foot on the wooden floor, his hand against the wall for support. There was a door at the end of the corridor. A flicker of light escaped from under it. A child's voice, saying the same words over and over: 'Mummy, Mummy, wake up.'

Michael pushed the door open. Inside it was dimly lit by a scatter of candles. The ceiling was somehow open to the stars, which were bright and infinite in the black sky. He could make out a shape on the floor. A body that had been posed. Pushed into a particular position almost like it was praying.

He saw the small shape next to it. The same words: 'Mummy! Mummy, wake up!'

There was a man standing over the posed body. In the dim light Michael could see that it was Ward. Or something that had been Ward. His head was shaved and his body was covered in wounds. Marks cut into his flesh.

He looked up. A knife in his hand. Ward's face was covered in blood.

'Michael. You've come to me. I tasted that emptiness in you. I knew.'

The man looked possessed. A bullshit word, but it was the first that came to mind. The face of every delusion, of serious mental illness.

'Ward?' Michael hobbled towards the child, attempting to shield her from the maniac. The huddled shape was still breathing. A horrible gurgling noise. The smell of incense mixed with that of blood, sinew and muscle.

Ward smiled at Michael, his eyes staring like a prophet's.

'Where's Nichol? He found out what you were doing? Didn't he?'

'Nichol. He was a good boy.' Ward pointed the knife at Michael. Held out his other hand in invitation. 'You want me to feed you to the universe. Don't you?'

There was a click from over Michael's shoulder. Don Cameron took a step forward, sighting down the shotgun. In the distance Michael heard the faint noise of a police siren. Then his own voice: 'Don't shoot him.'

Ward looked at Michael. Then at Don Cameron. The black sky overhead.

'Please don't shoot him.'

Ward smiled and opened his mouth to speak. Both barrels of the shotgun went off. Ward folded onto his knees. He looked down at the black mess of his stomach, and then as Michael watched in horror he got to his feet. One hand on his belly, holding his guts in. The knife still in the other hand.

Cameron reloaded the shotgun and stepped closer. Raised it to his shoulder. He said something. Michael never knew what – his ears were ringing from the blast. He realised that he was kneeling beside Monica. He put his arms around the child and covered her ears.

The gun went off again. Both barrels into Ward's face. This time he stayed down. Another heap on the floor.

Don Cameron turned to Michael and reloaded the shotgun for a second time. The sirens were closer now. Michael met his eyes. Tensed for the impact. But instead Cameron pointed the gun at the floor. He walked past and out into the dark.

Michael felt for Monica's hand. It was cold. The child was crying quietly. 'It's going to be OK. You're both going to be OK.'

He reached down and tried to staunch the wound in her stomach. There was a lot of blood under the black sky. And the comet went on burning.

Chapter 82

'You're going to be OK. You're going to be OK. Mummy's going to be OK.' Michael repeated the same words over and over like a mantra. Pushing down desperately on Monica's stomach to stop the blood as the sirens came closer. Finally there were voices and faces reaching through the void and back into reality.

He was cuffed again, dragged out and put into a van. Then the hospital, handcuffed to the bed after an operation on his foot and another one to reset the plate in his cheek. He passed in and out of consciousness. Buried alive under an eternal starry sky and through corridors deep under Ward's house. Ones that didn't end, didn't begin. Monica, Lucy. Always somewhere deeper, alive but gone bad. Changed somehow. The others with them. His father, his brother, Nichol, all lost down there. Lost in the void.

When Michael woke up again the cuffs had been removed. He turned his head and felt that familiar pain in his face. A man was sitting by the side of his bed. He was wearing a suit and glasses; he looked more like a young academic than a police officer. But his face was puffy and there were dark circles under his eyes. *Ben Fisher*, Michael realised with a strange feeling of synchronicity. Someone he'd known as a kid. What were the chances?

'Monica?' The word came out slurred. Michael's tongue felt like it had expanded to fill his mouth.

'She's going to live. That's all I know. Lucy's OK too. She's with her grandmother. It was Lucy who phoned the police. Monica taught her how to dial 999 in case anything ever happened to her gran. She heard her mother screaming from inside the house ...'

The house. That room under the black sky and the comet. Michael swallowed. The pain in his dry throat was like razor blades.

'My client, Nichol Morgan. I think Ward might have taken him.'

'We've found no sign of him at the house, or in Ward's car. That's all we can say for now.'

'There was a girl, Melissa ... Margaret Taylor.' It hurt even to speak. 'Ward was trying to use her to get to me. She was in—'

'She's fine,' Fisher said.

'How do you know?'

'She told her mother what had happened. She asked to come and see you earlier, but you were being operated on.'

Michael sank back onto the bed, enjoying the moments of relief. 'That's good.' Instinctively he went to tap his pockets for a cigarette. He stopped himself and laid his hands carefully down on the sheet instead.

'Why did Monica go to Ward's alone? Why didn't she bring someone with her?'

The detective looked down at the floor. 'DI Kennedy ... suspected that I might be involved somehow.' A range of emotions crossed Fisher's face as he spoke.

'You're not though? Are you?'

Fisher stared at Michael, obviously angered by the question.

'Ward was responsible for what happened to DI Kennedy,' Fisher said finally. 'He videoed the whole thing. He stabbed

Monica, then cut himself to ribbons and went out to the car to bring Lucy in. If you hadn't come when you did then ...' Fisher let his voice trail off. 'But so far we've not been able to find any incontrovertible evidence directly linking him to the other murders.'

Fisher took a breath then glanced over his shoulder at the open door of the room. He stood up to close it and sat back down.

'The investigation's a complete mess. DI Kennedy had been saying for days that we were focusing in the wrong places. I think someone tipped off Don Cameron.'

'Someone definitely told him that I'd killed Paul MacKay. Gave him my address,' Michael said. He'd worked that much out himself.

'Cameron's still missing. He's the only one who can say who tipped him off. My bosses don't know whether to keep after him or try to find evidence that Ward was responsible for the deaths. It would look better for them if it was Don Cameron and they could write Ward off as psychotic. There's no concrete evidence linking Ward to the boys. Those meteor fragments were the only thing ...'

Michael pushed himself up in the bed, pain in every part of his body. His foot was encased in plaster. He looked around for his clothes. Realised that they must have been taken away as evidence.

'My client Nichol Morgan, he knew what Ward was doing. He was too afraid to tell anyone, though. He left a phone with evidence on it, hoping someone would come looking for him.'

'The videos. DI Kennedy told me,' Fisher said.

'Do you really want to find out what happened to those boys?'

Fisher nodded. The fear was clear on his face, but he nodded.

'Help me out of here then. We can still get access to the videos.'

'But you've just had an operation ...'

'Am I under arrest?' Michael asked.

'No, I told you. Ward recorded it all.'

'So help me out of here.'

Chapter 83

Michael could read the hesitation on Fisher's face. Uncertainty over what rules he might be breaking. But finally he helped Michael out of bed, then down and out of the hospital into his car.

Michael waited in the car outside his flat while Fisher went in and came back five minutes later. He was carrying a pair of Michael's jeans, trainers, a sweater, what was left of the bottle of whisky and half a packet of cigarettes. He even helped Michael wrestle the clothes on and rip the jeans so they'd fit over the plaster cast and managed to keep quiet when Michael lit up a cigarette inside his pristine Volkswagen.

'Where are we going?' Fisher asked. His fingers hovering over the satnav.

Michael dry-swallowed two codeine tablets and chased them down with whisky. There was something comforting about Fisher's careful driving and the warmth of the vehicle in the gathering evening.

'Just drive.'

Fisher glanced questioningly at Michael but followed his instruction.

They took the long way to Henry's house. Through the mountains, along single-track roads. They doubled back several times until it was dark. Someone from the police had helped

Ward to feed Michael to Don Cameron, and Michael had no intention of passing on the favour to Henry.

Henry turned at the sound of Michael pushing his door open.

'I phoned you two days ago, Michael. I left a message. I thought you wanted to know about the videos?' His voice was outraged as he adjusted the Japanese bandanna, which was slipping down over his eyes.

'I do. I'm sorry – I got caught up,' Michael said.

Henry glanced at Fisher, seemed to implicitly accept that he was trustworthy. Michael settled down in a chair and took a mouthful of whisky. 'Can you show us the video of Alexander Allen first?'

Henry glanced at the whisky bottle, then at Michael's plastered foot. Without replying he clicked on one of his screens. Fisher edged closer to the monitor.

'This video was hidden in a link on the phone. The boy in it supposedly committed suicide six months ago. There was a piece of black stone found in his throat – like the other boys,' Michael said.

Fisher didn't take his eyes from the screen as Zandy Allen became visible through the window of his house.

'What else did you find, Henry? You said you'd phoned to tell me,' Michael asked.

'I phoned to tell you that I'd found more videos. A lot more videos.'

Chapter 84

Fisher sat down on the sofa in Michael's flat in Inverness. Over a month had passed since they'd watched the first of those videos on Henry's computer.

After thirty seconds they'd turned the sound down to mute the boy's pleas. After two minutes Michael told Henry to switch it off. He'd seen enough. Enough for any lifetime.

Michael had turned to Fisher. His own horror reflected in the younger man's eyes.

'Are you taking this on, or am I passing it to the press?' Michael asked.

The terror was plain on Fisher's face but again he had nodded. 'This is what the police are for.'

There was now a November frost on the windows, flashing red lights from the Kessock Bridge in the distance. The cold autumn evening had seemed to follow on with Fisher and the other detective, who sat beside him. The man's left arm in a sling under his jacket.

Michael recognised him. 'This is DC Crawford,' Fisher said.

Michael nodded. 'We've met.'

The two detectives seemed to carry their bad news between them like a physical burden. After everything, Michael wasn't sure that he was ready to hear it. Instead he reached for the bottle and splashed whisky into three glasses. Crawford pushed his away but Fisher drank his in one mouthful. Michael did the same and felt the burn in his throat, watched the long dark shadows on the wall.

'DI Kennedy's improving. She asked about you,' Crawford said.

Michael cleared his throat. The last thing he wanted to think about was that night. 'What can I help you with? Do you know who passed my name to Don Cameron yet?'

'It's very difficult,' Fisher said. 'Unless we hear it from Don Cameron himself, and as you know he's ...'

'Still missing.'

'We want to bring whoever did it to justice. But Cameron made two calls from that phone box. It's possible that it was on the second call that he obtained your name and address.'

'But you can't trace that number,' Michael said.

'You know that, Michael. It was a mobile phone. There's no record of who owned it.'

Michael nodded; he'd heard it before.

Fisher looked at the table, cleared his throat. 'You know that we've been tasked with investigating the videos you discovered. Investigating Kyle Ward. We've been making progress but we can't confirm his identity. It's complicated, but basically a young man named Kyle Ward disappeared in Australia twenty years ago. He was formally declared dead fifteen years ago. It was assumed that he committed suicide during a depressive episode. Now ...' His voice trailed off.

'Now you think he changed his name?' Michael asked.

'We think our man assumed Ward's identity. We don't know who he was before that,' Crawford said, leaning forward.

A nameless man wearing an identity as a mask. Like something from your nightmares.

'He used a fake identity to get work as a head teacher and no one picked up on it?' Michael said. He could barely believe what the detective had told him.

'There's a major investigation under way. Obviously there were some serious –' Fisher searched for the right word, he finally settled on '– oversights.'

'"Oversights".' Michael repeated the weasel word back to him. 'Oversights that cost how many lives?'

Fisher looked down at the table. 'As I say, there's a major review under way, and we can't comment on the details.' He looked up at Michael, obviously keen to move the conversation on. 'You said in your interview that Ward seemed to be delusional. Seriously mentally ill?'

'I used the word possessed. He seemed possessed. But I suppose it amounts to the same thing,' Michael said. Not for the first time he struggled to fit the two sides of Ward's persona together into one unified whole. How could someone wear a mask so well? Function in a position of authority while carrying out abductions and murders?

Fisher coughed. 'The toxicology report from his autopsy indicated that he'd ingested a cocktail of drugs on the night he died: amphetamine, Valium, LSD. It might explain some of his actions.'

'His actions?' Michael said, struggling not to feel serious dislike for the young detective. 'His torturing and murders, you mean.'

'We think he had … something like a delusion,' Fisher said, ignoring Michael's accusatory tone.

Crawford cut in. 'He was fixated on a particular meteor. A comet. It passed twenty years ago. The same time the man went missing in Australia. That was where the pieces of meteor were from.'

Michael nodded, letting his frustration fade. He remembered Monica telling him about it.

Fisher took over again. 'He mentioned it in his recordings, among other things. He believed that by murdering those boys, by placing them in those positions with the pieces of meteorite in their throats, he was communicating with the universe.'

'He was fucking insane,' Crawford said, now sounding angry. 'He made up some bullshit story to cover up the fact that he enjoyed hurting people, sadistically murdering young men.'

Michael watched Crawford. Somehow he envied the anger on the younger man's face. He didn't disagree with him. But glancing out of the window at the dark, at a universe of stars and galaxies, he felt a momentary disconnect from human morality. An almost psychedelic awareness of the infinite and our deep connection to it all – the sun, the seasons, the cosmos that made us, made every atom in our bodies – and maybe Ward was part of that cycle of the infinite. The grinding perpetuity of creation and destruction. Maybe the man would come back again in a different body. Maybe he was already here.

He reached for the bottle to dampen down the thought. He'd been having these notions since that night at the house. 'You didn't come to tell me about Ward though, did you?'

Fisher looked at Crawford. He took a breath, and Michael knew what was coming.

'You know we got access to a number of video recordings. Dozens of them?' Fisher said.

Michael felt reality tilt off by a degree.

'We've been focusing on identifying the men and boys in them, matching them with the missing persons you identified – Mark MacArthur, Lewis Fall, Iain Johnston.'

'I saw what was on that video. Nichol was on one too, wasn't he? He was murdered; he was tortured to death, wasn't he? What happened to him?' Michael felt the darkness then. Felt it coming in through the windows.

Fisher broke eye contact, looked at Crawford for a moment.

'Just fucking tell me what Ward did to him,' Michael said.

'Michael, Nichol was in several recordings ...' Fisher ran a hand over his face.

'He wasn't murdered,' Crawford said. 'Nichol was helping Ward. Acting as an accomplice. We think Ward was threatening him, or blackmailing him somehow. Forcing him to take part.'

Five Months Later

The seawater was ice cold. Michael stood in it until his feet ached and it was hard to breathe. He inhaled the smell of salt. The layer of frost on the beach. The water made a sharp black line against the frost as the sea rose gently with the tide. There was some kind of peace in that.

Michael waded ashore and sat on a rock. He dried his feet on his down jacket and watched the water rising and falling. He lit a cigarette and then another. The sun edged down in the west and a cold northern light crossed the dark water and sparkled off the frost.

He heard a footstep on the stones behind him. For a second he was sure it was Ward. Back in a different body. From his hiding place. Michael closed his eyes and tried to swallow the illogical thought. When he turned, Michael saw the ginger fur. Colonel Mustard had followed him across the moor and down to the beach. The cat shouted and nuzzled at Michael's hand. Finally he settled down on Michael's lap.

When he'd finished his last cigarette and the shadows had turned to black across the beach, Michael stood up. Colonel Mustard had fallen asleep, so Michael carried him slowly up to the croft house. His foot still ached. Especially when it was cold. The surgeon had shown Michael the X-ray. Twenty-six bones and more than a hundred ligaments in the human foot. Putting all the broken parts back together was a difficult process.

He stopped at the top of the hill and looked back down to the beach, at the sea and the stars in the purple sky. It was getting dark now in the gathering night. He felt in his pocket for the photo again. He'd found it among his father's papers when he'd finally made himself go into the byre. A shoebox of photographs that he'd never seen.

Memories of a different life. Of a different reality. Two boys smiling, shorts, T-shirts, a sunny day. A brother he'd almost forgotten. 'Joseph.' The name sounded strange in his mouth. He'd hardly said it since he was a child. He put the photo carefully back in his pocket.

It was almost dark when he got back to the croft and saw the dark car parked outside, engine running. Michael felt the prickles of unease. Paranoia seemed to come on easily these days.

Monica watched the moorland. The sharp line of the horizon was beginning to merge into the pale evening sky above the sea. She wondered if Michael was actually going to return to his house that night; maybe the drive out would be for nothing. Monica wasn't certain whether she felt annoyed or relieved. It would be the first time she'd seen him since the night at Ward's house. The memory triggered discomfort in her stomach. The throbbing of the stitched and now healed wound where Ward had thrust the knife, and the throbbing awareness of her own failures.

How could she have been tricked so easily by Ward's mask? The deeper horror when she considered her own arrogance in taking Lucy with her to his house. Her colleagues and the media had her down as the hero of the piece, the selfless DI who had risked her own life to catch a killer. It was simpler for everyone that way – to forget about the failures and the wrong turns in the investigation.

But Monica couldn't forget the look in her mum's eyes when she'd woken in the hospital bed: the relief that told Monica immediately that Lucy was safe, but also the recrimination – and the words that followed: 'Why did you take her with you Monica? Why did you go on your own?'

Monica had tried to reply but the words hadn't come out. Not that they would have made sense anyway when she didn't even know the answer herself. Something about trying to save Nichol Morgan maybe, or something deeper. Some idea only half-understood at the edge of her subconscious – of trying to play her part in holding chaos and evil at bay – whatever the cost.

'Maybe he's not coming back tonight,' Crawford said from beside her in the passenger seat. She had almost forgotten he was there.

She had turned to say something to him when Lucy piped up from behind her, 'Look! He's got a cat!' For the first time in a long time the kid's voice was alive with excitement as she scrambled forward to point over Monica's shoulder.

Monica climbed out of the car and watched as Michael walked slowly towards them. He was moving with a slight limp, his short hair a mess of brown angles. Wearing a new-looking down jacket – dark blue, better fitting than the one he'd had before.

He let the ginger cat jump down out of his hands. 'Don't worry, he's friendly,' Michael shouted as if the cat were a dog. It dodged past Monica's feet and into the warm interior of the vehicle.

She watched Lucy's face light up with delight as the cat barged up onto her knee. She tentatively held out a small hand. 'His name's Colonel Mustard,' Michael called as the cat pushed his head roughly against Lucy's fingers.

'We weren't sure you were coming back,' Monica said.

Michael lit a cigarette and breathed smoke into the night. Crawford had climbed out of the other side of the Volvo. He nodded at Michael and sniffed suspiciously at the wild country air. His hair was the blood red of an exit wound in the low northern light.

'I thought you were Ward,' Michael replied. He made a sound a little like a laugh, and Monica glanced back to the car to check Lucy hadn't heard. Luckily her daughter was entranced by the cat.

'Lucy's been having nightmares about a monster. They said she should see you. Change the context of what happened or something,' Monica said. *But how do you change the context of genuine malevolence?* she wondered. *When one malignant person can spread so much pain?*

Michael nodded. He looked tired, the lines at the corners of his blue eyes deeper than she remembered. His face a little more gaunt. He cleared his throat. Monica could tell that he wanted to ask about Nichol. She'd prepared an answer.

Instead he said, 'The police leak – have you caught anyone yet?'

Monica was somewhat surprised by the question. But of course he'd want to know; the leak had almost cost him his life.

'We don't know,' she replied, and not for the first time her mind drifted back to that moment on the road on the way to Ward's house. The officer who'd pulled her over at the flood – PC Duncan Gregg – and the rumours of corruption that surrounded him. She remembered the look that had passed between them, the little crumb of intuition she'd felt in that moment. Could Gregg really have given Michael's address to Don Cameron? 'It could be a coincidence that Cameron put in a call to the police. You know all this. We don't know if that's where he got your address,' she said finally, more than aware of how unsatisfactory her response was.

Michael seemed to accept it though. Probably beaten down by the bureaucracy of the multiple investigations and reviews that were now under way.

'You're back at work?' he asked as if they were casual acquaintances who'd met in the street.

'Not yet,' Monica said. She hated small talk. 'I've taken some time off to spend with Lucy. It's been ...' She thought about the sound of her daughter waking in the night screaming, the way she would stare at a fixed spot on the ceiling and talk about the man with the coal-black teeth who lived at the bottom of her bed. 'It's been hard for her.'

'What about Nichol?' Michael asked abruptly, finally finding the courage. 'Is there any news?'

Monica scanned his face, sensing Crawford's eyes on her. Should she tell Michael the truth? That the videos had shown someone wearing a mask fitted with horrible crooked teeth like those Dr Dolohov had modelled. That they had found no trace of the mask at Ward's house even though the videos clearly showed that was where the murders had taken place. They were working on the assumption that Nichol had worn the mask and had inflicted the bites. Had helped Ward to lure the boys to their deaths. Had helped him remove them from their homes.

Would it really help Michael to know any of that?

'Nothing,' Monica said finally. She glanced over at Crawford, whose eyes had dropped in relief. 'He disappeared ...'

'Or Ward killed him?' Michael asked.

'We might never know.' *Or hopefully you won't anyway*, Monica thought. *At least I can spare you that.*

Nobody spoke for a while. There was just the black sky overhead and the light from inside the house.

'Do you think I could have done something more? He must have messaged me because he wanted help ... There must have been part of him that was still a scared boy looking for a way out,' Michael said.

Monica nodded, but couldn't help thinking, *Maybe Nichol was a scared boy looking for a way out or maybe he was setting you up as Ward's next victim.* Because she'd watched those videos. She'd had a glimpse into the slice of hell that Ward – with Nichol's help – had created for those boys, and in her eyes some things were beyond redemption.

'I was supposed to be there for him. I was supposed to protect him ...' Michael said.

'So was Ward –' Monica caught Michael's eye '– and ulti-mately Nichol made his own choices. Same as we all do.'

Acknowledgements

I've been incredibly lucky in the help and encouragement I've had with my writing from so many talented people. Big thanks and appreciation to Ranald Macdonald, Gregor Matheson, Keshini Naidoo and Lulu Woodcock for feedback and belief in early drafts of my work. For years of adventures, enthusiasm and ideas thanks to Matthew Blackburn, Jana Guttzeit, Alisa Hughes, and Graeme Young. For artistic inspiration and hospitality on the west coast, Fiona MacKenzie. For being a well timed reminder of what teenage boys are like, Jack McCruden.

Huge thanks to my agent Camilla Wray and to everyone at Darley Anderson agency, also to my editor Jade Chandler and the team at Harvill Secker. I can't thank you all enough for everything.

Also big thanks to my family. My mum Evelyn Halliday for her encouragement and for her obsession with TV crime dramas in the mid 1980s, which familiarised me with the genre. My dad Ron Halliday for filling my head with this kind of thing, for telling great bedtime stories, and always encouraging my writing. My sister Tanya Baron for answering random text messages about stabbing, hanging, gunshot wounds, amputation, blunt force trauma ... And my brother Euan Halliday for his support and enthusiasm.

Finally, a huge thank you to my partner Sarah Woodcock. For all the love and support over the years, for reading endless drafts of my work and somehow maintaining enthusiasm, for expanding my tolerance of horror movies, exploring the highlands with me, sharing creativity and the vision for the story, and for giving me the idea to write a crime novel in the first place. I couldn't have done it without you.

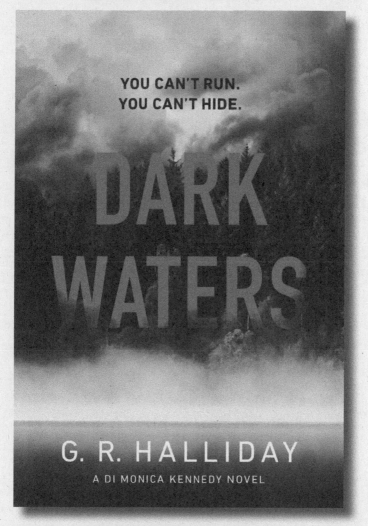

penguin.co.uk/vintage